PRAISE FOR NANCI KINCAID
AND
Balls

"At once a lovely but acutely perceptive story of a football coach's wife and a hilarious send-up on college football in the South. Creating dialogue is one of Kincaid's strengths, as is her ability to portray the struggle of these women in a world in which they are supposed to be silent helpers and stage props in their husbands' lives. The dialogue is so uncanny and earthy. In the end, this is not a book about football as much as it is about a woman's inner search." —*Lexington Herald-Leader*

"There's plenty of football, but the game itself takes a backseat to the novel's unique point of view. Much like the novel *How to Make an American Quilt*, *Balls* allows a myriad of women—young and old, black and white—to tell their story. The novel scores its points through the wonderful voices of these women." —*Birmingham Weekly*

"A superbly talented storyteller . . . *Balls* is not just a compelling look at the female side of the sport, or one that weaves a not-too-subtle thread of biography. It is a brilliant study into what makes the men who run football tick." —*Tucson Citizen*

"Engrossing . . . a terrific book . . . Kincaid's story is told through the voices of a wealth of characters . . . they are all dead-on authentic . . . unfailingly perceptive and deeply moving." —*Booklist*

Please turn the page for more extraordinary acclaim. . . .

BALLS

Also by Nanci Kincaid

CROSSING BLOOD
PRETENDING THE BED IS A RAFT

Balls

a novel by NANCI KINCAID

Delta
Trade Paperbacks

A Delta Book
Published by
Dell Publishing
a division of
Random House, Inc.
1540 Broadway
New York, New York 10036

ISBN: 0-385-33453-2

Reprinted by arrangement with Algonquin Books of Chapel Hill, a division of Workman Publishing

Manufactured in the United States of America

Published simultaneously in Canada

November 1999

10 9 8 7 6 5 4 3 2 1

BVG

For Percy

*I*t was not by accident that God created the world in the shape of a ball. I came to understand that early. All the men in my life imitated God in this way by making small worlds of their own out of balls. I never knew boys who dreamed of building skyscrapers, or campaigning for justice, or making music, or scalpeling into human flesh to repair hearts. Nothing like that. The boys I knew dreamed of one thing—balls. Getting them across the goal line, pitching them over the plate, sinking them in the hoop, putting them into the hole.

As a girl, when I watched men pass the pigskin, pitch the curveball, perfect the jump shot, I understood that they were playing war. What I didn't understand was that it wasn't just a stupid ball they held in their hands, but the whole world being tossed about from man to man—like a game of keep away.

From me.

—Dixie Gibbs, 1998

Contents

PREGAME

DIXIE

Mac runs onto the field. He's beautiful. The band plays the national anthem, the flag wilts in the heat, I mouth the words "bombs bursting in air." The first scream goes up, the coin is tossed, and somebody runs and kicks the ball into the sky. This is America, land of the free, home of the brave. My heart swells to nearly bursting with "Oh, say can you see."

One hundred college boys roar, run on the field, and butt helmets like a fistful of dropped marbles. The pep band plays "Black Bear Boogie" and the team charges through two rows of cartwheeling cheerleaders who glisten in the sun.

Like any decent girl, I'd once set out to be a cheerleader, but I got the flu the week of tryouts and missed my chance. I was afraid my life was ruined. But that same fall I was elected Shades Valley homecoming princess. A homecoming princess who was not a cheerleader? It was like if you got to be commander in chief without having ever been a soldier.

Daddy has expensive binoculars the better to watch Mac with. And Jett too. He passes them to me so I can see Mac's face, which I study, trying to imagine what he's thinking.

All other eyes are on Jett. People pick him out first thing—it isn't hard—the only colored boy on the field. They wait for him to make a mistake, to miss a pass or drop a ball or take a hangman's hit—anything that might give them permission to rip a paper cup to shreds and rage against a nigger on the field.

Lilly doesn't come to the games at all. She prefers to lie in bed at home, the lights off, the electric fan going, and listen to the game on the radio and nobody blames her at all. Jett's uncles come and friends I recognize from pickup games Mac takes me to in their neighborhood. They sit in a cluster, the colored people, and make me think of a dark freckle on a big pink face.

It's 1968 and the world's changing. It scares everybody. People say the rules are changing and it doesn't seem fair, to change now when people have finally gotten the hang of things with the rules they already know. I personally think rules are meant to be broken, even if I'm too chicken to break them myself. But not in football, of course, which is one good thing about it. It's something people can count on. In football the rules are the rules are the rules. So everybody can go crazy and relax all at the same time.

Heat bears down on the stadium. "Too hot for football," the man behind me says to his buddy.

"Never too hot for football," his buddy answers. "If hell put together a decent team I'd buy me a ticket and go down there to watch it. And so would you."

"I guess so," the man behind me says.

Mac's playing quarterback but the offense is sputtering. People are restless, waiting for the spectacular. I pray for the spectacular too.

Mac's sacked for what seems like the hundredth time by the Ole Miss defense in the second half. He lands shoulder first. I swear I can hear the crunch of bones. Afterwards he can't get up. Coach Bomar sends Vet, the trainer, to see about him. With the help of the managers Mac makes his way off the field, his arm dangling.

"If you can't take a hit, get off the field," a man yells.

"Get somebody who can throw the damn ball," somebody says.

"Ignore them," Rose tells me.

"There's no shortage of jackasses in this world," Daddy says with the binoculars pressed to his face.

The second-string quarterback runs in and the crowd cheers. I look two rows back at Mac's parents. Mr. Gibbs is going colorless, like a blank space where a man should be. Mrs. Gibbs is looking straight ahead, stiff as a board, tears rolling down her powdered face. She fumbles through her pocketbook for a tissue. Bobby's new wife, Lisa, is beside Mrs. Gibbs, patting her arm.

With Mac out of the game Coach Bomar takes Jett out too. The crowd loves this. "Sit your butt on the bench, black boy!" a man several rows ahead yells. Rose takes a handful of ice out of her lemonade thermos and throws it, hitting him in the back of the neck, which shocks me because it's not good manners and next to God, Rose mostly believes in good manners even at sporting events, which don't necessarily lend themselves much to courtesy. The man slaps at his neck like he's been stung by a bee. "Down in front," Rose says and then smiles.

Midway into the third quarter Mac comes back onto the sideline with Vet right behind him. Mac's still in uniform and has an adhesive-tape-looking contraption on his shoulder. Birmingham University is struggling to get a first down. Mac breathes down Coach Bomar's neck like a shadow. Jett stands apart from the other players, holding his helmet in his hand, sipping water from a paper cup.

When the second-string quarterback is helped off the field with an injured ankle people applaud him and boo. Then Coach Bomar puts Mac back in. They'll kill him, I think to myself.

The crowd's on its feet. Behind me Mrs. Gibbs yells, "Okay, Mac, let's go, Son." I look at her and smile.

Rose slides her sunglasses into her hair and claps. "All right Jett, let's do something now, honey."

The Ole Miss defense is in Mac's face, mouthing off with their plastic-coated teeth, lisping cusswords—I can read their lips through the binoculars—just before they grunt and knock the fool out of each other. I look at Mac's face. It's closed. He's refusing to hear them, refusing to see them. They sack him and grind into him, their knees, their fists, their ball-like heads hammering him.

"Get up, Mac," I whisper to myself. His name is spoken in a God voice over the loudspeaker again and again—"Gibbs stopped on the forty," "Gibbs sacked again," "Gibbs brought down by number thirty-three."

Mac throws the ball like a man with a double-jointed elbow. It's not pretty. The point is to get the pass off fast—short and fast, short and fast, get it to Jett, to Jett, to Jett—then take his hits. Again. Again. Again. Mac should not be getting up at all. Not anymore. Sometimes he waits for somebody to pull him up. He should be out cold. He should be dead.

In my mind I run down the stadium steps, jump over the rail, weave my way through the players and onto the field. My feet don't touch the ground as I go to Mac, throw myself over him where he lies trampled on the ground. I'm like Cornelia Wallace, who flung herself over George when the bullets started flying.

Then, late in the game, like a whisper, something begins to pass over the crowd. It's like a breeze through the stadium, where we're baking in our sweatbox seats, our wet clothes stuck to us. We begin—just barely—to believe. One simple thing.

Mac Gibbs will get up. *No matter how hard he's crushed into the ground, no matter how many times. He will rise again. It's a small, difficult thing to believe. But easier in Birmingham than in lots of other places because we're Bible people. Believing is in our blood.*

A boiled-faced man jumps up, spilling his cold drink. "You can knock him down, but damn if you can keep him down," he yells.

"Amen!" somebody says.

KICKOFF

ROSE

Dixie is a pretty girl. I hope it doesn't ruin her life.

There are worse things than not getting chosen, like getting chosen too early. Or getting chosen too often. But you have to live awhile before you can know that.

Dixie's smart too, which if she isn't careful can destroy her about as quick as anything else. I tell her, "Being smart can be a real detriment to a woman unless she knows how to go about it tactfully."

"Like you do, Rose?" she says.

"There are worse examples you could follow," I say. "Where do you think you got your brains in the first place?"

"From Daddy, I guess," she says.

"God knows how I wish that was the truth." I laugh.

Then Dixie looks at me sharp-eyed and that's the end of it.

She's my daughter and I love her, but without question she's got Bennett's sour blood. She's got that Carraway melancholy. Bennett Sr. might be the one that put the gun to his head, but they're all geared that way. Although there're just the slightest traces in Dixie so far, I see the signs and it breaks my heart. I'm afraid if she's not careful—in time—that Carraway despair might overtake her.

Now my family—if we all wanted to put guns to our heads, then yes, it would make sense. Nobody would question it. Most of us have good reason to try and hurry out of this life and on to the next one. Some of us don't have anything to lose but loss itself, if you'll excuse the expression. But the Carraways now. It's mysterious. They have everything to live for. Every reason in the world to be happy.

I'm planning Dixie's wedding. None of her grandparents are alive to see it. Nobody much in my family left to witness this. So mostly it will be Bennett's people, cousins, aunts and uncles, coming from miles around to see how Bennett is handling his grief and his father's estate. I think they'll be surprised. Bennett has good business sense, which I guess is better than no sense at all. He tells me there's no need for Dixie's wedding to be extravagant, but he knows I don't believe in extravagance. I believe in understatement. I want this to be something we all remember—forever. Bennett says, "Rose, don't try to make this into the wedding you and I never had, you hear me. It's Dixie's wedding. If you need to plan something for the two of us you can go ahead and start planning our funerals."

I've already planned his funeral a thousand times. In my mind I've given him an assortment of tasteful burials, chosen the casket and the music and stood right there and watched them shovel the dirt over him. So whether he knows it or not I'm way ahead of him.

Dixie, married. It's nothing I can really prepare her for. I can't decide if it's cruel for mothers not to warn their daughters, or if it's crueler to. Sometimes I get the feeling she wants me to talk her out of it. But I know if I tried she would probably never forgive me.

And Mac. He's a nice boy. I'm fond of Mac. If he'd been drafted into pro football he could have given her a good life. Some travel and excitement. Zale says Mac is a fine Christian and would make a good preacher if he was inclined. But no, he's inclined to make a good high school football coach. I just want Dixie to be happy. I don't know if football is going to be any kind of life for her.

Besides, I wonder if Mac really knows Dixie, knows about the notebooks she fills her room with. You can't call them diaries because there's no key to lock them with. I see those notebooks. Under her bed, in the back of her closet behind the laundry basket, closed away in shoe boxes. I could take one out and read it anytime, but I don't. Even when she leaves one of those notebooks lying wide open on her unmade bed, her thoughts right out there like so many birds poised for flight, well, I don't disturb them.

Dixie says, "Rose, you do like Mac, don't you?"

I say, "Of course."

"I mean *really*," she says. "Are you crazy about him?"

"I think Mac is just fine," I say.

"Well, sometimes I wonder. That's all. After what happened that night. It was like you hated him."

"That's over and done with," I say. "We've settled that, haven't we?"

"I guess so," she says.

I know she thinks about it. I know it didn't make sense to her at the time and might never. But when I woke up so late like that, an alarm ringing silently in my head, and went down the hall in the dark, the last thing I ever thought I'd see was a man in bed with Dixie. Every thought flew through my mind. *Save her,* I said to myself. *You've got to save her.* The idea felt like pulling a trigger and it made a sound like a gunshot too, the echo inside me. At first I went so crazy I didn't know it was Mac. It was just some thief in the night stealing my daughter's life. I wanted to kill him, to just rip into him, tear him apart—and make him regret everything right before he died from a bullet to his heart. Where was Bennett's gun? Where was the gun Bennett's daddy shot himself in the head with? Where was my sharp kitchen knife? I went at him with my fingernails and teeth. He wasn't Mac. He was every man I've ever loathed. He was every man I've ever watched destroy something beautiful.

And Dixie was screaming so bad I had to slap her to make her stop. That's what scared Mac, I think, seeing me slap Dixie that way. But she wasn't just Dixie. I was slapping myself too—that's what he didn't understand. I was slapping hell out of the stupid girl I had been, the one that now Dixie was going to be. Slapping sense into her. But she wouldn't stop screaming.

He says now I didn't actually hurt him, but God knows it wasn't because I didn't try. Just some scratches on his face and bruises that didn't amount to much. Afterwards I had his skin under my finger-nails. Zale says there's the power to kill in all of us. I know that now. I know that in a split second you can become somebody you don't rec-ognize and you can try to kill the stranger in you and the strangers around you. There was a moment, barely a flash, when I thought, *God, yes, this feels good. It feels right.* I have never killed anything but there is so much that needs killing. Mac kept saying, "Mrs. Carraway, it's okay. It's me, Mac." It almost makes me laugh to think about it now, Mac believing he's an exception, that he's different from all the rest of the men in this world. If Bennett hadn't stopped me when he did, who knows what I'd have done.

They all thought I was crazy. That's what Bennett kept saying "Goddamnit, Rose. You are fucking crazy." Bennett talks so ugly some-times. He pinned me up against the wall with my hands twisted be-hind my back while Mac got out of the house. I thought he might break both my arms.

"What the hell is wrong with you?" Bennett kept slamming me up against the wall. "Say? What the hell is wrong with you?"

Of all people, he should know.

DIXIE

The first time Mac opened one button on my blouse and touched my breast I thought it was a moment of genius. I think it must have been the way America felt when Columbus discovered it.

Even now, even though we're officially engaged, we still park up by the Vulcan on that road Mac knows, because of that time Rose caught Mac in my room and went crazy—and we weren't even doing anything but lying there talking—I mean crazy like a lunatic who belonged in an insane asylum, which I don't know if I will ever forgive her for or not, and she had on that see-through nightgown too, her nipples bouncing like two polka dots under there. Since then, we don't have any place much to go where we can be alone together. Except Mac's car, which sort of automatically veers up toward the Vulcan now.

"You are so sweet, Dixie Carraway, I could just eat you up," Mac says. It's not an original thing to say. It's what people say to babies, but he sincerely means it. In the last couple of years Mac has named his top lip Lewis and his bottom lip Clark because he says they are such a hell of a pair of explorers. They are too. He's like a man lip-led. Our mouths have taken over all other aspects of our love, like we are two infants in the world of passion—tasting, biting. I love that word, *passion*. It makes me think of a vine-ripened tomato on the hottest day of the year that last second before the skin splits open and the pulp oozes out. That fleshy red. All those little seeds.

Mac goes crazy if I suck his finger. You wouldn't think a little thing like sucking a finger could do to a guy what it does to Mac. But I don't just suck it, I really make it interesting, you know. I've developed what you might call technique. I just love what mouths can do—that the place that makes the words is also the place that makes the kisses. I watch him watch me while I suck his finger. For those few minutes it's like I rule the world. I mean if I said, "Mac, go run into that burning building," I think he'd actually consider it.

Before Mac, Daddy was mean to boys who came around me. He was rude. Rose was never rude and it really irritated her for Daddy to be—but too bad. Daddy was always telling boys it was time for them to go home, and no, I could not drive down to the shopping center with them. No, I couldn't go to the late movie. No, I couldn't go to the drive-in. No. No. No. Maybe that's where I developed my appreciation for the power of the word *no*.

But as soon as Mac came along, Daddy just sort of changed his tune. Sure, Mac could take me to the drive-in. Sure I could drive over to Tuscaloosa with Mac to see a basketball game. If it had to do with Mac, Daddy was in favor of it. I love Daddy and all, but the truth is this has never set right with me.

Since Daddy abandoned his fatherly patrol it has become my job to patrol things. I think I do it as well as any girl I can name who is fully human. Saying no is hard work. It can wear you out. As young as I am I'm already practically exhausted. No. No. No. God, how Mac loves hearing me say that word. Just the word itself seems to transform me into an angel and send me flying around in some heavenly sphere in his mind. Lucky for me *no* is Mac's favorite word. That's the kind of boy he is.

FRANCES DELMAR

I've put on a few extra pounds, so I need to find a bridesmaid dress that won't point that out. "All I ask is that you cover up
your breasts," Dixie says. "This is not a cleavage exhibition, Frances
Delmar. It's a wedding, thank you."

Is it my fault I might outshine the bride in certain areas? "Take it
up with God, Dix," I tell her. "Don't blame me."

See, the real truth is I'm scared to death of taking after my
mother, whose boobs make her look like a woman trying to shoplift a
couple of watermelons out of the Piggly Wiggly. And Dixie knows
I'm scared of turning into my mother—because she's scared of the
same thing.

Cleet says, "Frances Delmar, as far as I can see there's not one inch
of you to waste." He's the sweetest guy. He says, "Let's put it this way,
Frances Delmar. Nobody would ever mistake you for a boy. That's for
damn sure." Cleet's the best.

Anyway, I've cut out all french fries, Shoney's Big Boys, and hot
fudge cake until the wedding. Also no barbecue. That should take
these pounds off. But you know where I always lose first? Boobs.
Wouldn't you know it?

Dixie's letting Rose plan her whole wedding. That's just
like Dixie too. Do you think I'd just sit back and let my mother make
all the decisions about the biggest day of my life? But Dixie acts like
some kind of dumb Sleeping Beauty or something. It can really drive

me crazy if I let it. We've been around and around about it. I say, "Dixie, damnit, wake up and smell the coffee, child."

She smiles and says, "F. D., you smell it for me. You tell me what it's like."

Sometimes I think she lives her whole life through me. I do. Sometimes I wonder if I'd have done half of what I've done if Dixie wasn't sitting at home waiting for me to come over and tell her all about it. She likes her adventure secondhand, and preferably home-delivery. Like to Dixie a book is a real wild adventure, if that tells you anything. She's just so indifferent sometimes it really gets me. Curiosity might have killed the cat, but I swear if lack of curiosity hasn't killed more than just a bunch of stupid cats.

But don't get me wrong. I love Dixie. I really do. We've been best friends most of our lives. I used to spend practically every weekend at her house, used to go to all the Birmingham University football games with her family. Her dad's a real sports fiend. Has season tickets to everything. And Rose, well, I guess she liked to see and be seen. But whenever I think of Dixie and me as kids, I think of those afternoons at Legion Field when I taught Dixie how to smoke. We got in a stall in the ladies' room on the visitors' side, where nobody would recognize us. The opposing team's women were lined up waiting to pee. "You girls come out of there with those cigarettes," they said. But it's a free country. There's no law about how long you can stay in a bathroom stall. And I take credit where credit is due: it was me who taught Dixie to inhale and hold it in even if it hurt.

Dixie's parents were too wrapped up in the game to notice when later we smelled like a couple of Lucky Strikes doused in Shalimar. Her daddy was about three sheets to the wind by then. And Rose has been accused of being good looking all her life, but on game days she was guilty. I mean it. She was so beautiful sitting there that I went momentarily insane and started wishing she was my mother too.

Dixie and I wanted to grow up and be like the women we saw at Legion Field—lipstick bloodred, hair sprayed into helmets, fingernails painted, green-and-gold outfits with matching shoes and dangling gold bracelets. To Dixie and me, the ball game women were so glamorous.

We loved football, of course. The actual game. It was the most exciting thing there was. We memorized all the cheers. We studied the cheerleaders, rated their bodies, their kicks, their breasts. We took points off for sweat rings under their arms, failure to smile nonstop, fat thighs, or hair that frizzed in the heat. This seemed only fair. We knew even then that cheerleaders set the beauty standard that we were to aspire to. Of course I went on to be a cheerleader—high school and college both. But Dixie, she wasn't so lucky—even though she pretends it doesn't bother her. She pretends she'd rather be at home reading a book or writing some sort of weird poem or something. Dixie's practically gorgeous, you know, when she wants to be. But if you ask me she's never known how to make the most of it. Like she could have if she'd been a cheerleader.

Even when we were kids Dixie and I were certain we would grow up to marry football players. We swore neither of us would settle for less. We couldn't think of anything worse than ending up with one of the smart boys at school. Some guy like Porter Warren—even though Dixie swears he's a nice guy. If you ask me he's as queer as a three-dollar bill. Besides, smart boys were not *real* boys as far as Dixie and I were concerned. Some of our best friends were smart boys, but certainly neither of us wanted to grow up and marry one.

Once I said to Dixie, "You know where I'm going to have my wedding? On the football field, at halftime, you know, in front of the whole stadium. My future husband can run out on the field wearing his uniform and carrying his helmet in his hand."

"The coach won't allow it," Dixie said. "He'll make your future husband keep his mind on the game."

"Not if my future husband is a big star," I said.

"Yeah, but what if the Birmingham Black Bears are losing?"

"I'll call the wedding off. No way will I marry a loser."

To this day I think that it was at Legion Field that Dixie and I learned to be women. What we loved about football was mainly two things. One, you could scream all you wanted to. We screamed until we began to sweat and our raw throats could no longer be soothed by Dr Pepper. Sometimes now I wish I could just go someplace and scream like we did back then. Just scream and scream and scream.

But the second thing, the thing we loved even more than we loved screaming, was that we loved going back and forth to the ladies' room to comb our hair. Dixie has that straight hair that just lies still, obedient as some old dog that just knows one trick. But me, well, I have *this* hair. I've had to fight with all this curly mess day and night my whole life. If my hair was a dog it'd be a wet puppy, jumping, bouncing, yapping like crazy, running around chasing its own tail.

Ten or twelve times a game we walked back and forth in front of the concession stands to see who we might see—and more important, who might see us. We loved to roam the stadium with a swarm of friends and blend our small, nervous crowd into the larger, surer crowd, you know. We loved belonging. That was the magic of the thing —you could just buy a ticket and belong.

LILLY

Jett come around here and says, "So Mama, what you think about Dixie and Mac getting married?"

"Well, I hope it goes better for them than it does for most folks," I say. I was ironing Mr. Carraway's shirts. He don't like to send his shirts to the laundry, says they tear them up over there. He likes the way I do them, not too much starch. I ain't trying to make a shirt into a piece of plywood like they do over there and then go and charge you for the uncomfort of it.

"Like your marriage, Mama? You talking about yourself?"

"Just in case you hadn't noticed your daddy been missing out our lives for what—twenty years now. That's enough to make me think my marriage ain't going all that good," I say.

The boy laughs. If you ask me it's good when a boy can just laugh about the fool his daddy is. That wadn't always the way. There was a time when Jett was hurt not having a man to sit out on our porch in the evenings in a straight-back chair and worry about something. A man to eat up all the chicken breasts and leave us the wings, work a job until the first paycheck, then decide it ain't no kinda decent job after all, lay up on the sofa and watch some show on the TV like maybe it had anything at all to do with his own sorry life he was trying to live in some kind of big way. But Jett now, he don't remember none of that.

All he remembers is his daddy getting out that electric guitar and filling up the house with that good music. The house would soak up all them tunes like it wasn't nothing but a big cotton rag put down on a spill. Like you could hear the house drink it up, like you was living in a mighty thirsty house, like it was parched. You could touch your hand to the wall and just feel that music vibrating inside there like blood pumping, like the house was come alive. You could walk around barefoot and the music would go up right through your feet. I swear to God, you could feel it tremble your bones, like some kind of funny electricity shooting through you.

When Castro was making that music I thought I never seen any man look so good. It made good sense to love a man who could make that kind of music. I'd start to think he was a heavenly angel come down to earth or something—which he was not. He was just a music-making man. There was times we didn't have much else but music, but if we had that then we felt like we had something. I miss it as bad as Jett does, the music—but it's been so long now I can't hardly think of what else there was to miss about Castro. When he set out for Memphis saying he would come back to get us I didn't have no cause to doubt him. And that was the last we seen of the man too. Right this minute I couldn't tell you what he used to look like.

"Dixie says you coming to her wedding, Mama," Jett says. "Says you gon sit right up in the front with her mama and daddy."

"She didn't ask me nothing—not how I felt about that."

"Well, how you feel about it?"

"I feel all right about it, I guess. I can't think of nowhere else I ought to sit."

"Tell the truth, Mama." Jett laughs.

It don't mean a thing to me, if you want to know the truth. I am not one of those that wants to go everywhere with the white folks. Now I think the movie theaters and the restaurants, they ought to do right by colored and white both, and anybody else that pays taxes and counts themselves as American. But do I want to go over to that country club and swim in that swimming pool with them people?

I do not. I can't think of much worse than a bunch of wet white people. They get that smell and I swear if it don't make my stomach start to flip. And if not wanting to mix up with them makes me an Uncle Tom like Jett says, well then, that's what I am.

It's Jett that can't stand to be left out of nothing. I don't know how he got so determined. Sometimes I think it was me bringing him to work with me all those years, which I wouldn't of done if I'd had no other way, him playing with Dixie and seeing what all white folks have and where they go and how much they spend and what they eat, the next thing you know Jett is wanting every bit of what they got and more. He's most likely gon have it now too.

Already since he signed that contract he's paid off my house and my credit and bought me that condominium even though I am not a condominium type of a person. I like some ground with a place. I like something to stand on outside where you can grow you a little something if you want to. I like my morning glory vines and my bell pepper and tomato plants and some collard greens and all the rest of it. Where am I supposed to plant something in a damn condominium— and me the only colored in the building. If he wanted to buy me something he could of bought me a piece of land with a nice house on it—you know, out away from here someplace. But no, he's got to buy some kind of a showplace right in the middle of a bunch of yellow-haired white people. I didn't raise him to try and prove nothing to nobody that way. That's his daddy in him.

If I think about it too much it bothers me. Jett just a little ole boy, coming with me over to the Carraway's, seeing what all Dixie had up in her room. All those books. Them dolls. Every kind of toy. And I would make them up some lunch every day and they would eat together and pinch each other and aggravate me half to death. Then I would make them lay down for a nap on that sofa in the den, her head at one end, his at the other, and they would draw them an invisible line saying not to stick their toes over it or else. Jett would act like he was gon kill Dixie if she let her toe touch him. Then they'd finally fuss themselves off to sleep and when they woke up they'd have their legs tangled together and neither one of them a bit mad about it.

Then at night, at home, Jett would say, "Mama, who you love the most, me or that white girl?"

"That white girl is name Dixie," I'd say.

"Who you love the most—me or her?" He was so dead serious too, laying there with the sheet pulled up tight under his chin.

"There's nobody in this world I love much as I love you," I'd say.

"Why you so nice to her then?"

"It's my job," I said. "Her mama, Miss Rose, she pays me to be nice to Dixie. Dixie's mama is always off to church and don't have time to do nothing for her. So I do it. And they pay me. But don't nobody have to pay me to look after you, do they?"

"No, ma'am."

"That's right," I said. "I look after you for free. It makes me happy to look after you cause you're my own boy."

"I wish you didn't work over there," he'd say. "I don't like that white girl. That house is too big for you to clean."

I would kiss him and try and make him sing along with me, "Jesus loves the little children, all the children of the world, red and yellow, black and white, they are precious in his sight."

"See there," I'd say, "Jesus wants us to love all the little children. Even that little white girl, Dixie."

"Well, I don't," he'd say.

So I'd just finally turn his light out and leave him laying there worrying about it.

Rose, now, she's as peculiar as any white woman there is, but say what you want to, it never bothered her having Jett all through her house, playing with Dixie from eight to five and later on, when they got older, after school in her kitchen picking at each other. Rose is not afraid of the colored like lots of white folks because she comes from mill people herself and lived right down there where half the folks around her were colored. She grew up amongst the colored and so it's like she can't be bothered about it now. She has nothing to say about it. Not like Mr. Carraway.

And Dixie, she's none my own child. She don't have the place in my heart like Jett does, never will. But I know this, the child loves me. She loves me about as good as anybody white ever could. Her mama and daddy now, they like to pretend I ain't got eyes and ears, that I don't know the first bit of their business. It's like we all pretending we had a meeting and they said, "Lilly, you act like you don't know nothing." And I said, "Okay then, if that's the way you want it." But Dixie, she knows I don't truck with the truth. She knows if she asks for it, I'm gon tell it.

DIXIE

Rose says I can't possibly remember this. But I do.

Jett tied me to the porch rail in the midday heat and disappeared into the house. I screamed until I nearly melted like those crayons that get left in the back window of the car. It was the mailman who noticed I was draped over the rail, limp as a fish, my hands and feet tied with scraps of clothesline. When Lilly opened the door he pointed to me and said, "Did you know you had a child bound and gagged up on your porch?"

"I don't want to play with that baby," Jett cried when Lilly twisted his ear to make him say he was sorry. "She don't know how to play nothing. She messes up all the games."

It was Lilly who taught us to kiss and make up, standing with her hands on her hips ready to smack us good if we refused. I was willing to love Jett in the beginning. To let him love me. But no, he'd rather pick a fight. He'd rather make me cry. Or make me bleed. It was how I learned that you can hate a person that you love and love a person that you hate.

I liked to play love the baby dolls, rock them to sleep. He liked to play whip the baby dolls, pop off their heads. I liked to play dress the dolls up pretty, comb their hair. He liked to play strip the dolls naked, see if they will float in the toilet.

"Your dolls are all ugly," Frances Delmar said. "What did you do to their hair? I don't want to play with dolls with all that wild hair." So we locked ourselves in my bedroom, took the scissors, and cut off all the hair on my dolls' heads. Afterwards I had the nappiest-headed dolls in the world.

"Now look," Frances Delmar said when we'd lined the dolls up across my bed. "They look colored, don't they?"

They did. When Jett finally bothered us into opening the door he looked at those dolls like I was as evil as he'd suspected and at last he had the proof he needed. "What you mess up all them dolls for?" He looked at me like you look at a crazy person. "Miss Rose bought you all them dolls and you done tore them up. She ought to whip you for that."

Pain was one of Jett's main areas of interest. He liked to see me bust open and bleed some, to know he had left a white scar someplace on my white body. To this day I have scars on my legs where Jett dragged me down the gravel street behind a bicycle, and on my forehead where he accidentally dropped me headfirst off the top of the garage when he was supposed to be lowering me on a rope. I guess he would have killed me every day of the week if Lilly hadn't been there to stop him.

"Why does your mother let you play with a colored boy?" Frances Delmar would ask me. "Why don't you tell on Jett since he's so mean?" But I never did.

And Lilly didn't report to Rose either. She let Rose believe whatever it was Rose needed to believe. Most white people would think having a colored boy running all through your house bothering everything was not a good idea. But Rose didn't see a thing wrong with it. Rose has been accused of being a liberal more than once in her life, which tortures her, since she has never had the first liberal thought. Rose just believes in convenience. That's her politics.

Jett was always stealing books out of my room and taking them home with him, or hiding someplace in the house to read them. I heard Daddy say to Lilly one day, "I never saw a colored boy read like that, Lilly. If you ask me it's unnatural."

"It ain't no more unnatural than a lot of what goes on around here," Lilly said. She gets away with talking to Daddy like that. He lets her say anything she wants to to him.

"My daddy thinks you're unnatural, Jett," I said.

Jett was out on the side porch sitting in the metal swing with a book in his lap. "I ain't unnatural," Jett said. "I'm natural. Your daddy know that."

"Rose said she's missing one of her pearl earrings and she thinks you probably stole it," I said—which was a lie.

"What she think I want with a pearl?"

"I guess she thinks you like stealing for stealing' sake."

"If Ima steal something it ain't gon be no lady's ear bob. And you can tell her I said so."

"Tell her yourself," I said. Then I saw my library book in his hand. "I didn't say you could read that book, did I?"

"No need all them books to sit up in your room and go to waste cause you too blockheaded to read nothing."

"It's against the law to steal."

"Ain't nobody stealing nothing. Ain't Miss Rose taught you you spoze to share?"

"Rose has taught me everything religious," I said, "so just shut up, why don't you."

And so it was.

We played throw-the-ball-on-the-garage-roof-and-catch-it-when-it-rolls-off by the hour. I was as good as Jett. We also played dodgeball, but every time, he got to be the one to throw the ball and I had to dodge it in front of the closed garage door. If a ball was a bullet I'd have died a thousand deaths.

I knew every time Jett went to a dance or had a crush on a girl because Lilly told me. She showed me pictures of Jett dressed up in a suit and always standing by a smiling girl with an amazing hairdo and a corsage pinned to her dress. I knew the names of all the girls in the pictures. I made it my business. By this time Jett was already getting his name in the newspaper, which was unusual for a colored boy—something good, I mean. Lilly was always thumbtacking a clipping to the kitchen wall to make sure we saw it, to make sure we knew that Jett Brown, her son, was no ordinary boy. As if he hadn't driven us all crazy over the years proving that very thing.

Jett loves to dance just as much as Mac hates it. Mac says Jett's a dancing fool, but he watches him with the same sort of awe that I do. Mac says, "Ole Jett, he can dance the hell out of a song now, can't he?" And he can. He's the one that taught me what music I ought to be listening to. Lilly said it was his daddy coming out in him.

And it was Jett who taught me to fast dance too. By the time I was thirteen I had a reputation for being one of the best fast dancers of all my friends. "I swear you got colored blood," Frances Delmar said, jealous as she could be.

"Come on, Jett," she begged. "Dance with me too, son. I got all kinds of rhythm." She shook her hips like a hula dancer.

"You look like you got all the moves you need, girl," Jett said. "Can't nobody teach you nothing new, can they?"

"They can try." She grinned.

The truth is Jett never got much in the dancing mood around Frances Delmar. He watched her the way you watch a ticking bomb. He kept his distance like he didn't know what she might do next but he didn't want to be in the way of it when it happened.

"She's harmless, Jett, I swear."

"No such thing as a harmless girl," Jett said. "Especially not a white girl. Most especially not Frances Delmar."

"What about me?" I said. "How harmless am I?"

"You?" He laughed. "I'd say you pretty harmless, Dixie."

Of course, this was way before that time out in the garage when I was not so harmless, which seemed like it was as much his fault as it was mine, but no, he swears it was all my fault, like I set out to make it happen, which I swear I didn't. And it's the one and only thing that I have never told Mac about. It's my one secret.

Mac knows the part about the dancing though. That Jett taught me out in the garage, where we danced to the car radio. I got so I had a radar for Jett's body, what move he was fixing to make and how to copy him backwards. It was like mind reading, only it was body reading. We danced song after song until we were too hot to live and drowning in the music.

"You got to let loose of yourself," Jett said once, holding my hands and shaking my arms. "You dance like somebody got a body made out of boards. Loosen up, girl. Let the music get inside you some."

I thought the music *was* inside me some.

Lilly tried to get Rose to forbid me to go out to the garage and bother Jett when he was working out there. Rose thought that was the most ridiculous thing she'd ever heard. "For heaven's sake, Lilly," she said, "what's come over you?"

See, back then I guess Rose thought Jett was harmless. I guess she thought he would be like all the other colored boys she ever knew down in the mill town, who grew up and went off someplace where nobody could find them—just went invisible—and made you wonder if maybe you hadn't dreamed them up in the first place.

And now he's famous. Everybody is talking about him all the time. At least in Alabama. Next year he's going to make more money than Daddy. "I guess you could buy all of Birmingham if you wanted to," Daddy said as he stood in the kitchen and poured Jett a drink of whiskey to celebrate the good news, even though I knew Daddy didn't feel exactly right about any of this.

"If I'm going to buy some place," Jett said to Daddy, "it ain't going to be no Birmingham, Alabama."

When Mac and I told Jett we were getting married he acted a little upset about it. Like I know he thinks Mac's just marrying me since he didn't get drafted to play football. It's like Jett thinks I'm the booby prize or something. But it's not like that.

"I hope y'all know what you doing," Jett said.

"We do," I insisted.

So then he shook Mac's hand and hugged my neck. "You go easy on my man here, Dixie," he said. "Don't give him no trouble, you hear."

ROSE

I don't have a thing against Mac. For one thing, Mac is just wild about his mama and I have always liked that in a boy.

Maybe all you can hope for as a mother is that your daughter finds a boy who really loves her. Maybe Dixie's right, that that's all that matters. But there's love and there's marriage and they're two different things. If I thought Dixie would listen I'd tell her that. I'd say, "Take your time, honey. You don't have to say yes to the first boy who asks."

But I'm not sure how much longer Dixie can hold out. I know it keeps getting harder with Mac always holding on to her like he does. It's like he's got to touch her every minute to make sure, and that's in front of Bennett and me too, so I can imagine how he is when they're alone. I've said to them before that making that sort of public display is not becoming to them or anybody else. "You don't have to put on a show to let people know you love each other," I said. "You can be discreet." Mac looks at me like I am speaking some foreign language.

"I love your daughter, Mrs. Carraway," he says. "I want the whole world to know it too."

"Well, I suspect the world knows," I said, "whether they want to or not. You've pretty much seen to that."

"Good," he says.

I just want Dixie to walk down that aisle knowing it's her choice—marrying Mac. Not some trick nature has played on her.

Myself, I married into a civilized family with a good name. No mill boys for me—boys like my own brothers, who drank up their paychecks as fast as they could and drove around in their last-leg automobiles all night looking for a good clean fight. But Mama, she acted ashamed of *me* right up until her death. First it was that I had trapped "that rich boy." Next it was that "that rich boy" had bought me and if I'd been worth anything I wouldn't have been for sale. Bennett never got much from Mama, hardly a smile or a thank-you. Not that he cared. She had the same opinion of him that his people had of me. But we paid her hospital bill when she died.

Bennett says I'm disappointed that Mac didn't get drafted by the pros like Jett so he'd have the means to give Dixie a fine life. But the real truth is that Bennett's the disappointed one. He would have loved having a son-in-law playing professional football. It's no secret.

Now Jett's going to have more money than he knows what to do with. Next fall I guess we'll be watching Jett on our TV set. It just shows you what miracles God can perform.

So, yes, I wish Mac was going to be playing professional ball too. As long as his mind is going to be on football twenty-four hours a day he might as well get paid for his time. He had a good chance, I guess, but they said he's just too small. I hope he's not going to turn out to be a man who feels cheated all his life by his lack of size. Not that Mac *is* small. He's not a bit small.

So now that he's had to give up on his dream of pro ball he wants to marry Dixie right away and take her to Beasley to live. I don't know what the big hurry is.

MILLIE

Mac says the reason Bobby and Terry don't like Dixie is that they don't really know her. He says, "Mama, once we're married and they get used to having her around they'll see she's a good girl."

"Maybe so," I say. But I'm doubtful.

See, Dixie wadn't raised around boys, so she don't understand how they do. For example, it upsets her when Bobby and Terry get critical of Mac's ballplaying. So she clams up around them, crosses her arms, and goes into a little bit of a pout. See, she thinks they're hurting Mac's feelings, telling him everything he did wrong, pointing out all the errors of his ways, making fun of his mistakes. She doesn't think it's right for his own family to be talking like that. But that's how boys are. Except Marvin. Marvin's the only brother Dixie likes much.

Dixie is an only child, you know. She missed out on brothers and sisters and so she don't always read things the right way. I don't guess anybody in her family ever said a critical word to her, just *Honey* this, *Sweet honey* that. So she don't know thing one about the back and forth that goes on. That Bobby and Terry don't mean anything by it.

From the day I brought Mac home from the hospital Bobby and Terry have done nothing but love that boy. Sure they're plenty rough about it, but still and all, there's nothing in the world they wouldn't do for Mac. And he knows it. He knows they're just trying to teach him how to go about things, that this world is a certain kind of place and you got to know certain things to live in it if you're going to grow up to be a man.

When Mac was ten he got his first paper route. He was going to use the money to buy season tickets to the HamU home games. He figured it beat selling peanuts or programs, staying so busy counting change that you couldn't hardly glance at the field sideways. Next thing you knew the game'd be over and you wouldn't even know what happened. It was Terry that told him, "Forget that, man. Get you a paper route."

Bobby and Terry, they both had paper routes when they were young. It was Thurmond that made them do it. Thurmond, he never has been that big on handing out money to the boys when he could think of some way for them to earn it. Thurmond has his own ideas and the boys and I know that. He idn't the kind of father a boy would ever want to ask for anything.

Besides that, Terry told Mac that there was this one house on the route where the lady would come to the door naked sometimes. You know how boys talk. Said she would just open the door and let you stare at her while she stared at you. She'd get your money and give it to you and you'd say, "Thank you, ma'am," and the whole thing would happen like it was completely natural. And Terry laughed telling this, looking at me out of the corner of his eye. Boys do have certain curiosity—even my boys. And they can tell some stories too. And I don't know if there was a bit of truth to what Terry was saying, but Mac did get himself a paper route just the same. All he said to me about it was that he wanted those football tickets bad.

One day a boy from school, Laney Toombs, you know, a tough sort of boy, stole Mac's newspapers, just got on his bike and rode off with the newspapers hanging in a sack on the handlebars. Well, Mac couldn't let him get away with all those papers. People would be sitting around waiting on those papers. So he chased him. I mean he tore out after him, yelling, "Laney Toombs, you better get back here with those papers!" The weight of the sack sort of slowed Laney down a little, so Mac caught him, no problem. Slung him off the bicycle, papers went everywhere. Now Mac didn't want to fight him, I know that for a fact. Mac wasn't much of a fighter back then. He just wanted his bike back and his papers and to get on his way.

But this boy, Laney, you know, he's embarrassed because Mac caught him. He comes from a family that has a hard time, you know. His daddy is bad to drink. Now on top of it all he and Mac both know he's a thief. So the boy has to do something to save face. He clobbers Mac. He's not that big a boy. He's sort of skinny to tell the truth. But he pounces on Mac and so they roll around on the ground for a while. Pretty soon Mac has got him on his back and is sitting on him, you know, holding his shoulders to the ground.

Mac never did have the sort of temper Bobby and Terry got. He was always real even. So he just sat there on top of him, I mean for a long time. Mac doesn't say anything. Laney Toombs doesn't say anything. Pretty soon Laney takes his hands and begins to claw Mac's face. Runs his fingernails down his face and just, you know, claws the heck out of him.

So now Mac has got to do something, right? He shook him a few times, made Laney promise not to bother his papers anymore, and then let him up. He let him go. Laney Toombs jumped up and just started running like crazy. So Mac got up and delivered his route. And that should have been the end of it.

When Mac got home it wasn't quite dark. I was cooking supper. Thurmond wasn't home yet. Lord only knows what Marvin was up to, locked away in his room with his dog, Old King, probably dressing him up in some sort of costume. Marvin loved dressing that dog up and the dog didn't seem to mind too much either, but it would irritate the other boys so much that Marvin had to lock his door to do it. So Mac comes walking in the house and I'm trying to mash potatoes but I just drop that masher out of my hand and stare at Mac, his face. Bobby and Terry stare at him too. "What happened to you?" they say.

"Nothing," he says.

"What's that all over your face then?"

"What?" he says. "There's nothing all over my face."

"The hell there's not. Look in the mirror." My boys are bad to cuss when they get upset. It's not that I haven't talked to them about it.

It hurt me to see Mac looking like that, his sweet face just a swarm of claw marks. The flesh scratched right off his face, up underneath somebody else's dirty fingernails. "Son," I said, "who did this to you?"

"I rode my bike under a tree branch and it hit me in the face," Mac said. "That's all."

"You're lying," Bobby said. "You've been in a fight. Who you been fighting?" So Mac tells us. He says Laney Toombs. Bobby and Terry know the kid because he's got older brothers. They know where the kid lives. I know the family too. The mother works over at the hospital in the laundry department. The last time I was there she changed my bedsheets. Before I can say much Bobby and Terry grab Mac and throw him in the car.

"Where you taking him?" I ask.

"Mama," Bobby says, "he's got to learn to fight. If he don't know how to fight then he's gon get beat up every day of his life. We're not gon let that happen."

So I take off my apron. "I'm coming with you," I say.

"No way," Terry says. "You stay here. We'll handle this."

"I'm his mother," I say, "and I'll handle him—and you all too. I will not have my boys going around like a gang of hoodlums. We're going to go about this as nice as we can. Do you understand me?"

So we all get in the car and Bobby drives us over to the Toombs' house. Mac's about to cry by now.

"You mean you just sat on him and let him scratch you that way?" Terry said. "Why the hell didn't you hit him?"

"I don't know," Mac said. "I think I felt sorry for him."

"Can you believe that?" Terry said. "He's feeling sorry for a kid who's clawing his face until it bleeds like a damn river."

When we got to the Toombs' house I felt sort of sick to my stomach. I wished Thurmond was here to be doing this. "We're going to be polite about this," I say to my boys. "I don't want y'all to do anything to embarrass your daddy and me."

Bobby and Terry drag Mac up to the door of the Toombs' house. I walk along behind them. My hair isn't even combed. Mr. Toombs answers the door. It's like at first he thinks maybe we're selling something. Bobby and Terry tell him the story. They tell him they don't want any trouble. All they want is a fair fight. They want Mac and Laney to go at it again.

Mr. Toombs keeps looking at me standing there, a boy's mother. Idn't a boy's mother supposed to be against fighting? Shouldn't I be putting my foot down and saying I will not allow any fighting? But Mr. Toombs doesn't know how it is. I'm outnumbered. It'll either be this way now or some worse way that my boys will arrange themselves later. I know how boys are. "Hello, Mr. Toombs," I say. "I am real sorry about this trouble. I wish we didn't have to do this."

He stares at me and then grabs Laney by the neck of his shirt and drags him outside. I don't want those boys to hit each other. I don't want to watch them do it. I wonder what my blood pressure would read about now and I'm glad I don't know.

Right before Bobby shoved Mac at the kid he got up in his face and said, "Either you whip his butt or when we get you home we'll whip yours. Fight like you got some balls, damnit."

I guess old Mr. Toombs said something likewise to Laney and they went at it. It was kill or be killed if you ask me—those little boys, their pink arms flailing and their feet kicking. Mac was bigger than Laney. That was the thing. It didn't take him long to wear Laney out. I didn't want him to. I swear to goodness. Mac tore the kid to pieces. It was awful. I let it go on until I couldn't stand another minute, then I cried, "Stop this right now. That's enough of this. No more."

And Bobby yanked Mac off Laney, and Mr. Toombs snatched Laney up from where he was laying on the ground. And it was over.

I watched Mr. Toombs shove Laney into the house giving him a tongue-lashing. I bet he beat the living daylights out of that poor boy all over again for losing that fight.

And Mac was a bloody mess too. His nose was busted. But he had this look on his face that a mother knows. It was one of almost total satisfaction. It was like for this one moment Mac really loved himself. And Bobby and Terry loved him too. And maybe I did, but I like to think I'm woman enough to love my boys win or lose. But I saw it, how satisfying a boy's first real fistfight was. I wished Marvin had been with us to see it. Like maybe he could just learn something from Mac's example.

When I hear Mac tell Dixie this story about Laney Toombs, she doesn't understand. I can see she doesn't. But she understands him enough to love him. And that's mostly what a mother cares about.

"There's times people have to fight, honey." That's what I want to tell her. "It's not necessarily the end of the world either." But right now, the way she's looking at Mac with all that love in her eyes, she's in no position to believe me.

DIXIE

When Mac and I first tell Rose we want to get married she goes straight to the phone to make me what she calls a prenuptial appointment with the doctor. After what happened to her, Rose is a big believer in birth control. She thinks I don't know a thing about it, what happened, but it's not that hard to figure out.

On our way to the doctor's office Rose says, "I wish they'd had something like this in my day," meaning the Pill. It makes me sad to hear her talk like that. "Well, I'm glad they didn't," I say, "or I probably wouldn't be here right now, would I?"

I have no way of knowing, of course, but I'd say if Rose and Daddy make love once a year Daddy's lucky. Rose is above almost anything that has to do with the actual body. Maybe that explains why Daddy drinks himself to sleep almost every night. For example, I've never once seen Rose naked—unless you count that night when everything happened, but she wasn't totally naked even then. It just seemed like it. Even when she's driving me to the doctor's office I can feel her embarrassment. I started my period when I was ten years old, and Rose seemed so sorry about it. She gave me a book from the Baptist Church called *Becoming a Christian Woman*. Rose works at First Baptist Church. She's assistant to Pastor Zale Swanson, has been since right before I was born. She acts like Pastor Swanson's the most wonderful person on earth, but I think his hair is too perfect. The book had some diagrams of female insides and explained things the best it could without going all out and telling the truth.

Dr. Larry Durrell has been Rose's doctor all her life and he delivered me too, has known me since before I was born. He says I was born with something on my mind and when I was little he used to wink at Rose and ask me what I was so worried about. But I didn't know. So he'd tickle me and not stop until he'd made me laugh. He's also the one who gave Rose that pamphlet on alcoholism, which made her so crazy he had to call her up and apologize. Daddy's not an actual alcoholic. He just likes to drink. It relaxes him. He could probably stop anytime he wanted to. He probably would too, if Rose didn't stay on his nerves all the time.

When I'm called back to the examining room Rose says to Dr. Durrell, "Dixie's getting married, Larry." And he looks at me with his glasses hanging nearly off his nose and nods. See, if you know Rose you learn her code. How she says everything without really saying anything.

"Marrying the Gibbs boy, the Black Bear quarterback, are you, Dixie?" he says.

"Yes, sir," I say and go hot with humiliation. Rose waits outside while Dr. Durrell puts that cold speculum between my legs and looks to see if everything is all right. I know what he's looking for. Evidence. To see if I've let Mac do anything I wasn't supposed to let him do. So he can tell Rose.

But I am as pure as the driven snow.

Well, maybe not *perfectly* pure. Nobody's perfect, right?

When he finishes, Rose thanks him and he pats her shoulder and looks at her like he's in love with her, the way so many men do, which I've gotten used to. All my life people have stared at Rose. She dresses in that sort of good taste that borders on the worst sort of boring. Her hair is perfect too, short and very simple. She's medium height and slender and everybody wants to look at her. You have to. Rose is the only woman I know who thinks Jackie Kennedy is a little bit tacky the way she lets her hair get too long and dyes it so black. "Less is more," Rose always says. I don't always know exactly what she's talking about. But even so, it wouldn't surprise me if she was right.

So far not one single person has said marrying Mac is a bad idea. Frances Delmar says if I don't marry him, she will. She doesn't mean it. She's as crazy as she can be over Mac's friend Cleet James. He played defensive line for HamU. He's from Mississippi so he's really wild. He's also big. He has to send away to have his shoes specially made.

The only person who isn't very crazy about the idea is Porter Warren. He goes to Harvard now, but he writes to me all the time. He's not my type at all, but I've always sort of liked him for some reason. We used to sit out on the porch and he would get me to read my poems out loud to him. Now I send them to him in the mail and he writes back long letters telling me what they mean to him. He can find meaning in them that I never even knew was there. He's so smart he makes me feel like I'm smart too—which I secretly believe I am.

The bad thing about Porter when he comes over is that he tries to kiss me all the time. It seems wrong. Porter's very tall and thin and his hair is real long, but it's clean. He listens to opera even though it's in Italian and I know for a fact that he doesn't understand a word of it. He tries to get me to listen, but I refuse. "I'm not one to put on airs, Porter," I say. "I don't like things I don't understand."

"Of course you do," he says. "It's all the stuff people don't understand that they love the most."

"Oh yeah? Like what?"

"Like themselves. Like other people."

"You are too deep for me, Porter. I mean it."

"Not like Mac, huh?"

"Excuse me, Porter, but Mac is plenty deep," I say.

Then Porter smiles at me. "Sure. Sure he is, Dix."

I'm not about to let him pull me into that world of weird ideas where almost nobody I know ever goes. I prefer the regular world where people mostly think of the task at hand and not much else. At least a hundred times I've said, "No kissing, Porter. Let's just be friends." But you know how boys hate that. Saying *Let's be friends* to a boy is like waving a red flag in front of a bull.

Now he's written me these letters saying, "Dixie, you're nineteen years old. Your life is just beginning. You are nowhere near ready to get married, to give your life away to Mac or anybody else—and you know it too."

I don't get mad at him for saying that. Even when he calls and tries to talk some sense into me, as he puts it, I don't get mad. He means well.

I write him back, tell him the date of the wedding and that his invitation will be coming. I say, "Dear Porter . . . Mac really loves me. That's the main thing, isn't it?"

The newspaper says that Birmingham is sending lots of its native sons over to Vietnam, but so far I don't know a single one of the natives they're talking about. Not one boy out of my own personal life has been drafted. Boys I know are not soldier material, I guess. Most of them are going to college instead.

Daddy gets upset when he sees hippies on TV. He hates boys unwilling to be soldiers, unwilling to die for their country. He says, "Why don't you get a haircut, punk?" to the longhaired boys on TV. He says, "Looks like a bunch of ugly girls with all that dirty hair and those damn beads."

See, down here hippieness is more a look than anything else—a style, you know. People disrespect it too. So it's mostly the people who are already disrespected for other reasons that dress that way in the first place. It's sort of like a bad costume or something. Like being a hippie is a kind of game that requires a particular uniform. Like it's what you wear to smoke dope in and listen to your hair grow. And Birmingham has always been a place that believes in dressing correctly for every occasion.

Mac will not get drafted. He has a letter from his doctor about his shoulder falling out of the socket. So he's deferred, thank God. Jett and Cleet are too. Coach Bomar saw to that. So while other baby-faced boys are deep in a jungle way over their heads fighting one of America's small but sure enemies in a televised real war, Mac and Jett and Cleet and lots of other college athletes are distracting the American people, giving them a thrill or two by staging little harmless televised fake wars on the football fields of America. And people are loving it. Even people whose own sons are across the ocean in the muck of Vietnam buy tickets to watch college boys play a clean version of imitation war on a perfectly lined field of grass.

If you ask me, a boy has a much better chance of being considered a real hero for his dazzling performance on the football field than a boy does for his dazzling performance in the combat zone. This is one perfect example of when the imitation is more valuable than the real thing.

On the news it says that even the soldiers way over in Vietnam try to tune in to the football games every chance they get. They have a whole betting pool going too. It's like their recreation—betting their government checks on their home teams.

This doesn't seem right to me. So I spend a lot of my spare time thinking up alternative ways of fighting wars. Here's what I've come up with so far.

1. *The Trading-Places Plan:* What if right before a war started the warring nations agreed to trade a thousand families each? You know, a thousand mothers with all their children from each country would trade places. Then when the men started fighting they'd be afraid to drop bombs because they might kill their own wives and children, or their neighbor's wives and children.

2. *The One-Country-of-Endless-War Plan:* The world could set aside one small country that's just for wars. Nobody would actually live there. But when countries get mad at each other, they could book a war, you know, schedule it, and send their soldiers to this small country and just let them fight it out.

Frances Delmar says, "Dixie, this is just too far-fetched. It'll never work in real life."

But I say, "It's no more far-fetched than the way we do it now." I say, "Excuse me, but I can't imagine being able to hate total strangers enough to kill them in cold blood."

"It's like if you have to kill people to stay alive yourself," she says. Now that Frances Delmar writes letters to a bunch of soldiers she doesn't even know, she thinks she's an expert on war.

3. *The Death-Proof War Plan:* Instead of an army, every country could have a national football team made up of its finest soldiers. We could take all the guns away from everybody on earth. We could get rid of all the bombs and use the small country originally set aside for wars for football games instead. Only there would be something important at risk, you know. Like a territorial boundary. Or the right to a democratic election. Or removal of a cruel dictator. Or lifting of a trade embargo. It could be determined ahead of time exactly what was at stake, and it could be winner-take-all.

Any countries who wanted to could have national cheerleaders too. The Muslim women could cheer in their veils. The Hindu women could cheer in their saris. The island women could cheer in their grass skirts. The Dutch women could cheer in their wooden shoes. The Japanese women could cheer with their bound feet.

Here's what would happen. Countries with lots of money and resources would want to find ways to beat the other countries like always, so they'd start trying to recruit the greatest athletes in the world, not just in their own countries. This would slowly start getting people from different countries all playing on the same teams—you know, like a defensive line of Russians, Japanese sumo wrestlers, and Samoans and maybe a Kenyan running back and a kicker from India or Peru. Over time, if all went well, every country would have a multicultural team with players from everywhere. And by the time that happened then half of what countries go to war to protect would already be handled. I believe maybe this could actually work.

MILLIE

I'd of given anything if I could have got Marvin interested in playing ball like my other boys. He sang in the choir instead. It was practice, practice, practice, same as if the choir was some kind of team. And I'm a good Christian myself, so I was proud to have a son moved to sing in the choir. I mean it. Marvin has a real pretty voice.

But Thurmond, his daddy, was right. It was sports the boy needed. We should have insisted on it, I guess. Made him play whether he wanted to or not. But it didn't take much to see he was uninclined. Bobby would work with him out in the back yard, throwing the ball, trying to teach him just the fundamentals, and looked like every time he tried to help Marvin it ended up with Marvin hurt and crying, locking himself in his room or some such.

It looked for a while there like Mac might have a future in professional football. I still think he's good enough if the pros would've just had the courage to give him a chance. All his life coaches have been telling him he was too small or too slow and he's proven them wrong every time. He could prove it again, but this time since money comes into it, seems like they won't give him a try. It's nearly broke Thurmond's heart.

Now Mac has just given up on a pro football career. Bobby thinks it's Dixie that talked him out of his dream, that she didn't encourage Mac enough. But I say, "Mac is a grown boy, and he ought to know his own mind by now. If he says he wants to marry Dixie, then I say fine, we'll welcome her into our family the same as we did Lisa and Janelle." After this houseful of boys, I like having some daughters-in-law around here.

I guess this wedding Dixie's people are planning is going to be something. Rose Carraway called over here to ask me what color dress I was planning to wear and the truth was I hadn't even looked at the fabric store yet or the pattern book, but I just said pink right off the top of my head and she said, "Well, I was thinking I might wear pink too." So I said, "Fine with me. We'll just both wear pink then." But Dixie told me just the other day that her mother had gone out and got herself a beige dress instead. And I've got my dress cut out—when I got down to it, I got blue—and it's laying in there on the dining room table so all I got to do is find the time one day to sit down at the machine and stitch it together. I showed Mac the pattern and he said he liked it. "You and Dixie will be the prettiest girls there, Mama," he said. Mac's always talking sweet like that.

That first time Mac ever brought Dixie around here for supper it was a Sunday night back when he was still in high school and I'll never forget it. I made fried chicken and Jell-O salad and all Mac's favorites and it all turned out so nice and everybody sat around the kitchen table and talked very nice, out of respect for Mac, you know, who was bringing this girl to meet us. As many girlfriends as he'd had, you could count on one hand how many girls he ever brought home, so right off we knew this was real significant to him, this girl.

After supper we were all sitting around out in the carport drinking our ice tea when Marvin came outside on his way to Nativity rehearsal. He carried that Joseph costume I'd made him on a hanger, careful not to let it drag the ground. He was off to church, like I said, which never hurt anybody. But Bobby, right off, took objection to the shoes Marvin had on his feet. They were sort of like uncommonly modern cowboy boots with zippers up the front. I didn't think they were so bad. But Bobby starts ordering Marvin to take them off. And Bobby's bad to cuss too when he gets upset.

When Bobby and Terry get after Marvin about something, Marvin has this way of smart-talking them, saying, "It's a free country," which I don't know what ever gave him that idea, or why he thinks it's any kind of thing to say to his brothers when they're already upset. Now I don't want to take sides here, but it does seem to me that Marvin can aggravate a bad situation as much as anybody. His brothers are telling him to get rid of the shoes and he says, "Who elected you two queens for the day?"

And Mac's Dixie is just sitting there beside him with the sweetest smile on her face because she don't have any idea what's about to go on. Bobby was up out of his seat so fast his lawn chair folded closed behind him. He grabbed Marvin from behind and Terry sprang up and grabbed Marvin's kicking feet.

Thurmond got up out of his chair and went in the house and closed the door behind him. He believes in letting nature take its course. It was like his secret prayer that Bobby and Terry could pound Marvin hard enough in just the right spot so that he would miraculously be transformed into the sort of boy he ought to be. Bring his manhood to the surface some way. I don't guess you can blame a father for that.

Mac, bless his heart, tried to pull Bobby off Marvin, but he couldn't. It was like Bobby was saddle-breaking a wild horse and every second he could stay on his back was another point. "Get off him," Mac yelled. So Bobby hauled off and punched Mac. So then Mac punched him back. I knew how it was going to go. I'd been down this road more times than I could count.

Bobby shouted at Marvin and Mac, and Mac shouted back and I'm not telling what they said, because it would sound like they haven't had good home training, which they have. I don't allow ugly talk in my house and they know it. Of course, I guess technically, the carport is not the house, is it? And you know boys just do not have good self-control, not like girls. I say this because sometimes it seems like I'm the only person in this house who knows how to control myself.

Then, still straddling Marvin, Bobby shook him hard, banging his head up and down on the carport cement, looking Marvin square in the eye. And they both had tears in their eyes too.

Somewhere in all of this I did what I could think to do. I ran over and poured my glass of cold tea on them, ice cubes and all. "Stop this," I said. "I mean it now. Stop this."

Dixie, she just sat like she was glued to her chair, her face gone so pale and her eyes jumping from brother to brother. I knew Mac had wanted us to make a good impression, to make her feel at home.

Marvin's face was a deep shade of purple like it gets when he's so upset he can't think what to do. One eye was beginning to swell and his lip was bleeding. He mumbled something nasty and wiped his face with his shirttail.

"Son, don't talk ugly," I said. "That's not like you." See the younger boys, they learn from the older boys. That's part of the problem.

Marvin walked over and helped me pick up the Joseph costume. "It's all right, honey," I said. "See?" I held it up by the hanger and brushed it off the best I could with my hand. "I can press it again for you if you want me to."

"No, Mama," Marvin said. "It's okay."

And Mac, bless his soul, went over to where Dixie was sitting frozen in that chair and he pulled her up beside him. I'll never forget what he said to her. It made me so ashamed. "Welcome to the Gibbs insane asylum," he said. "You don't have to be crazy to live here, but it helps."

Then Mac and Dixie got Marvin in the car and drove him on to the church for his Nativity practice. I bet Mac had Marvin practically cheered up by the time they got there. He's always been good at that. Mac, he's a sweet boy. I saw Dixie's little made-up face there in the car window looking so bewildered. She waved good-bye to me as they pulled out of the driveway.

I hadn't raised all these boys without learning a few things. But my daughters-in-law, they'll have to learn this on their own and maybe they will and maybe they won't. It's not something you can tell somebody who hasn't lived any of it yet.

But inside all this fighting and ugly talk is a sort of hard love between boys that I had never known about before I had sons of my own. Even when Bobby had Marvin pinned to the ground and was practically spitting in his face, Bobby loved Marvin.

And Marvin, he makes himself into a test that's too hard for Bobby to pass. Then Marvin wins. Even with a black eye and a busted lip, he declared himself the winner—I could tell. And Bobby, with every punch he threw, with every stabbing word, he was saying, *I love you, you're my own brother. Why can't you just let me love you?* Men beating their love into each other. Afraid it won't be felt unless it nearly kills them.

See, not everybody understands this. Lots of young girls don't. And Bobby and Terry, even though they married two of the sweetest girls around, they don't really tend toward girls all that much. Girls make them nervous. I believe they think women are dangerous, which tickles me, if you want to know the truth.

But Mac—all this fighting around here is partly why Mac has always been partial to girls, I think. Because they were not brothers of any kind—or teammates either. Girls have always been the place Mac went to rest.

So after graduation when we put Marvin on that bus to New York City, where he'd always been talking about wanting to go, how did I feel? Was I sad? Just Mac and Dixie and me standing at the Greyhound station waving good-bye, Mac with his arm around me so tight like he thought losing Marvin that way might just make me collapse right there from grief. My baby off to New York City, where nothing good ever happens that I've ever heard of, but I thought, *Thank you, Lord. If this is your plan for Marvin's life then I'm grateful. If this is what you and Marvin want for him, then I will not interfere.*

I'd kissed his face and said, "I love you, Son. You're special to me. You've always been special."

"I know, Mama," he said. "I love you too."

We have not laid eyes on him since, but we got that note recently that said he was coming home for Mac's wedding. It seems like Dixie called him up and begged him to come and she got her Daddy to send him a paid ticket and so then there was no good reason for him not to. There's not a day goes by that I don't say a prayer for Marvin.

For all my boys.

DIXIE

Mac was raised Baptist like me but it came out different on him. Mac's mother thinks he is destined to be a preacher and just the idea of it gives her pleasure. Of course that doesn't scare me because I know that kind of thinking is essential to any decent Baptist mother.

Mrs. Gibbs is tiny, not even five feet tall. She dresses neat as a pin in clothes she makes herself. You can hardly tell except that she's inclined to mention it. Her glasses hang around her neck on a chain and her sweater hangs over her shoulders on a second chain. She wears her hair twisted up on her head more like a grandmother than a mother. She has a nice Southern look to her, just the barest suggestion of a nose on a delicate face gone soft. Mac says she's a country woman who moved to town after she got married, but who never really adjusted to town ways—which is something he greatly respects.

"Mama's the sweetest lady in the world," Mac says. "Anybody who can't get along with Mama can't get along with me either."

If that's a warning it's unnecessary. As far as I can tell, the only way not to get along with Millie Gibbs is to set your mind to it. She's willing to overcooperate with anybody in any circumstances. "There's two things I can't stand," she told me once, "and both of them are being at odds with somebody."

One time Mrs. Gibbs and I were standing outside the locker room waiting for Mac when Bobby and Terry passed us on their way inside. "Hey Dumb Bunny," Terry said. He kissed the top of Mrs. Gibbs's head.

"How's it going, Dumb Bunny?" Bobby winked at his mother.

I could feel a certain look come over my face.

Mrs. Gibbs patted my arm. "They call me Dumb Bunny because I don't understand football." She laughed. "It doesn't hurt my feelings, honey. Bobby got that started when he was a little boy. You know how boys love to believe they're smarter than their mama. 'Mama,' he'd say, 'for a lady who's been watching football all her life you sure don't know a thing about it.'

"I tell my boys that's the good thing about football—it doesn't require understanding it to enjoy it. I don't care the first thing about understanding it." She smiled. "Do you?"

"Not really," I said.

"If my boys didn't tease me I'd think they didn't love me," she said. "I wish I had a nickel for every minute I've spent waiting on my boys to come out of the locker room," Mrs. Gibbs said. "I'd be a rich woman by now." She reached for a tissue in her purse and began wiping off her glasses. "I hope you don't mind me asking"—her voice dropped to a whisper—"but did Mac tell you about his mountaintop experience?"

"Excuse me?" I said.

"You know. His conversion. It happened at a Gulf Shores Baptist Retreat a couple of summers ago. I have letters he wrote. He invited Jesus into his life. Mac's not an ordinary boy. He's special and I'd say so even if I wasn't his mother. He doesn't drink or smoke. That's not easy this day and age. You know how boys are."

Then she put her glasses on as if to study my face. "The Lord is at work in Mac's life. A mother can see these things. It wouldn't surprise me if Mac decided to dedicate his life to Christ. I wouldn't want anything to interfere with that. He'd make a wonderful preacher, don't you think?"

"Yes, ma'am," I said, even though I know it's wrong to lie to a boy's mother.

Sometimes when Mac and I are parked up near Vulcan I think about Mrs. Gibbs, how even after all this time she's still holding out for Mac to make a preacher. All the hopes she has for him. The way she hardly knows him at all. Not like I do.

The first night Mac ever unzipped his pants—or maybe I unzipped them, I can't remember exactly—I knew that nothing would ever be the same again. We held his penis in our hands—that's all—both of us, and petted it as gently as if it were a newborn puppy, man's best friend, one that would grow up to be a watchdog and guard and protect me all my life. Be loyal, just naturally.

I wasn't scared. It was like finding out Mac had a split personality or a fraternal twin I'd never met before. His penis was like his other self. A penis doesn't lie. I could tell right away. "This big guy loves you, Dix," Mac teased. And just like a dog who'd learned a handful of special tricks, his penis did everything to convince me—short of repeating those exact lines out loud.

There's so much power in my touch. I swear I'm magic. I personally count this as a religious experience. I don't know if Mac's penis is beautiful or not, since I haven't got entirely used to looking at it yet and don't have that much to compare it to, but I told him it was beautiful. "Thank you," he said, like it was a compliment he'd been hearing all his life.

"I love you more than anything, Dixie," he whispered.

I could tell by the way he said it that it was the God's honest truth.

LILLY

I could have married a hundred different times since Castro left. I've kept myself up. I can still open a man's nose and have him all up in my way, following me around like a little lost dog. So it's not that I don't have a man cause I can't get one. I can get as many as I want.

When I saw that Castro he wasn't thinking on coming back for us, then I said, "All right then." It was like what little trust I had in a man he packed up in his guitar case and took it somewhere in the vicinity of Memphis and lost it who knows where over there. I don't have no more. Trust is in short supply all around, if you ask me. And let me tell you this, if you want a man to lay down at your feet and cry and beg, then all you got to do is make it plain right up front that you do not trust him and you are not about to ever start trusting him, so it don't matter what he do or don't do. This will make a man crazy. A man can't hardly stand it. It is something useful to know.

I told myself, *Lilly, just raise up your son the best way you can. Make him into something. See if you can't put one man out into this world that would have something to offer a woman.* And all while I was raising Jett I didn't waver. There was no kinda man coming around my house at suppertime, nobody waking up in my bed in the morning or searching for his shoes in the middle of the night. I didn't want that example for Jett. I didn't want him thinking I loved nobody else in this world as much as I loved him. Cause I didn't.

Oh, there was one or two come close. There was a couple that I might have given a chance if I hadn't been all out of chances. A couple of times when Jett thought I was out of town with the church mission, I was no more out of town than he was. I was checked into someplace nice with somebody nice. But he never needed to know nothing about that. And it done me a world of good too. I come home singing. But eventually you gon get to the last line of a song. Then that was the end of it.

Girls is so different from boys too. Because Dixie now, she know things sometimes that don't nobody have to tell her. And Jett, sometimes he won't know something one minute after I just got through telling him. See, Dixie, she want to know everything. She act like she got to know or she'll die. But Jett, he only want to know what he want to know. He keeps it simple like that.

So on those mornings I come to work wearing something nice, wearing something besides my pedal pushers and flaps, she'd notice. She'd look me up and down, notice my hair was nice, notice I had on some nail polish, and say, "Okay, Lilly, what's his name?" Like the child could tell when I had a man sniffing around me. She wadn't never wrong. But Jett? Lord no. I'd leave the house in the morning all put together—good shoes, perfume, something extra nice that I don't ordinarily wear to work—but he wouldn't take the slightest notice of it. Of course all that did was make it easier on me. But still, I swear, it worries me a little bit that all the details of things just go right by Jett so unnoticed. His daddy was nothing like that. His daddy noticed everything and then went on and made up the rest any way he wanted to. Nothing got by him.

Dixie now, she'd want to meet these men when they come by the house to see me. I had them come by the Carraways for a cup of coffee maybe, you know. Maybe a little hot lunch or something. And Dixie would be right up in the way if she could, watching and listening. Staring a hole in these men, who might already be plenty nervous sitting in a white man's kitchen. Lot of mens are not that used to being stared up and down by a white girl. I mean she studied them hard. "Do you love him, Lilly?" she would whisper to me.

"No, darling," I would say. "I don't love him."

If Mr. Carraway come home when I wadn't expecting him then it was no trouble to say, "Mr. Carraway, meet Blythe here. He's come to fix the oven." Or "Mr. Carraway, meet James Spivey. He's trying to get me to buy some more life insurance." Mr. Carraway believes what I say. He don't never question me.

And Rose, just that one time she came walking in unexpected, which I can count on one hand the times she done that. Well, she saw that colored man there inside her house, and I swear if she didn't pause and look around to make sure she hadn't wandered into the wrong house, or wandered all the way back to when she was a little girl in the mill section and colored folks were everywhere she looked. "This is James," I said to her. "He's a friend of mine. We're just having some lunch."

"I see," she said. Then she looked at me like it was the first time she'd ever noticed that I was a woman the same as her. I ain't never scared of Rose, of what she might do. For one thing I'm pretty sure she won't do nothing. Besides, I know too much of her business to be worried about if she knows a little bit of mine. She said, "There's some rainbow sherbet in the freezer, if you think James might like some, Lilly."

Of course, we didn't want no sherbet. Colored folks don't truck with sherbet—it ain't enough to it. But I got that that was her way of saying, *I ain't seen nothing, Lilly. I didn't even come and go here today.* Which is sort of the best she knows how to act.

And Dixie, bless her, she never told not one word of my business to her mama or daddy, either one. Nor to Jett either, far as I know. And there was things she could of told if she'd wanted to. She can keep a secret better than I ever thought a white person could. So because of that I don't mind if she knows just the tiniest bit of my business either.

When I said I was gon wear the reddest dress I could find to Dixie's wedding, cause I look like something you can't forget in a red dress now, Rose said, "Lilly, red is not right for a wedding. Red is too much." That's the way she thinks and I know it, which makes me all the more set on red. If she thinks I'm coming to that wedding to play the part of her maid, she's wronger than she ever dreamed. I'm a guest like everybody else. And I don't think Rose has the bad taste to be telling her other guests what they ought to wear to a wedding.

Red is the right color. Idn't blood red? Idn't the heart muscle as red as a vine-ripe tomato? Idn't red the color of a stop sign? Cause there's things that's gon stop once you get married if you do it right. Idn't red the strongest color there is? Well, I think red is a good color for a wedding. Maybe if I'd of wore a red dress when I married Castro then he won't of had to go to Memphis looking for some other woman with sense enough to wear red.

"I love red, Lilly," Dixie said. "You'll look so good in red."

"I look good don't matter what color I wear, darling," I told her. It's the truth too.

DIXIE

Mac comes over one Sunday afternoon before the wedding with a page out of the *Birmingham News*. "Look at this." He hands it to me.

There is a small headline that says FAIRFIELD SOLDIER KILLED IN HANOI. I begin to read the article. It lists all the surviving family members.

"It's Laney Toombs," Mac says.

"Who?"

"You know. I told you. Laney Toombs, the guy who stole my newspapers that time. Bobby and Terry made us go at it in his front yard when we were kids. Remember? He's dead," Mac says. "Killed in action. The family is receiving people at the funeral home tonight. I'm going. Do you want to go with me?"

"I didn't really know him," I say.

"I didn't either," Mac says. "His family moved to Fairfield when we were in high school. I heard he dropped out. Hadn't seen him since."

"Maybe you could just write his family a note," I say.

"I'm going to the funeral home. Definitely. Mama is at home now making a chicken casserole and a Jell-O salad to take by their house. She remembers Laney because she liked to died when he got those tattoos put on when he was just barely in high school. He rolled up his shirtsleeve once to show her the word *Mama* wrapped around a rose. He'd flex his muscle and make the word jump. It made a real impression on her."

I dress in church clothes, including matching shoes and purse. I wear pearls. Rose wanted to plan the flowers for the wedding today, but I didn't feel like it since all I could picture was a funeral spray—the way they can make them stand up on easels like works of art, the way they bury the casket in flowers first, before they bury it in the ground. You should not plan a wedding when you have death on your mind like this. I could not get interested. So Rose said, "Shall I just make this decision for you, Dixie?"

"Go ahead," I tell her.

And I go with Mac to Fairfield Funeral Home. I haven't been well trained in death etiquette. My grandparents died when I was too little to remember. The only funeral I've been to was Frances Delmar's grandmother's. It wasn't half as sad as this.

Laney's mother sits in a chair beside the coffin. It's a closed coffin. She has no expression on her face. For all the world she could pass as a corpse herself. "We gave her some tranquilizers," her sister told me, "to calm her down."

I say to her, "I'm so sorry about Laney," and she doesn't say anything. She doesn't blink an eye.

But nobody has given Laney's daddy any tranquilizers. He's had whiskey, you can smell it on his breath, but it isn't really working. He's completely coming apart with every new person who walks into the funeral home. His crying sort of breaks out of him, totally unexpected, like until this very moment he hadn't even known he had any crying in him.

Mac shakes Mr. Toombs's hand and says, "I'm Mac Gibbs. I went to school with Laney." Then Mr. Toombs breaks down and cries. Mac tries to put his arm around him in a manly way. The sight of it makes me cry too. I know I have mascara running all down my face.

A couple of Laney's older brothers come over and take hold of their father. Mr. Toombs says, "This here is Mac Gibbs. He was quarterback for the Birmingham Black Bears. He knew Laney." The brothers shake Mac's hand. Then one of them yells across the room to his nearly dead mother, "Mama, this is Mac Gibbs. The Black Bear quarterback—you heard of him—come to pay respects to Laney." She doesn't so much as twitch at the information. "She's upset," the brother tells Mac. "This is real hard on her."

I sit in a chair against the wall while Mac speaks to this and that person. I can't do it. I am crying because Mr. Toombs is crying. I'm not used to that, seeing men cry over their children. It's terrible. I blow my nose and just sort of watch people mill around the room. I can see lots of family resemblances. The Toombs are a pretty big family. That's good.

Finally, Mac shakes Mr.Toombs's hand a last time and pats his shoulder, saying, "Laney was a good guy. I always liked Laney."

Mr. Toombs nods yes, yes.

As Mac turns to go, Mr. Toombs says, "Long as you're here, son, let me ask you something. Any chance you could get an old man a couple of tickets to the Birmingham–Tennessee game next season?"

Mac doesn't blink an eye. He's used to this request. "Sure thing," he says. "I can handle that. I'll leave you a couple of tickets at Will Call."

"I sure appreciate it," Mr. Toombs says. "I know Laney would appreciate it too."

"It's the least I can do," Mac says.

And if you ask me, it is.

FIRST DOWN

DIXIE

Our wedding was everything Rose wanted it to be. Frances Delmar wore a push-up bra that turned the tasteful bridesmaid dress Rose picked out into a dish and her breasts into ripe fruit artfully displayed there.

Bobby and Terry didn't much like it that Jett was Mac's best man. "The Shadow," they called him, like it was a joke. Jett stood next to Mac with the ring in his pocket. They were just like salt and pepper shakers, the nickname they'd been given by the press in college. A set you were not allowed to break up.

Pastor Swanson was his perfect self with his perfect hair. Rose arranged for the flowers to remain in the sanctuary for Sunday's church service. The bulletin would read, "Gift of Bennett and Rose Carraway in honor of the marriage of their daughter, Dixie Lee, to Mr. Mac Gibbs."

Rose thought I should wear my hair up. Mac wanted me to wear it down. I wore the top pulled up and the bottom hanging down. My dress was a fitted ivory satin. No beading, no lace, no razzmatazz. Rose saw to that. When I put on my veil I felt like one of those girls Daddy used to read to me about, who was rescued from her small, tattered life by the kiss of a dark-haired prince. Finally Daddy tapped on the door and said, "Okay, Dixie. Let's get this show on the road before one of us changes our mind." He shook like a leaf when he walked me down the aisle. I took comfort in the sweet smell of his bourboned breath. The church was packed. It looked like Rose had invited every person she'd ever met in her life.

My friends from high school came, and their parents too. And my Tri-Delta pledge sisters from HamU. Most of the Black Bears team was there. Mac recited his vows with his eyes so intent on mine that I was almost frightened by his sincerity.

Afterwards there was music and dancing. Mac was square shouldered and beautiful in his tuxedo. One of my favorite pictures is of him dancing with Millie. She told me her dress fabric didn't cost but $1.98 a yard and she hadn't needed but two and a half yards. She had silk flowers pinned in her hair. Mac picked her up off the ground and swung her through the air like she was a tiny pastel bird. The look on his face was something.

Jett and Lilly were the first two black people to ever step foot inside the Birmingham Country Club as genuine guests. Rose was smart enough to keep that a secret until it happened. Lilly wore a hot-pink dress (as close to red as you can get and not go full-force red) and a wide-brimmed hat and shoes dyed to match. She had to go all out since she was the only black woman there and all white women naturally expect a black woman to outdress them by a mile. There are certain ways that Lilly really hates to let white people down. "If I'm gon dress up, I'm gon show up," Lilly said.

Mac's parents don't drink. Obviously Daddy does. We compromised by having champagne and also fruit punch. As it happened Thurmond got as drunk as Daddy, maybe drunker. We have pictures. Millie said Thurmond wasn't used to free liquor and from the looks of him it was a good thing too. She said it was the *free* he was giving in to, not the liquor. Bobby and Terry stood at the champagne bar saying, "How much you guess this wedding set Dixie's old man back?"

Mac and I slow danced to "When a Man Loves a Woman." He whispered, "God, I love you, Dix," and I was so happy I didn't know what to do. We could both feel our hearts beating through our clothes. It was getting hot with all the music and dancing. Sweat was trickling down the sides of our faces.

Jett asked me to dance too because he said the best man was supposed to dance with the bride and sort of unofficially hand the groom over to her. We fast danced. Everybody stopped to watch Jett. He's something. When the dance was over Jett kissed my cheek and said, "Don't forget who taught you everything you know, girl." See, he can be sweet if he wants to.

By the time Mac and I left the reception the band was packing their instruments. The throbbing of the guests had become a murmur of general good wishes and sexual suggestions. We started our life together wearing brand-new clothes with the price tags still on them. With rice in our hair, JUST MARRIED shoe-polished on Mac's used Ford Fairlane, we sped into our life together absolutely drunk out of our minds with desire.

Our plan was to drive to Montgomery and then on to Panama City the next day, where a Black Bears booster had lent Mac his beach house, but we only made it as far as the Quality Lodge outside Besse-mer. We checked in, making a scene, since people recognized Mac. The management sent us a complimentary bottle of champagne—as if we needed more—and the delivery boy asked Mac for his auto-graph, which was sweet. We ordered hamburgers sent to our room too. Then I put on the special nightgown Rose had helped me pick out. It was white. Rose said if I had a pair of wings to go with it I'd have looked just like an angel. When I came out of the bathroom Mac was standing naked with a glass of champagne in his hand. The sight of him took my breath away. He walked over and unbuttoned my nightgown like a man unwrapping a Christmas present he hoped was going to be what he asked for.

We made love like love was food and we were starved. Nothing like five years of foreplay to get you in the mood. I bled a little, which surprised me—it looked like drops of rose petals in a bed of snow, like out of a fairy tale. Mac said the blood was beautiful. The next morning I was so raw I could barely walk. When I stood up a gush of evidence poured from between my legs. It made me dizzy. I was trembling. Mac's nakedness, his abandon, the moans he made when he was sat-isfied—this was what I mostly thought about.

We decided just to stay put and forget the beach. If we wanted to swim they had a pool at the motel. But when Mac found out the motel didn't get the channel with the golf tournament he wanted to watch that afternoon, we decided to move on. We checked in to a newly updated Howard Johnson just outside Montgomery. The tournament had started already. Mac went across the street to get a six-pack of beer for himself and Hawaiian Punch for me. I carried in my overnight bag and freshened up. So far Mac had never seen me without make-up and I never planned for him to.

We stayed at the Howard Johnson three more nights and never left the room except to get hamburgers and newspapers. We just made love and watched TV and made love and watched TV.

Frances Delmar waited until I got home from my honeymoon to tell me she was pregnant. She said it the way a person tells you she's failed a test and the teacher won't give her a makeup.

"What are you going to do?" I asked.

"I asked Cleet to marry me."

"What did he say?"

"I told him I was pregnant. That's all. He jumped to the conclusion that that was a marriage proposal. He also jumped to the conclusion that the baby is his."

"Isn't it?"

"The baby is mine," she said.

"Here"—I picked up a hairbrush off my dresser—"turn around." She sat on the bed and turned her back to me and I began to brush her hair, struggling with each knot as gently as I could, brushing her hair until it was detangled and beginning to fly wild with electricity. Her hair is best in its natural state of hysteria. I brushed her hair a long time, trying to put some *everything is okay* into my strokes.

Cleet and Frances Delmar drove that night to Biloxi, Mississippi, to be married by a justice of the peace—which when Frances Delmar's parents, and Rose too, found out would worry them out of their minds. No preacher? Cleet said later Frances Delmar cried all the way there and back. "You'd've thought we were on our way to a damn funeral," he said.

Two weeks later they moved to Laurel, Mississippi, where Cleet took a job as a high school driver's ed teacher and a part-time football coach. Frances Delmar applied for a part-time job as a weekend weather girl at the local TV station—at least until she began to show.

LILLY

The San Francisco 49ers drafted Jett in the first round, which everybody knows. There was a party at the church and the whole city of Birmingham was invited. Them government people came, because prejudiced as they are, they still like football, don't they? And nearly all Jett's white teammates come too, those boys that a couple of years from now will have jobs all over Alabama selling insurance or cars or barbecue chicken wings. They'll never make the kind of money Jett makes and I know that must seem inside out to them. The newspeople—Lord, like a swarm of gnats, all them big-eyed cameras everywhere. And all those girls looking for love too, prissing around—you know what I mean. And kids up underfoot of everybody getting autographs and eating up all the food.

Dixie sat like a lump on a log in the fellowship hall and looked everything over. "Lilly," she said, "looks like all the black people in the world are here today." I guess she hadn't never been outnumbered before. I think it done her good.

Well, Princess, she was there too. She goes to Tuskegee, getting a teacher's certificate. She's too light for me. And, Lord, acts light too. But Jett likes her. She's a preacher's daughter too, which you can tell that by looking at her. She carries herself that way, you understand, like whatever is happening in this world is of no concern to her because she got her eyes fixed on the next world—that mansion in the sky with them roads paved in gold. Only now that Jett has hit the big time it's like she thinks maybe she don't have to wait for heaven no more—maybe he can just up and buy her that mansion with them gold roads and she can move in right away. I hope to God he's got better sense than that. I've always told Jett, "Son, don't let some girl catch you by making you think you're catching her. Be smarter than that." So now I guess we'll see if he is.

Princess, she got herself introduced at the press conference too. Then stood right beside Jett for the picture they put in the paper. I don't mind telling you that got on my last nerve.

That was the same day Jett made me that presentation of the condominium. Right in front of everybody. Which I know set Rose and Mr. Carraway thinking I was gon quit my job with them. I could if I wanted to. I could quit anytime. I saw they were getting ready for it. Even now Jett's always saying, "Mama, why don't you quit over there. You don't have to clean nobody else's house." And I know that. I don't really have no good explanation for it, really. I might quit or I might not. I got that new car now, and I just come and go as I see fit and they act grateful whenever I show up.

Tell the truth, with Dixie gone, I am about the only link left between Rose and Mr. Carraway. They act like a couple of them science rats going through the halls of this house but never crossing up at any of the paths. Rose stays gone to church more and more. She's done forgot that that Zale Swanson is just a preacher. About half the time she acts like he's God hisself.

And Mr. Carraway, he getting downright spooky. About his only pleasure that I ever see is at the end of the day, right before I go home, when I sit down with him, take my shoes off, put my feet up on the Ottoman with them pink-flesh Band-Aids on both my big toes—and Mr. Carraway says, "Lilly, does that bother you, those Band-Aids being the wrong color like that?" See, maybe he acts like a dead man, but he notices things.

"This world is full of things that bother me," I say. Then we drink a Scotch and water and watch Walter Cronkite deliver the latest bad news. I get so tired of the evil people do. And now they got to film it and flash it in our faces every night.

"I don't know what's wrong with people," I say every time we watch the news. Because I don't. People have just all gone too far, if you ask me. There's too much going wrong. But do you think Mr. Carraway replies to that? No. He just sits and sips his poison. So I say, "Just everything, I guess."

Then I put my shoes back on to go home. I gather up all my bags and sacks because those people are pack rats and I'm forever weeding out batches of stuff they don't need but somebody else could use. I carry off who knows how much stuff to the church—and they don't ask me the first question about it either. If they did, I'd just say, *Y'all don't need that no more,* and I swear to God they'd say, *Oh. Okay then.* Because at this point they've run through so much stuff they don't know what they need or don't need anymore.

When I leave I say to Mr. Carraway, "You have a good night now. Don't do nothing I wouldn't do." Then I drive off in my nice car. By the time Rose gets home I know just how it will be. Supper will be heating in the oven and the Scotch will have Mr. Carraway transformed into a no-trouble zombie-husband, just the way Rose likes it. When she says, *Sit down,* he'll sit down. When she says, *Eat your supper,* he'll eat his supper.

Lord, they make me glad I'm a single woman.

It was Rose's idea for me to come with her down here to Beasley to see Dixie's new place. She wants me to help Dixie give the place a good cleaning while she stocks up the kitchen with some groceries and such. Rose is acting like Dixie has moved just outside of hell. I say it will do her good not to have it so fancy. Let her find out how spoiled she's been. Besides, she's young, and when you young you can live about anyplace and be happy.

But now, to be honest, I wouldn't live out here under no circumstances. Mac and her rented this little duplex that juts up to a cow pasture. I ain't never liked cows. And it's got that smell that drives most folks off the farm. It's gon take us more than one day to get this place clean too. I've lived in worse than this, but I ain't a

Carraway, am I? And I wouldn't allow myself to live in nothing like this anymore. Dixie needs to get her some curtains on these windows for one thing. And get her something planted in them beds out front. They look like little graves the way they are now, just heaps of dry dirt.

"So how you like being married, baby?" I ask Dixie.

She's making us some tuna fish for our lunch. She don't put in near enough mayonnaise. I see her look around to see if Rose is listening, then she says, "It's weird, Lilly. I really love Mac and all, but it's still a little weird."

So this makes me think there's some hope for the girl.

"How long did it take for you to get used to being married to Castro?" she asks. Lord, the things I let that girl ask me.

"I never did get used to it," I say.

She slaps some of that tuna fish on some white bread and starts to smear it. "Never?" she says.

"We wadn't right for each other," I say. "I married the wrong man and I knew it right off."

"That's sad," Dixie says. "But I married the right man, Lilly. Didn't I? Don't you think Mac is the right man for me?"

"You got too much tuna fish on there for one sandwich," I say. "Put some of that back."

So she does.

"Mac's the sweetest guy, Lilly," she says. "Isn't he? I know I'm the luckiest girl in the world."

"If you know it you don't need me to tell you then," I say.

I swear if that girl can't make fixing tuna fish look like one complicated job. It makes me nervous just to watch her.

On our ride home from Beasley Rose is mostly quiet. She'd bought sacks of groceries and put them away in the cabinets even though she knew Mac wouldn't like that. "They've got to eat, don't they, Lilly?" she says to me.

Then fifty miles later she says, "Lilly, tell me the truth. Do you think Dixie's going to be happy?"

I swear white people act like I know everything. "Well," I say, "I think she's got a better shot at it than some folks."

"We didn't see Mac the whole time we were there," Rose says. "Dixie says he stays up at the school every minute."

"She told me the same thing," I say. "Mac works harder than anybody you ever saw, Lilly," Dixie had told me, so proud. So now I say to Rose, "I believe Dixie really does love that boy—if that's what you're worried about."

"I know she loves him, Lilly," Rose says. "But you and I both know that love and happiness are two different things."

"You said a mouthful there," I tell her.

DIXIE

Hemp Sparks is meeting us at the Tastee-Freez, which he says is the heart of Beasley, Alabama. There are old men cleaning their fingernails with pocketknives on the cement picnic tables out front. Teenagers are circling the parking lot in homemade cars sitting up high on truck tires. Little, uncombed children are dropping french fries and scoops of ice cream and sobbing in protest. People stand in a long twist of a line at the window ordering chili dogs and onion rings, waving away flies. The air smells like wieners. When we drive up, people turn to stare at us like we're aliens landing in a spaceship. Like they've never seen a couple of normal people before.

It wasn't hard to spot Hemp Sparks. He wore his polyester coaching shorts and a coaching shirt with BEASLEY BULLDOGS stitched on the pocket over his heart—just in case of an unscheduled kickoff somewhere, I guess. "You come to the right place," Hemp says, shaking Mac's hand. "Welcome to Beasley, Alabama. Come Friday night you can't find a house with a light on. Everybody not laid up in the hospital is out at the high school. People around here support two things: the church of their choice and the Beasley Bulldogs."

"Sounds good," Mac says.

"I been helping coach the Bulldogs since the school opened," Hemp says. "I know everybody in the county—and everybody who's been run out of the county, coaches included."

Mac laughs.

Hemp takes us to his house for lunch, where his wife, Leeta, has fixed macaroni and cheese with bacon on it. Also sliced tomatoes, butter beans, and corn—all from her neighbor's garden, she says. We eat at the kitchen table with their five good-looking, yellow-haired teenage kids, who say *Yes, sir* and *Yes, ma'am,* even to me—which feels strange.

The four daughters are pretty—wide mouths with full lips and large, straight white teeth. When they smile or laugh it makes you think of lifting the lid on a piano keyboard. Three of the girls, Teresa, Carol, and Jo-Jo, are slim and angular, their breasts more like casual suggestions. You only notice this because China, the youngest daughter, is slightly plumper, her breasts like a commandment. And China's hair is not naturally blond like her sisters' either, but peroxided to a golden color. It's not trashy though. All the daughters look like they have a light on inside that shines out through their skin. And they are every one dressed in home-sewn clothes.

The son, Jeff, is a tall boy with hair as long as his sisters'. "Jesus had long hair," Hemp says to Mac when he notices Mac studying Jeff. "Can't argue with the boy about that, can I?"

"I guess that's right," Mac says.

Hemp looks across the kitchen table at Jeff, who's eating in a two-fisted style, his mouth just inches from his plate. "You ever hear of shampoo, Son? If you're going to wear your hair as long as a girl you ought to keep it as clean as a girl. Ain't that right, Coach?"

"I think you ought to cut it off," Mac says. "Then you don't have to worry whether it's clean or dirty."

"Jeff's a musician," Leeta says. "All the musicians wear their hair long nowadays."

"He pounds damn drums," Hemp says. "You call that music?"

"Daddy was expecting his son to be a jock," Jeff says, wiping his mouth with the back of his hand. "Wear his hair military-style. Eat dirt. Piss nails, you know. Ain't that right, Daddy?"

"Son, don't talk like that." Leeta points her fork at him. "Company's here."

"I wasn't expecting nothing," Hemp insists. "I take what God give me."

"Well, that would be me then." Jeff grins. "So I guess God's got a sense of humor, huh, Daddy?"

"Me and God both," Hemp says.

The macaroni and cheese is good. I eat everything on my plate. I'm thinking that it's good to have a sense of humor—we might really need one now. I hope to God I have one after all.

Leeta doesn't say much to me, but she watches me hard through a screen of cigarette smoke. Whenever I look at her she smiles. I can't think of much to say either. "This is mighty good," I say, "this lunch."

"How old are you, honey?" she asks me.

"Nineteen," I tell her.

Here is a list of our worldly possessions:

1. One king-sized bed (no headboard) that we are still paying on.

2. One twenty-five-inch color TV, which is more important to Mac than a car. I keep it going all day too, like it's a friend or something.

3. Yellow dinette table and chairs Millie gave us.

4. A hooked rug from Millie's attic.

5. A wooden plant stand Mac made in junior high.

6. A garage-sale dresser I antiqued avocado green.

7. Two gooseneck lamps.

8. A sofa Bobby and Janelle passed on to us that I don't like and didn't want, but Mac said it would hurt their feelings if we turned it down. We have a bedsheet over it to keep the stuffing from getting everywhere and so I don't have to look at it too much. It's Early American. Brown plaid. I hate it.

9. We also have fine china for twelve. (The same Lenox pattern that Tricia Nixon chose.)

10. Everyday china for twelve.

11. Good silver and stainless flatware, twelve each.

12. Fine crystal—red wine, white wine, champagne, ice tea, and water. Same pattern as Rose's.

13. Seventy-six pieces of silver service. From serving trays to coffeepots, casserole dishes to candleholders. And some silver items we cannot identify.

14. We have lace tablecloths and placemats every color of the rainbow. Mac says, "Dixie, you sure can set a pretty table. Now, if you could just cook us something fit to eat." Then he laughs. But we got some cookbooks too, which I study every night before going to bed. Rose says, "Dixie, honey, don't worry. If you can read, you can cook."

15. We have every kitchen appliance known to man. Mac likes the blender best. His new hobby is making banana daiquiris when he comes home from work.

It'll take me days more to unpack and organize our wedding gifts. And weeks more to finish writing the thank-you notes. But it's good that I'm busy since Mac leaves early every morning to go out to the school, where he meets with Hemp and O. D., his assistant coaches. They're looking at film and making up a playbook. And every night Mac comes home happy. We eat a sandwich and go to bed. We watch TV some, then we make love, then we go to sleep. Sometimes I dream, but by morning I've forgotten what.

LEETA

I've been married to Hemp for seventeen years, during which he has been a wood-shop teacher and assistant football coach at Beasley High School. Now they hire Mac Gibbs to come in here and be head coach, Hemp's boss. Why? Because he was a big deal college player? He doesn't have any coaching experience at all, but does anybody care? No. He's got a name. He's got Catfish Bomar's name behind his. That's all it takes. He's twenty-three years old for God's sake. I wish it didn't bother me, but it does. Hemp just says, "Leeta, nobody ever said life was going to be fair." Ha. As if I need Hemp Sparks to explain that to me.

When Mac and Dixie had us over for supper the first time, Lord, I didn't know what to think. We ate in the kitchen, where the floor sags and the linoleum is loose and coming up, sat at a rusty old dinette table that was set with china and crystal like nothing I've ever seen. I wanted to say, "Dixie, honey, this is Beasley, Alabama, not Buckingham Palace." I got all our dishes out of detergent boxes and from the IGA plate-a-week plan. But that's my problem, I guess, not hers. Dixie made chicken casserole. It was perfectly good. She lit candles and put out linen napkins and I thought Hemp would excuse himself and go home when he saw it all. He doesn't go in for that sort of thing.

Mac said, "Dixie is trying out some of our wedding presents here—hope you all don't mind." He took the edge off it, you know. I think he was a little bit embarrassed and I was glad to know he had sense enough to be.

And Dixie, she seemed so happy to have company that I couldn't stay annoyed for very long. She acted like I was her damn idol or something, which I hope to God she's got better sense than that. She asked me every question in the world—about Hemp and me mostly, and the kids too. She even bought a bottle of Blue Nun just because Hemp told her I liked it. And by the time we were through drinking it—just Dixie and me because Hemp and Mac drank beer—I don't know, I thought to myself, this girl, Dixie, is not as bad as all that. It's not her fault she had a rich daddy. It's not my fault I didn't. Maybe we'll do okay.

I'd been at the Burroughses' house all day, sitting with Lucy, who's dying of breast cancer and knows it too. She's got four kids watching her go—and a husband that wants to pretend there's nothing wrong. It wears me out. I sit with her from eight to five every day, which might not sound that hard, but it is.

I lit up a cigarette first thing and Dixie brought me a fancy glass ashtray, set it on the arm of the sofa beside me. "You just relax," she said. Then she sat down beside me and asked me all about my day. I can't think when was the last time somebody asked me about my day.

Here in Beasley I'm the queen of emergency situations. Anytime anything goes wrong anywhere, folks call me. You can ask Hemp. I've worked as a nurse's aide since we moved back to Beasley, when I was pregnant with Teresa, sitting beside people's beds all night, giving them sips of water, making sure they don't feel alone at the end. Some people think you can't die in Beasley unless I am sitting by your side. I mean it.

Watching all this death has not been good for me. It's taken its toll. Sometimes when my patients want to talk to me about dying, like Lucy Burroughs does on and off, I say, "Honey, there's nothing to be scared of." I speak with authority and people like that. I say, "Death doesn't scare me a bit. I could use the rest." Sometimes they smile when I say that. I tell my patients, "Don't worry, I'm right behind you. You just save me a place up there because I'm coming too." They think I'm just trying to be cheerful, but I mean it.

Hemp said to me not long ago, "Leeta, I don't know what I'm going to do with you. You're trying to get old on me, and let me tell you what—I am nowhere near ready to get old yet."

I wanted to say, "Damn you, Hemp. I've raised five of your kids on the fifty cents a week you make. I work all day at the health clinic and all night on the death patrol. All this so you can play ball all your life. Somebody around here needs to be a goddamn grown-up and it's clear it won't ever be you." I really hate Hemp sometimes. I swear I do. It's just that I still love him like a fool. I love him even more than I hate him.

Lots of nights when Hemp and Mac are still at practice or at school watching film, Dixie comes over to the house. If you ask me she's plain lonely—at home alone all day and half the night. Anyway, we drink coffee and tell about our families. Dixie talks about her mother a lot. For the longest time I thought her daddy might be dead because she never mentioned him. I tell about Hemp's mother because she was such a witch. But then I usually end up talking about my kids—the time Teresa ran away with that boy hitchhiking through Beasley, the time Jeff was arrested for buying drugs from an undercover cop he thought was a harmless guy just let out of the penitentiary (you know, he was trying to help him out and all), the time China's girlfriend's daddy killed himself with a double-barreled shotgun, which I understand from Hemp is no easy feat. His wife found him when she came home from church. He was sprawled out over the dirty clothes in the laundry room. I've never gotten that image out of my mind. I had night duty with him too, afterwards. He only lived four days, never even opened his eyes.

When I start talking about the kids, telling Dixie stories on them, they run for cover. They clear out like a bunch of startled doves. I usually cook while Dixie and I talk, macaroni and hamburger meat with a can of tomato sauce, or cold macaroni salad with diced tomato and cucumber. Dixie calls me teaching her to cook, which is a real joke. I tell her Hemp and I have raised five children on a prayer and a wish and because I know how to make macaroni fifty different ways. Usually I can barely get the food on the table before it's wiped out by my hungry-hearted kids. Dixie's learned to dive in fast if she wants any.

"Hemp's mother didn't want me to marry Hemp," I told Dixie. We were washing dishes and nursing cups of warm coffee while the kids scattered themselves around the house to talk on the phone and watch TV and play their stereos and radios, which is why I'm always saying, *How can I hear myself think in this house?*

Dixie's drying my chipped Melmac dishes like they're priceless bone china or something. Dixie's an odd girl in some ways—so careful. "To get Hemp to marry me I pretended to be pregnant," I tell her. "That's how desperately in love with Hemp I was. And he married me out of a sense of honor, after which I proceeded to get pregnant as fast as I could. I know he must have thought he'd married a white rabbit, the way I was in the beginning. I was just so scared of losing him. It wasn't until we had four babies, with a fifth on the way, that I finally confessed to him—by which time it was too late to matter."

Dixie stands very close to me when I tell her this, like she doesn't just want to hear the story, like she wants to feel it come off me, the waves of heat off my skin. And one thing I like about Dixie is how she hears inside of what's said. You don't have to draw her a picture or anything.

"When I think back on how much I used to love Hemp, it scares me," I say to Dixie. "I think loving him like that is the only truly terrible thing I've ever done. It's the only thing I'm really ashamed of."

Dixie listens to me as hard as she can and I don't think she knows what I'm saying, but I know she feels something. I don't think she believes me, but she doesn't believe me for my own good, which I sort of appreciate. "You still love Hemp now too, Leeta," she says. "Don't you?"

"Sure, I do," I say. I think any other answer would half kill her to hear it. "Hemp's a great guy. He's as funny as he ever was and just as sweet. He hasn't changed all that much over the years—he's still that boy I married, that handsome tailback. But I'm not the girl he married anymore, see. I grew up. I still love him though. I love him the same way I love my kids."

Sometimes Dixie stays at our house until time for me to go to my night job. We make instant pudding, listen to Jeff practice the drums, search his room for marijuana, or just sit in the yard and shell pecans.

So already it's like I've adopted Dixie or something. Like she's stirred herself in among my daughters, but not exactly that. Because I'm not Dixie's mother and she knows it and what I need with a friend who's just turned twenty years old I'll never know. But there you have it.

When Hemp comes home then Dixie leaves and goes back to the duplex to wait for Mac. Sometimes Hemp goes with her to drink a late-night beer with Mac as if he hadn't seen enough of him that day from seven in the morning until nine o'clock at night.

I swear if Mac was a dog Hemp would be his tail.

DIXIE

Mac and I live for Friday nights. We wake up like it's Christmas on Fridays. Neither of us can eat a bite of food. We just sip hot coffee and smile at each other like two people who will later have several hours of great sex. Only it's football.

Mac goes to school as usual. I clean the house for the party we'll have after the game—just the coaches and their wives and the Gibbs. I buy groceries—luxury items from the IGA like beer and onion dip. I make a cheese ball and roll in it pecans like they show in the recipe book. I sweep the driveway and clean out the car. I water the potted plants and arrange their leaves and sometimes smear mayonnaise on them like Lilly taught me, to make them shine. I arrange all the labels on the canned goods so that they face outward in the cabinet in case anybody opens the wrong cabinet when they're looking for a glass.

I pray all day too—sometimes out loud. It seems like God's my best friend now, just like Rose always said he was supposed to be. *Let the Bulldogs win.* I pray morning, noon, and night.

It's my job to drive the cheerleaders to the away games. We trail along behind the team bus and I listen to the girls talk about which boys are cute and quote the best sentences they've had spoken to them that week.

Frances Delmar and I had once been like the girls in the car—in love with a boy because he could run fast or throw a ball hard or take a hit and come away undamaged. None of these were talents we aspired to ourselves, but we admired these abilities in boys because it made them all the more our opposites—and allowed us to forgive them for all the small ways they disappointed us by being so opposite.

One of the girls in the car, Yolanda Branch, is beautiful. People in Beasley say she should forget about college and go to Hollywood and be a movie star instead. She's thinking it over. "You're really lucky, Mrs. Gibbs," she says. "Coach Gibbs is not like other men, you know. He's sensitive or something."

The cheerleaders like to arrive early to warm up. This doesn't mean practice their cheers. It means fix their makeup and spray their hair and wave to the boy of the week, whose number they'll look for all night. There's something interesting about boys who're willing to give up their names and become numbers for a night. "Look at twenty-two," the girls say. "I like number ten," Yolanda Branch says. "He's so bowlegged." I find myself a seat up high on the fifty-yard line and wait for the other coaches' wives, who will come to sit beside me like right and left guards. I feel sometimes like I'm impersonating an adult, that I'm still supposed to be one of the girls in the bathroom— Yolanda Branch maybe—but instead I'm a wife. Like there's been a mistake.

I like my time alone before games though, just sitting in the stands—sometimes the only person—watching Mac, who is so beautiful to me. He answers every question—the managers, the coaches, the cheerleaders, the parents, the newspeople, asking him, asking him, asking him. He's so calm. Not a rah-rah man like Hemp. Let Hemp go nuts jumping around, barking orders. I'm glad Mac doesn't do that. Jumping up and down isn't Mac's job. His job is to make jumping up and down happen to the rest of us.

The game is against Opelika—a mill town. It's mill workers' sons against farmers' sons, town boys against country boys. Sometimes Mac says, "It is just a game, Dixie." We both know that it's never just a game.

Here comes Leeta to sit next to me. And O. D.'s wife, Sandy, on the other side. They've been at this a long time. *Seasoned* is what they call themselves. "No pun intended," Leeta says.

Leeta and Sandy were both cheerleaders in high school—Sandy in college too. "It gets in your blood," Sandy says. "To this day I really miss it—cheering."

Leeta says, "My years as a cheerleader were some of the happiest times of my life. It's like my life has gone straight downhill from the time I could do a standing one-handed back flip and my thighs were as hard as two chair legs."

I laugh at Leeta like I don't believe her.

"I mean it," she says. "I swear to God."

I hold my breath at kickoff. This is the truth. When I watch Mac I'm so glad I didn't marry a banker or an insurance salesman or a doctor or a lawyer. What do they have to recommend them besides a lot of money? What can money do besides buy things? How many things can people buy before buying things gets boring? Mac has no money, but he has something money can't buy and it's never boring. He has the eyes of all of Beasley on him, their hearts to be ceremoniously offered up to him if his team can win the ball game—and their wrath to fall on his head if the team can't win it.

Being a football coach is not like being a banker, where if you're clever enough you can tamper with the credits and debits—and maybe get away with it. Mac's numbers are lit up on the scoreboard for the world to see. By tomorrow they'll be recorded in newspapers all over the state of Alabama.

Being a football coach is not like being an insurance salesman, where when a claim is filed you can point to the fine print and escape responsibility through a technical loophole—there's no loophole in football where the coach can ever escape being held responsible.

Being a football coach is not like being a lawyer whose job it is to carve himself a good life out of the heartache and tragedies of others. Even if a lawyer loses the case he still gets paid—so in the end it's only the client who really loses. Only the client goes to jail or goes bankrupt or heads for death row. It's conceivable that a lawyer could lose every case in his career and still die a rich man.

Being a football coach is not like being a doctor who can misdiagnose the problem and call for all the wrong treatments, unnecessary surgery, useless medicine, whatever—without anybody ever knowing, except the patient, who might end up dead and take the information to the grave with him. When a doctor loses a patient it's nobody's business how it happened. When Mac loses a game it's headlines in the Beasley newspaper that week—all his mistakes made public and offered up for analysis by everybody.

This is the sort of thing I think about when I'm supposed to be watching, maybe even understanding, the game. My mind always wanders. By itself football can seem ridiculous, but it's not by itself—it always means something more and bigger than what it is. You have to believe that to really enjoy it. At least I do.

Opelika runs back a punt to score. It feels like somebody shot me in the heart. I feel like an innocent bystander victimized by a gang of mill workers' sons. "Defense!" I scream. Opelika goes for the extra point. The ball veers off to the left like a damp firework that fails to explode. I give God the credit. "Praise the Lord," I say.

"Let's get some points, Gibbs!" a boy's mother yells.

"Put the ball in the air," a man screams.

"Just because Gibbs was a hotshot college player don't mean he can coach worth a damn," somebody says.

"He's scared to put it in the air," a man behind me yells. I look around to see that it's Pastor McBride from Beasley Baptist Church, where I go every Sunday. His son, Tom Allen, is a defensive lineman. Mac says size doesn't make you a football player. He said to Pastor McBride and Tom Allen once, "Football is not about size, it's about heart." They stared at him like he was crazy. See, if you ask me it's like religion. Religion is not about truth. It's about heart too. But naturally you would never expect a preacher to understand a concept like that.

Pastor McBride is on his feet screaming at Tom Allen, "Hit them like you mean it, boy!" You can see his words land on Tom Allen, who keeps his eyes pointed down, away from his father. "If that's the best you can do, Son, come on up here and sit with your mama," he screams. He's of the fire-and-brimstone persuasion. He believes winning is heaven and losing is hell.

Opelika goes around the end for a first down. Opelika fans go crazy. Pastor McBride goes crazy too. "Let's see some hitting out there, Gibbs," he screams. "Let's hurt somebody."

"I hope you brought your earplugs," Leeta says to me. "You're going to need them."

Opelika beats Beasley 13–0. It's our third straight loss and I wonder, *What is the point God's trying to make? Did the other head coach's wife outpray me?*

Afterwards Sandy and Leeta and I wait outside the locker room with the mothers and girlfriends of the players. We're all somber. Failure is very sobering. I can see through a crack in the door, the pink bodies in various degrees of nakedness.

Finally the players begin to file out of the dressing room—submitting to hugs from their mothers, slaps on the back and assessments of their performance from their fathers—and load on the school bus for the drive back to Beasley. Mac is last out, his hair still wet from his shower. He gives me a robot kiss, and says, "Meet you back at the house."

"Are you okay?" I ask.

"Look, Dix, don't worry." He smiles. "We're improving every game. Anybody that knows anything about football can see that—anybody who doesn't, then there's nothing I can do about people who don't understand the game."

I don't confess to Mac that I'm one of those people.

I gather up the wilted cheerleaders and load them into the car and trail the red taillights of the school bus all the way back to Beasley. This is my life, I think. It's not what I was expecting. When we get home Mac and Hemp and O .D.—and Bobby and Terry and Thurmond—will sit in front of the TV and rehash the game, while Sandy,

Leeta, and I sit with Millie in the kitchen and talk about something else. Sometimes the other women talk about their kids and I just listen. Sometimes we talk about food—where to buy it, how to fix it. Sometimes we tell what we did last week and what we're fixing to do next week, which is never anything extraordinary. Sometimes the talk seems so empty to me that I stop listening for the sense of it and just try to enjoy the sound of it, like it's music, their voices and laughing. Their bodies, their perfume and cigarette smoke and hair spray.

Then everybody goes home and Mac and I go to bed. Mac acts like we've had a great day—him and me—like we're in this together. I play along because, God knows, I wish it were true.

Tomorrow Mac will bring home all the dirty jerseys and towels for me to wash in our secondhand Kenmore washing machine. It takes me all day Saturday and most of Sunday. I hang them to dry on a line Hemp rigged up in the yard. They dry like sheets of plywood and Hemp stacks them like boards when he takes them back to school on Monday.

Before the season started Mac wanted new jerseys—a morale booster, he said—but the school had no money. So he brought home jerseys that should have been thrown away and the two of us dyed them royal blue in boiling pots on our kitchen stove with packets of Rit dye donated by the IGA. It took us nearly two weeks. They came out pale gray. Our hands were purple for weeks.

Mac told his team, "Look. Jerseys don't win games. Equipment doesn't win games. People win games."

I listen to Mac with great interest. As far as I know I've never won a game in my life. Unless you count all that foolishness when Jett and I were kids. Or you count that time I beat Mac at Scrabble and he got so mad he refused to play anymore.

Besides coaching football Mac teaches five health and PE classes. He lets me grade his students' tests and papers. I love this. I write thoughtful remarks—*Good work*, or *You can do better!* Things like that. Mostly Mac's tests are on the rules of the game. Mac knows all rules to all games. He tells his students, "You can't play the game if you don't know the rules."

But I personally believe there are exceptions to every rule. So if a test question can go either way I always give the student the benefit of the doubt. "Rules are made to be broken," I say to Mac. Then I carefully record the grades in his grade book.

Mac says, "Dix, if you could just keep a checkbook like you keep a grade book, we'd be set."

The truth about money is—we don't have any.

Mac makes four hundred dollars a month. One hundred goes for our rent. One hundred goes for the car payment on his Ford Fairlane. About fifty to seventy-five goes for electricity, which is too much, but try to tell that to Alabama Power. And twenty-five dollars goes toward our king-sized bed. So we have about one hundred dollars a month to live our lives on. Twenty-five dollars a week. That's food, gas, insurance, clothes, and fun. It's my job to make his money go as far as it will.

I'm not very good at it.

Twice this year when I was overdrawn I drove over to Auburn University and put up a sign to do typing at home for professors, but I was thinking they would provide the typewriter. Mac said it would cost more to buy a typewriter than I would earn typing. I also did about a two-week stint with Avon, but I found out fast that I'm not really a sales-oriented person. Besides, Beasley already has two Avon ladies. They let me keep my samples though.

I called Kirby Long, editor of the *Beasley Banner*, to see if I could work on his paper. I'm an English major. Or I was. But he said his wife does all his editing for him. I put in an application with the schools to be a secretary or an aide, but all the slots were filled.

The only luck I had was a callback from the IGA offering me a position as substitute cashier when their regulars get sick or go on vacation. It would be an on-call sort of thing. I said sure. But Mac vetoed that. "I don't want you working at the IGA," he said. So, so far, I haven't come up with a good method for a second income. I keep the nursery at the Baptist church, but that's not a paying job.

· The Beasley Library is a one-room annex next to the post office. I check out books like crazy. I also check them out from the high school library with Mac's faculty card. I've decided I'll just read books full-time and pretend to be getting paid by the hour. "If it makes you happy, Dix . . ." Mac says.

Mac is the only person I know who I would say is nearly perfectly happy. The only thing that would make him any happier is if the Beasley Bulldogs would get on the winning track. But meanwhile he's full of ideas. Like he wants to put out a little football guide that people can buy at games—the money will go for new uniforms. He wants me to write up a one-page profile of each player on the team. "You know, Dix," Mac said, "make it interesting." Then we'll mimeograph the thing ourselves, staple it together, and sell it. So I said sure. It'll give me something to do, interviewing every boy on the Bulldogs team. I'll write things up so that every one of them sounds wonderful.

Mac wasn't at Beasley High School one full year before the female teachers started dragging their classroom culprits to him so that he could straighten them out. All it took was Mac slamming a couple of troublemaking kids up against the wall in front of witnesses to rearrange some of the badass attitudes at Beasley. He was glad to do it too.

Hemp says Beasley is one of the last places on earth where people still respect authority.

MRS. CARPENTER

When they called me up to the school I thought, *Lord God, what is it?* I hadn't never been called up to the school before.

"It's about Jessup," they said. Jessup? He's my quiet one. My boys don't give me any trouble, most of all Jessup don't.

Mrs. Swingle—she's the librarian up at the high school—she looks on the verge of tears when I get up to her office, which all it is, is like a broom closet they set a desk in. There is sitting Jessup in a chair.

"I'm afraid you need to punish this boy," she says.

"What's his crime?" I say. He's not looking at me. Got a pick stuck on the side of his head. His shirttail is tucked in nice. He looks all right.

About then this man walks into the little office where we're standing—a young man I hadn't ever seen before. "This is Coach Gibbs," Mrs. Swingle says. "I asked him to stop by and help us straighten this out."

"Hey there, ma'am," he says.

"You know my boy Jessup?"

"Haven't had the pleasure." He looks at Jessup slumped in that chair.

Mrs. Swingle hands me a book. "Page two twenty-two," she says. "Look."

I flip to the page. I see it. Somebody has drawn some sex pictures on page 222. Men with big ole things. Titties the size of tractor tires. I look this mess over until Coach Gibbs takes the book out my hand.

"So, we got us an artist here, do we?" he says.

"That's not the only book Jessup has defaced," Mrs. Swingle says. "There's more."

I look at Jessup, but he pretends like I'm not standing there. I'm proud that he's got the decency to be embarrassed. I know he wouldn't ever humiliate me on purpose like this. Like him humiliating me humiliates him worse. "Boy, did you draw in these books?" I say.

He don't answer. So then I know. Whatever else he might or might not do, he don't lie. Not Jessup. I see him sit around about half the time with a pencil in his hand, scribbling up all his notebook paper, making pictures. Rockets mostly. Using up paper faster than I can buy it. But I ain't never seen no pictures looked like this. "What's making you draw mess like this?" I say.

Coach Gibbs speaks up then. "Everybody knows how people hate an unillustrated book. Ain't that right, Jessup?"

"He's drawn in a number of volumes of our *Encyclopædia Britannica* too," Mrs. Swingle says. I think for a minute she might cry. I think to myself that she must not have many real problems if she wants to cry over an encyclopedia page. I think to myself, *Why don't you just give the boy an eraser and set him to work erasing this mess?*

"I know he comes from a good family," Mrs. Swingle says to me. "I been knowing you, Mrs. Carpenter."

"We'll take care of this," Coach Gibbs tells Mrs. Swingle. "Me and Jessup and his mama will work this out." So Mrs. Swingle leaves. She's a old maid, you know. I bet Jessup's picture is the nearest she ever got to a man's thing. But that's not here or there. Because I don't allow my boys to mess with what don't belong to them. I don't allow them to ruin nothing.

"You got some talent, son," Coach Gibbs says to Jessup. "And a lot of nerve too. And one hell of an imagination."

Jessup's as silent as a dead man, his eyes cold.

"Your boy's not much of a conversationalist, is he, ma'am?" Coach Gibbs says.

"My boys was raised right," I say. "Jessup too." Then I look at Jessup, who is real busy studying his hands, the same hands that done all this drawing. Like he's occupied in his own thoughts. This child, my oldest boy, he's the only mystery child I got. The rest, I can read their minds faster than they can think anything up. But a quiet child, you know, they're the difficultest ones sometimes.

"You got an explanation for this, boy?" I say.

"No, ma'am," he says, sort of cleaning one fingernail with the other one.

"You tell the coach here that you wasn't raised to bother what don't belong to you."

"Yes, ma'am," he says.

"And I didn't raise you to be nasty minded neither, did I?"

"No, ma'am."

"Well, I will see to you when you get home then," I say. "Meanwhile, Coach, you do what you see fit to do, cause Jessup knows better than to do this right here." I tap the front of the book. "Page two twenty-two," I say.

"Let's get you out on the track and see if running some laps won't produce a little proper remorse, son," Coach Gibbs says.

"How many laps?" Jessup asks.

"I'll tell you when to stop," he says.

"No way," Jessup says.

"Let me tell you something, Son," I interrupt. "Either you get out there and run like the man says or else I'll run you myself. I don't know what's wrong with you, talking to people like you're talking."

"What'd you say, son? I didn't hear you," Coach Gibbs says. "Did you say, *I'm about to get my butt out there and run those laps?* Because let me tell you what, if you're not out there in five minutes then I got some other ideas about what to do with you that'll make you think running laps is a piece of your mama's angel food cake."

Ordinarily I don't like to hear nobody talk to my chirren like that. But Jessup is just not acting hisself. Cause you don't normally have to tell him nothing twice.

"You better make this good," Coach Gibbs says to him. "I'm gon be watching you."

I follow Jessup out to the track along with Coach Gibbs, like we're two shadows that push instead of being pulled. "Believe it or not, Mrs. Carpenter," Coach Gibbs says, "I don't like to be an asshole like this, but there's some kids that won't respond to anything less. Sometimes if you want a kid to stop being an asshole you got to start being one."

"That idn't no way for a teacher to talk," I say. "You spozed to be setting an example in how you talk."

"Yes, ma'am," he says. "You're right. I'm sorry." He might call hisself a coach, but he ain't nothing but a boy hisself.

Jessup starts running. He runs so slow. Coach Gibbs yells, "I didn't say jog. I said run!" So Jessup picks it up a little. The chirren at PE stop what they're doing to watch him. "Faster you go," Coach Gibbs yells, "the sooner you stop."

Jessup glares at Coach Gibbs. He has his silent way of talking and it don't require translation. All that anger is good fuel, I guess. Anger kicks in and Jessup picks up speed. Coach Gibbs is watching him. He says to me, "Your boy has got some legs on him, Mrs. Carpenter." The PE chirren are spozed to be playing something, but they're watching Jessup now, yelling, "Book it, man," and such as that. Every child out there is watching my boy run.

Here's what I say to myself. Jessup is my son and I love him. He's all bottled up and I don't know why. But he didn't kill nobody. He didn't rob no bank. He just got artistic. You can't go to jail for drawing pictures, can you? I know boys get an age and things get on their minds, but you can't be drawing your mind's contents out on a schoolbook. If he wants to draw dirty pictures he needs to go off by hisself and do it until he bores hisself with it. Boys is going to be nasty. I never met a man yet who didn't have his nasty side. But it ought to be kept more private. I guess Jessup knows that now.

I look at Jessup out there running, all them other chirren watching him, and I'm glad he's mine. I'd claim him now same as I did on the day he was born. He runs smooth like his daddy. Like he's got somebody after him but he'll die before he lets hisself get caught. For sure ain't nobody gon catch him today.

"All right," Coach Gibbs finally says, "that's enough, Carpenter."

But Jessup, just to prove a point, he don't stop. He runs another time around the field. It's his way of saying, *Okay, Coach, big man, so you can make me do it, but can you make me stop doing it?* I tell you right that minute I know, yes, this is my child, come from my blood, from his daddy's seed, got his daddy's stubborn ways. Jessup has something special to him. He drops to a walk. He's got his hands on his hips and he's sucking air real hard, walking away from where we stand, never saying one word. And I love the boy, I swear to God.

Coach Gibbs says, "Carpenter, wait up a minute."

Jessup looks at him stone-faced, but he's enjoying it and I know it—the show he just put on. He's enjoying proving that he can run, that he'll stop when he feels like it and not no sooner. But his face, I'm telling you, it's got his daddy's expression. I don't know where his daddy is right this minute, but I know where his daddy's face is.

"Know what I like about you, Carpenter?" Coach Gibbs says.

Jessup's looking at him now.

"You can run, but so what? The world is full of guys who can run. What I like about you is this—the more people watching you, the better you get. You got some showman in you, Carpenter. All you need is a full-time audience."

Jessup's breathing hard. Sweat's pouring off him like somebody poured a bucket over his head.

"You ever think about playing football?" Coach Gibbs says.

And this the way everything got started.

DIXIE

Mac leaves for school at six o'clock each morning and doesn't get home until after nine at night. Besides football he also coaches JV basketball and baseball and he helps out with tennis and golf—both boys and girls. He eats a big meal at the school cafeteria, where the women wearing those hair nets know exactly what they're doing. Vegetables, homemade rolls, desserts, the whole well-balanced thing. Now and then he gets them to fix me a plate and he brings it home for my supper. Sometimes I cook something here, but it alarms Mac, makes him think I'm getting bored and depressed, which sometimes I am. Most nights when Mac gets home we eat sandwiches or I heat a can of chili. We're usually in bed by ten o'clock. This is where our marriage mostly takes place.

Even though I've been married a pretty good while now, I haven't gotten completely used to it. I'm still a virgin in my own mind. I still think like a virgin. I think I still look like one too. I guess all those years of protecting my virginity from Mac sort of played havoc with my head.

Don't get me wrong. I love to make love with Mac. Sometimes he makes me think he is a scientist and I'm his experiment and if I prove his hypothesis true then I'll be written up in science journals all over the country. Sometimes I feel like a lost child Mac has found half-frozen in the woods and taken home with him to see if he can warm me up in front of the fire, put some rosy back in my cheeks. Sometimes he's an artist twisting our love into assorted body sculptures. Mac is not a boring lover like I hear other wives complain that their husbands are—like Leeta, who says she has to ask Hemp some mornings whether or not they had sex the night before because if they did she slept through it again.

But Mac now, he's a good lover. For one thing he's slow-slow. I mean backing-up, starting-over slow. I'm a guitar and he's Roy Orbison dressed in the black night, his fingers making me into some of the best music I ever imagined. And he's always thinking up something new too. He doesn't get stuck playing the same song over and over. And since he's a man of the physical world, already his body has begun to do more and more of his talking for him. I know exactly how to read his body too, how to hear it, how to answer the questions his body is asking—and how to translate it all into a pounding love.

In return for the adventure Mac brings to our bed, this is what I do for Mac. He probably doesn't even know it really, but I revirginize every day. I keep the new and the first time in things for him. No matter how much we make love, I remain as pure as the driven snow. He loves that about me too. I can tell. I'm like one of those flowers that the more you prune it, the more it thrives and blooms.

So Mac is the perfect man for me. I love the sight of him and the smell of him and the imprint he leaves on his side of the bed. I love the sure way he touches me and his weight bearing down, the way I feel so lovingly crushed beneath him. I love the funny things he says. And all the wordless sounds he makes. I love our sexless nights too, when we eat chips in bed or sardines on crackers and make fun of all the guests on *Johnny Carson*. I love falling asleep beside him, his arm tight around me, while he watches the late news and thinks about things he will never tell me, things that I cannot imagine.

I never confess what a terrible time I have remembering to take my birth control pills. Sometimes I forget for several days straight, then panic and eat a handful. Some nights I wake up in a cold sweat trying to remember if I've taken my pill or not. I stumble into the bathroom, study the dispenser, which is never astrologically correct, due to my haphazard forget-and-remember technique, so I just take an extra pill for good measure.

"Dixie!" Mac yells when I wake him with a flood of bathroom light and he sees me gulping down days of forgotten pills. "It's not *If one works, two work better.* You know that, don't you?"

Mac loves Jessup Carpenter and his brothers. I mean it. He's crazy about them. That's all he talks about—what they did in practice, what they said on the ride home, how they can transform the Bulldogs into a better team. I love listening to it, mostly.

He brings them over to the house nearly every afternoon. Columbus is my favorite. But I think Jessup's the talented one—art, I mean. They say he can hardly read or write, which doesn't make sense to me. Mac says he has a C average even though he can hardly spell the word *Carpenter*. Something's wrong somewhere. Anyway, Mac brings them by and we drink a Coke or something. Maybe eat some Fritos. Just try to talk a little bit, which is getting easier now.

Sometimes I feel hung between Mac and the boys who play football for him—not just the Carpenter brothers, but all the players— like I'm suspended somewhere between being a wife and an eternal schoolgirl. I don't know how to be motherlike toward them the way Leeta is, except to offer them food and drink like she does. I prefer to ask questions like a potential girlfriend might—questions about who they think is pretty, who they like to dance with, who they take to the movies on weekends. I know my questions have flirt to them, but I can't help it. The neutral in me will not come to the surface like I want it to. I feel like a girl doing a flimsy impression of maturity. Some boys, like Columbus, flirt with me right in front of Mac and I like it. Some quieter boys look me over like I am sixteen and still on the market and I like that too. I feel little surges of interest, but it goes sour quickly because they are boys and I now—married for the rest of my life— am supposed to be an adult, a grown woman with a husband. So I'm training my feelings to go underground, teaching my natural response to be unnatural now.

"Would you like a Coke?" I say to the boys. "How about a sandwich? Potato chips? An apple? A piece of icebox pie?"

One good thing: Kirby Long from the *Beasley Banner* bought one of those books of player profiles that Mac sold last year. He says my interviews were "intriguing" and now he wants to feature one or two of them in his newspaper every week. He'll give me a by-line and everything, like a column, you know. So now I'm polishing them up and making sure each one has a little anecdote to go with it— you know, human interest.

Yolanda Branch—Beasley's most beautiful girl—graduated from high school and, instead of Hollywood, goes to Birmingham University to study business. After she's safely gone, Mac brings home a collection of notes she'd written him that were very advanced. In one of them she lipsticked her nipples and pressed them to the page like kisses. "I may be young," it said, "but I'm not afraid."

"What the hell was I supposed to do, Dix?" Mac says.

"Marry her?" I suggest.

"It's not funny, Dix. I swear she scared the shit out of me. I mean it. Read this crap."

I did. And I saved them too, every note. I'm not sure why.

MRS. CARPENTER

Now most afternoons Coach Gibbs drives Jessup and Lavont and Columbus home after football practice since it cause them to miss the bus and I don't have my car running. Coach Gibbs tell me we gon forget about those library books. He's paying to replace them out his own pocket, but what he wants in return is Jessup out for his football team. And long as Jessup's staying late, then his brothers decide they might as well stay too. Ain't no harder to drive three boys home than it is one. And that Coach Gibbs, he act like he's in love with my boys. I mean it. Love what my boys can do for his football team.

At first my boys don't let Coach Gibbs drive them up to our actual house. They make him let them off out on the gravel road where a dirt path spirals off into that grove of pecan trees. Out here where the cotton fields are, right beside that man's cow pasture. I see him sometimes, he stop the car and let my boys out, and they wait for him to drive off before they walk the rest of the way home. They tell me this don't sit right with the coach.

They say to him, "Let us out right here, Coach."

And he says, "What you mean, right here? Y'all cows? This is a damn cow pasture. Where's your house?"

"We can walk the rest of the way," they say.

See, that coach wants to come up to the house here, but my boys are cautious. I raised them to be cautious. They say he already knows the name of every child I got and what grade he's in, who his teacher is. They say he knows Mary Virginia is my only daughter and that she's got a baby named Michael. It's like the man tries to know our business. But he's going to have to know it from the road. I swear if Coach Gibbs don't act like it hurts his feelings too.

"He wants to come up here to the house, Mama," they say. "He knows you work in the lunchroom at Lurleen Wallace, Mama," Columbus says. "He's been asking about you. Wouldn't surprise me if he showed up out there and tried to talk to you."

"What's he got to talk to me about?" I say. "I better not be having no kind of bad reports on none of y'all," I say. "He's got all y'all on his football team," I say. "And that's enough."

You can't force yourself into nobody's life. I know that. If he don't know it, he should. Especially him being white. He can't just go dragging up to our house and expect us to give him a big welcome. He's got to take it easy and let us decide if and when the time is right. And maybe we will and maybe we won't.

Now I guess Coach Gibbs has started taking my boys by his house, which all it is, is a duplex, like one-half a house, and not too nice either. People say his wife's daddy is rich, but you can't prove it by the way they live. So I guess if he can't come out to our house then he'll just take my boys to his. And they act like they like that. They got their curiosity.

Coach Gibbs's wife, she just a child. Maybe a year or two older than Mary Virginia. Her name is Dixie, which is no kind of name if you ask me. She tells my boys, "Y'all don't call me Mrs. Gibbs cause it makes me think you're talking to Mac's mother."

And this child, Dixie, she invites my boys in the house and lets them look things over. And she pours them some ice tea and such and she's like her husband about asking them one hundred questions about themselves.

I ask my boys, "What's that coach's house look like?"

They say, "His wife don't keep it clean, Mama. She got books all over the place and no curtains on none the windows and got a sheet on the sofa looking like a wrinkled up bed. And they got their TV in the bedroom." They always laugh telling this. Like it explains something about white people. "Yeah, you got to lay down in the bed to watch some TV," they say.

"Dixie," they tell me, "she like Jessup." Lavont and Columbus act out Dixie carrying on over Jessup. "You draw them pictures right there?" they say in a high voice, cause Jessup, he's always got drawings hanging out all his books. "Can I see them pictures? Will you show me?"

And even Jessup almost laughs at this. "That woman know some art when she see it," he says. "She ain't ignorant like the rest of y'all."

"You sure can draw good," they say in girl talk. "You sure do make some pretty pictures." Then they bust up.

So now most days after practice Coach Gibbs swings by his own house and gets his child-wife, Dixie, and she rides out here to bring my boys home. Ain't nothing wrong with her, I don't guess. She's one them blond women that makes you think of the color yellow every minute. She's one them white women who's all smiles. But I don't think she means no harm. Seems like my boys are easy with her. They say she asks them every nosy question—and I know they like that. They don't like that in a coach, but they like it all right in a girl.

The first time my boys let Coach Gibbs drive them all the way up to the house it's because Lavont has twisted his ankle and is hopping on crutches. "Y'all stop all this playacting and show me where you live," he said to them.

So here they come, driving up the road. I'm out in the garden getting together some early greens and the first of the tomatoes. I see the dust the car kicks up. Then Mary Virginia yells to me, "Here comes somebody, Mama." Little Michael is out on the porch already, waiting to see who it is. By the time they get up into the yard I see they got Dixie with them. She looks like she goes shy all of a sudden, but she waves me this little wave. Then I see Lavont try to get out the car, got them big ole crutches. "Oh, Lord," I think, "what now?"

"He's all right," Coach Gibbs says. He's out the car and walking up to the house even though nobody said, *Y'all get out and come on in.* "Lavont took a hit blindside," Coach Gibbs says, "twisted his ankle bad, but nothing's broken. You got a tough boy, Mrs. Carpenter. The doctor says a week on crutches to rest that ankle and he'll be okay."

I look at Lavont hopping along on them crutches. He makes me think of them Chinese people—how they eat with chopsticks, which comes so unnatural to me, that time I tried it down in Montgomery. I finally had to say, "Give me a fork," cause if I didn't I'd have starved to death. Lavont has got them crutches going every which way, like me with them chopsticks.

"You okay, Son?" I say.

"Just sore, Mama," he says. Michael is off the porch and grabbing ahold of those crutches, saying, "Let me try it."

"Mary Virginia," I say, "get this boy away. He's gon trip him up pulling on those crutches like that."

"Mrs. Carpenter," Coach Gibbs says, "this is my wife, Dixie. She's been wanting to meet you."

"Hey," she says. She's blushing too. Turns pink. She's so yellow and so pink all at once—you know them kind. It's just too much color going on for me. But I say hello.

Then I don't know what made me do it, but I say, "Y'all come sit down a minute. Have a cold drink. Mary Virginia," I say, "pour some tea for these folks. And Columbus, you and Jessup get a couple extra chairs out on the porch."

I'm thinking to myself, *Well, I guess Coach Gibbs hit the jackpot today. I guess his dreams is coming true this minute.*

His wife, Dixie, she's shy. Around me she don't talk like my boys are always saying. She's polite, drinks her tea, pets that cat which strayed up here and rubs itself on her chair leg.

But Coach Gibbs, now, he talks. He ain't gon miss his opportunity. "I don't want you worrying about Lavont," he says.

"Can't nobody hurt Lavont," Mary Virginia says. "He's too mean." This makes Lavont smile.

We can't get the talk going at first. Michael walks over to where

Dixie's sitting and he studies her. "Come back over here," Mary Virginia says. "Don't be bothering her."

"He's not bothering me," Dixie says.

All my boys were gathered up now, the little ones too, and Coach Gibbs is guessing their names, you know, who's who, cause he's made it his homework to know. And they're shocked, my boys, that he can name all their names.

Then he says to me, "If kids were dollars I guess you'd be a rich woman."

Dixie looks at him like he ought not to be saying that, but it don't bother me. I like the way the man just says what comes without thinking nothing over. When a man thinks before he speaks, that's when you got to worry about him. And besides that, I *am* a rich woman. There's ways I am for sure.

"You play your cards right, Coach," Columbus says, "maybe we'll make *you* rich."

"Say what?" Coach Gibbs is smiling.

"I mean you got to notice, see, the Carpenter brothers, we get improved right on down the line. Jessup, yeah, he's good. And Lavont, sure, he can run too. But don't neither one of them stand up beside me."

Lavont punches Columbus with his crutch and Columbus laughs.

"See, what I'm saying is, you stick with the Carpenter brothers and you can make the Beasley Bulldogs into something, Coach. By the time you get down to Michael—he's gon be the man now—you'll be done put Beasley on the map. People be thinking you know something about how to coach—when all it is, is you got an inside with the Carpenter brothers."

"Columbus the best at running his mouth too," Jessup says. "Don't nobody dispute that."

"You stick with the Carpenter brothers, Coach," Columbus says. "We'a make something out you."

Coach Gibbs laughed and it was a real good sound, his laughing —because it tells me he knows the same as I do that what Columbus is saying is the truth.

When they go, Coach Gibbs says to Dixie, "You want to drive over to that vegetable place in Tallassee for supper?"

She just lights up. "Sure," she says.

"My wife idn't much into home cooking," he says. "She's more the Tastee-Freez type."

"Well, it's hard to cook for two," I say. "Ain't hardly worth the trouble." And she smiles at me a thank-you.

"Let's go by and see if Hemp and Leeta want to go with us," Coach Gibbs says to her.

And I mean it, she got a look right then and she said, "I sure would hate to go anyplace without Hemp and Leeta." And Coach Gibbs, he sort of rolled his eyes heavenward.

Then Dixie says to me, "I wouldn't know how to act if we ever went anyplace by ourselves—just Mac and me. He's got to have his sidekick, Hemp, with him every minute." And she makes this fake smile.

I didn't say nothing to that.

Coach Gibbs winked. "Never mind her. She's in a mood."

And they finally left and we got supper on the table and sat down to eat and talked about white people. They an odd bunch.

MILLIE

I don't mean to talk about her, bless her heart, because Dixie's a sweet girl and I love her like my own, but Dixie's not taking very good care of Mac. I know her mother always worked eight to five—which I've never understood because it's clear they don't need the money—and maybe that didn't set the best example. I know Dixie was mostly raised by their maid, that Lilly. But when it's your son, well, you just wish the best for him. You wish him a nice, comfortable place to come home to, and a good supper on the table. Is that too much to ask?

They've been living in Beasley for more than three years. Mac's doing such a fine job too—and it's not easy either. Maybe they're not winning much, but he's building up the team so they can win. All that criticism, all the problems that go with young boys, and then the school part of it too. Mac has a lot on him. I just wish when he came home that Dixie had things nice for him.

Do you know she hasn't hung the first curtain in a single window? I don't mind telling you I don't sleep easy when we're there, not with anybody who wanted to able to look right in. Thurmond says the only person about to look in the windows out there is a cow. But that's not the point. I tack up a towel over the window every night, take it down in the morning.

Last year I brought some leftover café curtains of mine and while Dixie was gone to the store, I hung them up for her. Every window. It's true they didn't match, but I say any curtain is better than no curtain.

A man needs privacy in his own home. Mac seemed to really appreciate it, and Dixie was quiet about it, but she thanked me when I left. The next time we come back, every curtain was folded in a box, which she returned to me. "I sort of like seeing out," she said. "I hope you understand."

We try to see as many of Mac's games as we can. Bobby and Lisa and Terry and Janelle do too. Thurmond and I have always tried to support our boys in all they do, and they do the same for each other. We're a close-knit family—not like the Carraways, which I'm sure are nice people in their own way. During football season we take turns staying with Mac in the extra room. The rest of us get rooms at the Beasley Motor Lodge. (We bring our own Lysol spray and the people have gotten to know us over there. They try to give us a room where the TV works.)

And Dixie, bless her heart, she cooks spaghetti for us each time we come. We have spaghetti, rain or shine. Bobby and Terry tease her, "I didn't know you were a *I*-talian, Dixie? Did you know it, Mama? I believe Dixie's got spaghetti sauce for blood."

My boys like meat and vegetables. I know Mac does. Usually while I'm there I fix him a good supper, roast beef, potatoes, green beans, Jell-O salad, corn bread—the things he was raised on. I try to make enough to freeze, so later on all Dixie'll have to do is take something out of the freezer and heat it up. How hard is that?

There are so many ways she could be spending her days. If I was her living way out here, I'd put in a vegetable garden. I'd can some vegetables and make some preserves. It's a good way to stay busy and then you have something to show for it too. Not like reading books. Now, I'm not against reading books. It's just that what good does it do—going off into a fantasy world like that. I say what's the point of spending all your time reading about imaginary people's made-up lives when you ought to be living your own real life.

It wouldn't hurt Dixie to fix up around there a little bit. I know ironing is not fun, but it's fun to see your husband looking nice in a starched shirt. I know scrubbing the tub is not fun, but the more you do it, the less of a job it is each time. And I know Mac keeps odd hours, but he still needs to eat, doesn't he?

I wish Lisa and Janelle would talk to Dixie. They're churchgoing girls and make the sweetest wives for Bobby and Terry that I could ever hope for. They never come to Beasley empty handed either. They'll bring a cake or a Crock-Pot of soup. And football—they both love it. I do believe Janelle had rather go to a football game than win money. She's just crazy about football, knows everything that happens out on that field. She says she can't believe Dixie can enjoy the game not knowing any more about it than she does.

Don't misunderstand. I'm not comparing my daughters-in-law. My boys chose them with the help of the Good Lord—and so I'm grateful and just appreciate them with all my heart. I just wish I knew what to do to help Dixie along. You know, for Mac's sake.

ROSE

Since the Gibbs brought down those twin beds from Mac's old bedroom and set them up in the extra room at the duplex, they're usually settled in for every home game. Hardly miss a game unless Millie's in the hospital. Bennett and I usually get to only one game a season, just drive up and back in a day. Dixie says we can have Mac's and her bed if we'll stay overnight, but we don't. That's too much of a houseful, everybody on top of each other like that.

Bennett chooses the game he wants to see each season and we plan ahead to take the day off, usually arrive in Beasley early on Friday morning. Bennett goes straight out to the high school to see Mac. The Gibbs won't get here until right at game time. So Dixie and I have a little time to ourselves. She's straightened things up. I can see she's hung a few pictures since I was here last. Mac's team photos mostly. And one pencil drawing one of his players did of a rocket ship. She made this bookshelf out of plywood and cinder blocks. It takes up a whole wall. The place is getting a homey feel to it. She's painted the kitchen bright yellow—that helps. I sit down on her sheet-covered sofa while she makes coffee in the kitchen. I'd buy her a new sofa if she'd let me, but we've been all through that.

Here's one thing I know about Dixie. I can ask her how she's doing all I want to, but she's never going to tell the truth. Lilly says I ought to be grateful for that and just let it go. But I don't want to get off that easy. I'm her mother. I know this child. I know when something is bothering her.

The way Dixie talks about Mac you'd think he was running for office. "Rose, he's so good with those kids. He really cares about them, you know." When Dixie talks about Mac she always ends up talking about his players. I don't know those boys. I don't want to listen to every problem they have and the genius way Mac sets out to solve it. I just want to ask, "Dixie, honey, how are *you*, really?"

Dixie slices the pound cake Lilly sent and puts pieces on plates for us. All Dixie talks about right now is Tommy Eggleston. He's Mac's quarterback, who got his ninth-grade girlfriend pregnant. "Now he has to get married and go to work at the IGA and right in the middle of the season too," she says. "So of course, everybody's upset. No quarterback. No offense."

I guess I'm supposed to be distressed.

"It is so sad, Rose," Dixie says. "Tommy just sat right there on the sofa and told Mac everything. He kept staring at the second hand on the clock like he'd never known time chopped by in such sharp little seconds before. He was one of those boys," Dixie says, "that was planning on staying a boy forever—you know the kind—and he probably could have succeeded if Charlene hadn't come along and gotten herself pregnant."

"Girls don't get themselves pregnant, Dixie," I say.

"You know what I mean." Dixie drinks a lot of coffee now that she's become friends with that Leeta person. She pours me a cup too. "You know what's so sad, Rose," Dixie says. "Now Tommy will be one more boy who thinks of love as a trick women play on men. I hate that, don't you?"

"I do," I say, wondering when Dixie learned the things she's saying. What does she know about betrayal and the way men think?

"'Why'd Charlene let me do it, Coach?'—that's what Tommy kept saying. 'Why didn't she just say no, Coach?'"

"We women are ruthless, aren't we?" I say.

"Everybody's mad at Charlene," Dixie says. "I mean, she's one girl about to have one baby, true. She needs Tommy, granted. But the team is fifty guys who are depending on him too."

"Sounds like a rock and a hard place to me," I say. I wonder if Dixie hears herself. Does she know who she's talking to? If I haven't told her the truth it's partly because she's never asked. She shovels sugar into her coffee and offers me some. She's set everything out on a silver tray she got as a wedding gift and she's using her good china, Autumn, and some linen napkins. She's trying. I see that.

"If you want to know the truth, Rose," Dixie says, "this year alone three cheerleaders—one of them was homecoming queen too—got pregnant. Around here it's like even the good girls think if they don't get themselves a boy early all the decent ones will be snatched up and they'll be old maids at sixteen."

"As I recall," I say, "you picked out Mac when you were only about fourteen yourself. The only difference is you had the good sense not to pay cash for him. At least you had the sense to put him on lay-away."

"Good home training." She laughs.

I think to myself that I haven't heard Dixie laugh enough. It sounds almost foreign to me, her laughter. I look at this young woman in bell-bottom jeans with a scarf tied in her hair and I have to remind myself that this is my daughter. That she lives in this duplex out by this cow pasture. That she has married the boy she loves and he works all the time and doesn't make enough money for her to dress decent, or get a good haircut, or call her mother long-distance. He's all pride, Mac. But his wife, my daughter, is all that stands between me and mortality. Well, Dixie—and Jesus Christ, of course.

"You can't believe how many baby showers and shotgun weddings I've been to since moving to Beasley," Dixie says. She holds her coffee cup with two hands, like it's a bowl. "Pregnant girls don't get married in the church, Rose. It's bad form. They get married in their parents' living rooms with Bibles in their hands and tears in their eyes, you know. Then come the baby showers, oh my gosh, where the bride's mother cries into a Kleenex but everybody else tries to act artificial Christian-cheerful—no offense, Rose—including me. They get all these gifts they have never wanted in their lives, but they squeal and pretend to be happy over each plastic teething ring, each pair of crocheted booties. It is like virgins sacrificed to God. And these nice girls have their hearts set on making their way to heaven through loving deeds, you know, which is how they got into trouble in the first place."

Why is Dixie telling me this? Is she asking me a question inside all this talk? Is she accusing me of something?

"When you were pregnant with me," Dixie says, "did you have a baby shower?"

"I didn't," I said.

"Why not?"

"That's a good question," I say—but I hate the question. "Bennett's mother, Mrs. Carraway, sent out birth announcements for us. She put her own home address on them too, and goodness, you got the most presents you ever saw."

"But no real shower, Rose?" Dixie says.

"I guess nobody thought I needed a shower. I didn't know then what I know now. There's lots of things I'd do different."

"When I get pregnant I'm going to have the biggest shower you ever saw," Dixie says. "Mac and I have almost gone broke buying all these kids wedding gifts and shower gifts. They owe us big-time." She grins.

"Do you ever think about getting pregnant, Dixie?"

"Sure," she says. "Someday. But not now."

"Frances Delmar has two little girls already."

"Rose, since when do you want me to be like Frances Delmar?"

"I just want you to be happy." I sound like a fool saying this. It is not the sort of thing I say ordinarily. But sometimes I wonder whether or not Dixie knows I love her. It makes me mad in a way, her reluctance to know.

"You aren't craving grandchildren, are you, Rose?" she says. "You're not the type."

"Types change," I say. "When you're ready to be a mother I'll be ready to be a grandmother. You can count on that."

"Promises, promises," Dixie says.

I can tell she wants to change the subject, has got that imaginary door between us half closed already. There are so many subjects that are off-limits. Like Zale. She never asks me about him. Never mentions his name. And if I do, she just listens and moves on to something else. Zale has taught me so much about forgiveness. I'd like to talk to her about that. But the time is never right. "What about church, Dixie?" I ask. "Are you still going to church?"

"Never miss a Sunday."

"And Mac. Has he started going with you?"

"Mac grades film on Sunday, Rose. In the off-season he plays golf. You know that."

Mac's team won. All those Beasley people hugging Dixie, congratulating her, when all she did was watch the game, just like everybody else. And she's just beaming too, taking any credit that's offered her. It gives me a funny feeling.

She tries to get us to come back to the house, where she's having a get-together for the coaches—and of course all the Gibbs will be there. This morning I helped her make crab dip for the occasion. Lilly's recipe. But Bennett and I can't stay. We'll be late getting back as it is. Besides, I don't really want to stay. It's hard to explain why.

LEETA

It's midnight and I'm at work when the phone rings. I know before I answer it that something is wrong. My blood knows. China's crying so hard I can't hardly understand what she's saying. "Mama, Daddy has got a gun. He's gone out to the Carpenter place after Columbus. You got to stop him." It's funny how little explanation I needed. I knew all at once everything she wasn't saying. It all just came to me instantly.

"You get your things together," I tell her. "Go over to Dixie's house and wait for me. Get somebody to drive you."

She hangs up without answering me. But I know she'll do what I say. I know she won't give me any argument.

I have to get them to send a substitute over to look after Mr. Dozier. But he was out good already. His medicine keeps him pretty much asleep. Thank God. I'd hate to have to leave a critical patient in the middle of the night. But I'd do it rather than have Hemp Sparks go crazy and shoot a young boy.

I call Mac and say, "I need you to go with me. Out to the Carpenter place. I'm on my way to get you. Get dressed."

"What the hell is going on, Leeta?" His voice was rising out of a hard sleep.

"Hemp's gone crazy," I say. "I'll explain when I get there."

I should have known there was no way Mac was getting out of the house without Dixie with him. When I drive up she's waiting for me on the front stoop. She runs out to the car and says, "Is everything okay, Leeta?"

"What do you think?" I say. "I'm here in the middle of the night. I'm shaking like a leaf. Does everything seem okay to you?" I blow smoke at her, you know, to hide myself or something. I can be hateful, I admit it, but then I always hate myself for it. And Dixie, she's such an easy target, but she doesn't say anything, just gets in the back seat and says, "It'll be okay, Leeta. Whatever it is," which almost makes me cry.

When Mac comes out of the house I tell him not to lock the door because China will be coming over to their house to wait for me. So he doesn't ask questions, he just leaves the door unlocked and turns on the front light for her. Then he gets in the car and says, "Okay, Leeta. Talk."

When we pull up out at the Carpenter house it's lit up like a torch—every light in the house is on, and the trailer next door too. It makes me think of a giant fire in the middle of the black night. I ease the car up in front of the house. There's no sign of Hemp that I can see.

"Y'all stay put," Mac orders Dixie and me.

We watch him walk up to the door. We see Mary Virginia let him in the trailer. It's new, set up beside the old house—one of those deluxe models, double-wide. Mrs. Carpenter got the trailer about the same time Jessup went off to play football at Auburn. There was some talk about it, you know, like how could she afford such a thing working in the Lurleen Wallace lunchroom.

"This is spooky," Dixie says.

"Tell me about it," I say.

"Hemp wouldn't shoot anybody, Leeta. You know that. He's not that crazy."

"You don't know Hemp when he gets mad," I say. "You can't reason with him when he gets like this." I think of the time he shot his own hunting dog, Frank, for killing the neighbor's cat. Shot Frank between the eyes, because Hemp has ideas about things—how far you can allow nature to go. He cried doing it, but he did it, pulled the trigger himself. Hemp takes things personal, like Frank had let him down by doing what came natural to him. Like Hemp thinks dogs and people both ought to rise above their nature. Like nature is no excuse for anything.

"Hemp's the one inviting Columbus over to your house for supper all the time," Dixie says. "Every time I go over there, there's Columbus. Hemp's the one that sings his praises day and night. Says he's the best there ever was."

"The best football player, yes," I say. "But he never said it was okay for Columbus to touch China."

When Mac comes out of the Carpenter's house, he looks grim. He gets in the car, making the light flash on for a painful second, and then he turns to look at me in the relief of sudden darkness again.

"Columbus admitted it," Mac says. "This has been going on awhile. This is not the first time. But tonight when Hemp caught them China told Hemp that she's, you know, pregnant. I guess Hemp can't take it. He goes nuts, gets his gun, chases Columbus off. Then he and his buddy, Eddie Stuart, decide to pay Columbus a visit. Shoot a few stray bullets in the air, scare him a little, that kind of thing. You know Eddie Stuart," Mac says to Dixie, "from church?"

"Hemp and Eddie were trying to kill Columbus?" Dixie stares at Mac like he's a liar. "Hemp loves Columbus."

"He loves him on the football field, Dix, but he sure as hell don't love him in China's bed. Mrs. Carpenter had to call the police out here and they found Hemp and Eddie parked in the woods right where you turn off the highway."

"Eddie is a deacon," Dixie says.

Dixie's staring at that trailer where the story is hot, you know, like right off the presses. Dixie's nervous. See, she likes all those stories written in books—she can read the hell out of a tragic story confined to a paperback—but when the story is not in a damn book, when it's actually happening in real life, well, she freaks a little. She gets jumpy. But not me. I get this cold flood of calm. It comes over me like ice water.

Finally Mrs. Carpenter comes out the front door with Jessup one step behind her. She looks dressed for church. They get in the back seat beside Dixie.

"Hate to hurry you, Mrs. Carpenter," Mac says, "but the sooner we get down there, the less chance Columbus will say something to make matters worse."

"Can't get no worse," Mrs. Carpenter says.

"This is China's mother, Leeta." Mac introduces me.

"I know who she is," Mrs. Carpenter says.

When we pull up in front of the makeshift police station, a former gas station with the ghost pumps still in place, the first person we see is Hemp standing out front. He's crying like a baby. *Thank God*, I think.

"That's the girl's daddy," Mac says, "Hemp Sparks."

"I been knowing him," Mrs. Carpenter says. "We was little together." She gets out of the car, her head steady and looking straight ahead, and she walks by Hemp like she never noticed him standing out there crying his eyes out. I tell Mac and Dixie to go ahead and look after Columbus, that I'm not ready to get out of the car yet. It'll take me a minute. So Dixie pats my arm and they get out and walk a respectful distance behind Mrs. Carpenter and Jessup like this is a funeral procession or something. If I didn't know better I would think Mrs. Carpenter owned the jailhouse and was just stopping by to be sure things were running smooth. I remember Hemp saying once, "She's a pretty damn good looking woman to have one hundred kids like she does. She knows it too." Now Hemp is watching her walk by and I am thankful to God that I don't know what he's thinking.

I see Mac stop there in front of Hemp. "What the hell is going on, man?" he says.

"It's that goddamned Columbus Carpenter," Hemp says.

"Leeta is in the car over there." Mac nods toward me. "You need to go talk to her."

• • •

"What you want me to say, Leeta? China, your baby girl, has been fucking a nigger boy?"

"Did you hit her, Hemp?" I ask. "What did you do?"

"I hope I slapped some sense into her," he said. "I just saw that boy pasted to her like that, his black self all over her, and God knows what I said or did. I ain't holding myself responsible. I took that boy into my home too. I tried to do right by that boy." His eyes are hard and red.

I don't know this man. I know he isn't my husband. He's not the kind of man I would marry. But even the stranger that he is, somehow manages to break my heart.

"She claims she loves that boy." Hemp chokes on his words. "Can you believe that? He rapes her and she says she loves him. I can't let China ruin herself—all of us—like that."

"*You* love him, Hemp," I said. "Why can't China?"

"If you'd've been home nights like a mother ought to be wouldn't none of this happened," Hemp said. "A mother belongs at home. Idn't no paycheck in the world worth this."

When I get inside the station the young officer on duty— I home-nursed his grandmother—says, "This way, ma'am," and signals me back to a small room where Columbus is seated at a wooden table. Columbus looks like a man waiting for his supper. The officer opens the door. "Go in," he says.

Everybody looks at me. Mrs. Carpenter and Jessup, Mac and Dixie. But I don't say anything. If Columbus is scared he doesn't show it. He's quiet, which I know is all wrong for him. I know he's a boy with plenty to say.

"What you doing here, Mrs. Sparks?" he finally says to me.

"I was about to ask you the same thing," I say.

"Coach Sparks," he says. "He thinks I got China pregnant."

"Did you?" I ask.

Columbus doesn't answer. The silence swells like a blister.

"Somebody did," Mac finally says, "unless God is setting her up for the Second Coming of the Lord."

"According to Coach Sparks," the young officer says, "he's chased this boy away more than once. Is that right, son?"

"Where is she at now?" Columbus asks. "China."

"You got more important things to worry about, boy," the officer says. "If you got the idea you're gonna get in touch with her then you'd better get rid of that idea. She's got enough trouble already, thanks to you."

"Mrs. Carpenter," the officer says, "Mr. Sparks is charging your son here with rape. You might ought to get you a lawyer."

Mrs. Carpenter takes a deep breath but doesn't say a word.

"Beasley is a small town, and a thing like this—well, it concerns us all," the officer says. He's got the exaggerated sincerity of a young preacher. Then he looks at Mac. "You got lots of colored on your team now, don't you, Coach? Well, that's fine and good. I ain't got nothing against the colored. Slavery bred them into some mighty fine athletes, so okay, I understand that. You can't hardly win today unless you got you some colored boys. But maybe you ought to make some kind of rule about colored boys chasing after white girls."

"Look," Mac says. "What Columbus did was stupid, but it sure wasn't rape."

"She's underage, Coach. The law is the law. Rape is rape. Black or white. Lot of white girls around here, you know, they get curious. They act like a black boy might have something a white boy don't. That's all I'm saying. You're the only person out at the school who might could put a stop to some of this."

"Sex?" I say. It's like I'm laughing, but my voice sounds too mean to be laughter. It's part laughing and part screaming—not screaming for help, just screaming about helplessness, how much helplessness there is, how helpless I am. "You want Mac to put a stop to sex?" I shout. "How about love? While he's at it, you want him to put a stop to love too, Officer? And stupidity. He might as well stop stupidity too as long as he's stopping things. Why don't you get to work on this, Mac? Right now. Time's wasting."

MRS. CARPENTER

I've lived here all my life. Everybody in this town knows me. And my kids too. We hadn't never had any trouble with the law except a little tax mix-up once or twice.

So the police release Columbus into my custody and I sign the papers. The girl's mother takes her fool husband away. And Coach Gibbs drives everybody else home. Columbus, he sits stone silent in the back seat and stares out the window like he's waiting for a vision to appear. I tell you the truth, I didn't know right then whether to hug him or slap his face.

When we get home Mary Virginia's waiting up with a pot of coffee. I tell Coach Gibbs and his wife to come inside. There's things we need to talk about, I say. We circle around the table and Mary Virginia pours us all some coffee. She's got Michael asleep on the sofa. That child can sleep through a train wreck.

Columbus, he sits at the kitchen table and stares at his hands, doesn't say a word.

"Hell of a time for palm reading," Coach Gibbs says to him. I think Coach is like me—don't know whether to try to reason with the boy or just to knock his head off and watch it spin.

None my boys have ever had a bit of trouble with the law. Mary Virginia, she run off that time when she was fifteen and so wild and crazy I was half-glad to be rid of her. She got to where she had too much attitude to work with. I mean it. And I called the police to bring her home, and they did, and I said to her, *Look here, this is how things going to be in this house, and this is the way you going to act, and if you ever worry me this way again, running off like this, I will not send a soul after you, and I mean that thing. I'll just act like I never had a daughter and don't have one now.* Since then she's pretty near straightened herself out— what with having a child of her own to look after. Motherhood, now, it can put a head on your shoulders where there didn't used to be nothing but a hat rack.

My boys, they never did act out too much or get an ugly attitude that I couldn't handle. Something bothers them, they bottle it up, or maybe they get outside and punch at each other until they get the thing settled. Jessup, he used to just sit and draw, make up a picture world and go inside that picture and you couldn't hardly get him out of it. Calling him to supper was about the only way I knew to get him to put that pencil down and say something to the rest of us.

But Columbus, he's got a mouth on him, talks when he ought to be listening. But he wouldn't hurt a soul. He most definitely wouldn't rape a young girl. I'd like to think he's got sense enough not to be lovesick over some pale white girl either, but I said my boys are *good* boys, I never said they was perfect.

My kids been around white chirren all their lives, but they stay preferring their own. But then they get this idea about playing football out to the school. Coach Gibbs, he entices them, you know. And next thing I know they are having their pictures in the newspaper and their names on the loudspeaker and I see all those white girls, those cheerleaders, bouncing up in their faces. Hugging their necks and rubbing all up against them. White girls, it's a sight what white girls will do.

"Wouldn't none of this be happening if you'd just let Columbus be," I say to Coach Gibbs. "Why you got to go dragging my boys into playing ball? They used to be stick-to-theyselves sort of boys. You should have left them alone."

"How'd I turn into the bad guy here?" Coach Gibbs says.

"You got Columbus and them out there trying to turn your sorry team into winning a few ball games," Mary Virginia pipes up.

"I'd rather they had them little after-school jobs to earn some spending money," I say.

"I must be hearing things," Coach Gibbs says. "It's football that's getting Jessup a college education, isn't it? You think he'd be enrolled at Auburn right now if it wasn't for football?" He looks at Jessup. "Speak up, son." But Jessup, he keeps quiet.

Coach Gibbs looks at me like I'm the unreasonablest woman in the world. See, you can't make white people understand what you're saying. They hear right over the top of things, when you got the meaning of it low. Down at the beginning. At the root.

"If Columbus was a white boy what you guess they'd do?" Mary Virginia asks. I *know* she's looking for a fuss.

"They'd put a gun to his head and make him marry the girl," Coach Gibbs says. "This time next week he'd be sacking groceries down at the IGA."

"They try to make him marry her and I believe he'd like that." Jessup is disgusted with his own brother. "Columbus acts like he loves that girl."

"I didn't raise him to be stupid like that," I say.

"China is a really sweet girl, Mrs. Carpenter." Dixie, usually she don't say too much.

"If Columbus is looking to find a sweet girl," I say, "he don't need to look at a ghost of a girl like that Sparks child. There's plenty of sweet colored girls, if sweet is what he wants."

"If y'all gon talk like I ain't here, then I mize well go to bed." Columbus gets up from the table where he's been sitting like the cat's got his tongue. "Y'all know everything. Y'all got all the answers." He leaves the room.

I don't hardly see how I can stop him. "We gon talk in the morning," I yell to him. "You got till morning to think up something to say that I want to hear!"

"He didn't used to stay so moody," I tell the coach's wife.

"Football is not all bad, Mrs. Carpenter," Dixie says. "Look at Jett Brown. You've heard of him, right? He lives like a king out in California. It's all because of football. And your boys, maybe they have a chance at a life like that."

"Does he run with white women?" I ask. "Mr. Jett, the king?"

"Sometimes," Dixie says. "Jett says out in California everybody mixes up."

"Well, we're in Beasley, Alabama, honey," I say. "In Alabama, it's only dogs that mix up."

"I been blamed for a lot of things," Coach Gibbs says, "but I swear you're the first one to blame me for your son getting a girl in trouble. That's a new one."

"Football, football, football" I say. "That's all I hear."

LEETA

Dixie's at my door first thing this morning. I'm still dressed from last night, haven't closed my eyes a minute. When China called Mr. Dozier's house my heart stopped cold. Mr. Dozier's an old man with testicle cancer. He cries sometimes, but he was sleeping real sound last night. I listened to my child's voice and I swear to God, hadn't I prayed every night that this exact moment would never come?

I put China on the bus to Bluefield at three o'clock this morning. My twin sister, Reeta, lives in Bluefield. "China will be with family there," I tell Dixie. "She won't be alone." I see Dixie staring at the sweat rings under my arms.

"She's gone?" Dixie says.

"I was scared what Hemp might do," I say. I look in the mirror and try to shake my head but my hair has gone flat against my skull. I run my hands through it trying to revive it. I keep on until Dixie reaches over and takes my hand down.

"Your hair is fine," she says.

I grab my purse and a sweatshirt off the pile of unfolded laundry on the floor. "I called in sick today. People are just going to have to find a way to die without my help. I need to get out of this house or I'll go crazy."

We get in my car and Dixie drives us to Tastee-Freez to get hot coffee. "Where do you want to go?" she asks me, but how can I answer that? Back in time. I want to start over, everything all over again. My whole life erased.

"It doesn't matter," I say. "Just drive."

So we head for nowhere in particular, and neither of us talk for the longest time. Dixie looks in the rearview mirror and she looks over at me and she watches the road. I can feel the questions swimming through her head because they're swimming through mine too and it makes waves between us. It's so humid and heavy, the air, that it's like the car is a boat and in our minds we're paddling.

Dixie turns off on smaller and smaller roads until we're on a semi-gravel two-lane that leads us into Macon County, right into Tuskegee. I've smoked half a pack of cigarettes by the time we get there and I'm beginning to cough. This town has always made me nervous. You can't tell what the people here are thinking. Everybody here is black.

"You need to eat something," Dixie says. So we stop at Hardee's to get cheeseburgers even though I don't really want to.

We get our cheeseburgers and sit at a table in the front by the window. "Jett's old girlfriend lives here," Dixie says. "Princess. She's as light as I am."

Dixie always talks about this Jett guy like he's the road not taken, but when I ask her about him, she laughs. "He's Mac's best friend," she says. "And in case you haven't noticed, he's black." I've noticed, I tell her, because she won't hardly let us miss a single 49ers game on TV. It's like she thinks he can't play if she's not watching. That's because this guy Jett, this black guy, means nothing to her. Nothing at all.

"A lot of these people are half-white," I say, looking around me. "You can tell by looking at them." I nod toward a table where two pale black women sit, one of them with hair as straight as mine. "She's as white as I am," I say. "Look."

"Are you thinking about China's baby?" Dixie asks.

"My grandbaby." I lift the bun off my burger and remove the onions like I'm taking a couple of white zeros out of an equation. "Hemp wants China to have an abortion. He made her promise. Reeta knows somebody."

"Is that what you want?"

"It's full circle," I say to Dixie. "In a way, I was my own mother putting myself on a bus, you know." I light a cigarette and lean back in my chair picking at my cheeseburger, pinching off bits of bread like little Communion bites. "I guess everybody in Beasley knows what happened?"

"Gossip is the lifeblood of Beasley," Dixie says. "You're the one who told me that."

We're the only white people in Hardee's. When I begin to cry it doesn't matter because I'm a stranger here. Dixie has never seen me cry and when I start, she starts too. She cries open-faced, fully exposed. Her face shines wet and clear and it is strange to say but it pleases me, almost cheers me up a little, her tears, because I know she's crying for me, for my pain. I love Dixie at this moment. My own girl on a bus that will take two and a half days and deliver her to a strange new land. "I'm sorry, Mama," she said a thousand times.

I ask myself what I would do if a man—not Hemp—wandered into Hardee's at this exact moment and saw my misery, the way it shines off me like a light, and he scooped me up in his arms and promised me a better life. What if he said, *Baby, you can count on me. Let me take you away from all this?* And he really meant it. I would go with him and forget everything that ever came before. But no such man ever comes, does he?

When we get through crying and calm ourselves down, we get back in the car. We drive through Notasulga, Tallassee, Milstead, and Shorter. Cotton fields are everywhere. And woods. And houses of the poor and the not-so-poor, one kind next to the other. If houses were dreams people lived inside of, most of the ones around here would be too small and in bad need of repair, like something you could get trapped in, something that, as shabby as it might be, you could not afford—a dream you had to keep hammering at and screwing together with mismatched screws. No matter how modest a dream you build, seems like it always falls apart—and you just keep on patching until you die.

We pass big, old white houses with pots of flowers and such, and a swing on the porch, and the grass mowed perfect and you know all the bills are paid at that house and you wish you could knock on the door and they would take you in and love you. Why do people with money always paint their houses white? I've never seen Dixie's Birmingham house except in pictures. It's hard to love people who grow up in houses like that. Sometimes I don't think I can.

"See that house there?" I point to a shack where the doors hang open on the hinges and there's more stuff strewn in the yard than there is inside the fall-down house. "I was raised in a house worse than that. Mama used to like to say that we didn't know we were poor back then, not until the government set out to tell us, but that's a lie. We knew."

"We'll be back to Beasley before long," Dixie says. It's like she wants to find a route where we won't pass anything else depressing, you know, a route where nobody is poor and everybody is happy. Sometimes Dixie is ridiculous.

"You don't have any kids, Dixie," I say when we reach the Tastee-Freez sign that says WELCOME TO BEASLEY. It shows a giant hot dog with a smile on its face and little shoes on its feet. "But someday you will have kids and nobody can tell you how that changes things."

"Write down China's address for me, Leeta," Dixie says when she lets me out in the driveway at home. "It would be all right if I wrote to China, wouldn't it?"

"Sure," I say. "She'd appreciate it." I feel suddenly nervous. I fish in my purse for a check stub and write Reeta's West Virginia address for Dixie. All the while I see Hemp standing in the window, watching me, waiting for me to come in the house. "Damn him," I say.

"Who?" Dixie says.

I nod toward the window where Hemp has planted himself.

"Do you think it bothers me, Dixie? China's baby being half-black?" She doesn't answer me. "It doesn't bother me one bit," I say. "It's just that this is a screwed-up world we live in. And I am about to go inside to the screwed-up man I live with and take up where I left off—being his screwed-up wife."

Then I put one foot in front of the other and walk into that house where my life waits for me.

DIXIE

Fornication is one of Pastor McBride's hot topics these days. The truth is I like that one better than the ones hinging on football metaphors and using the Beasley Bulldogs as living religious lessons. More than once he's twisted a sermon out of one of the harmless anecdotes I've written in my newspaper column—"Notes from the Coach's Wife."

And Leeta, she's in church every Sunday like always. And all her daughters too—except China. They wear those dresses Leeta sews them that make them all look cut from the same cloth in an economical sort of way. And they pray so *hard*. It's a show of support, you know, for China. They pray for China and I do too. But I also pray for Columbus.

Mac says Columbus never misses a football practice. Even with all that's happening he's at practice every day and ready to go. On game nights he outplays himself like nothing anybody around here has ever seen. He runs right through people, like his reward for playing hard is going to be everlasting life. Folks cheer for him right along too—not turning on him near as bad as they would if he was pussyfooting around out there. People don't love that in anybody—personal defeat. They love trouble, of course—somebody else's. But they don't like to see anybody give over to trouble completely.

It hardly seems to matter much that Beasley is losing almost as many games as we're winning because Columbus is such a spectacle he softens the blow of the losses for the rest of us. Even the people who hate Columbus—people who think he ought to be sent straight to prison for what he's done—forgive him, more or less, for a couple of hours each week while he runs like a madman up and down the playing field.

I know it's corny to say, but it is almost like you can see Columbus turn into, well, almost a man. Like pain can do that. You'd never know that lots of afternoons when Mac drives him home after practice he breaks down and cries like a baby.

In today's particularly athletic sermon Pastor McBride suggests that we imagine that *the football* is sin—you know, the leather ball itself—and asks us to watch the way people want it and take it over the line when they get the chance, which he warns us in the end is nothing but a touchdown for Satan. He asks us to notice the way people gather up to watch other people struggle with their sins, to notice how we all lust for the excitement of sin. Pastor McBride is just driving me crazy.

Of course Mac's never at church to defend himself when Pastor McBride decides to get creative with a sermon. Mac hasn't stepped a foot in church since our wedding, except to speak at the men's prayer breakfast now and then. So it's up to me to defend our family name—and the team too.

I say to Pastor McBride after the service, "I'm sorry, but I've decided to try the Methodist Church for a while. I won't be able to keep the nursery on Sundays anymore."

"Try the Methodist Church?" he says. "Churches aren't like shoes, Mrs. Gibbs. You don't try them on to see which one goes best with the dress you're wearing that day."

"You criticize Mac too much," I say.

"Even Jesus was criticized, honey."

"I know," I say, "but Jesus didn't have a wife, did he?"

Shortly after I become a Methodist Rose gives me a sewing machine to prove she has a forgiving heart. Leeta teaches me how to use it and loans me all sorts of patterns and fabric remnants. Before I know what's happening I have not only made curtains for every window in the duplex but I'm making my own clothes too and bragging about it, saying, "You'll never guess what these slacks cost me."

I've even gone so far as to make Mac and Daddy a couple of cotton neckties out of scrap material. It's like right before my eyes I'm turning into Millie, Mac's mother. At night I dream of thread—the way it holds pieces together, the tiny stitches almost invisible, the double knots, the amazing power of something so insubstantial.

LILLY

I know a 7 and 3 season ain't nothing to brag about, but it's the best they done so far. And them people in Beasley have give Mac five hundred dollars and a new toaster oven. Dixie called me up to tell me. She says Mac has invited Jett to be the speaker for their high school sports banquet and he said sure, he'd come. So it's natural she would want me to come too. So I drive over the night before.

Next morning we all go to Montgomery to pick Jett up at the airport and who do you guess is there ahead of us? Princess. I thought for sure I'd seen the last of her. She hugs my neck and says, "Oh, Mrs. Brown, it's just so good to see you." *Well,* I think, *if you been wanting to see me so bad I been sitting in Birmingham these last five years right where you saw me last.* When Jett get off the airplane, you could tell he was surprised to see her. But oh, he looked good. He looked Hollywood-ified now that he's making all them commercials, but he still looked good just the same. He about hugged the daylights out of me.

Mac slaps Jett on the back and says, "J. B., baby," which is what they call him in them commercials. "Welcome home, man."

"You damn whistle-neck," Jett says, "how's it going?"

Then Dixie hugs his neck and he says, "Hey there, white woman. You're looking all right for a married lady." And she laughs and says, "When did you start talking like *that?* Your accent is gone. I hope you still got some Alabama in you."

Then Princess comes over to him and makes a show out of herself. She kisses him like he is a cough drop and her throat is just about killing her. I thought for a minute there she might just swallow him up. You don't expect nothing like that out of a preacher's daughter.

If anybody invited Princess to come back to that duplex with us I don't know who it was. I know it wadn't me. But here she is, little suitcase in hand, riding back to Beasley with us, taking Jett in her car. "Jett and I got a lot to talk about, Mrs. Brown," she says. "I hope you don't mind."

They had me a place up at the big table in the cafeteria where Jett give his speech. I sit right next to Dixie, then Mac on her other side. They introduced me and everybody clapped, but I don't let that go to my head any. They don't know me. And I don't know any them people.

The name of Jett's speech is "What It Means to Be a Winner." I think he gives a real nice talk. But Dixie, that child cries through the whole thing. I can't hardly listen to what Jett's got to say for her carrying on beside me, fishing around for another Kleenex. Mac, he gets right irritated with her and whispers, "What the hell is wrong with you?"

"I don't know," she says and proceeds to cry twice as hard.

I tell you the moment that gets me. It is not when all them white people stand up and clap their heads off when Jett is through talking. It is while they are sitting there, listening to him. I think to myself, *This is what that boy has wanted all his life — all these folks listening to what he's got to say about things.* Afterwards they line up to shake his hand. They have those cameras flashing.

But Dixie, Lord, that girl is a mess about now. She must have something to cry about that don't none of us know the nature of. I have to excuse myself and go off to the ladies' room with her, see if we can't get her toned down. She has already about embarrassed Mac to death. She goes in one them stalls and like to never come out. There's a long line waiting too, them women listening to Dixie inside there, crying like all get-out. "Baby, what is the matter with you?" I keep saying.

"Lilly, I don't know what's wrong," she says. "Everybody is being so good to Jett. All these white people, you know."

"Got to be more to it than that," I say.

That man at the newspaper wants to take a picture of Dixie because I believe, the way he is acting, that he's sweet on her, but Lord, she is not about to let nobody snap her looking like she does with them swoll eyes. So he takes a shot of Jett with that boy Columbus. He's got a scholarship to go to Birmingham University next year and they are making like he's gon be the next Jett Brown. Seems like a nice boy. And I meet his mama too. She comes up and tells me her name, says Dixie is all the time talking about Jett. She is nice enough. She don't dress worth anything. I guess she sees Dixie is upset. I hear her say, "Now honey, I hope you the one that writes up this story for the newspaper. I think you write real good, honey."

It is as close to a smile as Dixie manages all night.

By the time we get back home I am wore out. And Dixie, she kisses me and goes straight to bed. It's the only way she can get away from Mac saying, "I don't get it. Just tell me what the hell you're crying about." If he really wants to know, I think, he'd quit talking and listen. But he don't know how to go about anything with women. Never has.

The next morning Dixie is better. She makes everybody a big breakfast. Eggs and sausage and grits and them biscuits out of a can. It wadn't bad. And she is smiling and you would never know she had ever had a sad minute. Like whatever was the end of the world yesterday is not the end no more. We sit down to eat and Mac is so glad to have Dixie acting right he's ready to forgive her for crying in front of all them people.

Before anybody can say anything, Dixie gets up from the table in a hurry and goes down the hall to the bathroom, where in a minute we hear her throwing up.

This was not the kind of visit I was wanting to have over here. Plus I was looking forward to driving Jett back to the airport, but when I say so, Princess tears up too and gets pitiful and I swear to God, I just don't have the patience for all this. We all watch while Jett and Princess load her car. Jett hugs everybody. When he hugs Dixie— she still has a Kleenex over her mouth—he says, "Girl, take care of yourself now. Ima call you next week." And she nods.

Jett and Princess drive off toward Montgomery, where their paths will split apart, thank God. We see Princess is crying. I'm the only woman around here who's not. I guess Princess'll go on and live her down-to-earth life over in Tuskegee. And Jett, he'll soar on up into the sky, which will reduce Princess to nothing but a little speck—right before she disappears altogether. I guess that's what she's crying about. But I don't believe in it myself, crying over a man for any reason, even if that man is my own son.

I don't leave until after lunch, when Mac has gone up to the school to do whatever he does up there. Dixie is laid out on the sofa with her legs tangled in a quilt. I made Mac go get her some ginger ale before he left. Now she's sipping it and saying, "Princess makes me sick, Lilly—the way she monopolized Jett. We didn't hardly get a minute with him."

"He's the one let her do it," I say.

DIXIE

Mac says China shows up at school just as suddenly as she left. He says people act like nothing ever happened. China practices her cheers, does her homework, and makes the honor roll like always. The only difference is that she's stopped bleaching her hair blond. She's letting it grow out to a natural, noncolor brown. It looks terrible too, as if a scarlet letter could take the form of dishwater-brown hair. Her face is as pretty as always, only now there is something knowing and wise around her eyes—at least people like to say there is.

Hemp dropped the charges against Columbus under the condition that he stay away from China, no contact at all, not even at school. Mrs. Carpenter told us she had to make Columbus sign the papers. He didn't want to. "You need to forget all about this white-girl predicament," she told him.

Suddenly I have a pair of breasts like something out of a trash magazine. Every time I undress I stare at myself in the mirror. And Mac—when he comes home at night my face is the second thing he looks at. He makes love to me like I'm some new woman who's made him forget all about his wife.

I'm in my fourth month and I'm beginning to show. We can feel the baby twist and kick, like already he is running through the place looking for the way out. A human house. That's how I feel, like a house on feet.

I get in the bathtub and lie there for hours. It's the only way I know to get cool. In the tub I'm not just a house. I'm more like a houseboat. I lie still, let my mind float, rub my hands over my belly, and talk to the half-person, half-tadpole swimming inside me. I use the same kinds of love words I would use if I were trying to coax a fish to the top of a deep river—only I am the river *and* the houseboat floating in it. And Mac, he is some handsome guy waving to me from the shore.

When the call comes, at first I think it's a joke.

"Dixie, I'm sorry to have to call you," China says. "But if it was me I'd want to know."

"Know what?" I have a sudden icky feeling and grab for the saltines I leave sitting out.

"I don't want to cause trouble, I swear," China says. "But Coach Gibbs, he's always in Coach Epperson's office. They lock the door. I think they're having an affair."

I actually laugh. "Are you talking about Barbara Epperson? The softball coach?"

"I know she's not pretty," China says, "but a lot of men like her."

"I'm sure it's not what it seems," I say.

"I'm not the only one who thinks so," China says. "Everybody does."

"You know people love to talk," I say. If anybody knew she should. "I'm sure there's nothing to it."

"I'm glad you're not upset. I was afraid you'd be mad."

"I'm used to rumors."

"Okay," China says. "Daddy said not to call you. I'm real sorry."

"It's okay, China," I say and hang up.

Bobby Epperson. In the land of harmless women, she seems the most harmless of all. Her strong point, according to Mac, is that she can tell a great joke. So why do they need to lock the door to tell a few jokes? I dial the school and have the secretary track Mac down, something I've never done before.

"Dix?" He's out of breath when he gets to the phone. "What the hell? Is everything okay?"

"I want you to come home," I say. "Now."

"Right. Okay then. I'm on my way."

Part of what makes our marriage so good is the fact that I rarely ask Mac for anything, especially any of his time. Now he's rushing home to me and I feel this surge of power. Maybe I should get mad more often. That's one good thing about being pregnant—all my feelings just come out whether I want them to or not. It feels like the first time I've ever had feelings—you know, like anger or anything.

I'm sitting on the sofa, waiting, when Mac drives up. He comes in the house like he's expecting to find me bound and gagged. "Dixie?" He stands in the middle of the room in his wide-legged stance. "Are you okay? You scared the hell out of me."

"I got an interesting phone call today," I say.

"Yeah? You gonna tell me who from?"

"China. She wanted to let me know you are having an affair with Bobby Epperson."

Mac looks at me like I've finally gotten to the punch line of some convoluted joke. He lets loose something like a laugh.

"She said you two close yourselves up in her office."

"Good God," Mac says. "I thought you were going to tell me you had a brain tumor or something."

"So, is it true?"

"Dixie, give me a break. She's a nicotine fanatic. We go at a few cigarettes, talk a little shop, you know. You're not taking this seriously, are you? Believe me, if I was going to have an affair it damn sure wouldn't be with Bobby Epperson."

"I put up with all your football crap, Mac, but I'm not putting up with this other kind of crap. I mean it." My voice shocks me. It's so strong the words just shoot out like bullets.

Mac hasn't moved from his spot in the center of the room, like he wants to keep proper distance between us. "God, if anybody ever told me you'd be jealous of Bobby Epperson I'd've said they were crazy."

"I'm not jealous. I'm mad."

"Okay. No more smokes with Bobby. It's done. What else?"

"I want this rumor to stop."

"What am I supposed to say?"

"I don't care what you say, Mac. I want you to make sure everybody knows you're married and thinks you're crazy happy about it. Lie if you have to."

"Dix, my God . . ." He just stands there staring at me. It's like he doesn't recognize me. "You're really mad about this," he says. He looks at me like I'm some new offense and he doesn't know what the hell defensive play to call.

School's out and summer is so hot Mac lets Rose and Daddy buy us air conditioner units. I'm already working on the football profiles for next year. Mac's players are into it. They come over, let me interview them and take their picture. Their mothers make them wear nice shirts and wait for them in the car.

I sit in front of the air conditioner and write all morning, then I sew all afternoon. I've made some unique baby clothes. Leeta says she's never seen anything like them in her life. But I don't want my baby looking like every other baby in the world.

China comes by the duplex selling raffle tickets for the Baptist church. I promised her I'd buy two. She stands in the doorway while I rummage through my purse for two dollars. I'm short twenty-six cents.

"It still seems weird," she says, "that you don't go to church with us anymore."

"I decided to try the Methodists."

"Is that all?"

"I don't think church is supposed to make you feel rotten."

"Of course it is," she says. "It's like penance."

"You'll have to make that one raffle ticket," I say. "I can't find enough change."

"That's okay." She makes no move, just stands in the doorway like she's waiting for a miracle.

"Do you want to come in?" I say. "Have a Coke?"

"Okay." She closes the door behind her, steps toward the sofa, and runs her hand over the sheet, smoothing the wrinkles before sitting down.

I get us Cokes and Vanilla Wafers on a saucer and set it in front of China on the sofa. "You're growing your hair out?"

"Nobody likes it," she says.

"It's your hair," I say.

"Do you have a cigarette?" she asks, which is strange because she knows I don't smoke. "It just keeps me from eating, you know. I'm trying to lose these pounds." China takes an ice cube out of her Coke with her fingers and drops it back in like a rock in a puddle. She speaks quietly. "You never asked me about my baby, Dixie. How come?"

"I guess I didn't think I should."

"What did Mama tell you?"

"Your daddy wanted you to get an abortion."

"I just pretended it was too late," she says. "Daddy was going crazy. And Mama, she kept talking about those little orphans in the pictures of Vietnam, you know, the ones whose fathers deserted them and all and they've got those sad eyes. Little brown babies like that. That was in Mama's head."

"It was a hard thing," I say, sounding stupid.

"You know how they give abortions?" China looks at me hard. "They put this little vacuum cleaner thing up inside you and it really hurts and then they just suck the other life out of you."

"That sounds terrible," I say.

China leans back against the sofa sort of shaking her glass so the ice rattles. "You like Columbus, don't you, Dixie?"

"Sure I do."

"Can I ask you something? Do you think it's possible to love somebody at my age?"

"I loved Mac when I was your age."

"Pastor McBride says Columbus is going to ruin my life. Columbus cried when I told him that. He wouldn't cry if he didn't love me, would he?"

"I don't think so."

China sets her drink on the tray and tucks her knees beneath her. "I had a baby girl," she says. "They let me meet the people who adopted her."

"That's good," I say.

"They're black, the people. Aunt Reeta knows them. You should have seen how happy they were."

MARY VIRGINIA

Me and Mama go to Birmingham to every one of Columbus's games we can. This week Coach Gibbs and his wife, Dixie, go with us. Dixie's big as a house and can't sit for long without her ankles swelling up. It don't seem like pregnancy suits her.

Watching the game up in the stands with Coach Gibbs and Dixie —that's something. See, Coach Gibbs, he don't never sit up in the stands, you know. It's his first time. And he hates it. Everybody is on his nerves so bad, you know, saying stupid things. They say anything stupid about Columbus they got me and Mama to answer for. We don't truck with that.

"You don't realize what asses people are until you listen to the talk up here," Coach Gibbs says to us. "I couldn't take much of this, I tell you."

But what gets me most is that his wife, Dixie, she doesn't know shit about football. She's reading the program and asking Coach Gibbs about the Power One. He laughs, but damn. "It's the Power I," he says. "You know, like *eye*. We run the Power I at Beasley." The girl is in a fog or something up there. It sort of shocks me.

After the game we go down to the locker room and I swear if we don't see China Sparks down there first thing. She's wearing one of those dresses her mama makes for them girls—look like missionary dresses if you ask me, but let's face it, China ain't no missionary. A dress can lie now. I seen many a lying dress. Fact is, I worn a few myself.

When Columbus comes out of the locker room the first thing he does is go over there and kiss China. She looks almost scared, her eyes jumping around to see who all is watching. Every eye is on her because every other eye is on Columbus. I can feel Mama bow right up. "Be nice, Mama," I say. "This ain't no place to start nothing."

So Columbus comes over to us and he brings China with him, got his arm around her. "Hey, Mama," he says and kisses her and me too. "Y'all remember China?" he says. But we see what he's saying—*Y'all don't say or do nothing to upset this white girl.*

I don't know about Mama, but I ain't about to lose my little brother arguing with no white girl, I can tell you that.

Kids are lining up for Columbus's autograph. They see China Sparks like a streak of white lighting standing there. That missionary dress don't fool them kids.

"Is that your girl?" a boy asks Columbus, got a program stuck out for him to sign.

"Sure is," Columbus says. "Pretty, idn't she?"

"She's white," the kid says.

"I know," Columbus winks, "but don't tell nobody. Let's me and you keep it a secret, okay?"

The kid never takes his eyes off China, looking at her like she is about the scariest thing he's ever witnessed firsthand, scarier than a dead girl, or a naked one. China is blushing to almost purple, looking sort of bruised all over, like all them stares was fists pounding her.

Then this black kid says, "Ima get me a white girl too when I play ball at college. Ima be a tight end."

"You're not either," the white kid says.

"I can get a white girl if I want to. Tell him, Columbus."

"First of all," Columbus says, "get you a good education. Then don't neither one of y'all have to bother with picking out a girl. You just let the girls pick you out. You might get black, you might get white, but you'll definitely get plenty."

Mama slaps at Columbus. "That is not any kind of way to talk to kids," she says. "Behave yourself."

DIXIE

It's like being stabbed within an inch of my life every thirty minutes or so. Even before we get to Lee County Hospital and the doctor puts a gas mask over my face and knocks me out cold, I'm already numb.

While I'm lying helpless on the delivery table, I split in half, make two people out of myself. It's like I multiply and divide at the same time. They put me to sleep so I won't see this happen. But I know.

When I come to, I have a daughter, Sarah Blakney Gibbs, who looks like she's clawed her way out of me, little scratches on her swollen face. The nurse lays Sarah in my arms and I feel my body contract around her like a cracked hull trying to reclaim its place around a tender pink peanut.

"You did good," Mac says and kisses my forehead. All those times Mac has been called to Millie's bedside because her heart has threatened to give out on her again have made him jumpy in hospitals. Like he thinks they're places women go to punish you with their pain, make you feel miserable. He seems ready to bolt from the building any second, like he fears they'll lock the doors to the place and never let him out.

He can't come to see us the next day because Beasley has an away game, but he gets Leeta to bring roses and write "I love you" for him on the card.

When Mac comes the next morning to drive us home, he brings the game ball from the night before. Leeta's daughter Jo-Jo has painted on it in fingernail polish, "For Sarah, Happy Birthday, Love, Daddy. Beasley 21, Notasulga 16."

Until now I've never thought of breasts as anything practical. I considered them mostly ornaments. Now that mine are full of milk I'm changing my mind. They are so heavy that sometimes I walk around carrying one in each hand. The slightest movement causes milk missiles to shoot from me like artillery that fires before it's aimed.

Mac and I wake up to find ourselves sleeping in a little sea of milk. "Can't you do something about this, Dix?" he says. "Are you sure this is normal?"

I start to cry.

"Come on, Dix," Mac says. "I didn't mean anything." I get the feeling he can't wait to get away from me. Like for the first time in his life he's afraid of my body. I am too.

When I nurse Sarah, her sweet pink mouth like a vise on my raw nipples, sucking hard with her eyes closed, I can feel something deep inside me tighten and shrink with each tug.

"Doesn't that hurt?" Mac asks me again and again. Only once, late at night, when I'm drifting in and out of this new kind of semisleep, do I feel his mouth on my breast, sucking gently, tasting me, then pulling away silently, as if he hadn't done it and hoped I hadn't been awakened by it. What he doesn't know is that the touch of his lips on my breast cut through me like a knife.

I'm a wreck, but for the first time in my life I can honestly say I feel married.

"Can I come over and see the baby?" China asks. She calls almost every day but hasn't wanted to see the baby until now.

"Sure," I say.

"Can I bring Columbus with me? He's in town."

"I guess so," I say. "Sure."

When they arrive Sarah is asleep in her bassinet. I lead them into the bedroom and let them look her over. China is squeezing Columbus's shirttail in her fist.

"Man," Columbus says, "she looks like a baby bird."

"She's pretty," China says.

"She's tiny, man. Look at her foot. It's about the size of my finger." He lays his finger beside her foot.

China puts her hand on Sarah's head. She's like a girl reaching for an apple. She runs her finger over the pulsing spot in Sarah's skull. "There it is." She takes Columbus's big hand and runs his finger over the same spot. "See? It's her soft spot," she says. "You can feel her heartbeat there."

Before they leave they give me a present for Sarah, a set of plastic keys on a chain. They walk outside and get in Leeta's car. For the longest time they just sit there in the front seat, China wrapped in Columbus's arms, her face buried in his neck. They stay that way for almost an hour.

Mac hasn't touched me in weeks. When he comes home at night he goes straight to pick Sarah up, even if it means waking her up, then he rocks her back to sleep. He's never home when she's awake, so to make up for that, it's like he's fathering her in her dreams. I guess he thinks that counts. I guess he thinks what works for her should work for me. He sneaks into bed with me like he hopes to God I'm asleep. And I pretend to be.

I hate how unchanged his life is. Baby or no baby, he has the same body he's always had, keeps the same schedule he's always kept, thinks the same thoughts he's always thought. Nothing has changed, except that when he gets around to coming home there is a baby in the house. I swear to God, some days it is all I can do not to get a gun and shoot him.

Frances Delmar calls me every few days on the Mississippi State WATS line at Cleet's office. "How's parenthood?" she says.

So finally I blurt out, "Mac has got the Elvis Presley syndrome, Frances Delmar. He's got it bad."

She laughs. "What is that? He breaks out into sudden song—'Love Me Tender' or something?"

"Hardly," I say. "It's the Elvis Presley syndrome, F. D. I read about it in a magazine. When Priscilla gave birth to Lisa Marie and transformed herself into a mother, Elvis never could think of her as desirable again. The Elvis Presley syndrome, you know. You've heard of it."

"Oh God, Dixie, is that what's bothering you? Enjoy it while you can, child," she laughs. "Men get the idea that you can be either a mother or a wife, and they never know which one you're going to choose, especially not at first. I've had to retrain Cleet three times now."

"Here's the thing," I say to Frances Delmar. "I don't feel any desire for Mac, you know. None. It's just that I want him to desire me again and it's driving me crazy that he doesn't. The less he does, the less I do. What if it's gone forever? What if it never comes back?"

"It comes back, Dix. I promise you. Some things you can't beat to death with a stick. But if it bothers you so much why don't you tell him?"

"If I tell him, Frances Delmar, then if it happens it will be perfectly meaningless. You know that. If you have to ask for what you want, then it doesn't count when you get it."

"You still got that great logic, Dix," she laughs. "I guess the only thing left to do is say your prayers and sit back and wait for the magic."

I don't go to Beasley's last game. It's too chilly to take Sarah out. And I'm too moody. Since Millie's been sick, Thurmond, Bobby, and Terry just come for the game and drive back afterwards. They don't spend the night with us like they used to.

Beasley is winning too—without me. Mac's best season so far. I guess that should be comforting. He's got two Carpenter brothers on his team this season, Cleveland and Charles. They're good. But lately I feel like if I never see another football game it will be okay with me. So instead of bundling Sarah up in her tiny Bulldogs sweatsuit, I cuddle with her in bed, wrapping myself around her like an ocean around a small island, and we listen to the last game of the season on the radio waves.

Beasley wins again. They finish with a 9–1 season.

      I don't hear Mac come home, but I feel him lift Sarah from the curve of my arm and put her in her crib. Then he comes back to our bed and from the moment he lays down beside me I know the hiatus is over. I know it by the way his fingers land on my skin like tentative astronauts on a new planet. He can say Dixie so that all I hear is the X that marks the very core of me. The explosion is good. His into me. Mine back into the world again.

MRS. CARPENTER

If they don't stop showing it on TV over and over again I'm going to call up somebody and complain. Them newspeople forget folks have families watching—that his mama is watching. They got that picture firing frontwards, backwards, then frontwards again like a machine gun so you have to watch it happen a hundred times before those TV people are satisfied and stop the film. His knee is bent forward, you can see that, and then two them big boys, they just dive on top of him and snap the knee joint in two. You can see his leg swing up when the bones break. It makes you look away from the TV and bite your lip.

Columbus had surgery that same night. Coach Gibbs drove me and Mary Virginia and Michael to Birmingham and we got to see him just before they took him in. Coach Catfish was there too. He didn't stay, but he stopped and told me how sorry he was. "These things happen," Coach Catfish said, which is no kind of thing to say to anybody's mama when her son is being rolled into surgery.

Somebody had the good sense to bring some Krispy Kreme doughnuts. Michael can eat a boxful by himself. Coach Gibbs, after a while, I guess the cat got his tongue. He sat there and read a bunch of newspapers, as quiet as a mouse, which ain't like him. But when he went to call up Dixie I heard him say, "It's not good, Dix. I can tell you that right now."

• • •

"You got to do something," I tell Coach Gibbs. I'm sitting in that little duplex on that pitiful old sofa they got. You'd think with what they pay him he could get a decent sofa. It ain't that I'm nervous. It's that I'm aggravated. So I rub my fingers together this way—it's a habit.

"They got Columbus so upset he don't know what to do," I tell Coach Gibbs. "Them people at the college. First they got his knee so bummed up he couldn't finish out last season. He let his marks go, you know, cause he missed so much class, was working so hard on his recuperation. So now they up and took his scholarship away. They saying it's his marks, but it wadn't his marks when he was busy playing every game for them.

"And now won't none of them pro scouts talk to him no more like they been doing. Too chancy, they saying. Got to wait and see, they say. You know that's done broke his heart. You know he's been dreaming that dream a long time."

"I don't know what to tell you," Coach Gibbs says. His wife is sitting there holding that roundheaded child. That girl is only a year old, but she's big. Dixie, she is listening to every word I say. But I don't care who hears it, because it's every bit the truth.

"Now Columbus say Coach Catfish done turned on him too. You got to talk to that man. Tell him he can't do my boy like that."

"Like what?" Coach Gibbs says.

"He told Columbus—we got witnesses that heard this when we was up at that hospital last year—not to worry about nothing, that he had a place for Columbus on the Black Bears football staff, you know, a job, since his hopes for pro ball was vanishing. Seemed like the least the Catfish could do, seeing my boy played his heart out and got his body tore up trying to help that man win. If you ask me Coach Catfish owes him.

"But now he's saying he don't have no place for Columbus after all. You know why?" See here, this is the part that's hard for me, but I got to say it. I got to get myself used to it. "This sickens me to say it, Coach Gibbs, but he knows Columbus runs with that white girl,

China. They on. They off. But the Coach is saying he can't have no black coach that runs around with white women like that. He says won't nobody stand for it and he sure don't want folks questioning him over it. He said Columbus got to get rid of China or he don't have no job at HamU."

"I guess Columbus doesn't want to get rid of her?"

"He talks like he's gon marry that girl. I hate it worse than anything, but I look at it like this. If I can get myself around this thing and put up with it, then I think Coach ought to get hisself around it and put up with it too."

"Coach is not too modern on some points."

"That girl ain't done nothing but cause Columbus trouble from day one," I say. "Seems like the more trouble she causes the better he likes her. It's like to drove me crazy."

"They've stuck together a long time," Coach Gibbs says. "Must be something to it."

"The boy can't take much more heartache," I say. "You reckon you can talk sense to Coach Bomar?"

"I'll put in a good word for Columbus," Coach Gibbs says. "But, Mrs. Carpenter, you got to know I can't promise anything."

This ain't a bit satisfactory, but this is what happened. Coach Gibbs talked to Coach Bomar, then Coach Bomar called some high school coach he knows over in Montgomery. Now Columbus got the promise of a little coaching job over there—a black high school, so you know they can't pay no real money.

"This ain't nothing I ever thought I'd be doing," Columbus told me. "But I guess it beats a bullet between my eyes, Mama."

Like I told Coach Gibbs, I'm disgusted with all this football mess.

DIXIE

After a second 9 and 1 season Coach Bomar offers Mac a job as quarterback coach at HamU. For one thing Mac's a good coach—the best. For another thing it's Mac that sent Columbus to HamU and he was as good as any player they ever had—then his injury and all. So I guess Coach Bomar thinks he owes Mac, you know. Mac says yes on the spot. I've never seen him so happy. It makes me happy to see him happy. Saying good-bye to Beasley won't be easy though.

The Bulldogs Booster Club is trying to lure Mac into changing his mind with incentives like membership in the Montgomery Country Club, use of somebody's cabin on Lake Martin, and a guaranteed thousand-dollar bonus every year. But they're beginning to give up and get used to the idea that we're leaving. Already Kirby Long's newspaper has started speculating about who the replacement coach will be. Mac has recommended Hemp.

Mac calls a special team meeting to say good-bye to his players. It seems like this might kill him in a way all those losing years never did. He's emotional and it startles me—not to mention the team. Afterwards they file out of the locker room silent and dazed—like Mac. It's as though Mac has announced his death to them and as a result they're giving serious consideration to dying themselves.

In the spring the townspeople give Mac a going-away barbecue at the stadium. They present him with a football signed by his players and a second football signed by the booster club members. They also give him a lamp a player's mother has made out of a Bulldogs helmet—you pull the chin strap and the light comes on. Most of the town comes, and Mac says good-bye over the loudspeaker. He's eloquent, I think. Then folks, including me, get teary and there's hugging and well-wishing all around. Sarah is only two and a half, too little to understand what's happening.

Mrs. Carpenter and Mary Virginia come by the duplex with a pound cake wrapped in tinfoil. Mary Virginia's son, Michael, comes with them. He's ten years old now, still making the most of being the baby of the family. He's a handsome boy who stares at Sarah like she's some weird brand of house pet.

"I feel the same about losing you as I did when Jessup went off to Auburn that first time," Mrs. Carpenter says to Mac. "Now most all my boys off someplace. But I sure wadn't expecting you to go off too. We done been through some times."

"That's the truth," Mac says.

"I been mad at you more than once." She laughs.

"That wasn't hardly a secret." Mac grins. "Nobody around here could give me a bad time like you could."

"Well, I just say to you the same as I'd say to my own. Now you going down yonder where Columbus used to be at. If he hadn't of hurt his knee I reckon he'd be off playing pro ball someplace. I reckon he'd be rich about now."

"It was a terrible thing," Mac says. "What you hear from him? How's he liking coaching high school?"

"He don't think much of it," she says.

Mary Virginia holds Sarah on her lap and Michael feeds her bites of cake like she's a little cat. "Why her hair fly out like that?" He holds a wisp of her hair in his hand. "Fly away. She need some oil on her hair to make it lay down."

"Hush, boy." Mary Virginia laughs. "White folks don't put oil on their hair."

"They ought to," Michael says.

"They like it to fly out like that," she says. "It's spoze to do like that."

This strikes Michael as funny. He lifts up strands of Sarah's hair, then blows on them so they fly across her face. She loves it. "You got a nice baby," he says. "She got some funny hair too."

Just when I've about got this duplex looking decent. It looks like a home now, not like the campsite it started out as. Now Mac says we can buy a house in Birmingham, you know, with a dishwasher and a fenced yard and two bathrooms. I think about it every minute. I think about what colors to paint things, what style curtains to make, what kind of new sofa to buy. We'll move Sarah out of her crib and into a real bed. I'll have some tomato plants in the back yard. I'll set the table with our good china once a week and cook something for real. We'll invite Rose and Daddy over.

Here's what I haven't told Mac yet. I don't want my news to get buried under his news, so I'm waiting until the time is right. But I'm pregnant again.

The day the moving van comes to load us up Hemp is there at seven o'clock sharp, already crying, with a cup of coffee in his hand. He cries most of the morning, can hardly look at Mac without tearing up. "Wish to God I was going with you," he says.

See, the truth is it's like Mac has been married to Hemp all these years in Beasley and I've mostly been married to Leeta. It was like we just had a big four-person marriage or something, and now the marriage is breaking up. It's sad. But I'm secretly glad because I think maybe now, when we get to Birmingham, Mac and I can be married for real, you know, like people are supposed to be. Just him and me and our kids.

When Leeta comes by with her grandbabies we just look at each other and begin to spill like two glasses of water—one half-full, one half-empty—knocked over by the shaky hand of a dreaded good-bye. Leeta watched me become a mother. I watched her become a grandmother. We know nearly every secret the other one's got. "We've been through everything together," Leeta says.

By noon the moving van is loaded. People have gathered to say good-bye. It's painful, like a planned death you'd thought you were prepared for but found you were not.

Mac begins to say good-bye to Hemp, to shake his hand and say, "Take it easy." I don't know who cracks first. I think Hemp. It's like something unnatural. Then it's Mac. He's crying and Leeta lets out a sob at the sight of him, puts her grandbaby down on the floor of the empty room and goes to Mac, her footsteps echoing, and she cries with him like it's been rehearsed. It's like some sad slow dance they're doing. And from one person to the next, we all join in the kisses, the tears.

Finally we back out of the driveway, waving our hands the way magicians wave theirs right before the magic happens. We drive silent miles. I'm holding Sarah in my lap and clutching a sack of drapery samples Leeta gave me—you know, to make curtains for our new life. Finally Mac speaks. "We're not ever going to find people any better than that," he says. "They're as good as any people on earth."

"I've never seen you cry like that," I say.

"Everything's happening, Dix," Mac says. He reaches for my hand and squeezes it. "All our dreams are coming true. I promise. We're on our way, baby."

SECOND DOWN

DIXIE

We bought a small house in Homewood not too far from Rose and Daddy. Rose found the house. I loved it from the minute we stopped the car out front. It has crepe myrtles and dogwoods and grass so green it's blue. It has flower beds lined with monkey grass and a homemade mailbox in the shape of a birdhouse. Daddy loaned us the down payment.

When we moved in Mac let Rose *lend* us some furniture too, "until we can get our own," he said. The nicest thing is an antique glass-front china cabinet that's been in Daddy's family for years. I think it'll go in the dining room and we'll display our hardly ever used china and wedding gifts in it. But when it's delivered Mac says, "I tell you what, that would make a great display case."

Next thing you know it's in the den with his collection of game balls in it. His first football. The ball from the Shades Valley High School championship game. You know. He arranges the balls himself, each of them inscribed for the occasion.

When Rose sees this she looks like she might faint, but she doesn't. You can always count on Rose to rise above. She's turned rising above into an art form. She hopes I can learn to do the same.

And Daddy—I think he's looking forward to his first HamU sideline passes, to being, at last, a football insider.

Mac's summer routine: morning staff meetings, racquetball games, free lunches of barbecue sandwiches or home-cooked vegetables at any of dozens of Birmingham restaurants, afternoons of golf and cold beer, a quick supper at home maybe, and evenings of supervising the weight room and watching game films until late, learning the players by name, number, and anecdote.

Late at night when Mac enters our air-conditioned house and climbs into our cool-sheeted bed he whispers into my hair, "See you in the morning, Dix," although usually he's up and gone before I wake up. But he kisses my hair and then sets about dreaming the dreams he'll draw patterns of tomorrow, like an artist in a sketchbook—the arrows pointing the way to freedom, the Os crashing against the Xs at the intersection of the curved lines, the broken lines, the invisible lines. Sometimes I look at Mac's playbook and see that he has drawn my face there, two O eyes, an X nose, and a wide-sweep-left smile on my face.

Mac's a happy man. It's like he's got new life stirring inside him too, ideas swimming around his head day and night—a former big fish in a small pond, now a bigger fish in a bigger pond—so that in a weak moment he looks at my swollen belly and believes he understands what it is to be pregnant.

When Mac agrees to go with me to Lamaze classes I'm so surprised I almost cry. It feels like a miracle—as if Jesus has gone to the river not just to be a fisher of men but also to take a dip in the deep water with Mary Magdalene, who loves him. Only I think Jesus wasn't quite as lucky as Mac since Jesus never had a real girlfriend or a wife and was doomed to be an eternal son, never to mature and evolve into a father like Mac.

I hug Mac's neck and kiss his face with gratitude. "Don't worry. Football will still come first," I promise.

I've become a Baptist again. There's a limit to how far I'm willing to carry religious freedom. Not after all Rose is trying to do for us. So I'm back in the fold at Birmingham First Baptist Church. Pastor Swanson issued me a special welcome at the eleven o'clock service the first Sunday I was there. I enrolled Sarah in church playschool three days a week and myself in a Bible study class because Rose really wants me to. There are three other coaches' wives in the class—Romalee May is one. She used to be Miss Georgia.

The night of our first Lamaze class I'm pretty excited. It's a steamy Birmingham night, the air full of black-and-white memories—you know, swing the statue, hide-and-seek, stand on your head, catch fireflies in a mayonnaise jar. Tonight the world smells of fresh-cut grass and wild onions and rain when it hits the asphalt and turns to steam. It smells of wild honeysuckle and hamburgers on our neighbor's grill and fresh dirt from the holes I dug to plant a row of geraniums at the back door today. I walk to the car carrying my pillow in my arms, thinking that life is good and I'm lucky to be living it.

When we arrive at the hospital it's too cold and has the antiseptic smell of crisis that you always expect in a hospital. We go inside the bare classroom and find ourselves in the midst of hand-holding couples with serious, satisfied expressions.

The instructor, a pretty woman named Julianne, has posted a sequence of photographs of her own delivery on the bulletin board in the front of the room. Mac's not adequately prepared for this sort of personal revelation on her part. "I can't believe she wants the world to see her with her legs spread like that," he says. "Don't you think that's a little bit sick, Dix?"

The childbirth film, *The Birth of Joey*, is the final blow. Mac alternates between subtle moaning and audible gagging. The last half of the film he looks away, out the window in the direction of the HamU football stadium, which sits high in the cityscape, like a crown on Birmingham's head.

When the class is over Mac doesn't linger to talk to the other fathers the way Julianne suggests. He's the first man out. On the way to the car he says, "What I want to know is what was wrong with the way Sarah was born? She turned out fine, didn't she?" When we get back to the house, where Romalee's baby-sitting Sarah, she says to Mac, "So, how was your baby class, mister?"

"Gory," Mac says. "The goriest damn thing I ever saw."

Romalee looks at me and winks, as if somehow this should not surprise us, two bloody women like ourselves, as if we should smile and think it's funny. "Men are such sissies," she teases. "A little blood and they're all to pieces."

But that isn't true. Mac spends his life in a locker room full of naked men. He's seen broken bones jutting through flesh, skin scraped off in sheets, pus pouring from wet wounds—none of that phases him at all. It isn't the blood, I think. It's the female body doing something more substantial than wearing lingerie or a swimsuit.

Suddenly I feel the same way I felt when after having been married to Mac for almost five years, during which I made baked chicken for nearly every special occasion, he casually mentioned to me one night that he had never liked baked chicken. "What?" I yelled. "I've been baking chicken for five years now. I didn't know you hated it. Why didn't you tell me?"

"You never asked," he said.

Mac's first Lamaze class was his last. So now I go alone, carrying the pillow off our bed, acting perfectly cheerful about Mac's absence. The other couples accept that Mac is a hardworking man. He receives the forgiveness that coaches always receive—so busy. So I don't have to be embarrassed to be there alone. And I'm not.

The other women's husbands are called their coaches. What a joke. Of course, if they were really coaches, they wouldn't be here in the first place, I think. "It's your job to coach her breathing," the instructor says to the husbands. "Remember, coaches, she's going to be depending on you." It's all I can do not to laugh.

I like to think a lesser woman might be disturbed by this turn of events. She might feel abandoned and she might be really angry. A really desperate woman might throw a fit and demand that her husband get over his aversion to the female body and treat the upcoming birth of his child as something important. But I pride myself on being able to deal with the small personal adversities. Maybe I'm like Rose that way.

I have learned Lamaze breathing by myself and I've gotten so good at it—I can get so absorbed in my focal point—that I don't even need any coaching. In Lamaze class it begins to look to me like all those husbands bent over their wives, whispering, tugging, rubbing, are just in the way. I start to feel like those other women are envious of me—left alone to do things my way. Nobody else to try to horn in on my pain.

Our first season I roll my pregnant self over to the stadium and climb the steps to my seat as if my getting to the game were an athletic event in itself. I grip the underside of my belly and carry it up the steps as if I'm holding a small world in my arms. I settle into my seat and situate my belly on my lap. Then, along with the other assistant coaches' wives, I relax for what seems like the first time in my life and enjoy the game. Losing doesn't occupy my mind. At last I'm free to think about other things.

I remember the way, as a young girl, I used to be charmed by physical excellence—the agility, the grace, the instinctive human insistence on overcoming obstacles. I was moved by it. It was as if football were a performance of high art, that spontaneous sort of art that occurs when, as the saying about luck goes, preparation meets opportunity. But football's about desire too. It's the desire I like now. It's very satisfying, seeing men trying hard to do something difficult—no matter how inconsequential in the overall scheme of things. And I like being fairly certain they'll succeed.

If I could pretend the ball was something other than a ball maybe I could really love the game. Sometimes I tried to believe the ball was *love, truth,* or *beauty* so that I could look at the game, and the men playing it, differently, as if it—*what men could do with their balls, and stop other men from doing*—would make the life I was living something worth devoting myself to. This has always been important to me. In my secret heart I plan to live a life that matters. Mac probably doesn't know this. I was born to be audience. But that doesn't stop me from longing to do something remarkable.

Romalee and I sit together at every game. She's a fountain of information. She knows every player and his entire history. She knows every formation and can predict with pretty decent accuracy what the next play will be. When the official's whistle blows, she knows why. It's like going to the theater with someone who's actually read the play before coming, who's seen it performed dozens of times and knows how it should end. But Romalee's experiential expertise lasts only until the rum and Coke she's sipping sets her free from it all.

We're sitting at the HamU–Florida State game with the other wives, most of us relaxed into a near stupor because HamU is leading by three touchdowns, so nobody is worried. Romalee has gotten suddenly quiet and serious. "Has Mac ever come to watch you do anything?" she asks me.

"What do you mean?" I say.

"I mean, you watch every game he coaches, right?"

"Only missed one."

"And what has he ever watched you do?"

It seems like a trick question. "I don't know," I say. I didn't want to say that the only time I ever remember Mac being an audience to one of my significant moments was when I was crowned homecoming queen at HamU my freshman year, which seems too small to mention alongside the former Miss Georgia.

"That's what I thought," Romalee said.

"It's not because he's not interested in what I do," I insist. "It's just that I don't do anything that interesting—you know, worth watching."

"You're going to give birth to a child," she says. "Some people might think that's almost as remarkable as coaching a football game."

YOLANDA

The Bomars—you should see the parties they give. Celeste dresses to kill—I am telling the truth—and when she opens the door to the coach's house you feel like you've walked into a Lauren Bacall movie. You feel like the camera is rolling. Like if you can get close enough to her you can be a star too. I never saw anybody like her. There was definitely nobody like her in Beasley. I know that.

Sometimes Celeste will stand in the doorway, hold a gin and tonic in the air, and welcome people by singing out, "Give me your tired, your poor, your huddled masses yearning to breathe free!" I get a kick out of Celeste. People act like she's just as amazing as the real Statue of Liberty, standing there like that. I admire her too—even when she passes out in a chair and has to be taken upstairs by Catfish or their maid, Levinnia.

Except for Celeste, the parties at the Bomars's are never wild. Anybody feeling a surge of wildness coming on knows to excuse themselves and go elsewhere to indulge it. I never let myself get wild over here. The unspoken rule is that Celeste and Catfish are entitled to get drunk if they want to. Who'd blame them? They've *earned* drunkenness. They're the stars of the damn show. They write their own scripts. But nobody else does. Guests are careful that way. Happy, but in moderation.

When I see Dixie Gibbs she's so pregnant she looks like a big pink football herself. Puffy, you know. She's hard to miss because she moves about the party the same lopsided way a rolling football moves. If she stands in one place for long she looks like she's braced for kickoff, just waiting for the big foot of fate to kick her across the finish line into motherhood—that end zone of end zones women are always talking about.

While Mac's busy talking postgame football, Dixie mostly chats with the other wives. She laughs at jokes, which sort of shocks me. Maybe it's hormonal, her new sense of humor? She used to be so serious all the time. *Deep*, people said. *Coach Gibbs's wife is mighty deep.* Well, they ought to see her now.

I nibble on finger food and stare at her until I finally get up my nerve. I tell myself it's been a long time. People change. She must know that. Okay then. So I walk over to her.

"Mrs. Gibbs, I bet you don't remember me." Her ankles are swollen and she's sitting in the corner of the room with her feet propped on the windowsill. She's squinting, trying to place me.

"In fact, I almost hope you don't remember me," I say. "I made such a fool of myself—Mac said he told you all about it."

"Yolanda Branch?" she says. "Is it you?"

I laugh. "You've probably never seen me out of my Beasley Bulldogs cheerleading uniform."

"My goodness, you've grown up. You've changed your hair. You've changed, period."

"It's been a long time," I say. "I'm working at HamU now, in fundraising. And I promise you, I don't send love letters to married football coaches anymore."

"I saved those letters for the longest time," Dixie says. "They were just—amazing."

"I'm really embarrassed about that," I say. "I was a real case back then." I thought of the lipsticked nipple prints I'd closed my letters to Mac with. Actually, if you want to know the truth, the genius of it still sort of satisfies me to this day.

"Does Mac know you're here?" Dixie asks.

"I went by his office," I say. "I think I scared him."

"Probably," she laughs.

"Now I see him all the time. You know, in my job." It occurs to me then that Mac hasn't mentioned me to Dixie. Hasn't told her that I'm working for the university, that I see him a couple of times a week. He should have told her. "It's wonderful that you're pregnant again." I smile.

Walker May's wife, Romalee, is sitting on the windowsill where Dixie has her feet propped. She's watching me that way she always does. "Yep," she says, "we childless women always act like pregnancy is the greatest thing since sliced bread. But the truth is, Dixie, honey, you look miserable."

Dixie smiles at Romalee. "Do you know Yolanda?" she asks.

"Everybody knows Yolanda," Romalee says. If she thinks I'm impressed because she used to be Miss Georgia, I'm not.

"I want you to meet my husband," I tell Dixie. Husbands can be good for sort of neutralizing things, you know. I tug at Ralph's sleeve. He's standing behind me talking to Walker. "Honey," I say, "this is Mrs. Gibbs, Mac's wife."

He turns to look at her and she says, "Call me Dixie."

I can see what she's thinking. Ralph is more than twice my age. "This is my husband, Ralph Moseley," I say. He shakes Dixie's hand. He knows what she's thinking too. Ralph's not a handsome man. He's used to people thinking, *What in the world?*

Dixie's probably thinking, *He must have money,* which is what people always think. "Ralph owns Moseley Communications," I say, as if I'm reading her mind. "I used to work for him."

"Now I work for Yolanda," Ralph says, grinning.

It went all right, I think. I was nervous for nothing. I was just a stupid kid when I sent those letters. A little fool, actually. It was a long time ago.

Before the party's over I speak to Dixie again. "How's Coach Sparks doing?" I ask. "He was the sweetest man."

"He still is," Dixie says. "And his wife, Leeta, is twice as sweet as he is. We really miss them."

When I last saw China I said, "How is your sweet daddy?" And she said, "Daddy used to dream of being a college coach, you know, like Coach Gibbs. Now he dreams of inheriting a fortune from a dead relative. He's sort of given up on things." I thought to myself, *China, after what you put him through it's no wonder.*

It wasn't until the party was nearly over that Mac looked for Dixie and went over to where she sat like a beached whale and pulled her to her feet. It's clear Dixie has been eating for two, but Mac is as good looking as ever.

DIXIE

I try to call Leeta once a week, but lately I've missed a few times. So I dial her when we get home. I know it's late. Hemp answers. "Hey," I say, "I'm trying to catch up with Leeta." He gives me the number where she's working home-care—a newborn with everything wrong who's been sent home to die—and I dial the number. Leeta answers. She says she has the baby in her arms, but it's okay, she can talk. The teenage parents have taken painkillers and gone to bed. "They're too young to have to deal with this kind of thing, Dixie," she says.

"You'll never guess who I saw tonight, Leeta."

"Jett Brown, man of your dreams?"

"Hush," I say. "Yolanda Branch—remember her?"

"The girl destined for Hollywood?" she says sarcastically. "Miss Movie Star in the making."

"She's in Birmingham, working for the university. She asked about you and Hemp. She sees China sometimes."

"I never liked that child," Leeta says.

"She's not a child," I say. "She's married to a man old enough to be her daddy."

"Surprise, surprise," Leeta says.

For some reason Leeta makes me laugh. "Yolanda's changed," I say. "Grown up. She was nice."

"A leopard can't change its spots," Leeta says.

I love Leeta. I miss her so much sometimes it startles me. Since

I'm pregnant I don't ask her much about the child in her arms. I can't bear to hear about it—everything gone wrong with the divine plan.

"Beasley has a scandal brewing," Leeta says. "Guess who?"

"You?" I say.

"Don't I wish," she laughs. "It's Mary Virginia. She got into a scuffle with the guy she calls the one good white man in the world. I don't know what it is with the Carpenters and white people. It's the beatingest thing. I don't know all the details, just that the man's wife found out about Mary Virginia and came over to her house. Michael got in a fistfight with the guy. Mrs. Carpenter had to call the police. I was at the hospital when they brought the man in with a possible skull fracture. So he left, followed his wife back to Dothan."

"Poor Mary Virginia."

"Yeah, so much for the one good white man in the world. Mary Virginia can't walk down the street in Beasley without people saying, 'That's the woman that got involved with that white man, broke up his marriage too.'"

"What women do for love," I say.

"We're a pitiful species sometimes." Leeta takes a deep breath. "Me, I'm in recovery."

I laugh.

Leeta says she's started wearing bifocals and her hair is gray now, no more artificial blond to confuse people. She says Hemp stays on her nerves every minute. "Maybe I tricked him into marrying me. But now he tricks me into staying with him." There's no mistaking the sadness in her voice. "Did Hemp tell you I've stopped going to the Beasley games? He says, 'I guess Leeta has a date with her boyfriend every Friday night. She can't be bothered with a stupid football game anymore.' God, I wish that was the truth," Leeta says.

ROMALEE

The truth is I always thought I'd have some babies too, you know. But when I married Walker he made me promise—no kids. He has kids by his first marriage. Two boys, David and Trey. They're a couple of nightmares. I mean, I love them and all, but they've pretty much single-handedly helped me get rid of the notion that I want kids.

Dottie, Walker's first wife—God love her—is raising the boys pretty much by herself. She's not going to win any prizes for the job she's doing either. I don't know what Dottie has to gain by letting Walker's boys become a couple of first-class brats. But I swear, David and Trey are as good as gold for me. Really. After they got over the shock of things—you know, the divorce and all—they came around. I guess they know I love them. I guess they know I'll knock them into the next world if they give me a hard time. And if I don't their daddy will.

We get the boys a couple of weeks every summer, and Walker arranges it so that it's the weeks of the football camp, so usually they stay in the dorm with the other campers instead of here with us. The truth is I don't think Walker is the father he ought to be, but under the circumstances what can I do about it? It was all pretty messed up before I ever came on the scene.

Last year at football camp David got caught smoking marijuana. We were lucky it didn't get into the newspapers. It would, like, ruin Walker's reputation as a disciplinarian—his own kids, a couple of regular hellions, arrested or something. It's not good for a coach, you know, having his own family spiraling out of control. But, like I said, it's Dottie that's raising them. She lives in Florida, in Gainesville. It's her alimony check that put that swimming pool in her back yard. And I'm the one that sees that she gets that check every month.

I spend a lot of time with Dixie. She doesn't work either—I mean, outside the home. We're the only wives who don't. Mac and Walker get along really great too, play golf all the time and everything, so it was sort of natural that Dixie and I would become friends. Dixie's the most pregnant woman I've ever seen in my life. She swears she loves the whole thing—being fat and swollen and tired all the time, going to Lamaze class all alone. She can almost make a person believe it. Watching her, you know, has given me some mixed feelings.

But I just don't know if I could let go of my body that way. That's how Dottie lost Walker. After Trey was born she couldn't lose the weight she'd gained—and she just kept gaining more. The first time I met her I was sort of startled. I mean, she's a pretty woman, has a pretty face, but her body, it's just gone.

And Walker, he did everything to try and get Dottie to lose the weight, but she just wouldn't. She said, "I gained this weight to give you two sons, Walker May! I sacrificed my body for you." But she should've known that that kind of logic would never work with Walker. He's a body man, he really is.

I used to work out down in the HamU weight room. Nobody gave me permission, I just started going, and the weight coach was real good about helping me out. And I admit it, I wore some leotards that probably ought to have been outlawed. I was just divorced, you know. I was trying to get myself back, not just my body, but my head and everything. I hate to think what I spent on all those leotards—there wasn't more than fifty cents' worth of fabric in any of them.

Anyway, Walker loved the show I was putting on. "Strut your stuff, baby," he'd say to me with a big smile on his face. He didn't know me then either—not at first. "You got these guys eating their hearts out," he'd say to me, talking about the other coaches lifting weights. But I knew whose heart he was really talking about. I wasn't Miss Georgia for nothing.

He swears he was going to divorce Dottie anyway. He swears it had been coming for a long time. It just took him a while to get up his nerve. And I helped him get it up, I guess.

Funny thing is, now that we're married, Walker sort of bugs me all the time about what I eat, about whether or not I'm working out. Some days I don't blame Dottie for getting fat, just to get back at him for all that nagging. But I'm not like that, you know. I've got too much pride to let myself get fat. That's one reason I smoke. The other reason is my nerves—they stay torn up. A cigarette helps.

I sit with Dixie at almost all the games now. She spends more time watching the people in the stands than she does the game. Myself, I take the game seriously. Our future rides on these games. "You don't know what stress is, Romalee," Dixie says to me, "if you think HamU football games are nerve-racking. When is the last time HamU lost a game anyway?"

It's true we win most of the time. If we didn't there'd be a lynch mob after Catfish Bomar and I'm sure he knows it. Even if he loses one game everybody starts saying, *The guy is too old, he's lost his touch,* and crap like that.

Dixie's in my Bible study class too. Most of my prayer requests are for the team, and if Dixie stays here long enough hers will be too. All the wives pray for our husbands' players and their families and all. But Dixie, she always wants us to pray for some Leeta woman whose baby was born with everything wrong and this black woman who lives with a white man and this gay guy that works in New York and a whole host of strange-sounding characters. So far she's never said the first prayer for Mac's players or the team or anything like that.

But before it's over, she will.

LISA

Shoot, there was nobody in this world happier than Bobby and Terry when Mac got the job as quarterback coach at HamU. That's been their dream for him as long as I can remember. Now their baby brother is back in Birmingham. Bobby and Terry can get inside HamU practices every afternoon, and so far this season, I don't think they've missed a day.

Since Mother Gibbs stays so sick they don't always get to the games anymore, but you can believe Bobby's on the phone after each one, giving them a play-by-play. They're all so proud of Mac they don't know what to do. The Black Bears will be playing in the Gator Bowl this year too. We're all going. Except Dixie. Her doctor doesn't want her to get too excited.

We're having our Christmas dinner early, you know, because we'll be in Jacksonville on Christmas Day. Mother and Daddy Gibbs drove over this afternoon, their car so loaded with food I swear the tires looked flat. "What we don't eat, we can freeze," Mother Gibbs said. Marvin, of course, he usually can't get away from New York this time of year. Sometimes he sends a card. Anyway, we've all been cooking for days. There's no feast like a Gibbs feast. Even Dixie brought pies. She gets her maid, Lilly, to make them. They're decent. It's like Dixie, you know, to act like she can't be bothered with cooking anything herself.

Before we say the blessing we each take turns saying what we're grateful for. There's so much to be grateful for. I say I'm grateful that

Mother Gibbs is feeling good, well enough to come over and be with everybody on this special day. Bobby's grateful that Coach Bomar had the good sense to hire Mac.

Dixie says she's grateful to have one beautiful child and another one on the way. And Mac says he's grateful that Georgia missed that field goal or else we wouldn't be going to the Gator Bowl after all. I love this part, you know, when everybody pauses to give thanks and we all realize how blessed we are. We're all so blessed. Then we're ready to eat.

Usually we put all the men in the dining room so they can talk among themselves, you know, the men and boys. We fix our husbands' and sons' plates and take them to them. Then while they eat, we serve ourselves. Mother Gibbs likes to sit in the dining room too, on a footstool by the door, in case anybody needs anything, *more tea*, *more butter*, so she can jump up and get it. She loves doing this. She's done this since I've known her, carry the sweet pickles or the cranberry sauce from place to place, serving her husband and boys that way. She doesn't like to eat until after all the men have finished. Never has.

The rest of us, the women and girls, after we get the men situated, we sit at the kitchen table. That way we can talk about what we want to. I've never known the Gibbs to do it any other way. So that's why it sort of shook everybody when Mac, right after the blessing, got in line to fix his own plate.

"Sit down in here, Son," Daddy Gibbs calls from the dining room. "Dixie'll get that for you."

"My arm's not broken, Daddy," Mac says. "I can get it."

Dixie blushes red as a beet and everybody gets silent. It throws the whole family ritual totally off rhythm. It's about like Marvin showing up wearing some girl-like clothes like he used to. But as if that wasn't enough, the next thing Mac does is sit down at the kitchen table right next to little Sarah in her high chair—at *our* table.

"Mac, come here," Terry yells. "That's the women's table."

"Long as they're integrating the whole world," Mac says, "we might as well integrate Lisa's kitchen table. Ain't that right, Mama?" He grins at Mother Gibbs, who looks startled. "I'm gonna sit with the women and see if I can't learn something," he says.

I don't mind telling you I feel sorry for Mac about half the time. Dixie's my sister-in-law and I love her, but sometimes I just don't think she does right by Mac. She claims to be a Baptist, but I swanney I can't hardly see evidence of it. I've tried to talk to her about this, wife to wife. I tell her about that time I got Bobby to go with me to the marriage retreat at the church. It was wonderful. Our husbands told us all the ways they appreciated us, and the ways we could become even better wives—you know, just small things, but they can make a big difference to a man. "Just because a man acts like he doesn't appreciate anything," I tell Dixie, "doesn't mean he really doesn't. Men just have trouble showing appreciation."

Maybe Dixie told Mac before they arrived that if he wanted to eat, he better fix his own plate. I've known her to say things like that before, but used to be Mac ignored her. So I just reach over and pat Mac's shoulder and sit down across the table from him. If this is the way he wants it, okay then. Janelle and I look at each other and sort of shake our heads. We'll talk about this later—that's for sure.

Meanwhile we watch Mac's plate to see if he needs seconds on anything. He loves dressing and gravy more than any man I ever saw. So don't get the wrong idea. We weren't mad at him or anything. It was just weird, Mac sitting there in the middle of us like that. For one thing it killed the conversation dead. Having a man sit at a table of women is about like having a policeman sit in the middle of some outlaws who'd ordinarily be planning their crime.

I know Bobby and Terry will find a way to forgive Mac. They always do. But Dixie now—they're too mad at her. Dixie just sits there by Mac and stays pretty quiet. Even when Mac looks at her and winks she just barely smiles.

I don't know what Dixie and Mac are trying to prove, but they're ruining our Christmas Eve dinner. I hope they're happy.

After dinner when they leave to go home and the rest of us are all sitting in the den, Bobby says, "Lord, I don't know what Mac sees in Dixie. I wouldn't put up with her for five minutes. Somebody needs to do her a favor and tell her she's not the Queen of Sheba."

"Dixie's an only child, Son," Mother Gibbs says. I have to tell you, I get tired of hearing that. That's Mother Gibbs's answer for everything. Since when is being an only child an excuse for everything? That's what I want to know.

Right then I see that Dixie has come back in the kitchen door. I see her reach under the kitchen table and get Sarah's shoes, which I guess the child kicked off during dinner. I know Dixie hears us talking. I see the look in her eyes.

DIXIE

"Since when do you care what Bobby thinks?" Mac says. "If you cry every time he says something stupid you'll be crying all your life."

See, Mac thinks I am upset because of my hormones. He thinks pregnancy is what makes me so emotional. This makes it impossible to explain anything to him. He can't really listen to what I'm saying when he thinks he already knows. Besides, he's on his way to the Gator Bowl tomorrow and now is not a good time to get anything started.

"Ignore Bobby." Mac closes his suitcase. "It works for me."

Ignoring people is one of Mac's great strategies. I'm never as good at it as he is—especially ignoring family members. You're supposed to love them, aren't you? Maybe I *am* an only child, but I know that much.

"Who says you can't love them and ignore them at the same time?" Mac says. "Sometimes the only way you can love a person is by ignoring him."

Sometimes Mac is so deep it almost kills me. He has this total commitment to sanity. His specialty is making molehills out of mountains. No matter how complex anything is, Mac will find a way to see it as simple.

This is what I've learned, not just about Mac but about men in general. It's their job to play dumb, see. But Mac—who can play dumb with the best of them and has probably fooled many a foolish person—I know, without a doubt, is not dumb, or at least he's never any dumber than he wants to be.

That's one thing I really love about Mac.

Recruiting heats up the split second the bowl game is over—which, by the way, we won. Now Mac leaves town on Sunday and stays gone until the following Friday—he goes everywhere, stays in nice hotels, eats in restaurants, meets interesting people, has adventures. Right now he's in California, staying with Jett, looking at a couple of guys out there both named Tyrone. I can't help but be slightly jealous. So I call them on the phone.

"Lord," Mac says, "the wonders of silicone. You ought to see the bodies on these girls Jett knows. They'll stop traffic."

I'm scheduled for induced labor when Mac gets home. Earlier Dr. Haskell said, "You sure you want to do this, Dixie? A baby can be born just as long as his mama shows up. The daddy is a bonus."

"I want Mac to be there," I insisted.

So Mac lets me off at the hospital early Sunday morning, then goes to his office. By the time he gets back, my Pitocin drip is full throttle and I'm already in transitional labor. Jack Haskell is serving as both obstetrician and Lamaze coach. He's held my hand nonstop. Now I'm practically in love with him. He hasn't left me for a single minute. Not one. I'm so grateful that I begin to pretend that Jack's my husband, that this baby we're delivering belongs to him.

By the time Mac arrives the nurses are wheeling me into the delivery room and I've stopped caring where Mac is, whether he's with me in the delivery room or not, whether he's even in the world or not. At this moment Jack Haskell makes a better pretend husband than Mac does a real one.

"If you want in on this you better come on," Jack says to Mac, who goes pale and stands in the hall like a man in a trance. "This baby is not waiting for you."

Minutes later I see the nurse lead Mac into the delivery room dressed in his green hospital garb. She has him sit on a stool and arranges a mirror so he can see the birth when it happens. "No," Mac says, "I don't need to see."

Jack presses my hand into Mac's. "Hold on, now," he says.

I think I'll die. I think there's no pain so huge it can swallow a person this way and have them survive. Jack cuts me but I tear anyway— my head, my heart, my lungs, my legs, everything tearing open to let this child into the world. I split in half—again. But this time I'm awake and I feel it.

In less than fifteen minutes Buddy is born. The nurses wrap him in a warm towel, clear his breathing passages while he screams, and carry him to Mac, who sits perfectly still, satisfied in a distant sort of way. He looks Buddy over a long time.

When Mac hands Buddy to me I know him completely, instantly —my own son, that worried look on his tiny face. Is it possible to be born worried?

Mac leaves thirty minutes later. He has a plane to catch. Chicago. A couple of great prospects there.

Two days later I go home to Rose and Daddy, who'd had Sarah with them all week. Mac arranges for a graduate assistant named Mad-Dog to drive us from the hospital. Mad-Dog is young and bewildered and can't think of a thing to say, so he keeps his eyes on the road. I feel like an alien in his small economy spaceship.

We stay at Rose's almost a week and let Lilly spoil us with good food and endless advice. At night we take turns passing Buddy around the dinner table, like a sweet dessert to be sampled. When it's Sarah's turn she sits still in her chair and kisses Buddy's face with loud sister-kisses. Rose takes a thousand pictures. Anytime Buddy cries, Lilly comes in and takes him away from all of us, carries him into the kitchen. It's like she thinks white people should not be trusted with babies.

Buddy's bassinet is so full of balls that there's hardly room for him in it. This is as close to having a son as Daddy has ever come. It's clear he isn't taking any chances.

"Mac and Walker nearly got themselves killed up in Chicago," Romalee says. She comes over every day, brings Sarah a treat, "just to make sure she doesn't get jealous of Buddy," as if I'd let that happen. Romalee takes Buddy out of my arms and holds him, even when he's asleep. She keeps me posted on the world. Mac and Walker are out recruiting, and she makes recruiting her personal business. (Mac says Walker couldn't recruit a starved dog with a bucket of beef. He says Romalee is Walker's ace in the hole when it comes to recruiting.)

"Ordinarily," Romalee says, "Southern coaches don't care a thing about recruiting Northern boys. They prefer homegrown boys trained in their local churches to love God and football above all things." Romalee speaks with authority and makes me laugh.

"Have you ever noticed how when Northern boys come south it doesn't always work out? Trying to mix attitudes is like trying to stir gravel into a bowl of soup. You can stir all you want to but they're still two separate things," she says. "And why do Northern boys talk like they think everybody in the South is hard of hearing? Tell me that. 'I'm not deaf,' you have to tell them over and over again. And they talk so fast too, like they've got a hatchet for a tongue, good Lord. I'm always saying, 'What's your hurry, boy? You got a fire to go to?'"

"So if all this is true," I say, "what are Mac and Walker doing up in Chicago?"

"Don't get me wrong, Dixie," Romalee says. "Yankee boys are sweet. It's just that they don't know how to do down here."

"So why are Mac and Walker in Chicago?" I ask again.

"Fenzo Nichols," she says. "They worship him."

After Mac and Walker get home from Chicago I hear the story of Fenzo Nichols. Walker and Romalee come over with beer and pizza. When we get the children in bed, Mac builds a fire in the den and the four of us sit around like a small, happy family.

"Chicago is cold as a harlot's heart," Walker says, sitting on the hearth in front of the fire, doing an imitation of shivering, with a beer in his hands.

"Fenzo lives in the cement jungle," Mac says. "We know that going in. But my man Walker here, he rents a car and gets us a map. So we find the Nichols's place, which, let me say, was no easy task. We go in, right? Meet his mother, try to make Birmingham sound like a football mecca, garden spot of the world, right?"

"The kid is nervous," Walker says. "He isn't used to white people coming around his house and suddenly he's got this trail of white coaches after him, lined up at his door, including Mac and me—two rednecks from Birmingham."

"Speak for yourself," Mac says.

"Fenzo's mother was so suspicious," Walker says, "I swear I think the woman was sitting there with a pistol in her purse. No question she'd just as soon blow our heads off as have to look at us. This wasn't a visit where the mother makes a pot of coffee and offers you a cinnamon roll, if you know what I mean."

"I felt like I was sitting there with a sheet on my head," Mac says.

"When the visit's over we're sweating, man," Walker says. "I mean, you could cut the tension with a knife. Afterwards Fenzo walks us down to the street and we were damn glad. People sort of looking out of their apartments from behind their cracked doors, trying to figure out who the hell we are. If Fenzo hadn't been with us you'd probably be looking for our bodies in a Dumpster right now. If looks could kill we'd be six feet under. "Go eight blocks that way, Coach," Fenzo says, "then get on the interstate. Forget the red lights, man."

"We shook the kid's hand and took off," Mac says. "I like the kid. Doesn't talk too much. Good-looking kid. Great speed too. Don't ask me how we could mess up 'go eight blocks, then get on the interstate.' All that damn snow everywhere. We hit a slick spot, slid into a pile of slush, the tires spinning like crazy, ended up with the car stalled out.

Now there's not a sign of life on the street. It looks like a damn sky-scraper ghost town. But there's a bar on the corner. So we decide to drink a beer while we wait on somebody to come jump-start the car."

Listening, I begin to remember Mac, the boy I married. He was the best storyteller in the world then. Even now, it's like watching a live performance on a stage, hearing him tell this story. I miss him so much suddenly—this part of him that's mostly gone now. I know I'm star-ing at him with a goofy grin on my face. Because the truth is I've al-most forgotten about this—the way I love to hear him talk.

"So we go walking into the bar, right?" Mac says. "You talk about some black folks now. They're looking at us like they've just been waiting to stumble up on a couple of white guys that need a good killing. And Walker here—he gets a little low on brainpower some-times—he says, 'Don't bother about us, y'all. We just want to use the phone. Trying to get home to Alabama.'

"'Yeah,' I say"—Mac grins and slaps at Walker—"'announce it, man. *Alabama* is the magic word. Why don't you go on and say your great-great-granddaddy was Robert E. Lee? Why don't you get out the Confederate flag and wave it in their faces.'"

Walker shakes his head and laughs. "I was scared, man."

"About this time we're sweating for real," Mac says. "We don't know whether to spit or whistle 'Dixie.' I mean it."

"Then this guy—I mean a big damn guy—gets off his bar stool and walks over to us." Walker's eating pizza while he talks. "I'm thinking, *Good-bye, world*," he says, wiping his mouth. "I'm thinking to myself, *Walker, man, why couldn't you just sell insurance like your daddy said?* and the guy—he's a giant now—he looks us over good, and about when I think he's fixing to pull a gun and shoot a couple of holes in us, he says, 'I'm from Alabama, man. Whereabouts in Al-abama you from?'"

"Walker almost kissed the guy on the lips." Mac laughs.

Walker's laughing too. "I tell the guy, 'You are about the best-looking thing I ever saw in my life.' I swear it was all I could do not to hug his freaking neck."

" 'Y'all a long way from home, brother,' the guy says. Then we shake his hand. We just about shake it off."

"You won't believe who he was," Mac says to Romalee and me, like he wants us to guess. "Clarence Taylor."

Romalee and I have blank stares. We don't know who Clarence Taylor is.

"Played for Grambling," Mac says. "Did a couple of years with the Redskins. He had great feet too, for a guy his size."

"Hell of a player," Walker says. "He got our car started for us, led us on out to the interstate. He's as good as they come. We told him, 'Look, you find your way south, Clarence, and we got a couple of HamU tickets for you—any game you want.' He said he's got a nephew playing for Mississippi State—our third game next season. We said, 'Come on, man. We'll set you up.' "

Mac and Walker are in high spirits. They talk and Romalee and I listen and laugh with them. "Hell, we're just glad to be alive," Walker says. "Glad to be back in the bosoms of our wives." He winks at Romalee.

"Sad thing is," Mac says, "I don't think we got a chance with Fenzo."

"Naw," Walker says. "I don't see him coming down here, although we could showcase him as well as any team in the country. But those inner-city kids, you know, they got an attitude."

"Fenzo's attitude is not going to get in his way," Mac says.

"I guarantee you he'd be dating white girls," Walker says. "Those kinds of kids, they always do."

"What kind of kids?" Mac says.

"We got too much of that already," Walker says. "Jenkins and Smith from New Orleans and Blocker from Atlanta—those urban types—they all got white girlfriends. If you ask me Coach Bomar ought to put a stop to it. Any nigger who gets mixed up with a white girl, I'd just pack his bags and send him home. Wouldn't have to do it but a couple times. That'd stop it quick enough."

"Get rid of any *who*'d you say?" Mac looks at Walker. "Would you repeat that?"

"Any colored guys. I meant to say colored guys."

"Any *who?*" Mac says.

"Black guys," Walker says.

Walker and Romalee brought two large pizzas and they're both nearly gone. Romalee just eats the toppings off hers. So Walker takes what's left, her crusts, eats them like crackers. "Speaking of black guys"—Walker grins—"y'all hear the one about the old boy locked in a truck full of basketballs?"

He told this joke last time we were together. But it's part of what Walker does—he jokes. He wouldn't tell this if Jett were sitting here, I think. He'd be kissing Jett's feet. He'd be getting his autograph, nodding like he does, yes, yes.

"You better hope none of your players hear any of your stupid jokes," Romalee says. "You or Catfish, either one."

Walker shoots her a look. "So I tell a joke now and then. So what? Look, you think the black players don't sit around telling white-man jokes? Don't give me that, Romalee. Black players are as racist as anyone else and you know it."

"So, you're an expert on minds of black players?" she says.

"It's not their minds that interest me. They're not here because of their minds, if you'll excuse me for telling the truth."

"If that's true, it's pathetic," Romalee says.

"Don't get me wrong," Walker says. "I love these kids. I love Caesar like a son. I mean it. I'd do anything for that kid. But I don't fool myself into thinking he gives a rat's ass about me. As good as I've been to him he'll walk away from here in a couple of years and it'll be like he never knew my name."

"Caesar may not be book smart," Mac says. "But he's got as much common sense as anybody we got."

"Look, I'm not blasting Caesar. Who you think got up and went down to the jail that time his daddy got locked up? Y'all remember that? Who you think paid his bail? Y'all trying to make me out to be a racist, but I'm not. I'm a realist."

"You're becoming a damn philosopher, man." Mac smiles. "Maybe you ought to skip the talk and write a book."

"I could write a book," Walker says. "There's plenty of people who'd buy what I'm saying.

"Well, there's the KKK, for one," Romalee says.

"You mize well get off your high horse, missy," Walker says. "You can try all you want to to pass yourself off as some sort of bleeding heart. If I'm a racist, then you're damn sure one too."

"Go to hell, Walker," Romalee says.

"All I'm saying is *it takes one to marry one*."

"Obviously not," she says. "You married me and I've got a brain, so according to your theory you ought to have one too."

"Looks like we're out of beer," Mac says, pretending to search the refrigerator. So Walker and Romalee go home. The evening always ends when the beer is gone.

Signing date comes. Mac's like a kid at Christmas. Both Tyrones from California sign and six other top Alabama players Mac recruited. But the miracle of all miracles is Fenzo Nichols. He called Coach Bomar, said he wanted to come to Birmingham. Something about the weather, something about the football tradition, something about a phone call from Clarence Taylor.

So Mac has taken to recruiting like a fish to water. The *Birmingham News* writes an article about him, GIBBS CAN RECRUIT. His picture is in the paper. He has a big smile on his face.

Coach Bomar is so pleased he writes Mac a bonus check from his personal account as a way of saying thank you. He stops by the house to give it to him in person. Sarah sees him first and says, "Daddy, Fish Man is here." She recognizes him from TV.

"You got a future, son," Coach Bomar says to Mac. "Anybody can coach if the players are good enough. But unless you can *recruit*, the players won't ever be good enough."

"Yes, sir," Mac says.

When Coach Bomar leaves, Mac gives me the check to save for

our vacation. A week at the beach this summer. Our first real family vacation—ever.

Sarah's playing in a house she's made by turning all the patio furniture upside down. I'm greased and lying out in the sun while Buddy takes his nap. I'm working on my tan, getting myself psyched up for our trip to Gulf Shores, making lists of what to take, when Mac and Walker come home unexpectedly. At first I think they want some lunch. Then, looking at their faces, I think someone has died.

"Hey, Dix. How's it going?" Walker says.

"What's wrong?" I ask.

"Dix, there's been a change in plans, but hear me out before you get upset," Mac says.

I stand up and put on the old shirt of his that I wear over my bathing suit. "Go ahead," I say.

"We got word today from Coach Bomar that there's a coaches' trip down to Point Clear. Golf and fishing with some money guys—everything paid for. I didn't know a thing about it when I planned our trip to Gulf Shores, but Dix, it's the same week."

"Do you have to go?" I ask.

"It's not a good idea to miss it, Dixie," Walker says. "Coach wouldn't look too kindly on one of us not showing up."

"Listen," Mac says. "I was thinking. Just because I can't go to Gulf Shores doesn't mean you and the kids can't still go."

I'm just standing here in my baby oil, Mac's shirt stuck to me, my hair falling out of its pins. I'm trying to think.

"Mac was upset when he found out about this trip, Dix," Walker says. "He brought me with him for moral support. And I was thinking, as long as Mac and I are both tied up, maybe Romalee could go with you. You know, a girls sort of thing."

"With two little kids," I say. "Nonswimmers."

"Right."

"What do you say, Dix?" Mac looks so childlike at this moment that it makes me turn my head. He takes a boy vacation and I take a girl vacation—is that what he's proposing? I take the kids and the diapers and the peanut butter and the toys. And he takes his golf clubs.

"Nice," I say and walk past him into the house.

ROMALEE

There is golf.

Just when I think football is all there is to Walker's life he proves me wrong. Golf. Never let it be said that Walker is not a man of dual interests.

When Mac picks him up for their trip to Point Clear Walker's like a kid off to camp. It's like he thinks he's getting away with something and I don't know it. To tell the truth, I look forward to a week to myself. I love it when Walker's gone.

Before they leave, Mac takes me aside, says, "Romalee, look after Dixie for me, hear?"

So I go over to Dixie's every evening. We decided we didn't need to go all the way to the beach and spend all that money just so we could chase Sarah twenty-four hours a day and mop up Buddy's diapers and spit-up around the clock. I mean, we can do that here. "Next year," Dixie says. She wants me to think she isn't so mad at Mac she could kill him.

We feed the kids their supper and bathe them and get them into pajamas and Dixie rocks Buddy off to sleep. I can hear her in there singing to him. I read to Sarah until she finally gets sleepy and drifts off. My record so far is eight books—some of them twice—before the child gives in to pure exhaustion. Then I kiss her little face. Her cheeks are like marshmallows.

Finally Dixie and I sit out on the patio in the pitch dark and we drink vodka on ice with twists of lemon. She always lights a citronella candle, but I keep telling her those things don't work. We put our feet up and listen to the crickets just singing to beat the band. I love that sound—crickets.

"You know they have women down there, don't you?" I say.

"What are you talking about?"

"At Point Clear," I say. "It's money people all right—and their girlfriends, and their girlfriends' girlfriends. Don't tell me you haven't heard the stories?"

"Like what, for example?" Dixie sips her drink.

"Last year when Kathy divorced Virgil, it was because of a woman he met on the Point Clear trip. He kept on seeing her. And Kathy found out."

"That's Virgil," Dixie says. "That's not Walker or Mac."

I laugh. "I don't trust Walker as far as I can throw him."

"Maybe you've got your reasons," Dixie says. "But I don't worry about Mac. He'd never do anything to hurt the kids or me."

"Give me a break, Dixie," I say.

"He wouldn't. He's a family man, Romalee."

I can see she's set on believing this. "I hope you're right," I say.

After a while I make us another round of drinks. Dixie nurses her drink so long the ice melts. She's not a drinker. But if you ask me, a few drinks would do her good. Help her sleep, since she stays nervous at night with Mac gone. She says she hears things. I take the drinks outside where she's sort of rocking her chair, humming something.

"So Romalee," she says, "if you don't trust Walker, then why do you stay married to him?"

I'm not sure I hear her right. Since when is trust a requirement for marriage? "I said I don't trust him, Dixie, not that I don't love him. He likes it that way too. He gets a kick out of it, my mistrust and suspicion. It makes him feel like I really love him a lot. You know, like I'm watching his every move. Besides, we've got a lot in common, Walker and me. And I think our future is bright, real bright."

"Bright how?" Dixie asks.

"Walker will be a head coach one day. There's a good chance he'll get the job at HamU when Coach Bomar steps down. Coach Bomar as much as told Walker so."

"Really?"

"Well, not in so many words. But Walker's been with Coach Bomar longer than anybody. He's the logical guy."

"Romalee May!" Dixie raises her glass like she's making a toast. "Head coach's wife!"

"I'll be a damn good one too." I clink her glass with mine. "You watch me, honey."

And then, I don't know, we just get the giggles. We laugh until I think we'll wake up the children, until we have tears running down our faces.

DIXIE

Mac comes home from Point Clear suntanned and happy. He gives me six hundred dollars he won on the golf course. "Spend it on yourself," he says. I know he's buying my silence, but it's the most money I've ever had of my own. I count it with him standing there, watching. "It's yours," he says again.

Then it's back to normal. We only see Mac at suppertime. Two nights a week he mows the grass before going back to the office and we watch him. Buddy's afraid of the lawn mower, so he sits in my lap and Sarah distracts him by standing on her head in the freshly cut grass. Her hair smells like onions.

In Mac's daily absence the children and I carve ourselves a life out of trips to the grocery store, swimming lessons, vacation Bible school, afternoon naps, ice tea and tomato sandwiches, cartoons, and bedtime stories. We make a home where Mac is a welcome visitor. "Drop by anytime," we seem to say.

I make curtains and casseroles and drive car pools. I plant flower beds and paint bedrooms and set out the sprinkler at night. I push the stroller for miles each day with Sarah running at my side like a happy puppy. We stop and talk with our neighbors who are walking their dogs, or weeding their yards, or pushing strollers of their own.

Several nights a week we eat with Rose and Daddy, delicious suppers Lilly cooks. On Sunday nights they eat with us. Rose comes straight from church, Daddy straight from the golf course. Sometimes they don't speak to each other all evening. Rose focuses on Buddy and Sarah, and Daddy looks up at the night sky like he's searching for something—the taillights of a plane heading for another continent, or a particular constellation that has eluded him all his life. We eat peach ice cream out in the yard while Sarah catches lightning bugs in a peanut butter jar and Buddy watches her and shrieks. We're mostly happy.

When Mac comes home he seems delighted to have stumbled upon such a happy household where everything's clean and pretty and he's treated as if he were one of the family.

When the *Wives' Itinerary* arrives in the mail it's the size of a small book. I read it like a novel—all the bowl-game activities they've planned for the wives while our husbands are busy, every activity segregated, like something a bunch of Baptists would plan. But I am a Baptist, so I'm used to it. This is my first bowl-game trip—the Orange Bowl in Miami.

The fourth night of the trip I'm seated next to Celeste at an official team dinner. She's drinking bourbon and water, which I think maybe she's been doing all afternoon. She orders one for me each time she orders one for herself. I have four hardly touched drinks surrounding my plate.

"My head's killing me," Celeste says. She raises her glass over her head, sloshing it. "Winning's everything!" she shouts. I see Coach Bomar glance at her out of the corner of his eye. He's at the head table waiting to speak to the crowd, stir the hearts of the ticket holders. "It's such bullshit, isn't it?" she says. "Winning is the hobgoblin of little minds, honey. You know that, don't you?"

"Well," I say, "winning does beat losing, I guess."

She laughs. "That's the spirit, honey. Spoken like a true coach's wife." She takes a gulp from her drink. "You want to know something?" she says. "I think winning is crap. Winning is a lot of hollow, empty nothing. There's nothing at all interesting about winning. Now losing, honey—losing, you can work with. But winning—it's for the stupid and the shallow."

I feel myself go pale. Celeste is getting louder. People are beginning to stare. She holds her glass up again. "To losing!" she shouts. "To the guts it takes to lose!" A murmur ripples through the banquet hall. Coach Bomar says something to Mac. Mac nods toward the exit, a signal for me to get Celeste out of earshot of the crowd.

"Celeste," I say, "let's go to the ladies' room."

"I'm embarrassing you?" She smiles.

"We can't really talk here. Come on." I hook my arm through hers and we make a conspicuous exit. She carries her drink, lifting it in salute to Catfish, who's now making his way to the podium, ignoring her in that polished way that comes from practice. The crowd roars with applause when they see him.

"They love the son of a bitch," she says. "Listen to that."

Once in the ladies' room we sit on a bench as if we're about to fix our hair. Celeste lights a cigarette. "It gets old," she says. "It gets so goddamned old."

"I guess you've heard it all a thousand times," I say.

"Sometimes I think if I have to listen to one more stupid sports cliché I'll get a gun and start shooting people. You know the worst thing that ever happened to Coach Bomar, honey?"

"No," I say.

"Some people think it was marrying me." She laughs and blows smoke at her face in the mirror. "But it's not that. The worst thing that ever happened to him was all this goddamned *winning* crap. If he hadn't been so busy winning football games he might have really made something out of himself."

"Lots of people worship him," I say.

"I know." She shakes her head. "How stupid is that?"

"He seems happy."

"He's not," she says. "He's dead." She slams her cigarette into the ashtray and crushes it. "He's as dead as this cigarette butt." She holds it up for me to see. "He doesn't want anybody to know it though. I'm the only one who knows it. And you know what else? He's killing me. I am one step closer to dead every fucking football season."

I'm almost afraid to breathe the same air she breathes. "Does he know you feel this way?" I ask.

"'Does he know you feel this way?'" She mimics me.

What's wrong with her? She has everything to be happy about, doesn't she? Practically the most successful husband in the whole profession?

"Let's get a cab," I say.

"Good idea," she says. "Let's get the hell out of here."

On our way down the hall we hear Coach Bomar say to the audience, "My wife, Celeste, is not feeling well tonight. She's sorry not to be here." Then he says in classic Catfish style, "And I'm sorry y'all don't get to see her too. She was going to wear her red dress, and there's no woman in the world now that does for a red dress what Celeste Bomar does." The crowd applauds with wild approval. It's like they love a man who is never too busy to appreciate a good woman— his own good woman.

Celeste looks at me. "Does this dress look red to you?"

HamU lost to Oklahoma in the Orange Bowl. I don't remember much about it. Romalee says our offensive line couldn't protect the quarterback. Oklahoma was just too much up front.

MRS. AUGUST

Randolph is named for my brother. He was shot down when he wadn't but seventeen. That like to killed me. So I named my first baby after him.

Now Randolph's own daddy is in prison and the truth is I hope he don't ever get out. Since Randolph was little I been telling him he don't act nothing like his sorry daddy. He's got his uncle Randolph's ways. Good ways.

And he got talent too. I didn't hardly know how much until he started playing ball. Them coaches at the high school, they love my boy. Now he's got college coaches coming after him from all around. We don't have no phone, but they call up his coach and he tells me. They drive over here in their nice cars and make us a bunch of promises. If I haven't learned nothing else in my life I've learned this—don't listen to no man making promises. So a promise now, it goes off me like if I shoo a fly.

We got Mr. Walker May coming around here from over at Birmingham. He's the same white man I been dealing with all my life. He thinks because he puts on a necktie maybe I ain't gon recognize his kind. But I do. Can't no necktie change nothing.

"The thing about being poor, Coach," Randolph said to Mr. Walker May, "is that it is just so unconvenient."

You think I wouldn't like to give him what other boys got? I tell him, "Randolph, them other children out at the high school got everything money can buy, but money can't buy talent, Son. And you the one got the talent."

Until Randolph got on that high school team, hadn't any of us had cause to leave Troup County. Next thing I know, every Friday night we're watching Randolph play ball—and it don't matter where the game is, we go. I find us a way to go. And I start to see there's more ways of doing than I been knowing. I see these nice restaurants and I think I ought to get me a job working in a nice kitchen and quit the mill. I been at the mill too long. I know I can cook as good as anybody they got in there now. You can ask my boys, if you don't believe me. I can flat cook.

All the people around here know me. They say, "Mrs. August, Randolph was outstanding tonight. I know you're proud of him."

I say, "Sure am," but that don't tell the story. Randolph has turned me into somebody—made being his mama mean something.

The truth is I got all the dreams knocked out me young. My own mama slapped the dreams out of me whenever she saw the slightest sign of one rearing up, which is what drove me to the mill so early. I wadn't the only one quitting school to work in the mill. It was everybody. Back then my paycheck was just spozed to keep me going. Now it's got three more to keep going and I swear my boys can eat up my whole paycheck at one sitting—they all got big appetites. I done some things wrong, told them wrong because I didn't know no better at the time. But now, with all these colleges after Randolph, then it give me the opportunity to rethink things. I can tell my boys different from what was told to me. "Dream if you want to," I say to them. "Get you a dream and just hang on to it hard." That's what I'm doing.

See, I always dreamed of a painted house with a modern bathroom. I dreamed of a car that would start when you turned the key. I dreamed of a job where your paycheck would last more than one day—wouldn't be no line of folks waiting to take their parts out of it, you know. Like you would have you a little bit extra. You might could buy you some nice shoes, or go eat in a fish restaurant. Or send your mama a little something she could set aside. Oh, I dreamed lots of things, but none of it seemed possible until these white coaches get swarming around Randolph.

When Coach May comes to supper the first time, he brings his wife, Romalee. She's got a sister lives in La Grange. So it's a small world. She's skinny. No black man would look at her twice. There ain't enough to her. But she eats good.

I serve them venison and gravy on white bread. Randolph shot the deer himself. It's so tender you can cut it with a fork. And we have collard greens and corn bread too. I know they can't get no better supper at any restaurant in Georgia.

"I don't guess I got to tell you what kind of opportunity this is for Randolph," Coach May says to me.

"No," I say. "You sure ain't."

"He'll see some of the world, and if he stays healthy, then the world will see some of him and what he can do."

"He can do plenty," I say.

"I'd like for him to have the chance to prove it at Birmingham University," Coach May says. "You make this pickle relish yourself? It's as good as my mother's."

"Have more," I say. "There's plenty."

While Coach May is talking to me, his wife, she talks to Randolph. It's nothing about football. I hear her telling him that handsome as he is he'll have to fight the girls off. I hate to tell her, but that's no news to him. He been fighting the girls off for several years already.

Since that first supper Coach May keeps coming back. Sometimes he brings Kentucky Fried Chicken or a pie from Piggly Wiggly. He don't come empty handed. Randolph has taken a liking to his wife too. She sends him articles out of the Birmingham paper and writes notes that say, "Randolph—this could be you."

Half the schools in the South wanted Randolph but he signed with Birmingham University. People think they paid me money but they didn't. It was Mr. Eggers, a HamU booster, that offered me that job working in the kitchen at the Ramada Inn. We do banquets and everything. He said Coach May told him I wanted to work in a nice kitchen. I make twice the money too. So we rent a place from him and he gives us a deal on the rent. It's nothing illegal about it. Mr. Eggers is not with the university in any way. He's just a good Christian man and a football fan.

LILLY

It don't bother me to go to Birmingham games now that Jett ain't playing. I don't mind watching a bunch of boys I don't love bang each other up. So I go with Mr. Monroe. He's a fool for football. All we hear is this Bobby C. Shaw. Mac says, "Bobby C. is a great-looking kid." So naturally I think he means the boy's handsome and so forth. After the game I notice this white country boy. Got that backwards way you can't miss.

Coach Bomar requires all his boys to wear a coat and tie on game day. He wants them looking nice, not like a bunch of hoodlums. So this boy is standing there in about the nicest suit you ever saw. It's a suit that cost somebody something. But he's got his pants legs rolled up in a wad just drooping over his shoes. Them other boys see it too and you know how boys will do.

"Bobby C., man"—they laughing—"what you doing in them droopy pants? Y'all look what Country got on."

The boy just grins. "I thought these pants must been designed for one tall dude. Look here, man." He unrolls his pants legs while his teammates holler. There's at least an extra foot of pant on both legs. He has on nasty-looking shoes too.

The other boys pat him on the back and laugh like they love him or something. "Bobby C. scared they're going to charge him to hem them pants up! They hem them pants free, man," they say.

"They didn't tell me it was free," Bobby C. says. "Ain't nothing ever free."

I about love this boy myself right then, white as he is. So I say to Mac, "Bring that boy around to the house so I can hem them pants. And you get him some decent shoes too."

Mac looks at Bobby C. "That's a great-looking kid, Lilly."

"I seen handsomer," I say.

Mac laughs. "I didn't say he would make a movie star, Lilly. But look at the bones that boy's got. He's nowhere near through growing. He's got those long arms and some great hands."

So I get it. *Great-looking* don't have nothing to do with a boy's face. A coach says *great-looking*, he means from the head down. I ain't used to considering people like they was headless.

Sure enough, Mac brings Bobby C. around to the house so I can hem them pants. I make sure Mr. Monroe is there too. I feed them and Bobby C. eats good. I love to see a boy eat.

I say, "Where'd you get a expensive suit like this, boy?"

"Mr. Chamberlin bought it for me," he says.

Mr. Chamberlin is a white lawyer in town. His wife is in the Bible study with Dixie. They got a child Sarah's age.

"Yeah," Mac says. "Jerry Chamberlin in an all right guy."

When I get those pants hemmed and pressed, then I wrap up the leftovers and give them to Bobby C. too. He's a nice boy. I believe anybody would like him. He makes me miss having Jett around the house eating everything up.

TRISH HANNAH

Lorenzo won't talk to no coaches unless they meet him up at the high school or over at McDonald's or the mall. I know he don't want nobody to meet Granddaddy, who is losing his mind. Done lost his hearing. He's old and sometimes acts a fool—you can't never be sure when he's gon bust loose and go crazy—but he's all we got. Me and Lorenzo. We been with him since we was small. It ain't been no picnic either. Granddaddy likes to take a drink. Sometimes I think he's got booze where blood ought to be. Like if you cut him open, then whiskey would pour out. And he's old now too. Too old to change his ways. Too mean.

Now Lorenzo is about to get away from here, go off to play football at some college, so all of a sudden he's too good for me and Granddaddy. Like he don't want nobody knowing we're his people. I don't know what Lorenzo got to be so mad about. I'm the one got good reason to be mad. I'm the one gonna be left to look after old Granddaddy by myself.

It ain't right. It's me that studies and my teachers say I got potential. I'm smarter than Lorenzo and everybody knows it. Who you think does his work for him?

I'm the one got the message about Coach Gibbs coming to take Lorenzo's family out to supper. His coach give the message to me to give to Lorenzo. So I think, *Okay, it says his family right here. We're his family.* So when Lorenzo gets ready to go meet this coach out at the mall, then me and Granddaddy are ready too. "We going with you," I say to Lorenzo.

"Ima go myself," he says.

"You embarrassed over your own family?" I ask.

So then he has to let us go. Lorenzo, he's the miserable type. Not like me. I know how to make the best of things. But he's quiet and all he does is study his problems and worry and sleep his life away every chance he gets. Now all of a sudden everybody gets crazy about his moody self just because he knows how to run. Damn. I can run as good as he can.

So we get a cab over to the mall. I got Granddaddy looking pretty nice. I make him put his teeth in. I make him wear his hearing aid. It is like I'm his mama. Both their mamas. Lorenzo, he can't even look at Granddaddy he hates him so bad.

Coach Gibbs is a good-looking white man. I don't like him. I just say he's good looking—for a white man. And his wife is there. She makes me sick. She's the kind of white woman you can't help but hate her guts right off the bat. I don't know what she thinks she's smiling about.

"Good to meet you, Mr. Hannah." Coach Gibbs shakes Granddaddy's hand. "I know you're proud of your grandson here." Granddaddy don't say nothing back because he can't hardly hear.

We go to Morrison's Cafeteria. Coach Gibbs says, "Get anything you want." So I get one piece of cherry pie, one bowl of peach cobbler, one slice of chocolate cake, and also some coconut cream pie and some garlic bread. He said get what you want. He didn't say nothing about no balanced meal.

Granddaddy, even if he can't hear, he knows what's going on. He hears that part about get what you want. He gets everything. He gets roast beef and fried chicken and turkey and dressing and every vegetable they got. He has to get a second tray, so I say, "Granddaddy, don't get no second tray. That's too much." But he acts like he can't hear me. He acts like he never had nothing to eat in his life until right this minute.

I look at Lorenzo and I think maybe he's gonna die—he looks like he might. Granddaddy tortures Lorenzo good, just embarrasses the fool out him—been doing it all his life. So I see what Lorenzo gets. One piece of fish. Some french fries. Like he wants these white people to know that he knows something about moderation. That he is no hungry nigger. Like me and Granddaddy are niggers, but he's not. I want to slap his face.

We sit down and eat. Granddaddy, he blanks out. Just eats his food, but he's not that good at eating with his teeth in. He makes noises and such. So Lorenzo pouts. He stares down at his plate, just nods his head yes or no if Coach Gibbs says something. So it's up to me. I swear to God, it's always up to me.

I talk to these white people. Mrs. Gibbs says to call her Dixie. But I don't. I ain't giving her the satisfaction of thinking we're personal, her and me. I want her to know that she don't stand a chance with me. She asks me questions—you know how nervous white people do. What grade am I in? Do I like football? Do I have a boyfriend? Just shit like that. It's how white people do when they're trying too hard. I give her some answers. I ain't about to be rude and mess up Lorenzo's future.

Also, here's what I'm thinking. They'll see how smart I am, see how I can talk and how nothing bothers me and I can handle anything that comes my way—like they'll be impressed and go away from this supper thinking, *We got to find a way to get Trish into college too.* I'm like dreaming my own dream right in the middle of Lorenzo's dream.

Coach Gibbs is all right. He sees Lorenzo is the agony type. He tries to keep it easy, you know. He's probably thinking Lorenzo don't have a bit of personality. Like he's dull. Which it's true. I'm the one got the personality. If Lorenzo keeps on being so dead-acting I start to think Coach Gibbs might change his mind, might stop wanting his ass at Birmingham. That would serve Lorenzo right, sitting there feeling sorry for hisself.

Mrs. Gibbs says, "Trish, if Lorenzo comes to HamU, I hope you can come see him play. We'd love to have you stay with us."

"I'm going to be pretty busy," I say. I don't know why but I get this sad feeling, almost get started crying or something. I hate her for doing that. What's next? Is she going to offer me some of her old clothes, or ask me do I want a job cleaning her house, or give me advice about turning my life over to Jesus, or slip me a twenty-dollar bill so I will go away feeling fine? One my white teachers does that. Put me twenty dollars in an envelope and slip it in my homework on Fridays. I hate that.

When we have nearly finished eating, Coach Gibbs says to Lorenzo, "Let's me and you take a little walk." So they get up and walk toward JCPenney's. Coach Gibbs puts his arm around Lorenzo's shoulder. Lorenzo is so stiff he's like a mailbox post. We all watch them walk off. That leaves me with Granddaddy and Mrs. Gibbs. I want to go with Coach Gibbs too. I want him to put his arm around me and talk to me about a future. But there they go without me.

Mrs. Gibbs wraps up the dessert she didn't eat so Granddaddy can take it home. He says to her, "You a pretty lady." She says, "You're a nice man." I think I'll throw up. I mean it.

When Lorenzo and Coach Gibbs come back I see Lorenzo's in an improved state. He looks the same but there's something comes off him, like a good smell or something. Coach Gibbs hugs me and says, "Trish, I hope we're going to be seeing a lot more of you." But I'm down here in Mobile. How they gon see a lot more of me?

Then Mrs. Gibbs, she hugs me too, but I go stiff. She knows I hate her guts. She knows there's nothing she can do about it either. I make her helpless.

I get Granddaddy away from doing anything worse than just making a big mess at the table. He's confused all of a sudden. Don't know where he is. He holds on to me and I lead him on out to where Coach Gibbs called that cab to get us. We get in the cab and Lorenzo waves good-bye but he don't smile or nothing.

"So what did Coach Gibbs say?" I ask.

"I'm going," Lorenzo says. "I'm gon sign my name and go."

I look out the window the whole way home. When I get in bed Ima cry my eyes out. But not until then.

MRS. JONES

Tug's always been big for his age. His name is Corbett Jones Jr., but since he was little people have called him Tugboat. We'd go to the river and he'd wade right in, paddle around like a natural swimmer, and since he was so big and sort of quiet and slow, he got the name Tugboat. He's strong too. I've seen him lift the back of a car so a man could remove a flat.

We're fairly well off. I work at the courthouse, issue marriage licenses. Been there twenty years. Corbett, he's in the car business. We own our own home and the eighteen acres it sits on. Tug is the last of our kids to go to college. His sisters set him a good example. Tug wants to make a veterinarian. He'd be a good one too.

When Coach Gibbs comes around here talking about a football scholarship, my husband is ready. I hear what he tells that coach. "Only recruiter ever took a interest in me was the army recruiter. Before I could turn around, my butt was clear off in Germany. That's why I want to go about this here different. I don't want my boy, Tug, missing out on no opportunities."

"I can sure understand that," Coach Gibbs says.

"Don't nobody appreciate opportunities like somebody who hadn't had many," Corbett tells him. "Trouble is, if you hadn't seen much opportunity before, it can be hard to spot."

"I hear you," Coach Gibbs says.

Corbett wants Tug to go to school over at Clemson. They have a good veterinarian program for one thing. But also, Corbett says, *they know how to sweeten the pot.* That don't mean anything to me. I can't be getting off work every Friday to drive all the way to Clemson. It's too far. I tell Corbett, "It's a fool that sends his son off to play ball so far away he can't even watch him do it."

I see Coach Gibbs is discouraged after talking to Corbett. I take him aside before he goes and say, "Don't worry, Coach. Let me talk to Tug's daddy."

I get Corbett to agree to let Tug visit HamU. I say we'll all go over there for a recruiting weekend. They pay for everything—motel and all. "What can it hurt to visit?" I say.

The weekend we go, there are six colored boys and four white boys visiting. I think they're all nice boys. But right off Corbett gets upset. "What you guess they're giving these colored boys when they sign?" he says. "I bet they're getting cars and ticket deals and money on the side. If they going to do all that for the colored boys, then they better do that for Tug too."

"Tug already has a truck," I say. "He doesn't need a car."

"What's fair is fair," Corbett says. "If they want Tug so bad, then let them prove it."

From then on, the rest of the visit, I'm miserable.

We meet with Walker May. Tug will play for him if he comes to HamU. Right off I think he looks at Tug and misunderstands him. He thinks Tug is a bully because he's so big. But Tug's a sweet, sensitive boy. Coach Gibbs knows that.

Coach May says to Tug, "You ready to bust some butt, son?"

Tug looks at me like he just wants to get away from this coach. Coach May doesn't notice. He says, "If you like to kick ass, this is the place to be. All we need is a few good men."

I'm disappointed that a coach would talk this way. I've always discouraged Tug from talking ugly. We follow Coach May while he shows Tug the stadium and the playing field. He insists we walk out on the field and try to imagine seventy thousand people in those bleachers cheering us on. He tells us to picture it, to close our eyes and see if we can't hear it—all those people screaming Tugboat's name. I myself can picture it.

Then Coach May says to Tug, "Come on, son, let's go head-to-head right here, you and me."

"Sir?" It's like Tug's hard-of-hearing.

"You think I'm old," Coach May says, "but I'm not old. I been hit by the best. Show me what you got." He gets down in his stance and grunts, "Come on, come on, hit me, hit me."

Tugboat doesn't want to do it. He looks at his daddy and me like he wants us to say something to stop this, but what can we say? "Go on, Son," Corbett says. "Hit the man."

So Tug gets in his stance too. He has on his good clothes. Coach May mumbles something, then Tug lurches forward and smacks into that coach so hard I let out a scream. The flesh sound is awful. He knocks that coach on his back and I see Coach May's nose is bleeding. He shouldn't have made Tug do it. Now he's laying there trying to get his breath. And Tug says to his daddy and me, "Let's go."

I think everything is ruined.

At the dining hall that night Coach Bomar comes over to our table and says, "You got a fine son. I like him." Then he bends toward us and says, "Don't let Coach May scare him off. Coach May is more bark than he is bite."

Corbett takes Coach Bomar by the arm then and says, "Can I talk to you a minute, Coach? I got a couple of concerns." They go off together and I pray Corbett isn't messing things up for Tug. See, if HamU is looking for killer instinct, then Tug doesn't have that. But what he does have is survival instinct. That's what he was showing out there today. That he'll do what he has to do.

I don't know what was said that evening, but afterwards Corbett seems peaceful about Tug playing ball for HamU. He's ready to give up his dream of Clemson and all that foolishness.

On Sunday Coach Gibbs has us over to eat dessert. Tug has Coach

Gibbs's girl, Sarah, hanging on him like she's a monkey and he's a tree. She's squealing and all. I see he likes that.

I study the pictures on the wall. Coach Gibbs's team pictures take a whole wall. They also have pictures of him with other coaches and some famous people, playing golf. They have pictures of Jett Brown too. He's in all the commercials on TV.

Dixie says, "If Tug comes, we'll put his picture up too."

"Where you put the pictures of your own kids?" I ask her.

She says, sort of shocked, "That's a good question."

I wasn't meaning to be rude.

MRS. GREGORY

I don't want Richard to go to Birmingham University. I definitely don't want him playing football. He's too smart a boy to waste opportunities just so he can play ball. It's a brutal, violent game. I hate it. Football is for boys who can't get in to school otherwise— poor boys. Medical schools won't take a HamU degree seriously. Playing football is like working your way through school and Richard doesn't need to do that.

He won't listen to me. I blame Hastings. He encourages Richard. Would Hastings have gotten in med school and had the success he's had if he'd cared more about sports than academics?

Hastings says, "Eleanor, the only reason I put academics first is that I wasn't worth a damn as an athlete and I knew it. I'd have played if I could, but I just wasn't good enough. But Richard, he's got real ability, Eleanor."

"He's got a brain too," I say.

"One doesn't cancel the other, Eleanor."

"He could get hurt."

"So could we. Lightning could strike. A bus could hit us."

"Why can't he play at Vanderbilt or Duke—a good school."

"Duke's got too many Yankees."

"Be serious," I say. "You went to Duke."

"I am serious. You don't go to those schools if you're a football player, Eleanor. Richard is a football player."

"I hope you enjoy Richard wasting his life living out some sick jock fantasy of yours," I say.

Richard went to a small private school. They didn't really emphasize sports that much. So when he went out for football I didn't see what harm it could do. But then his junior year he started talking about transferring to public school, playing on a good team, where he could prove himself. And Hastings let him transfer.

Now Coach Gibbs is recruiting Richard. I don't have anything against Coach Gibbs personally. But I see the trap you can fall into. First you're a player, then you want to be a coach. It's like an addiction or something. I want more than that for Richard. So much more.

"Mother," Richard says. "I have a chance to play for Catfish Bomar. He's the winningest coach in the country and he wants me. It's a great opportunity—guys would kill for this opportunity."

See, that's the problem. Richard and I have very different definitions of opportunity.

DIXIE

Romalee is the best wife at recruiting. The players love her, partly because she's good looking. But also, she bakes for them. But all the wives do. Romalee just makes every player her personal business. She knows their families, their grades, their classes, what they drive, if they have girlfriends, what they worry about, what they like to eat. All of it. She knows.

Number one, Romalee's the only wife who doesn't work. I don't have an official job, but I have two kids, and Pastor Swanson has me writing the obituaries for the Sunday bulletin and now and then an article for the *Baptist Bugle*. I don't get paid anything, but I work.

Number two, Romalee doesn't have any kids of her own and sort of wishes she did. So she lets the players be the kids she never had. She mothers them like crazy. And they like that. So I've learned a lot from watching her. She knows how to do.

"A black boy," she tells me, "you got to win his mama over. A black boy will go where his mother says go. You got to see to it she likes your husband. But a white kid, now—no. A white kid, you got to play to his daddy."

"I know that," I say.

"Also," Romalee says, "boys talk best when they're not around the coaches—or other players. Try to get them away from the others—in the kitchen if you can. You'll be amazed what they say when they're helping you mash potatoes. You don't have to ask them anything either. Give them a chance to say stuff they can't say around all the others. They appreciate that."

"Okay," I say. "What else?"

"Feed them," she says. "Food is the universal language. It makes boys relax. The more relaxed they are, the better."

"Right," I say.

And mostly Romalee is right. But the thing that works best for me in recruiting is my kids. Sarah loves these boys—all of them. She climbs all over them, drags them to her room to show them things, wants to sit by them while they eat, plays hide-and-seek, and bothers them with a million questions and a million "Hey, watch this's." And even though she's only eight, she flirts with them. I swear. I look at that child and she's flirting.

And Buddy's getting used to having them come and go all the time—boys, all colors, sizes, types. It takes him longer to warm up to them, but when he does, he becomes their shadow. So if I just turn my kids loose, they can relax these boys, make them feel welcome and sure. And in a way, over time, we fall in love with each one. It sounds corny, but it's true. I start to love them like they're part of my family— the younger brothers I never had, sons, nephews, cousins. I want everything for them that I want for my own kids. Everything good.

The football family, the football family—get so tired of hearing about that. "An all-male family is not a real family," I've told Mac a thousand times. But when the players come to our house to watch TV or eat spaghetti, then it feels good, like an actual family. Anybody's problem is everybody's problem. Anybody's good news is everybody's good news. It's very nice.

And Mac, here's his secret: *recruit the mothers.* Black boys or white boys, Mac recruits their mothers. If you ask me he's a genius. Players' mothers love him. If the mothers love him, soon their boys will. The mothers invite Mac to supper, call him up day and night, write him notes, ask to borrow money from him, tell him all their troubles, ask his advice, bake him cakes—everything. And he listens to them, mostly. That's what does it, I think. He listens to these boys' mothers the way they deserve to be listened to. Like he has all the time in the world. Like he's genuinely interested in what they're thinking and feeling and worrying about. He listens to them the way I wish he listened to me.

Then they turn their sons over to him, knowing he'll look after them and treat them fairly. And he does.

Here's a list of some of Mac's recruiting violations. I personally think of it as a list of good reasons to love him.

1. Sent Tyrone's mother a plane ticket to Birmingham so she could see him play one game before he graduated.

2. Got Jerry Chamberlin to buy Bobby C. a winter coat and some shoes.

3. Got Lorenzo Hannah a summer job working for Bobby at Jim Walter Homes.

4. Paid for Eddie to fly to his grandmother's funeral.

5. Arranged to get Orlando's teeth fixed.

6. Got three boys' mothers and one boy's father better-paying jobs. A few calls to some alumni.

7. Loaned some boys Christmas money. Then forgot it.

8. Paid hospital bill when A. J.'s girlfriend had baby.

9. Paid for baby's medicine—all four years.

10. Got Kevin's mother's electricity turned back on.

11. Arranged for Eric's mother to get a decent car.

12. Sent Trish and her granddaddy bus tickets to see Lorenzo play.

Romalee says this is probably just a drop in the bucket, and it probably is. Like Romalee says, "Sometimes the Christian thing is just not the legal thing, Dixie."

I know a lot of stuff Walker has done too, although I don't make a list in his case. After Coach Bomar named Mac offensive coordinator, Romalee and I made a silent pact not to compare offensive performance to defensive performance. Walker has been defensive coordinator a long time. HamU is known for its defense. So we're not going to line up on opposite sides of the ball too. We're not going to compare and contrast. We'll leave the criticism to the fans and the press.

I think all the coaches, offensive and defensive, are just trying to help these boys get their lives off to a good start. I don't see anything wrong with that.

Jett comes to Birmingham every recruiting season and stays at Lilly's house, or if he brings a girl, he stays at the condo he bought Lilly, which she's never moved into. He gave Mac a key too. I've never seen the inside of the place.

Sarah and Buddy love it when Jett comes. He brings them jerseys and silver dollars. He likes to lie on the floor in the den and wrestle with them. He likes to hold them and refuse to let them loose. It's how he played with me when we were little.

"You ought to have kids," I say. "You were born for it."

"Funny, I know a couple women say the same thing."

"I suppose they're volunteers."

"You could say that." He grins.

"I don't blame them," I say, "for wanting to marry you."

"Why?" Jett's holding Sarah and Buddy by their legs like a couple of fish.

"What kind of question is that?" I say. "Because you can be sweet when you want to."

"And?" Jett's looking at me with those smiling eyes.

"You're rich."

"What else?" He grins.

"Sort of handsome. Okay? Is that what you want me to say?"

"Nearest to a compliment I ever got out of you."

"Lord, you'd think you'd heard it enough in your life."

"But you always say, 'You look good for a black man.'"

"At least I say you look good as some kind of man. You never say I look good as any kind of woman."

Jett laughs. "You look pretty good, girl. For a white woman."

"I guess coming from an expert on white women like you've become, that's a compliment."

"Now you sound like Mama," he says.

When Mac gets home I lose Jett. I get the kids to bed while Mac and Jett sit and talk football. They talk so far into the night that I give up and go to bed too.

I wish Mac had never taught me the importance of keeping score. I was happier before I was forced to think of the world as divided into winners and losers. I managed to resist this for a long time. Then it was like I woke up one morning and couldn't resist anymore.

I don't know exactly when this huge marriage scoreboard appeared in my head. My name is in the home-team slot and Mac is the visitor. I don't know if we have mascots or not. Maybe I'm the Dixie Do-Gooders (Mac's accused me of that before) and he's the Mac Mess-Ups (which I've accused him of). I know this is lopsided and wrong, but I can't help it. What makes the marriage game different from a football game is that it's never over. You have to keep score endlessly, all your life, whether you want to or not.

This is the way it works.

Every time I forgive Mac for anything he gets six points. Forgetting my birthday, six points. Forgetting Sarah's or Buddy's birthday, six points. Missing Christmas morning with the family, six points. Falling asleep when I'm talking to him, six points. Ruining our beach vacation, six points. Not calling home once for two weeks while he's off recruiting, six points. Missing every one of Buddy's special moments—his first step, his first word, his first day of playschool, his first T-ball games—six points. Not visiting Millie in the hospital, six points. Playing golf instead of coming to church when the kids are baptized, six points. Calling me Norma, his secretary's name—twice in one day—six points. You get the idea.

Sometimes he gets the extra points too. All it is, is saying, "I'm sorry, Dix." He gets one point for every *sorry*. The insane thing about this game is that every time I forgive him, *he* gets the points. So far it's a slaughter. He's winning the marriage game by a mile.

So I send off to Unity Prayer center someplace in Missouri. Romalee told us about it at Bible study. Also I saw it advertised in the *Baptist Bugle*. You can send a prayer request and get professional prayers said for your particular problem. I write in, "Please pray that I can stop keeping score in my marriage." But I don't sign my name in case somebody tries to figure out who I am.

THIRD DOWN

DIXIE

Sometimes good news comes at you like a snake you don't see until you step on it. GIBBS GETS GO-AHEAD, the *Birmingham News* says. Mac is named head coach of the Birmingham Black Bears. Nobody seems really surprised except me, and maybe Walker, who'd been campaigning for the job himself. The press had ideas of their own about who should succeed Catfish Bomar when he retired. But Catfish handpicked Mac for the job—he made that clear—so nobody could argue with the choice too much.

HamU holds a press conference to introduce Mac as the new head coach. I stand behind him wearing a green wool dress and gold earrings, with Sarah beside me, the green bow in her hair all but nailed to her head. Buddy stands on the other side, bored, with his wet hair neatly parted. We look like people on a Sunday school poster.

When Mac steps up to the microphone I feel dizzy.

"On behalf of Dixie and myself—and our children, Sarah and Buddy—I want to thank Coach Bomar and Birmingham University for this opportunity," Mac says. He says all the right things.

"Mrs. Gibbs," a reporter shouts after the press conference, "do you have a comment?"

"It's wonderful," I say.

Mac and I are invited to dinner at the Bomars' to celebrate the announcement. Nobody is ever invited to dinner at the Bomars', so this is an occasion. When we get there, Celeste is "not well," as in pleasantly drunk and one second away from passing out. She's dressed for dinner, lively and sloppy happy when she opens the door, beautiful in her loose-fitting sort of way, but within minutes she's collapsed on the sofa and is for all practical purposes asleep. I've witnessed lesser versions of this. She always passes out gracefully, with such poise, unconsciously arranging herself in some elegant reclining posture that actually makes me envy her style. Coach Bomar puts an afghan over her. "Tell you what," he says. "Celeste isn't feeling well. Let's go out to the club for supper."

"Will she be okay?" I ask.

"Levinnia will look after her," he says.

Coach Bomar and Mac are a spectacle at the country club. All eyes are on them. Midway through dinner Coach Bomar says to me, "How's that new baby of yours, honey?"

"Buddy's wonderful," I say. "He starts school this fall."

"Good," he says. "Waiter, let us have another round over here." The waiter brings fresh drinks, Scotch for them, chardonnay for me. Coach Bomar lifts his glass. "To the future!" he says. And we all drink to that.

"Dixie"—he looks at me—"let me tell you something. There's lots of good coaches in this world. Mac here, he's more than a good coach. He's a good person. You understand what I'm saying?" I smile to signal that I understand. "A lot of people think you have to be an asshole to be a head coach—I used to think so myself. Hell, I *am* an asshole. But hey, this profession has got some sorry individuals in it, and Mac here, he's no angel, but he's not sorry either. You got you a good man here. He's smart. Be proud of him."

"I am."

"And don't forget this—a wife is important in this profession. A wife can make all the difference in the world. It's not a bed of roses, being married to a football coach, honey. Celeste could tell you that. Do you like football?"

"Sure."

"Do you love it?"

"Well, I love Mac."

Coach Bomar's laughter is a growl. "Good answer," he says. "Football's just a stupid game. Don't let anybody tell you different."

He smiles at Mac. "Boy," he says, "how'd you get a pretty girl like this to marry you? I might've said you were smart, but I damn sure never said you were anything to look at."

"I know when to beg, Coach." Mac smiles.

"I hear you, son," he laughs. "Sweetheart," he says, "I'm too old to beg anymore. If you don't believe me, ask Celeste."

On the ride home our car becomes a living, breathing person whose brain we occupy, whose imagination heats things up until the car windows are sweating. We're inside something big and alive and we know it, our own yeasty happiness swelling to meet the outer limits of what we'd only dreamed of. Or what Mac had only dreamed of.

I straddle Mac in the driver's seat. He can hardly get his pants unzipped fast enough. My blouse unbuttoned, my breasts swollen, Mac saying my name as he kisses me and bites my lips like a man in search of the source of all this magic and good fortune, his mouth hot on my skin, I loosen his tie and try to tear his shirt open. I'm a woman starring in a movie I've never seen.

It's as exciting as if I'm making love to a total stranger.

Celeste Bomar invites me to lunch and makes tuna fish salad party sandwiches, without the crusts, and mimosas. She's just one woman but lives her life like a pair of twins—one wild, one civilized, both wise. Celeste isn't as young as she used to be but she's dedicated to staying beautiful. I think she's like a woman who started out as a perfect green leaf, then, when her fall came, shocked everybody by refusing to wilt and instead turned hot, screaming yellow or fire-red, and while everything around her died and fell, she just held on and refused to let go of the high branch.

She sets our lunch out on the glassed porch, where a parakeet chirps and occasionally bites at the wires of his cage, making a ping-ing sound. It's a beautiful room, the porch, full of potted plants and hanging ferns. The outside brought inside and air-conditioned. We eat at a small table made from on old sewing-machine stand. "Here," she says, raising her glass. "To change." She taps my glass. "May you be very happy in this house."

"And may you be very happy too—wherever you go," I say, which sounds stupid.

This is what Celeste says to me during lunch. "Darling, no sense in trying out for the team yourself, you know. They won't let you be on the team. You might as well learn that early."

I laugh. Then she says, "Did you know Mussolini had a photographic memory?"

"No, I didn't."

"Coach Bomar says Mac has that too."

She's not the only head coach's wife I know of who calls her hus-band *Coach*. I hope I die before I'm reduced to calling Mac *Coach Gibbs*. She says *"Coach Bomar"* like it's the only way I'll understand who she's talking about, like if she says *my husband* it'll mean nothing to me and I'll have to stop and figure out who she means. I guess nobody can re-ally think of coaches as husbands, not even their wives after a while. It's like if she called him anything other than *Coach* she'd be telling a big lie.

"A photographic memory," she says. "Coach Bomar says all it takes is one time and Mac learns. Never forgets a thing."

"That's true," I say, although I don't know if it is.

"Let me tell you something else," Celeste says. "I could tell you more than you ever wanted to know. But listen, darling, remember this—Mac might have to win over everybody in this town, but you don't. He gets paid to kiss ass so that he can get his ass kissed. That's his job. It's not yours. You can't please people. Don't bother to try."

I sit there as if she has just announced that there is no God. How do you have lunch with an atheist?

"And the money people," she says, "watch out for them. Their money can buy them lots of things. Sometimes they start thinking it can buy the football coach too. And if you're not careful, it can. Never underestimate the money people, darling. Never start thinking they're your friends because they're not. They're just friends to your husband's job. It's the job they love, not the man who has the job. Remember that."

"I will."

"And another thing," she says. "They're going to carve the win-loss record into *his* headstone, not yours. You're never going to win a game and you're never going to lose one. Because, like I said, you're never going to be on the team. If you forget that, you're doomed. Try to remember that."

For being married to one of the winningest coaches in Alabama history Celeste certainly does talk a lot about doom.

"This is great tuna fish," I say.

"Curry," she says, "that's the secret."

After lunch she takes me on a tour of her house, which is becoming my house. I'm thinking, *I can't wait to redo everything.*

Mac's keeping Walker as defensive coordinator, even though Bobby and Terry tell him that's a mistake. "He's after your job, man. Even a blind man can see that."

"So he's ambitious," Mac says. "You want me to hold that against him?"

Already Mac's gotten over three hundred calls and letters for the seven remaining assistant coaches' jobs. Columbus Carpenter calls first thing. "Small-time football is killing me," he says. "I been biding my time, waiting for a chance like this."

"This is not high school, Columbus. You know that, don't you? You think you can recruit anybody?"

"Coach, are you kidding? Give me a break, man."

"What about China?"

"You behind the times, Coach. She's married a redneck that calls himself a preacher. You remember Tom Allen? She married him and made her daddy a happy man."

"Well, there's lots of fish in the sea," Mac says.

"I'd like to be going fishing over there in Birmingham. If I can't outrecruit anybody you got hired, you can fire my ass."

"I'm gon hold you to that," Mac says.

"Man," Columbus says, "you already know I can talk to black kids. What you don't know is I can recruit the hell out of some white kids for you. White kids love me. I'm telling the truth."

"Come on home then," Mac says.

Cleet's an assistant at Northwest Mississippi Junior College—it's the fifth place he's coached because he has the uncanny knack of working for coaches that don't last long. Fired four times and has the scars to prove it. Each time, I've spent hours on the phone with Frances Delmar, listening to her lament the insecurity of her life, the constant humiliation and upheaval. "I swear," she says, "you can't trust a living soul in this profession. It all comes down to every man for himself."

Now Frances Delmar has a community-service TV show that she loves. She and Cleet have three kids—Jane, Lydia, and Joe—and have just built a house. But Cleet says yes to Mac's job offer in a heartbeat, no need to talk anything over. In less than a week Cleet's in Birmingham living in the Bear Cave, eating at the training table, driving his dealer car. He is as happy as a wild creature who has at last been returned to his natural habitat.

Frances Delmar will have to give notice at the TV station, wait for the kids to get out of school, sell the house, and pack for the move. It'll be months before she and the kids arrive.

"This is going to be great," she says when I call her. "Just like we always imagined. The only thing is, well . . ."

"What?" I ask.

"Well, Cleet's salary. I always thought assistant coaches at a school like HamU would make more money."

"Oh," I say.

Hemp calls Mac at home late at night. It sounds like he's been drinking to get up his courage. "Listen, Mac," he says, "save me one of those coaching jobs you got, how 'bout it? I'll work as hard as anybody you got over there—harder. There's nothing holding me and Leeta here—the kids are grown. We could all be together again. Like old times. What do you say, buddy?"

From the look on Mac's face you'd have thought Hemp was dying. "Hemp, man, if I was hiring the greatest guy around then I'd hire you no questions asked, but man, I got to hire some coaches with college experience. You understand, don't you?"

"Sure," Hemp says.

"Listen, how about some other job—like equipment manager?"

"No way, man," Hemp says. "I'm a damn coach."

The next afternoon Hemp shows up at the house with his suitcase. "Look," he says to Mac, "I'm here to help you, man. If you don't think I'm a coach, okay then, tell me what the hell else to do. I want to be a part of this. I been waiting on you to get your chance so I could get my chance. I know I'm not getting any younger, but I got a lot left in me. I can help you. I swear. The only way you can get rid of me is to shoot me."

"I hope it won't come to that," Mac says.

"Where's Leeta?" I ask.

"She's home drawing up divorce papers, I reckon." He smiles.

Mac wants to hire a second black coach, a guy with experience to coach defensive secondary. "Coach, nobody hires two black coaches," Walker says. "I'm not trying to tell you what to do, but one black guy, that's all anybody expects."

"You got something against black coaches?"

"Heck no. All I'm saying is there aren't that many qualified black coaches out there. Just because a guy used to be a great player doesn't mean he'll make a good coach. A lot of these black coaches, they got natural ability, but they don't really know the game, the Xs and Os. That's all I'm saying."

I'm in Mac's office when a call comes in from Baltimore. "I'm going to be honest with you," Mac says into the phone. "I want a black guy for this position." Then he says, "Well, you sure don't sound black. Where you from?"

The following weekend Jasper Shirley comes for an interview. Neither of us has ever met anyone like him. He speaks with such immaculate diction—no trace of accent at all. I know we stare at him like he's from Mars. How will he do with Alabama kids who speak homemade English? Will they be put off by Jasper's good dressing, good grammar, and general fanciness? Jasper grew up in Washington, D.C. His father was a military man. He's traveled the world. "But my wife is from North Carolina," Jasper says, trying to soothe us.

We take Jasper to dinner at the Bright Star in Bessemer and his table manners put ours to shame even though the Bright Star doesn't require high etiquette. During dessert I say, "Jasper, how many years have you been married?"

"Eleven," he says. "Two great kids. You'll love Alice when you meet her. She's proof I can recruit, Coach."

It isn't until Jasper arrives in Birmingham with Alice (who claims to be black, and we take her word for it since there's nothing about the way she looks to go on—pale skin, green eyes, red hair) and she mentions that next week will be their one-year anniversary, and I look puzzled, that she says she's Jasper's third wife. He has children by each of his first two.

"Jasper," I say later, "I thought you told me you'd been married eleven years."

"You didn't ask me how many years I'd been married to Alice." Jasper laughs. "You asked me how long I'd been married period. So I just added all the years together. I want credit for all the hard time I've done," he says. "Every last minute."

"I can't do a thing with him," Alice says proudly.

Catfish stops by the house one night after dinner and sits at the kitchen table sipping Scotch, giving Mac advice he never asked for, while I clear the dishes and Buddy and Sarah watch TV upstairs. "You don't want to hire a whole staff of guys itching to be head coaches," Catfish says. "They'll be too busy competing among themselves to pay full attention to competing on the field. Naw, you want a couple of older guys, who've missed their chance at being a head coach, know it, and have learned to live with it. But you don't want a whole staff of guys with more experience than you've got either, cause they'll think they ought to be running the show." He pauses and hands me his glass. "Dixie, honey, you got a couple of ice cubes handy?"

"You want a couple of young guys," he says to Mac, "former players maybe, who are already loyal to you—not just loyal to the team, but to you, Mac Gibbs, the guy that gave them this chance of a lifetime. Any young guy who doesn't know this is the chance of a lifetime, you don't want him.

"And you need one straight shooter, a church guy—you know the type. But too many Bible beaters and you're doomed. Especially look out for Bible beaters from Texas—whew, you talking about trouble. Avery Drake, Lord, what a mess he was."

"I heard he was preaching out in Dallas now," Mac says.

"I didn't know he was out of jail," Catfish says.

"The girl's daddy dropped the charges," Mac says.

"He could recruit," Catfish says. "I'll give him that."

"And nowadays," Catfish says, "you got to have at least one colored coach. Too bad you couldn't talk ole Jett into coming back to Birmingham. Naw, I guess he's too rich to turn back now. Can't hardly turn on the TV without seeing his grinning face. Hell, I guess I'd be grinning too if I was pulling in what he's pulling in. I hear he's knee-deep in white women out there."

"He's doing all right," Mac says.

"Black kids being recruited these days look for a black coach on the staff and you've got to have it. Columbus Carpenter, he's a good bet. But this Jasper Shirley, he looks like he ought to be working in a bank somewhere."

"Jasper's all right, Coach," Mac says. "He's smart."

"Well, you want a couple of smart coaches—you know, Xs-and-Os types that get off on drawing up plays and watching film, like ole Haymaker, stay locked up in their offices until the wee hours plotting, but who don't necessarily click with the players that much. Players start to think, *Okay, that guy's the brains. Don't have a bit of personality. Good enough.*"

Mac laughs. "Did Haymaker ever sign anybody?"

"Are you kidding me? Haymaker couldn't have signed his own mother. If he hadn't been so damn smart I'd've had to get rid of his ass, but hell, the guy was a genius.

"And wives," Catfish says, "look out for the wives. You get a pussy-whipped coach out there and you'll never get more than fifty percent out of him cause his wife's got his dick in a sling. Myself, I like to see a coach married to a Southern girl. Some of these Northern women, man, they don't know when to quit. A coach that can't control his wife—well, all I'm saying is you don't want him. Ain't that right, Miss Dixie?" He winks at me.

ROMALEE

Nobody ever said life would be fair, right?

Celeste is one thing. Celeste is Celeste. But Dixie? She's the head coach's wife now, which is a real joke. She was content the way things were. It was me that wanted more. I guess this is what you get for having a little ambition.

Walker's putting on a good face. He could've gone to coach at Florida again. But Mac practically begged him to stay. So here we are, watching Mac and Dixie move into the house we ought to be moving into. It's awkward as hell.

The new coaches' families are trickling into town now. It's supposed to be Dixie's job to see that the wives are happy. They've got to be willing to make reasonable sacrifices for the good of the team without complaining too much and disturbing the delicate equilibrium of team morale with any personal dilemmas of their own. That was hard for Alice. When she got her mammogram back and found out she needed a biopsy she debated a long time about whether she should tell Jasper and go ahead with it or wait until recruiting was over. It was a tough decision.

And it was me Alice turned to. Not Dixie.

I told Alice, "Don't wait on Jasper. Get you an appointment right away—and I'll go with you." When we found out Alice needed a mastectomy Jasper was in Baltimore recruiting. I couldn't tell you where the hell Walker was.

I've met Frances Delmar before. She used to come to Birmingham to visit. I've heard every story in the world about her—Dixie thinks the sun rises and sets in Frances Delmar. But I personally think she has attitude, you know.

"Who, Cleet and me? Are you kidding?" This is how Frances Delmar talks. "I don't see him enough to get pregnant again. We've moved from lovemaking to tension releasing. We've got things pared down to three minutes, start to finish. He's on the road recruiting every minute except when he brings his laundry home. Cleet says if I turn up pregnant he's hiring a private detective to find out whose baby it is."

See what I mean.

DIXIE

We're moving into the coach's house soon. I have to decide whether I want to recarpet or have the wood floors stripped and refinished. These are the sorts of decisions I've always dreamed of making. I have long suspected deep in my core that my life would be spent transforming the ordinary into the beautiful. It's like a calling. Now I lie awake at night overwhelmed at the enormity of the task. The coach's house is large and charming. I plan to make it look like a picture in a magazine—you know, magnificent yet homey. I spend days studying wallpaper books like there's going to be a test later. Each morning the university sends over workmen to do my bidding. I am deep into the science of color. The philosophy of fabric. What impact a window treatment might have on our outlook on the world.

Sarah's in fourth grade at her new school. She wears a Black Bears T-shirt nearly every day, no matter how I try to talk her out of it. Every morning I force a bow into her wispy hair. Every afternoon she comes home without it—lost, she says.

We decided to enroll Buddy in church school because he's small for his age and shy, so he's enrolled at First Baptist Christian Elementary—and he's terrified. Buddy's like me—slow to adjust. He cries every morning when I drop him off at First Baptist. It's like tossing him into a sea of children. He begs me to take him back home, to yank him from these too deep waters and set him back on safe, dry land, in front of the TV at home. He clings to my slacks so tight he has to be peeled loose.

"Go ahead," his teacher says, "he'll be fine the minute you're gone." I try to believe her.

Two or three nights a week Mac flies in the university jet to talk to booster organizations, alumni groups, or quarterback clubs. I worry about the plane crashing. Several times a month Rose or Lilly keeps the children and I go with Mac to a country club, a VFW, or a high school auditorium. We travel the whole way in virtual silence. I assume Mac is collecting his thoughts for the talk he'll give. I assume the silence is golden as far as he's concerned, even though this enlarged silence between us is a bleak turn of events for me. But silence seems a small price for me to pay. I think of it as my own flimsy contribution to the team effort. By the time we arrive I always have butterflies, no matter where we are, no matter who is there waiting, like me, to hear Mac *say* something.

But once Mac's in front of the microphone, looking out at the audience with his boy face, people grow quiet and attentive. The men fold their arms across their chests, and the women cross their legs, put their hands in their laps, and massage their cuticles, preparing to listen. The room's alive with low expectations. Then Mac begins to talk, and he's like Jesus casting his net into the sea—a fisher of men. As the net of his words falls over their heads, people smile and warm up to him.

"I bet you're sitting out there wondering, *Who the heck is this guy who thinks he can replace Catfish Bomar? Right?* Well, let me tell you something," Mac begins. "I don't have any intention of replacing Catfish. I'd be a fool to try. Catfish Bomar was my coach for four years and he taught me more than I could begin to tell you. I love the guy. There's nobody in this room that loves the guy more than I do. So the last thing on my mind is replacing him. I just want to honor him and his faith in me by building on the tradition he worked so hard to establish at HamU. And I want you to help me. I can't do it without you.

Black Bears fans are the best fans in the world. I want us to field a team that will pay tribute to the greatest coach who ever lived." The room bursts into applause. The faces of the people in the room swim forward like a formidable whale of a thing.

"Millie Gibbs didn't raise any dummies," Mac says. "I don't know how your mama raised you, but my mama raised me to believe Catfish Bomar sat up there at the right hand of Jesus." The crowd shouts "Amen."

See, I think, the truth *will* set you free.

FRANCES DELMAR

I ring Dixie's doorbell flanked by my kids. Dixie welcomes me like I'm the millionaire bringing her a cashier's check. There she is, her hair pinned up on her head like a messy crown and that damn smile. She's laughing when she opens the door, saying, "Oh, F. D., F. D." I fall into her arms like she's forgiveness and I deserve it at last. We spin around like two clumsy square dancers, squealing, "Oh my God, oh my God." Our children back away from the scene.

"Good grief, Mom," Lydia scolds me.

We herd the children inside to the kitchen, where I study Sarah and Buddy, and Dixie studies my kids. She says, "It's like if you dismantled you and Cleet and used your separate pieces to make three conglomerate children. They're beautiful."

Jane's fifteen. She's tall and blond like Cleet but has my wild hair, bless her heart. She's a splendid-looking girl, even if she is my daughter. But she's bookish. Don't ask me where she got that. It's awful when your daughter is a head turner. Men just zoom right in on her, stare like fools. But I swear she'd rather read a book than live a life.

"She's wonderful," Dixie says.

"She's a goody-good, Dix, like you. I knew you'd like her."

Lydia's just a year older than Sarah. She wears her hair pulled back in a low ponytail. She and Sarah clash instantly. "Those leg warmers are out of style," Lydia says. "Nobody in Mississippi wears them anymore."

"I don't care what rednecks in Mississippi do," Sarah says.

Joe's a box-shaped boy with the buzz cut Cleet insists on, a small replica of Cleet. He's the kind of boy you automatically offer food and he automatically accepts. "Joe hates girls," I tell Dixie. "You know what that means, don't you?"

"What?" she says. "He's gay?"

"Lord no. It means he'll grow up and be a ladies' man. All the ladies' men really hate women deep down."

"How do you know?"

"I notice things," I say.

"Oh God," Dixie says, "you haven't changed a bit."

DIXIE

It's late when the phone rings. Mac and I answer it at the same time. "How's it going, man?" It's Jett.

"I'm running around like a damn chicken with its head cut off," Mac says.

"How's Dixie?" Jett asks.

"She's fine."

"How are the kids?"

"Bradley broke his ankle. I thought he was faking, but X rays show it's broken all right. He's out for the rest of the season. And Smith pulled a hamstring."

"Man, *your* kids," Jett says. "I'm talking about Sarah and Buddy."

"Oh," Mac says. "They're fine. Just fine."

ROMALEE

I've studied this. What a head coach should be in the state of Alabama. It just proves Walker's a natural.

If a coach doesn't have strong Alabama connections, then he doesn't belong in Alabama. I call this the *No Yankees need apply* rule. A coach should be rural or at least act rural. This is no problem for anybody in the state—even folks from B'ham and Mobile, no matter what they say. A coach should not try to dazzle anybody with good grammar or an impressive vocabulary. A coach should hunt, fish, chew tobacco, play golf, and have the guts to scratch what itches, cameras or no cameras. A coach should perform a few acts of symbolic cruelty early on to set the tone for later so people will take him seriously. (Alabama people respect this more than making money.) FOUR PLAYERS HOSPITALIZED FROM HEAT EXHAUSTION. COACH DENIES PLAYERS WATER IN 98-DEGREE HEAT. LAWSUIT PENDING. It was Walker this article was written about. An Alabama coach should talk to boys about their mamas. A coach should tell his players after every game, "Don't do nothing tonight you wouldn't want your mama to know about." And he should mean it. Alabama likes old coaches better than young coaches. If a coach has at least one brother sent to prison, that really helps. Alabama likes coaches that harp on players going to church and dedicating their lives to Christ. Quoting or misquoting the Bible a lot is also good. A coach should develop a personal cursing style. A defensive coach is better than an offensive coach. Alabama loves defense. Most of the South loves defense. This is because people here are always more interested in stopping forward movement than they are in making any forward movement of their own. An Alabama coach should not be too good looking. People hate that. Look at Catfish. But he should have a good-looking wife and she should be a churchgoer. It's okay for him to have kids if they pretty much stay out of sight and out of trouble. He should be nice to black people, but not so nice people start to think he's a liberal. He shouldn't really have any politics, but if he does, they should be predictable. He should stick with whatever he was raised to think.

Now let me ask you, who fits this list best—Walker or Mac?

DIXIE

The moment Mac takes the reins a handful of key players quit the team. It'd be a lie if I said it didn't upset me.

The truth is recruiting had fallen off the last years before Coach Bomar retired. The decline was fueled by coaches from competitor schools. "When the Catfish goes, he'll be taking his legend with him," they said. Now, for every person who seems to hope Mac will succeed there're ten who expect him to fail. Nine of them work for newspapers.

The newspapers start in after Mac before he's played a single game. There's already article after article on low team morale. I read every word of it too. When I try to discuss these articles with Mac he says, "Look, Dixie, I listen to people harp all day. When I come home I don't want to hear it."

So I call Jett out in California and make him listen while I read articles from the newspapers. "Listen to this, Jett," I say. "They're after Mac bad. Players are quitting."

"Payroll players," Jett says.

"What do you mean?" I ask.

"I mean when a new coach comes in, players that had a little something coming under the table from the old regime come in to check things out with the new coach, see if certain boosters are still in line. Mac thinks he can field a team without any handouts. He wants to run a clean program, Dixie, and I'm not saying whether that's smart or stupid. But it's costing him."

"He never told me."

"I never told you either. You understand?"

"Then what should I do?"

"Do what you do best, woman. Smile your way through it."

Jay Byrd (that's his name), a sportswriter from the *Birmingham News*, comes to interview me. It's supposed to be a human-interest story, he says. So I serve him coffee and pound cake on a tray in the den. He has pen and paper and a small tape recorder with him. I sit on the sofa across from him with my coffee cup on my lap. Then he proceeds to ask me penetrating questions.

"What does Coach like to eat before a game?"

"I beg your pardon?"

"Food. What does Coach eat on game day?"

"I don't know. He eats at the training table."

"I see. Does he have any superstitions, like parting his hair a certain way on game day or carrying a lucky coin?"

"Not that I know of." (I wasn't about to tell Jay Byrd about the sexual superstitions so many coaches have—including Mac. If they happen to make love to their wife the night before a win they'll make love to her before every game until it proves useless. Likewise, if they don't make love to her before a win they'll refuse to make love to her before the next game too—until the theory is thrown into reverse. But somehow this didn't seem like it would translate well into print.)

"No lucky socks?"

"Don't think so," I say.

"What are Coach's hobbies?"

"Golf."

"Just golf?"

"That's all he has time for. Maybe racquetball at lunch."

"Golf and racquetball." He writes on his pad. "So how did you meet Coach?"

"He spoke on behalf of the FCA at training union when I was in junior high, but I didn't meet him until high school."

"So you went to Shades Valley too? Did you know he would be a coach when you married him?"

"I knew he wanted to be one. Yes."

"If he hadn't been a coach what you think he'd have been?"

"His mother thought he might be a preacher."

"Did you think so?"

"Not really."

"Does Coach have any particular sayings that sum up his philosophy? You know, something he says around the house?"

"He doesn't say that much around the house."

"You mean he's quiet around the house."

"I mean he's not really around the house that much."

"Can you think of anything?"

"Well, sometimes he says 'The less you say, the less you have to take back.'"

"Great!" Jay Byrd smiles and scribbles on his pad.

I am near hysterics when I call Rose. "Honey," she says, "I think it's a nice article. The picture sure is good. Even your daddy remarked what a good picture it is. If they got a few things wrong, there's nothing you can do but rise above it. Just insist on standing in the light, honey. And remember this in the future. The less people know about you, the more they think of you. Silence is the best way I know to assure a good reputation."

I guess Mac thinks silence is the best way to assure a good marriage too. "Listen," he says when I try to talk to him, "I've got worse problems than a few misquotes in a story. Just forget it." He slides his lips across mine as he goes out the door.

The university sends over a list. It comes directly from the president's office and is hand-delivered to me by Yolanda. It's a guest list for parties we'll be giving at our house after games. "Here it is," Yolanda says. "You better learn this by heart. The money people."

I feel like she's handed me a lighted firecracker.

The list groups the names according to their financial contribution, the most important people first. Wives' names are in parentheses. The whole thing gives me chills, but by the next morning I've memorized nearly all twelve pages of it.

I wake up nauseated. If I didn't know better I might suspect morning sickness. Mac's first game as head coach is against the Georgia Bulldogs and they're favored by two touchdowns. "Good luck," I call to Mac in my sleep. He leaves the house before daybreak wearing a coat and tie and carrying his briefcase. He looks like a man on his way to a courtroom trial.

Flowers are delivered for the after-game party. Butch and his staff are in the kitchen in their white aprons. The catering truck's in our driveway, and the smell of cocktail wieners wafts through the neighborhood like a public announcement. HamU's sent over maintenance men to rake the yard and sweep the walks. Later workers will direct cars to parking spots with long-handled flashlights. Immediately after the game the Black Bear Beauties—handpicked girls who earn scholarships by acting as hostesses for athletic-department functions—will arrive in flawless makeup and what are loosely called church dresses to smile, smell good, pass plates of hors d'oeuvres, and help watch after Sarah and Buddy for me. Everything's meticulously organized.

On the drive to the stadium I listen to Mac's pregame interview on the radio. "Shhhh," I say to Sarah and Buddy. "Let's hear what your daddy has to say." He always makes sense. This is where I get my information and the children get theirs—just like everybody else.

ROMALEE

More than once CeCe's invited me to watch the game in the athletic director's box and mingle with the rich and powerful. But it can be agonizing. The world's too full of rich men with blond wives, who like to tell me they can buy and sell Walker a thousand times over. "I thought about being a coach," they say. "But there wasn't enough money in it. I won't settle for less than the best and I knew I couldn't have the best on a coach's salary. Yeah, I was defensive back. I was fast too."

Money's just another style of jockstrap. It wouldn't have surprised me to have one of the money men unzip his pants and pull out his credentials just to show me that even though he might be too small to play football, his bank account's plenty big. In fact, I could imagine the whole press box full of men holding their credentials in their hands while they sipped their drinks and watched the game, criticizing the stupid coaches and bumbling players. It's the universal game behind every game—"mine is bigger than yours."

I shouldn't drink so much.

CeCe, bless her heart, is a saint. Week after week, win or lose, trying to keep the money people happy. They pay Sly to do it, but nobody's paying CeCe. I swear I think she likes it.

I'm not surprised to see Dixie in her usual seat right next to me. Dixie's a basket case in that quiet way of hers. "Here." I offer her a plastic cup. "Think of it as a tranquilizer."

Frances Delmar is always late. With three children, she runs her own personal three-ring circus on game day—on every day. It's the end of the first quarter when she comes up the steps two at a time, a million-dollar smile on her face. I don't know why she never combs her hair. "Bite 'em, Black Bears!" she shouts, waving her pom-pom over her head. She does have her moments.

You'd think we were headed for a country-club luncheon instead of a ball game, especially Frances Delmar. She's overdressed. So is Alice. All the kids race up and down the stands to get hot dogs or cold drinks, drop pennies through cracks, collect plastic cups. They drive me crazy. The coaches' sons are allowed to stand on the sidelines during the game, unless they're too little, like Buddy. Frances Delmar's, son, Joe, is on the sidelines, but he's big for his age and Cleet wants him down there. Buddy has never expressed any interest in being on the sidelines. Instead, Dixie brings books about insects and sharks to keep him busy since he loses interest in the game minutes after kickoff and begins saying, "How long until it's over, Mom?" I don't have the heart to tell the kid it's never over.

Some of these new wives hardly know their husband's own players. That's inexcusable. As far as I'm concerned it's our job to know who has a mother dying of cancer or a father running around with a younger woman or a sister who's pregnant and unmarried or a brother on drugs. The players' problems are our problems. Any wife who doesn't understand that *should*.

Frances Delmar, she gets it. Already she's been on the phone to the mothers of all Cleet's players, inviting them over for coffee before the games. She'll make those boys' business, *her* business. I see that. So good for her.

But Dixie, the chosen one, mostly just prays for them. She prays like a religious fanatic all of a sudden. Dixie says Frances Delmar's going to join Bible study too. And Alice is thinking it over. Since Alice is black our white Bible study might be too tame for her. Half the time it's too tame for me.

Mac wins his first game as Black Bears head coach. HamU 32, Georgia 21. It's the sort of game where the outcome was never seriously in doubt. The Black Bears lead all the way—thank you, Jesus! —so we squeeze each other's hands, hug each other, breast to breast, run our fingers through the hair on the heads of children who are not our own, smile at strangers.

LILLY

Butch, he runs the training table over at the Bear Cave. All Dixie has to do is get out her silver service and have it ready for Butch to fill up with food. "Butch is an artist," Dixie tells me. "Food's his medium, Lilly."

"Is that so?" I say.

She says, "Butch says he likes giving these parties because his esthetic side is wasted on the training table. 'There, all they want is plenty.' Butch went to chef school in San Francisco, Lilly. Ice carvings are his specialty."

"Well, how about that," I say.

On this here occasion he's carved a growling bear head out of ice, with huge fangs hanging down. Inside the mouth he has put a bunch of fruit. It's something all right.

Rose and Mr. Carraway, they here early too. Rose is nosing into everything, and Mr. Carraway, he done got into the bar. I know it's none my business, but I say to Rose, "Listen here. You can't let him drink bad like he does. He's liable to embarrass Dixie and Mac if he gets sloppy."

Rose just looks at me. "What do you suggest I do, Lilly? Handcuff him to the kitchen table? Tie him into a chair?"

"Just tell him," I say. "If you don't, I will."

DIXIE

I hurry up the walk to the house, barking orders to Sarah and Buddy on how to negotiate the onslaught of people who'll be arriving at our house momentarily. My nerves are like a serrated knife blade. I thank God for the win as if I am thanking him for saving the life of one of my dying children. I brush my hair and put on lip gloss before the first guests arrive.

Jackson Smith and his wife, Elsie, are owners of a chain of restaurants that span the South called Mama's House. Jackson is also chairman of the board of trustees. "Come in," I say.

They barely acknowledged me when Mac was an assistant coach. Now they embrace me as if they've known me forever and loved me the whole time. "Great game," Jackson says. "We're off to a hell of a start."

Within minutes the house is full of people. The party is in full swing: kinks oiled out, liquor flowing, food plentiful, Black Bear Beauties smiling like girls getting paid by the tooth, assistant coaches in huddles for postgame talk, their wives relaxed for the first and only time all week, guests roaming the house and studying the decor, the pictures on the walls, the contents of the medicine cabinets.

Buddy and Sarah make endless trips to the buffet table for plates full of cocktail wieners, meatballs, and maraschino cherries. Lilly and Rose scrutinize Butch's kitchen work. Daddy is drunk. The smokers are smoking, the jokers joking, the talkers talking, the laughers laughing, the good-lookers looking good, and the watchers watching. All's right with the world.

Then Mac walks in. He's like a magnet entering a room full of paper clips. If he can get to me he'll kiss me and say, "Hey, woman." But instead he looks at me across the room. He holds a game ball and mouths, *for you*. It touches me down to my core. Somebody gets him a drink. Yolanda, I think. The Beauties head his way with their trays of salmon puffs and cheese spread. The women blow their cigarette smoke in his direction. The men freshen their drinks—pour them themselves this time and forget the ice. Sarah wraps herself around Mac's leg like a snake on a fence post. "Hey, girl," he says, and kisses her cheek.

While Mac holds court I mingle. Make a mental note to speak to everyone present. Make sure there's plenty of crab dip. Introduce shy people to talkers. Rescue Black Bear Beauties from the occasional man who mistakes them for appetizers to be sampled. I have an ear for the too high giggle that means, *Help me, somebody*. It's that universal woman's laugh that only other women recognize as a distress call.

Daddy stands with other men and listens to them talk. His eyes are glassy and he's virtually silent, but I interpret his wide-legged stance and folded arms as signs he is enjoying himself. I go over and kiss him. "Hi, Daddy," I say.

"Good game," he says, nodding.

I go upstairs to check on Sarah and Buddy, who are sprawled on the floor watching TV with plates of hors d'oeuvres in front of them. I kiss them and say, "Try not to spill."

Eddie King, Mac's car dealer, is coming out of our bedroom. "Somebody was in the bathroom downstairs," he says. "I didn't think you'd mind."

"Of course not," I say, wishing I'd locked the bedroom door.

He puts his arm around my waist as I start down the stairs. "Dixie, honey" he says. "I love Mac as much as the next guy, but I'm still a man, right." I pull away from him, my hip hitting his with every step I take. "Wait," he says. "I want to be honest with you, all right? I think you're a fine-looking woman."

"Thank you." I step ahead of him down the stairs.

"I'm trying to pay you a compliment," he says. "I do a hell of a lot for the Black Bears!"

"Thank you," I say.

"Maybe a compliment doesn't mean a damn thing to you," he says angrily as I turn the corner into the kitchen. Eddie's drunk. Mac says Eddie King is okay. He provides half a dozen dealer cars for the coaching staff. And he's so wrong about me. The truth is I would almost die for a compliment.

I spot Frances Delmar and Alice sitting in the corner with their shoes off. Frances Delmar is sipping her drink and rubbing her feet. "Well"—she smiles at me—"one down and ten to go."

Butch begins to wind down and pack up. The crowd dwindles. I stand at the door singing a series of melodious good-nights. Romalee's pretty drunk by now. She's stabbing smoked oysters with toothpicks, holding them up with a knowing look. "I'm going to have to put my diaphragm in in the car on the drive home," she says. "I've done it before. I swear, winning is the only aphrodisiac Walker understands. He thinks football is foreplay."

Frances Delmar's yawning but hanging on. Flirting always exhausts her that way. She's tossed her hair in the faces of half a dozen smiling men. She knows how to laugh a certain way that makes a man believe he's actually funny.

At a certain point Mac excuses himself. "Some of us work for a living," he says. Then he goes upstairs to bed.

I wait out the last guest. It seems like the only decent thing to do. I savor their reluctant exits, the little kisses I collect at the door. "Love you, Dix," Romalee says as Walker navigates her outside. "See you at Sunday school tomorrow."

"Does she always get that drunk?" Frances Delmar asks.

When the house is cleared of guests at last, I stand in my stocking feet with smudges of mascara under each tired eye, looking like someone who's fought her way through the evening. I look around at the ashes in the plastic cups. I look at the plates of half-eaten food littering the room, the crumpled paper napkins in the chairs, the dropped cocktail wieners ground into the rug, and I feel satisfied, successful. Like a woman who's done a good job, given a moving performance, contributed to the world in some small way. It's a Scarlett O'Hara moment.

ROMALEE

So I drink a little. I'm no alcoholic like Celeste Bomar. But it's no wonder she had to check in to the sanatorium and "rest." Who in their right mind turns their life over to a bunch of eighteen-year-old boys, then just sits back and watches what they do with it? It's enough to make anybody drink.

I don't let anybody get by with talking trash about Celeste. I stand up for that woman. Nobody ever wants to think badly of Catfish Bomar—noooooo. But everybody's willing to believe he married a crazy woman.

Celeste Bomar is like Birmingham's madwoman in the attic. She miscarried four times and never delivered Catfish any progeny. So as a form of what people consider self-banishment, she's inclined to take long journeys alone to places normal people aren't interested in, like Iceland. When everybody else heads for Gulf Shores, Celeste's buying a ticket to Afghanistan.

As a childless woman myself, I sort of understand Celeste. There's more to her than all that ruckus she keeps stirred up.

She lived most of her life in the coach's house Dixie's living in now. She haunts the coach's house like a cold spot in a warm river— you never know when you'll wade into it and get this sudden little shiver of loneliness.

Dixie feels it too. She told me so.

DIXIE

On Sundays the papers come. It takes me half the day to read through the sports sections and clip out any articles pertaining to Mac or the Black Bears. I keep them in a box under our bed and am planning to make a scrapbook eventually. This is Millie's idea. She saved news clippings when Mac was a boy and now her heart is set on my doing it too. So I do. I started the day I married him. It is not a healthy activity, though—reading the printed word. It is like positioning myself on a spit that will rotate me over fires stoked by the awkward jabs of sportswriters everywhere. So many of these sports experts have never played a sport in their lives, and you don't have to wait for them to tell you that. The pen is the only power they've ever had, and if you ask me, it is too much power to come so unearned.

Even so, I clip out newspaper articles like a surgeon cutting out cancers. The benign articles I appreciate and read to the children. The malignant ones I stuff into my cardboard box like so much decay into the compost heap.

When you've been married to a coach as long as I have, you understand that there're just so many sentences available to a coach, and that his sentences are exactly like the sentences of all other coaches, so it's pretty unlikely that you can ever read anything you haven't read a thousand times already. It's like a sentence-recycling program especially for football coaches. I tease Mac about going to *coach school*, where they teach all the football coaches in the United

States the fifty sentences from which they are to construct a public life.

The newspaper quotes Mac: "They were bigger on the line and faster in the backfield. They whipped us, plain and simple."

"Is that the devastating-defeat paragraph?" I tease. "Did you learn that line at coach school?"

"The less you say, the less you have to take back."

This has stopped being just something Mac says. It has become his philosophy of life.

And the less we talk, the more I write.

I was invited to write a column for the *Baptist Bugle* once a month. It is called "The Gospel According to Gibb"—which means Mac, of course, not me. It was Pastor Swanson's idea. Already I work on the church bulletin gathering birth and death announcements from the Sunday school classes. But in this column I write an inspirational don't-forget-to-stop-and-smell-the-roses football anecdote kind of thing, where I draw positive messages from broken bones, broken hearts, missed extra points, and even mothers dying of breast cancer who come to the games in wheelchairs, scarves tied over their bald heads, to watch their sons play ball, maybe for the last time. Maybe the son scores the winning touchdown and the mother dies the next day. Like that. I tell the truth. My goal is to bring the reader to tears. To show the human side of football. I forgive myself small inaccuracies because my stories are designed to be uplifting.

It's amazing how many people read my column too. Now and then the *Birmingham Post-Herald* reprints something for the semi-Baptist world at large. I enjoy it so much I've signed up for a writing class in the English department at HamU.

Romalee told me I needed to get involved in community affairs. She's in every club in town. I was already active in Christian Women's Club, but after becoming head coach's wife I was elected president, which terrifies me. I think I do Christianity a disservice by putting myself forward as a product of the faith. But what can I say?

I'm also homeroom mother for Sarah's class. I judge the Miss HamU beauty pageant and the Miss Alabama pageant too. Luckily Daddy trained me to evaluate the physical beauty of other women. I'm ashamed to say I consider myself an expert. As does Romalee.

I go to aerobics three mornings a week with Frances Delmar. I put our house on the Birmingham tour of homes at Christmas to raise money for the Alabama Home for the Incurables.

My marriage has become a series of small games I've invented and play alone. For example, some nights when Mac comes home I don't say anything at all. I wait and see how long it'll take him to notice my silence and correct it with some words of his own. Trouble is, Mac doesn't notice my silence and doesn't correct it, and never knows he's failed a simple test.

I have trouble sleeping. Fear of dreaming is what keeps me awake. Everything I thought I'd forgiven and forgotten comes back to life in my dreams. Suddenly it seems like there're so many things I should have been mad about but wasn't. But now there's no more storage room left for me to hide things away. A thousand times I try to say to Mac, "We have to talk."

"Dixie, all day I listen to problems. It's like people think I'm a psychiatrist instead of a football coach. The last thing I need is for you to bitch and moan too."

"Mac," I say, "I don't care if the world is falling apart, I want ten decent sentences from you each day, half of them about you and me, a couple about Sarah and Buddy. I want you to look at me when you speak these sentences. If you don't have time to speak them, write them down before you go. If you're out of town, call them in by phone. I mean it, Mac."

Mac laughs. "Dixie, baby, I love you." He goes into his study and closes the door. Minutes later I hear his film projector jerking through the motions. I picture his thumb on the stop and go buttons.

LISA

Marvin came to only one of Mac's football games this year. He actually came down to see Mother Gibbs, who's in the hospital. Dixie wanted him to go to the game with her, so he did. I was nervous because you can't ever tell how Marvin will act. Nobody has to sit around and wonder whether Marvin is homosexual either—he makes sure of that.

I wish he could see his way to get right with God. You know, give up his sick lifestyle. Doesn't he see how much it breaks Mother and Daddy Gibbs's hearts? He's so selfish sometimes I just want to shake him.

But Dixie's crazy about Marvin.

At one point this afternoon Marvin puts his arm around me and says, "Lisa, is Dixie happy? Is my boy Mac good to her?"

"Of course," I say.

"You wouldn't lie to me now, would you?"

"Mac's as sweet as he can be."

When the game's over—we lost—Marvin has us distracted from the loss and we're grateful. Even me. Afterwards he won't come to the party at Mac's house. I think he's afraid he'll embarrass Mac, which is true. He hugs the kids and Janelle and me. Then he turns to Dixie and says, "Some things your best friend won't tell you. But, honey, you got to do something with that hair of yours."

"What do you mean?" She's shocked.

"I mean, damn, girl, you got the same hairstyle you had back in high school. That pageboy is tired. You need a change."

Dixie's always had organized hair. People praise her for it too. It's sort of trained in the way to go, because all her life it has gone the same way, like something you can count on. Hair.

The only thing I really like about Dixie is her hair.

FRANCES DELMAR

We're five games into our second season when Tennessee beats us 37–6. That makes us 1 and 4. Romalee sits there laughing at a joke, three sheets to the wind. I'm sorry, I just can't stand it.

"What is Walker's problem?" I shout. "The defense couldn't stop anybody if they were the only players on the field!"

Romalee looks at me like I'm speaking Spanish. I should know better than to try to have a conversation with a drunk.

"Come on, F. D." Dixie tries to pull me away.

"I swear, I don't know what Walker's doing up there in the press box, but it wouldn't surprise me if he was asleep."

"You're blaming Walker for this loss?" Romalee asks.

"It's not Walker's fault," Dixie says. "And it sure isn't Romalee's fault. There're eleven men on the field and half a dozen coaches, so don't blame Romalee."

"I can't stand the way Romalee drinks herself into a stupor while her husband's defense loses the game for us—again."

"You're being ridiculous," Dixie says.

"I think Mac needs to put the fear of God into some of his defensive coaches." I grab Jane and Lydia. "Let's go," I say.

"What's your problem?" Romalee shouts to my back.

"She hates to lose," Dixie says.

DIXIE

Frances Delmar doesn't come to the party after the horrible Tennessee game. Cleet comes alone. I hardly have time to worry about it. Entertaining people whose team has just lost its fourth game takes every ounce of stamina I have. I send Buddy and Sarah upstairs and ask Hedonna, their favorite Black Bear Beauty, to take them plates of food. Then I welcome the guests, who come out of obligation and curiosity to rehash the game with the razor precision of onlookers who have all the answers after the fact.

"People dragging in here like it's a funeral," Lilly says.

Dell Barr, the basketball coach's wife, hugs me. "Chin up," she says. "When the going gets tough and all that." I know it pleases Dell for the football team to lose. The worse we look, the better they look. Yolanda has explained this to me. *Watch out for Dell*, she said. I smile and say, "Thanks for coming."

I see Eddie King coming up the walk. My instinct is to run. "Hey there, darling," he says. "I tell you what, it's time you cut Mac off. Tell him no more nooky until he wins a damn game."

I swear I could be nice to a mass murderer who holds a gun to my head. I believe I could listen to the story of his tragic life and come to love him fully right before he shoots my brains out. I can be nice to people who don't deserve to live. I absorb hostility like a woman made of sponge—like it's my purpose and I'll somehow be empowered by it. I can even siphon off the anger reserved for Mac, since Mac isn't here to do it and likely wouldn't do it if he were.

Hedonna taps my shoulder. "The phone's for you, Mrs. Gibbs." I hope it's Mac. *Where in the world are you? I'll* say.

"Dixie, it's me."

"Frances Delmar, are you okay?"

"I just can't stand it, Dixie. Cleet and I uprooted everything to move here, and the thought of getting fired again . . ."

"We're not going to get fired. Mac has a contract."

"I take it you don't listen to the postgame call-in shows."

"No, and you shouldn't either."

"There's a lot of talk out there, Dixie. I can't start over again. My kids barely get settled in school, then wham, Cleet's on the job market again. I don't know how much more I can stand."

Mac walks into the room then like he's just signed a takeover clause and now owns not just the house but all the people in it. "Frances Delmar, Mac just came in. I've got to go."

"You understand, don't you, Dixie?" she says.

"You've had a hard time," I said. "I know that."

A strange calm eases over the crowd, like all is better now that Mac's arrived to carry the load of disappointment for everybody, to accept all the blame they've come to deliver.

"Where have you been?" I whisper.

"Don't start, Dixie," he says.

"What the hell happened out there, Coach?" Eddie King says.

"You got eyes, King. Haven't you ever seen an old-fashioned ass kicking?"

There it is. The half-laugh that spreads over the room like semi-relief.

I don't tell anyone about the numbness I feel in my arms and legs. It's like they've gone to sleep and when I move they wake with the force of a thousand stabbing pins. At night I wake up terrified, my heart pounding like a fist with a boxing glove on it, beating against my chest like something trying to bust out. My legs are so numb I have to rub them before I can even stand up. I walk through the house, looking out the night windows, while Mac and the children manage to keep dreaming.

I have no real problems compared to other people. Look at Alice. Two years ago she lost her breast to cancer. She's just glad to be alive. So HamU is losing a few ball games. That isn't the end of the world, is it?

I'm not sick, my children aren't sick, I pay off the credit cards most months, my husband loves me, I'm not fat, my house is nice, I have friends. I should be happier. But instead, I sort of hate myself. After the children go to school I get in my car and drive the interstate circling Birmingham. I play Don Williams's "Lord, have you forgotten me?" or Lionel Richie's "Hello, is it me you're looking for?" Sometimes I cry for no good reason.

Sarah comes home from school with a black eye. She storms into the house, slams her lunch box on the kitchen table. "You have to teach me football," she says.

"What happened to your eye?"

"I'm not a loser, Mom."

Sarah's prone to handing down declarations, but this one's profound because it's punctuated by the purple knot on her face. "They always choose me for their team—the boys—when they pick sides," she says. "I can't tell them I don't know how to play—I don't even know the rules. It's the only time they like me—at recess—you know, because of Dad."

"If they were smart they'd like you all the time."

"Mom, listen! I ran the wrong way. I scored for the other team. Then Gabriel—he's a boy in my class—said I was a loser just like Dad's a loser. He said, 'Give Mac the Ax.' They all started singing it, 'Give Mac the Ax.' So I hit him. I hate Gabriel." She released a breathy cry and went steely again. "He hit me, Mom. I ripped his shirt. We had to go to the office for fighting." She pauses to leave me space to start yelling.

"I have to learn how to play, Mom. It's for Dad too. So I don't embarrass him."

"Okay. We'll tell Dad. We'll get Dad to teach you."

"When?"

When is a terrible question in our house. "We'll ask him tonight, okay? Here"—I hand her an ice cube wrapped in a wet paper towel—"put this on your eye. It's a pretty great shiner."

"Dad will love it, right? Do you think he will?"

"I think he'll say it's a beauty." I kiss her stringy hair. "I love you, Sarah Gibbs."

"Mom?" she says. "Are they going to fire Dad?"

"No, sweetheart, not if they're smart."

"But Mom, what if they're *not* smart?"

It's midnight before Mac gets home. Even if HamU wins the rest of our games—which would take a miracle—there's little chance of undoing the damage. It's grin-and-bear-it time. I do the grinning. Mac does the bearing it. He looks calm like always, but I know he won't rest well this night, that his dreams will jolt him awake and he'll sit up and punch the air until I touch him and he remembers that this is night and we're supposed to be sleepers in it.

"You have to wake Sarah up," I say. "She got in a fight at school. She wants to tell you."

Mac takes off his shirt and hangs it on a chair. He takes off his shoes and leaves them in place on the floor. "She okay?"

"She wants to learn to play football. Defense, I think."

"Don't we all," Mac mumbles. He goes to Sarah's room and lies beside her on the NFL bedspread she chose herself. I follow and stand in the doorway. "Potato head," he whispers, "wake up."

She rolls over and sits up, a wild creature with her night hair and purple eye.

"I hope the other guy looks worse than you."

"Mom said you'd teach me to play football."

"Can't you find something better to do? How about tiddly-winks?"

"Dad, I'm serious."

"Why do you want to play football? Can't you be a cheerleader?"

"They already have the cheerleaders. It's all the goody-good girls, Dad. They think I'm a loser because I ran the wrong way."

"Did you score?"

"For the wrong team!"

"Well, at least you scored." He smiles. "Maybe I ought to get you to come out there and play for the Black Bears."

"Dad!"

"What kind of boy gets in a fight with a girl?"

"Every kind, Dad. Mostly Gabriel."

"Next time he wants you to play just tell him you don't want to. You don't have to prove anything to them, potato head."

"I do, Daddy. I'm the fastest girl out there. Only two boys are faster than me. They were calling me a loser."

"Well, you're a winner if I ever saw one." Mac kisses Sarah's black eye. "If anybody hits you again you tell the teacher, you hear me? No more fighting. Okay? Running the wrong way is not the end of the world."

"It seems like it," she says.

Mac smiles. "I know what you mean." He kisses her cheek and stands up. "See you in the morning," he says. But of course he won't see her in the morning. He'll have been at the office for hours before she wakes up. Mac walks by me and we kiss one of our automatic good-night kisses.

I go to Sarah and she pulls my face close to hers and whispers, "Mom, try to cheer him up. Okay?"

FRANCES DELMAR

I'm no racist, okay?

But I swear now is not the time for Mac to get political on us. Not everybody in Alabama knows Smokey Hubbard like we do. Not everybody loves him, and even those who do aren't ready for a black quarterback. Especially not when we're having the first losing season anybody can remember.

I know. I know. Mac's got his so-called reasons. First our quarterback gets sidelined with a knee injury. Then our backup guy gets this viral infection. (Cleet calls it the scared shitless infection. He says, "There's kids that play hurt and there's kids that play hurt.") So that leaves us a true freshman, Eric Baber. He's got talent but no real experience. Cleet begged Mac to play him anyway. "He's all we got, Coach." I heard him say that myself.

"Baber's not ready," Mac said. "It'll destroy him if we throw him in there now."

"Then who's our quarterback?"

"Smokey," Mac said.

"Oh, shit," Cleet said, "I was afraid of that."

We were all afraid of that.

Smokey's been starting at defensive back. He's good. The week Mac moves him to quarterback—good Lord, the newspapers, the radio shows. The day of the game it looks like they're letting black people in two for the price of one. It looks like National Black People's

Day. They make their own section in the stadium—you can't miss them. Seems like they're all kin to Smokey or something, chanting, "Where there's Smoke, ah-ha, there's fire!"

Help us, Jesus.

Smokey's tall and thin, has deer legs too. It looks like one good hit and his shins will splinter like matchsticks. But they don't. He can change directions faster than most people can change their minds. He can jump over a pileup like a deer over a fence. Seems like he can do everything—except win the game for us by himself.

My daughter Jane doesn't like football. But she's watching Smokey. "He's the best player out there, isn't he, Mom?"

"He's one of them," I say.

"He's definitely the cutest," she says.

Oh great, I think. *My daughter who's immune to men finally notices one—and he's black. Terrific.*

After the game I'm sick. Vanderbilt beat us, which is pretty damn serious. I swear I'm running a fever. My nerves can't take all this. We go to the locker room and there's Smokey's family. They make a relative wall around him, but even that can't keep the loss at bay. We lost. Again. Bad. I see Dixie talking to Smokey's family, trying to say something to convince them that *white people are not all bad.* They're not likely to believe it after today. The abuse was the worst I've ever seen.

When I saw Smokey's mother, she said, "Look here, can't no one man win no game."

Afterwards a white woman I don't even know said to me, "It's bad enough to lose with a white boy at quarterback, but when you start losing with a black boy at quarterback then there's no excuse for it."

On the ride home Jane turns on the radio and we listen to Mac's radio show, as if the game itself wasn't torture enough.

"I got faith in Smokey," Mac says.

Well, you're the only one, I think.

It's not just the white people who're mad at Mac. The colored people are mad too. One black man calls in and says, "Hell yeah, that's how white folks do—wait until they got the ship sinking, then call up the only black boy on board to be the damn captain."

"Turn that off," I say.

It's a wake at Dixie's house after the game. Cleet always says, "In football it's not good for anybody unless it's good for everybody." I wish he'd tell Mac that.

Mac hasn't been home ten minutes when a call comes for him. He takes it in the study with the door closed. When he comes out he's white as a sheet. "It's Smoke," he says. "I got to go."

"Oh my God," I said. "Somebody shot him."

DIXIE

I'm in bed with all the doors locked when Mac finally gets home. "Is everything okay?" I say. "I've been worried."

"Smokey was closed up in his dorm room," Mac says. "I guess people thought he was in there slitting his wrists or something."

"What was he doing?"

"Thinking," Mac says. "There's precious little of that going on these days."

Mac undresses, folding his clothes neatly over a chair like he always does. "I said, 'Smoke, let's take a ride. Get the hell out of here.' We rode halfway to Montgomery and back. I asked him, 'Do you want me to get this monkey off your back? Because if you tell me to, I will.'"

"What'd he say?"

"He said no. Just like I knew he would."

"He reminds you of yourself, doesn't he?"

"Heck no. Fans hated me because I didn't have enough talent. They hate him because he's not who they want him to be—a white boy."

"Get some sleep," I say. "You're worn out."

"I'm going to start Smokey next week, Dix. Be prepared."

"I am," I lie.

Mac lies down in bed, folds his hands behind his head, and stares at the ceiling. "Sometimes I wonder why the hell I'm in this profession. Nights like tonight I almost remember."

"Good," I say.

R O M A L E E

The homecoming game is against an undefeated LSU. I bundle up and go with Dixie and Sarah and Buddy to the pep rally and bonfire. Buddy loves the bonfire—a stack of burning wood as tall as a water tower.

Sarah spent extra time fixing her hair and even let me spray it. Until now she's acted like having hair was nothing but a big inconvenience. "You're a vision," I told her.

There's been talk in the newspaper about whether Smokey will wear a bulletproof vest tonight. It's like out of a bad movie or something. Mac brought home a handful of hate mail too—Dixie showed me. Letters from guys inviting Smokey to meet them at various spots in Decatur and Gadsden and Mobile.

Dixie watched Mac hide the letters in his underwear drawer and for an insane moment she said she imagined he was hiding love letters. When he went downstairs she got the letters and read them. "What are you doing?" Mac snapped. He'd come into the room without her hearing him.

"I found these," she said. "I thought they might be love letters," she confessed.

"Well, they're not," he said.

• • •

Sarah finds her friends—mostly boys and Frances Delmar's daughter Lydia—and goes off with them. We agree to meet on the steps of the library after the bonfire.

The police are everywhere. Mac says a few words and the pep band plays, so you don't notice how meager the applause is. Walker and the other coaches introduce the players. Smokey gets booed, but not as bad as I expected. Then the president welcomes the alumni, and all eyes turn to the bonfire. The party.

Buddy wants to get up close. He stands with his chest against the yellow tape the police used to rope off the area. It's a spectacular sight. The roar of gasoline-soaked wood shoots orange flames into the night producing sudden, intense heat that forces us all to step back. People oooh the way they do when Christmas trees are lit in dark rooms, only this is a fire the size of a building.

I don't see them coming. I'm as absorbed as Buddy is in the sight before us. I don't notice the commotion until I feel a push and the whole crowd stumbles a little, then gasps and laughs as fraternity boys with their faces painted black, wearing white plastic fangs in their mouths—their black bear costumes, I guess—break through the safety rope. The band stops playing and people begin screaming and chuckling as the boys run toward the fire carrying a fishing pole with a dummy hanging on the end of it—a dummy wearing sunglasses and a sign around his neck that says MAC GIBBS. We watch them dip him into the fire.

Buddy reaches for my hand but doesn't turn his face to mine. Dixie puts her arm around his shoulder.

Afterward we wait for over an hour for Sarah. Dixie's beginning to worry. The crowd's thinned and the bonfire's settled into a steady blaze. We sit on the library steps and watch the fading revelry in silence.

"Mom, do you think Dad saw?" Buddy asks.

"I don't know," she says.

I've almost decided to ask one of the policemen to help us look for

Sarah, when she comes walking up from behind the library. Dixie reaches for her, but she says, "Don't, Mom." She turns away from us so we won't see her eyes.

We drive home, Buddy and Sarah silent for a long time.

Finally Sarah says, "They used to do that to the slaves. Only for real."

"Who?" Buddy asks.

"The white people. The KKK."

"Are you going to tell Dad?" Buddy asks.

"No way," Sarah says. "Don't you tell him either."

"I'm not," Buddy said. "No way."

We ride silently for a couple of blocks, then Sarah lets out a sigh. "Sometimes I really hate people," she says.

"Me too," Buddy says.

"Me too," I say.

There was no need to tell Mac. Just in case he didn't see it himself, there was a picture in the newspaper—his likeness going up in smoke.

LILLY

I been helping out some at Dixie's house. She the one with the kids and the stay-gone husband. I run out of something to do over at the Carraways'. Mr. Carraway, he's in rough shape, but he get up and go to work every day.

Dixie didn't say nothing to me about Buddy starting to wet the bed. That boy is close to eight years old. I just found them wet sheets under his bed and I said to Dixie, "What's this here?"

Now I see how Dixie's trying to cure him with love. But you know, don't matter what folks say, love don't cure everything. Every day she lets Buddy pick out three books and she reads them all twice. Some nights after she turns out the light she sits on his bed and makes up stories about a bunch of great heroes who wet the bed when they was boys. She got every hero in the world wetting the bed— George Washington, Abraham Lincoln, John Glenn, that astronaut, even President Carter. Lord, to hear her tell it, about every man who turned out to do anything noticeable used to wet his bed.

"Mom? Is that the truth?" he asks her.

She tells Buddy, "It's the little boys with problems who grow up to be big men with solutions." Then she comes out of there and says to me, "Lilly, I bet Dr. Spock's turning over in his grave."

"I don't put no store in Dr. Spock," I say. "Idn't no telling how many children he messed up."

This makes Dixie smile.

"No drinks after seven o'clock, Buddy." That's one Dixie's new rules. Every time I come over here they got some new rule. Dixie tries setting the alarm during the night and waking Buddy up to go to the toilet. Sounds like one of that Mr. Spock's ideas, if you ask me. But it's a waste. They both wake up out of sorts in the mornings. Then Buddy starts begging not to go to school.

"I don't feel good, Mom. For real," he says.

"You don't look sick to me," Dixie says.

He twists his face into a bunch of sick expressions. He clutches his belly or limps and say his legs hurt, both of them.

"You're good at that," Dixie'd say. "Maybe this Halloween you ought dress up as a hypochondriac!"

"Mom, you're going to be sorry when I die," he screams. He sounds so desperate that Dixie gives in and lets that child stay home and read books in his bed all day.

"You can't let that child hide out thataway," I tell her. "You got to make a child do what that child don't want to do. He's got to know he can get past it. Don't you be letting him play hooky this way."

"He's only seven, Lilly."

"Seven is old enough to do what you don't especially want to do. You going to ruin him if you let him start hiding out."

One morning Buddy claims his legs is paralyzed and he won't get out of bed all day long. Dixie calls me and I go over there. That evening he wants to be carried to the supper table. Dixie props him up in a chair and watches him eat. He seems too happy imagining himself a crippled boy. I can see it myself. It idn't natural. And it makes Dixie get started thinking, *What if something really is wrong with the child?*

I said, "Look here, you call the doctor and have him look that boy over. He don't seem right."

So I go with her to take him to the pediatrician. He don't want to go. Cries the whole way.

The pediatrician says, "Buddy's small for his age, Dixie. That's not easy on a boy—especially a sensitive boy."

"Okay," she says, "so he a little undersized. He'll grow. Right? Mac was the smallest of Millie's sons, but he grew up to be the largest one of all."

"There's a lot of stress at your house," the pediatrician says. "It's hard on Buddy."

"What can we do to help him?" Dixie asks.

"The best thing I can think of"—that doctor smiles—"would be for Mac to win a few games."

Dixie just stares at him like she didn't hear him right.

"I hope you ain't planning to send no bill for that advice," I say.

DIXIE

Our eighth game Smokey runs for two hundred yards and we win. His mother's crying outside the locker room. We all cry then. Even Romalee, who never cries, cries now. So we all know—and the fans do and the press too—that it can be done. We can win with a black quarterback.

At the party afterwards the mood is good for a change. People pour into the house with smiles on their faces and drinks already in hand. Now and then somebody lets loose a whopping "Bite 'em, Black Bears!" and everybody lifts their glasses in a swell of team spirit. I feel alive again. Maybe that's why I notice him when he comes through the door. The minute I see him I feel like he's somebody I know and I've been waiting forever for him to get here.

He's wearing a black cowboy hat and looks like he's just tied his horse to the porch rail. He's with a pink woman whose trashiness is deluxe. Miniskirt over absence of hips. She looks like some prominent judge's daughter who as a young girl was sent off to some elite private school, but who'd always dreamed of growing up to be low class and wild. I understood because I'd grown up being jealous of free-spirited girls who wore cheap shoes, dime-store earrings, and clothes one size too small. This woman knows what she's doing. Her makeup makes her look sort of like a not-so-perfect cake that's saved by lavish swirls of lickable icing. I'm instantly jealous.

A pause in the noise signals their arrival. People turn to stare at them. Who are they? They look like they've wandered into the wrong place. I half expect them to look around, then ask Mac for directions to the Country Wigwam, where they can Texas two-step all night in the bright company of people wearing snap shirts.

Mac extends his hand. "How's it going?"

The man shakes Mac's hand, mumbles something, then says, "This is my friend Rudy Long."

"I want you to know I'm a big Black Bears fan." Rudy squeezes Mac's hand. "I just love football."

"Well, that's all I ask of anybody," Mac smiles. "Come on in, Rudy Long, and liven the place up."

Rudy swings her happy hair and enters the room breasts first. But it's not Rudy—it's the man. It's the way his eyes scan the room and slam headfirst into mine. It's like he's looking for me. He looks familiar and dangerous. He tips his hat in my direction, then takes it off altogether while Mac introduces him to an assortment of car dealers, tax accountants, and restaurant owners. Across the room I pick up a toothpick and absentmindedly stab a cocktail wiener.

As the night inches along, no matter where I stand in the room I can feel the man's presence. I'm like a heat detector and he's the hot spot. Every time I glance in his direction—just to be sure—he's looking at me. "Who's that?" I ask Romalee.

"Beats me. Looks like he took a wrong turn at Dodge City or something. Look out, child. He's coming over here."

I use Lamaze breathing to stay calm. I've always been a sucker for people who travel the edges, one boot on this side, one boot on that side. I love people who don't fit in—if it weren't for Mac, that's the kind of person I hope I'd be.

Rudy Long is chattering with Sly and CeCe. Sly's sloshing his drink down the front of his suit, laughing, and CeCe's eyebrows are raised high enough to merge with her widow's peak. I feel this man approaching the way you feel a grass fire coming your way. It's not smart to just stand here and wait.

His hatband has left an indentation on his forehead. His hair is dark and threatening to curl in the humidity of the crowded room. "I've been wanting to talk to you," he says.

"Dixie Gibbs," I say. "So, I guess I must be in luck, since you seem to like blonds." I nod in Rudy's direction.

"A friend of the family," he says.

"Not your sister?" I smile. "You could have fooled me."

"I guess I *have* fooled you."

"I beg your pardon?"

"You don't remember me, do you? Here I was thinking you'd run across the room and leap into my arms when you saw me." He smiles. "And you don't even remember me. Porter Warren."

"Oh, my God." Porter Warren, smartest boy I ever knew. The boy who'd made me feel like a poet, who'd gone off to Harvard to ruin himself a million years ago. I reach out and touch his shirtsleeve like I'm checking to be sure he's real. "Porter! Yes, I remember you. You used to scare me to death," I say. "You've changed."

"Oh, so now I don't scare you?"

"Maybe a little bit." I smile.

"Good," he says.

"What in the world brings you here? You're the last person I would expect to see at a football party."

"I've moved back to Birmingham. Got to do as the natives do," he says. "But I have ulterior motives. I'm up to no good."

"Now that's the old Porter I remember." I laugh.

"So you're a married lady," he says.

"Been married forever," I say. We both glance at Mac, standing in the foyer smoking a cigarette, surrounded by a group of men with drinks in their hands, reliving fourth and one—again. As soon as the antismoking campaign took hold across America, Mac took up smoking. I never tried to talk him out of it either, although the American Cancer Society sent letters and made calls protesting his smoking on the sidelines during games. I love the way he holds the cigarette in his square hand, the way it bounces in his mouth when he mumbles scraps of conversation, the way smoke gets in his face and makes him squint his eyes. And I especially like the way he lights cigarettes for women who have been fumbling through their purses looking for their lost lighters. I've seen women walk all the way across the room just to get Mac to light their cigarette. Yolanda, for one. I didn't blame her either. He can light a woman's cigarette without missing a beat in the conversation too, his eyes saying, *Here, let me do that.*

It's past midnight when the party begins to wind down. Only the diehards remain, those few who hope for a little private drunken conversation with Mac, a story they can repeat straight from the coach's mouth at the golf course tomorrow and again at the office on Monday. Men, mostly, linger. Rudy Long had tried to get some dancing started but the room was too crowded so she'd settled for animated swaying.

"See that woman?" Frances Delmar nods toward Rudy Long. "You'll never guess what she does."

"She's a table dancer who lives off generous tips?" I say.

"She's studying American literature. They say she's read every book you can name."

"Good for her," I say.

"Looking at her I swear I feel like the old woman in the shoe," Frances Delmar says.

"You are the old woman in the shoe." I smile.

"Don't laugh," she says. "You are too."

Sly and CeCe glad-hand themselves to the door, where they look at Mac—that private look that means, *How in the hell do we do this week after week?* Mac kisses CeCe and shakes Sly's hand and never loses his place in the high-investment conversation of former high school quarterbacks who've grown up to be frustrated millionaires, love nothing better than telling Mac what play he should have called to start the second half and how it might have changed the whole momentum of the game.

Lilly orders the Black Bear Beauties to pick up the room, empty ashtrays, get coats for anybody not able or not inclined to get out of his chair or his sentence and get his own coat. After saying an appropriate assortment of good-byes I take off my shoes and carry a plate of ham-wrapped asparagus into the kitchen, where I try to juggle it into the refrigerator.

"I'm looking for the hostess."

I jump, knocking a jar of mustard to the floor. It rolls across the room and lands at Porter's feet. He picks up the jar of mustard and sets it on the counter. "There's something I want to say, Dixie." He reaches over and turns off the kitchen light.

"What are you doing? Turn the light on."

"What I've got to say can't be said under bright light. I don't want you to see me blushing." He takes a step toward me.

"Well, you can say it from there. Don't come any closer."

"I don't think this is something you want me to yell across the room."

"This better be good," I say. My heart's pounding so loud I'm afraid he can hear it.

He puts his hat on the table, then folds his arms and leans against the counter. "I know you think I don't know you anymore, Dixie. But I got eyes. I know what I see."

"And what do you see?" I tear a paper towel off the roll and begin to wipe my hands.

"All these folks here tonight see you walking around with that god-awful apron on, and they think, *That's the coach's wife. Isn't she sweet.*"

"And?"

"I know you're walking a damn tightrope, afraid any minute you might fall off. I just want you to know that I see that—you know, that *somebody* sees that."

He might as well have set a match to the hair on my head. "You have no right to analyze me," I snap. "That's what used to drive me crazy about you in the first place!" My voice shakes, which always happens when the truth makes me furious. "You should go now." I turn my back to him and swipe at crumbs on the counter. "Where's your girlfriend?"

"She's not my girlfriend."

I sling the paper towel into the sink and turn around to face him. "I want you to know I'm a very happy woman. No matter what you think."

He reaches for my apron string and pulls it so the apron falls off. He holds it in his hands like a kite that's just crashed out of the sky. "Get your coat and come have a drink with me, Dixie. Coffee. Anything."

"You're crazy." I stand paralyzed. He really *is* crazy.

"I know a place that stays open all night. We can tell the stories of our recent lives. We can talk about our mothers if you want to. We can tell the truth or we can lie."

"I don't even know you anymore." I snatch the apron from him. "Besides, if I want to talk to somebody I'll talk to Mac."

"You *are* scared of me." He smiles. "I'm flattered."

"I'm not scared of you. Why would I be?"

"I don't know," he says. "Maybe because I'm scared of you, Dixie Gibbs. You scare the hell out of me."

Heat rushes to my face. I must look like a ripe tomato. I love what he's saying. Why? Why can't I be clever and respond like a woman in a movie? What I need is a script and a little rehearsal. I hook a strand of hair behind my ear. As far as I knew nobody in the world has ever been afraid of me—not for a single second. I want to believe him.

When I get to bed Mac's nearly asleep. "Good game," I whisper. He growls. "Did you have a good time tonight?" I ask.

"A party's a party, Dix."

"Did you talk to anybody interesting?"

"Nope."

How should I go about this? I want to sound casual yet refreshingly honest. I put my arm around Mac, positioning myself. "That Porter Warren guy, Mac—what does he do?"

"Takes blonds to parties, I guess," Mac says.

"Right." I sigh and close my eyes. "He went to Shades Valley with you," I say. "I guess you don't remember."

"Sure I do. He was a brain. He's the new partner—at Homewood Medical."

"He's a doctor?"

"Trauma specialist or something."

"Boy, does that sound right," I say.

"He'll be rotating with the other team doctors. Why you asking? He call me names or something?"

"He flirted with me."

"Zat so?"

"And Mac"—I roll up to face him in the darkness—"it scared me because I liked it. He wanted me to go have coffee with him tonight—that's what he said."

"Coffee. That's pretty tame."

"He just wanted to talk."

"Friendly guy."

"Mac, I really liked it—the attention. I just wanted you to know."

"Never knew cowboys were your type, Dix."

"Me either, but I stood in the kitchen wishing I could go."

"What stopped you?"

"You. I guess."

Mac brushes a semikiss across my forehead. "Sleep good, Dix." He rolls back down into his cave of quilts.

I lie perfectly still facing the ceiling with my eyes closed. I'm remembering my conversation with Porter Warren and improving it in all the places it needs improving. I'm smiling to myself in the pitch dark. I have no idea if I'm remembering things the way they actually happened.

About the time I'm sure Mac's dead to the world, he whispers, "Dix? You don't have to tell me everything, you know."

One week later on Friday morning I get a phone call. "Dixie? This is Porter Warren. Look," he says, "I owe you an apology.

I had things on my mind, I drank too much, I saw you—and I don't know. I'm calling to say I'm sorry."

"I see."

"I didn't want to see you tomorrow without clearing things up between us. I was out of line. It won't happen again."

"I see."

"Does that mean I'm forgiven?"

"I guess so."

"I'll see you after the game then. And I swear, no repeats. You don't have to dread seeing me."

I hardly dreaded it.

We lose the ninth game. HamU's first losing season in longer than anybody cares to remember. The after-game party is wakelike. I'm doing my best not to die trying.

"Dixie, come here." Frances Delmar leads me to the upstairs bathroom. "Here." She takes out a tube of what looks like flesh-colored lipstick and strokes it under my eyes. "We've got to do something about those circles," she says. "Is it your period?"

"Is it that bad?" I say.

"You look like Mac uses you for a punching bag. Wait." She digs in her purse for her compact and pats powder under my eyes too. "That's better. You should get some of this," she says.

I look in the mirror. I see a woman with white ghost skin smeared under each eye. I smile at the improvement.

"Put on some lipstick," Frances Delmar says. "And some blush. Now is not the time for the natural look, Dixie. If you'll forgive me for saying so."

I avoid Porter the best I can. He came alone. He isn't as handsome as I remember. He only smiles and nods, nothing else. He stands first in one spot, then in another, chatting like a totally civilized person. He looks like a doctor too, now that I know he is one. It's a little disappointing because generally speaking I have a low opinion of doctors. I want him to be the man I imagined he was—a smart guy dressed up like a cowboy.

I don't see Porter to speak to him until the end of the evening, when he comes in the kitchen to pay homage to the hostess. "Thanks for letting me back in the house." He smiles.

"Why do you come to these parties?" I say. "I wouldn't be here if I didn't have to, but you, you don't even like football."

"No," he says, "but I like you."

Butch and some of his assistants come through the kitchen just then with boxes of cups to be loaded into their truck. "You can go out this way, Porter," I say. "I'll walk you out."

He follows me out of the kitchen past the catering truck to the end of the driveway. The cold air feels so good I think I might be running a fever. We stand in the driveway, two awkward silhouettes. I don't care what Butch is thinking as he watches me stand silently next to a man who's not Mac. I suddenly wish we were going on a long trip someplace cool and far away.

"Dixie," Porter says. "I'm cold sober. And I still want to say something to you."

"Oh, God," I moan. "Go ahead then."

"You're a lovely woman."

I nearly cry. "Is that it?"

He laughs. "Were you expecting more?"

"No, I was expecting worse." If his words had been warm water I'd have volunteered to drown in them.

"I've got a feeling you're a woman looking for trouble." He smiles. "Could that be right?"

I wanted to say to him, *Say that again. Say I'm lovely.* But instead, I say, "I don't know what you're talking about."

"You know exactly what I'm talking about." He puts his hat on, tips the brim, and says, "Good-night, Dixie."

I hurry into the house. The last of the guests won't be leaving for hours, but I whisper to Mac, "I'm going to bed now."

He nods. I feel his eyes on me as I go upstairs to bed.

SARAH

We wake up on Sunday morning and there's this crop of FOR SALE signs planted like rows of corn in our yard. I see them first. Daddy went out the back way when it was still dark and missed seeing them—thank God. "Mom!" I yell. "Look what they did."

While Buddy and Mom and I yank the signs up and put them in the garage a reporter from the *Birmingham News* snaps our picture, and it's in the paper the following day—the three of us dressed for church, our arms full of real estate signs. I have my head turned away, so you can't really see my face. Buddy counted thirty-two signs in all. Each sign Mom yanked from the yard she slammed to the ground, one on top of the other, making a clanging sandwich of signs, like a metal bonfire waiting for a match. It's a wonder she didn't wake up the whole neighborhood.

"Sorry about this," the photographer said as he snapped away. I thought Mom might take one of those signs and knock him in the head with it. I thought if she didn't, I might. He was such a punk. It's the first picture of Mom I've ever seen where she isn't smiling. Mom *always* smiles. I had on a pair of Mom's heels and she never even noticed. I'm not allowed to wear heels yet. Like shoes are a big deal or something.

"Don't mention the signs," Mom said to Buddy and me on our way to Sunday school. "No need to upset your grandparents. Just pretend nothing happened. Act like nothing's wrong."

Mom is just like Grandmother Rose. They're so twisted.

"Let me speak to that pussy Gibbs." That's what the man says to me when I answer the phone. I've heard worse. I hear worse than that at school all day long. The calls that get to me are when they say stuff like, "I hope you have fire insurance," and then hang up. Junk like that.

Once a guy said someone had put a homemade bomb under the hood of our car. Mom called Hemp to come look and see. "Just a jackass prank," he said. But just the same he looked pretty nervous when he started up the car just to ease Mom's mind.

We've had our phone number changed but that doesn't help. Mom wants to trace the calls, but Dad said, "Just ignore it."

Good luck, I think. Telling Mom not to worry is about like telling the pope not to pray.

Now Mom keeps the phone off the hook all night and most of the day. She's getting sort of weird, if you ask me. Last Tuesday night when she walked into the PTA meeting at school the room went silent. I pretended not to notice, but I noticed.

Looking at Mom sitting alone like that—no one coming over to sit with her, not even my friend's parents—I could have killed everybody in the room. I mean it.

D I X I E

       Senator Billy Harrington and his wife, Arvell, come to the party at our house after our last game. We've just beat Chattanooga— a small, humiliating win. The four of us stand in the kitchen for a few minutes of private conversation. "Mac," Senator Harrington says, "I got a player for you."

       "Who's that?" Mac lights a cigarette.

       "My sister's boy, Banks Cochran. He's a natural athlete."

       "Get him to send me some film. I'll take a look."

       "Well, technically he doesn't have any film."

       "He didn't get along with the high school coach," Arvell says. "The coach was completely unreasonable."

       "What makes him think he can play for us?" Mac taps ashes into an ashtray on the counter.

       "Like I told you, the kid is a natural athlete."

       "It's unlikely a kid who's never played high school ball is going to make it as a college player," Mac says. "But there's nothing to stop him from walking on—if he wants to try."

       "He wants a scholarship," the senator says. "I'd consider it a personal favor."

       "Banks is very special," Arvell says.

       "I'm sure he is," Mac says.

       "How many kids you got on the team whose uncle is a senator? Let's face it, you can use all the help you can get. I don't have to tell you there's a lot of rumbling around the state."

"Goes with the job." Mac smiles.

"I'd like to see my nephew out there," the senator says.

Just as I'm leaving to make rounds in the other room, Arvell touches my arm. "Dixie, sweetie," she says. Her smile is so genuine. "Try to talk to Mac, will you? Banks is the sweetest boy. You'd just love him."

"I'm sure I would," I say.

The death knell sounds at the end of our 3 and 7 season. It's like a clock striking midnight twenty-four hours a day. Mac has two more years on his contract, but the papers are full of talk of alumni buying him out—a lively crusade led by prosperous ex-players, some of whom had played with him in the sixties, who've gone on to become big-time car dealers and barbecue-restaurant owners. The six o'clock news is unbearable. We all live life like there are nooses around our necks and any sudden move might leave us hanging.

One afternoon just as I'm about to pick up the children from school, CeCe screeches to a halt in front of the house. I look out just in time to see her leap from the car and run up the walkway. I open the door before she rings the bell, my stomach churning as if I know she's bringing me news of a tragic death.

"Oh, Dixie." She hugs me. "I'm so sorry. It makes me so mad and I just want you to know it's not true—it's just stupid talk, and I'm just furious about it."

"What?" I stand like a board while she hugs me.

"On the radio? I guess you weren't listening, thank God. It doesn't matter. I just couldn't bear to think of you sitting here listening to the call-in show—those idiots."

"Oh," I say, hoping she will *not* tell me more.

"Sly is behind Mac all the way, Dixie. We're both standing by you and Mac until the bitter end no matter how much pressure they put on Sly to fire Mac. I just want you to know that."

"Thank you," I say.

"How are the kids?"

"Fine," I lie. What should I say? That every personal essay Sarah has written since Mac was named head coach is about the football team, the score of the last game and whether or not her father is happy or sad? That she spends hours in her room writing inspirational letters to Mac? *Dear Daddy, Don't be sad. You're a great coach. Your team just needs a little practice. It's not your fault. I love you, Sarah.* She leaves these letters on Mac's pillow at night and he reads them in silence and saves them in his underwear drawer. Sarah's standard sentence before entering any room is, "Is Dad in a good mood?"

Recruiting becomes a matter of life and death. Mac goes at it with divine inspiration—and a touch of terror too. As Cleet likes to say, "The best coach doesn't necessarily win the game. The coach with the best players wins the game." I desperately want Mac to be the coach with the best players. I send a five-hundred-dollar check to Unity Prayer asking them to pray for recruiting every day until the signing date.

I don't see how a player can resist Mac. I personally would love to have been recruited by Mac Gibbs. He calls prospective players on the phone, writes letters to them, goes to see them, spends time visiting with their parents, invites them to get away for exciting weekends full of dinners and parties and lots of one-on-one personal time. He has heartfelt conversations with his recruits, asks them about their hopes and dreams, listens to even the smallest things they say—and understands. And he never forgets a word of it. It's because, in a way, he loves them. And needs them too. They're real to him in all the ways I wish the children and I were.

During the season Sarah and Buddy and I go to watch afternoon practices, so we have some sense of having seen Mac, of being able to pick him out in a crowd. We see him leaning out of the coaching tower watching over practice in his dark glasses. If Sarah can get his attention he waves at her. "I wish Dad would let me go up in that tower," she says.

"Maybe someday," I say.

She glares at me. "Mom, you know *someday* means never!"

Now that the season's over Mac stays on the road and we only see him on Sunday nights at suppers at the Bear Cave, where the coaches' families gather to help convince recruits that HamU is a great place to play football. It's called family night, sort of like Wednesday nights at the Baptist church.

It started early in the afternoon—the pain—like a needle sticking my heart, making it jump like crazy for a minute. I'd freeze, submit to voluntary paralysis until it passed. Now the pain's less sharp, and instead it feels like my heart's locked closed and won't open enough to let the blood pass through. It feels like if I lie down, my heart will stop altogether.

At the recruiting dinner Mac sees me put my hand on my chest and asks, "What's wrong?"

"My heart," I say, "hurts."

"Ask Vet to give you something for heartburn."

But the pain subsides and I forget about it. Then on the ride home it starts again. "What's wrong, Mom?" Sarah asks. "You look funny."

"Nothing," I say. "Just a twinge."

As the evening wears on, my heart becomes more alarming. It's beating so weakly I think it'll stop altogether, especially if I lie down. So I don't. I walk. Sometimes it gets a catch in it, like a door's trying to slam shut but there's a sharp object blocking it. This has never happened before. I chew some of Mac's Rolaids. He eats them like candy, buys them by the carton. I take a couple of aspirin. I drink a glass of red wine.

When Mac gets home I'm waiting. "I don't know what's wrong with me," I say. "My heart's sore. It won't stop hurting."

"Go to sleep," he says. "You'll feel better in the morning."

An hour later he's asleep, just like the children, and I'm walking around the house, afraid to lie down, afraid to even sit down. I wake Mac up. "Maybe I should go to the emergency room."

"Call them," he says. "See what they say." He rolls over and falls back to sleep.

I call the emergency room and speak with the nurse. "I know this is crazy," I say, "but my heart's doing strange things."

"We can't diagnose you over the phone," she says after I try to describe my symptoms. "You'll need to come in."

It is two o'clock in the morning now. I wake Mac a second time. "They said I should come to the emergency room."

He's half-asleep. "You don't need me to go, do you?"

What am I supposed to say? *No, Mac, I don't need you for anything—ever?* "I can go myself," I say. "You sleep." I feel like I've broken out in involuntary song, a rousing chorus of "I am woman, hear me roar!" Only I'm scared.

"Can I help you?" the nurse says.

"I called," I say. "It's my heart."

Next thing I know I'm in a thin hospital gown sitting in a chair in a curtained cubicle. The nurse asks me to lie down, but I'm afraid. "The doctor will see you in a minute," she says.

By the time he gets to me I'm clutching my heart like it might fall out of my chest. "I'm Dr. Warren," he says. "Here, let me help you." When I look up at him I want to run from the room. *Not Porter! Please, God.* I wonder if maybe I'm exaggerating the pain and the whole stupid thing. But while I'm considering saying, *Excuse me, there's been a terrible mistake,* my heart sputters like a motor choking, and it scares me. "My heart," I gasp.

"Dixie?" He glances at my chart to make sure I'm who I seem to be. "You're going to be okay," he says. "Here." He helps me sit up on the examining table. "Tell me what you're feeling."

I look at his face. I want to hate him. He doesn't smile. I think for a moment about how awful I must look. "It's my heart," I say. "It feels like it's going to stop."

"I see." He puts his stethoscope to his ears. "Let me listen." He places the stethoscope against my back. "Sorry," he says. "It's cold." I can't bear to take my hand from my heart.

"Now the front," he says, taking my hand in his. "Do you mind if

I move this?" He's touching the flap on my gown. I look away. I feel the stethoscope land on my heart. He listens for a long time. I try to relax. Of all the people on earth.

"You've got a little murmur," he says. "Has anyone ever told you that before?"

"No."

"Never had an episode like this before?"

"Never."

"Are you feeling especially anxious about anything?"

Is he crazy? "No more than usual," I say.

"Do you think you can lie down now?"

"Maybe. I'll try."

"I want to give you something to help you relax and then listen to your heart when you're in a resting state. I'll speak to Mac," he says. "Tell him you're going to be here awhile. Is he in the waiting room?"

"No."

"Who drove you here?"

"Nobody."

"You drove yourself?"

"Yes."

"Where's Mac?"

"At home."

"Does he know you're here?"

"Yes."

"Why didn't he come with you?"

I'm not going to let the tears come. I don't want this man to feel sorry for me because my husband's at home asleep while I'm busy having a heart attack. "He couldn't," I say. "Somebody had to stay with the kids. It's okay. Really."

"Do you want me to call him to say you'll be here awhile?"

"That's not necessary."

"All right then," he says. "The nurse will be right back with something to help you relax. We'll see if we can't have you feeling better."

He squeezes my hand and I squeeze back. Then he leaves. I close my eyes and wait.

When I wake up again, it's five o'clock in the morning. My heart's tender, but not as bruised and aching. Porter's sitting in a chair in the cubicle writing on my chart. "Hello," he says. "How do you feel?"

"Better."

"I'd like to schedule you for some tests," he says. "I don't think there's anything serious, but we want to be sure."

"I need to get home," I say. "It's almost morning."

"I want you to call my office and arrange for the tests. The office opens at nine." He looks like he's the principal and I'm tardy or something.

"Okay," I say.

"You'll need somebody to drive you home. Can you call Mac?"

"I can drive myself."

The way he looks at me then, I feel like an unsolved mystery and Porter's a detective tracking down the prime suspect. "Get dressed," he says. "I get off in thirty minutes and I'll drive you home myself."

"It's not necessary."

"Just get dressed," he says. "I'll be back."

It's full-fledged morning when we walk to the parking lot. The sun seems cruel. "This is it," he says, pointing to his truck.

"The vehicular choice of a country gentleman doctor," I say.

"I don't know about the gentleman part," he says.

We ride in silence for a while. I've never felt uglier. I feel foolish and ridiculous too, like I've faked an illness, even though it didn't feel fake. All the talk that goes on between coaches and players sort of works on the minds of coaches' wives and children: *If you can't play hurt, don't get hurt. Get up. That didn't hurt. You big baby. No pain, no gain. He's faking. He's a sissy. He's a wimp. He's a girl. He's a pussy.*

"So, do you think this was all in my head?" I ask.

"No"—Porter's twisting the radio dial—"I don't. Your symptoms are not uncommon. It can be pretty frightening."

"I'll say."

"We'll run some tests just to give you peace of mind. Call my office. Don't forget."

When he pulls up in the driveway none of the lights are on in the house. "I'm sorry to put you to this trouble," I say.

"No trouble."

"Listen," I say. "I don't know what you're thinking, but I want you to know I had no idea you'd be working at the hospital when I came in last night. If I'd known—"

"You wouldn't have come?"

"I just want to make sure you don't think—you don't misunderstand, you know."

"That I don't get the idea that you wanted to see me again, so you faked a heart attack." He smiles.

"Right."

"Because you didn't."

"Right."

"Want to see me or fake the heart attack?"

"Neither."

"Fair enough."

"And one more thing," I say. "This is confidential, right? It's not going to be in the newspaper tomorrow, is it?"

"I won't tell if you won't," he says, "but I think Mac should know."

"Of course," I say. "I tell Mac everything." I put my hand out to shake his, even though I know I look like a fool.

I walk into the house expecting to see some signs of life, but there are none. I wake up the kids. They have just enough time to get themselves together so I can drive them to school. "Hurry," I tell them. "We overslept."

I look in the bedroom. Mac's already left for work.

It isn't until the kids and I get outside in the driveway that I remember my car is at the hospital in a no-parking zone.

SARAH

The school nurse called Mom to come pick me up. When she gets there it makes me start crying all over again. I hate that stupid nurse. I hate Mr. Hardy. I hate this whole school. Now Mom's all freaked out. When she sees me she gets tears in her eyes right off the bat, before anybody even tells her what's going on. That's how Mom is.

"Mr. Hardy's a fine teacher," the nurse tells Mom. "He didn't mean any harm, Mrs. Gibbs. He told some jokes," the nurse says. "He had no idea it would upset Sarah like this."

"Mac Gibbs jokes," I say. "Gabriel told me."

"Sarah confronted Mr. Hardy in the lunchroom," the nurse explains. "She was very disrespectful, I'm afraid."

"Bullshit," I say.

Mom looks at me that way she does. If I'm not careful she'll be crying her head off too. She asks me what happened like she really can't stand to know. But I tell her anyway.

"I just asked Mr. Hardy when he last coached a game," I say. "He's a total creep, Mom. He said he understands how Dad feels because last year he coached seventh-grade girl's volleyball! He said he knows how it is to be a coach. So I called him a total loser, Mom, just to see how he liked it, and he sent me to the principal for being rude. The principal said I had to apologize to Mr. Hardy and I just started to cry. This is such a stupid school. Now I can't go back to my classes because everybody will know I've been crying. I have to go home."

"You'll have to sign her out in the office," the nurse says. "I'm sure Mr. Hardy didn't realize how sensitive Sarah is."

Mom ignores the nurse. She puts her arm around me and we walk out of the building. Sometimes I love Mom. Like now. I swear she's nice to everybody—even that nurse today who needed somebody to knock her block off. Mom wouldn't hurt a fly. She's not mad either. She just says, "Sarah Gibbs, I love you. I wouldn't trade you for any other daughter in this world."

That got me, you know.

More than one car passes us with an AX MAC or a GOOD-BYE, GIBBS sticker on the bumper. We notice them.

"Mom, are they going to fire Dad?" I ask.

"I think they're going to try, sweetheart," she says.

DIXIE

When Millie died, Thurmond called to tell us—Mac on one phone, me on the other. "Mac"—Thurmond's voice breaks—"don't bother with trying to come home for your mother's funeral, Son, you hear? I know you're in the middle of a tough recruiting season. You've got enough pressure on you right now. There's nothing you can do here. Bobby's already on his way over."

"Thurmond, I think Mac can take time out from recruiting to bury his own mother," I interrupt. "Can't you, Mac?"

Mac is silent.

Sarah's picked up the phone in her room. She sobs, "Granddaddy, don't be crazy. Daddy is *definitely* going to Granny's funeral. Aren't you, Daddy?"

Millie had been dying since I first met her. She'd had more ailments than I could keep track of. Mac claimed she'd been dying his whole life, as long as he could remember. He'd somehow quit believing her death would really ever happen.

"She's in and out of the hospital like other women are in and out of the grocery store," Mac said once. He stopped rushing to her bedside just because she checked in to the hospital. He teased her instead. "I know you just check in there so people will wait on you hand and foot. You're just on a little vacation. You don't fool me." Sometimes she laughed when he said this. Sometimes she cried.

• • •

Mac's late for Millie's funeral. I begin to think he's been killed in an automobile accident or stricken deathly ill himself. "Where's Mac?" people ask all morning. He arrives just as the family's being seated in the church. Wearing his dark glasses, he shakes Bobby's and Terry's hands, shakes hands with Marvin, who's flown in from New York, shakes Thurmond's hand like he's being introduced to him for the first time in his life, then follows the children and me to our seats.

Sarah and Buddy have studied their grandmother long and hard as she lay waxed into a sleeping position in her coffin. They've cried and touched her and whispered their good-byes. So have I. It seems that in death she can know what I'm thinking and everything I've ever thought—and at last understand enough to forgive me.

Gibbs men don't cry. But on this day, watching their mother lie still in her coffin with too much rouge on her face, like a painted doll—eyes closed, lips stitched closed—all four brothers break apart. Thurmond does too. They'd nearly survived this funeral service designed to test a man within an inch of his own life, but at the very end—when the organist plays "Amazing Grace," Millie's favorite song, as Bobby requested—like dominoes in a line, the sons fall forward in their seats and weep.

Mac cries so hard his crying has sound to it, like a gasping. It terrifies Sarah. Buddy peers around the edges of me to watch this thing happen. Mac shakes the pew crying. Sarah and I circle him with our arms and try to hold on to him, although we're crying nearly as much as he is. He squeezes our hands so hard he crushes our fingers. The pain is excellent. Even then I believe Mac's crying about more than his mother's death—he's crying about the other smaller deaths in his life too, including the one happening between us, which we don't know how to stop.

Mac drives straight from the graveside back to the university. This upsets me. I want him to stay longer like his brothers. "They have jobs too," I say and then hate myself instantly.

Mac drives away as fast as he can. I stand in the road at the cemetery with the children beside me and watch his exit until he's reduced to a swirling cloud of red dust.

I'm mad, in part, because I think Mac isn't doing his fair share. He's not taking any responsibility, leaving everything to Bobby to decide. "Mac, you can't just run away from this," I say to him before he drives off. It's not at all what I'd wanted to say. I know better than to speak the truth like that.

That night when I try to call Mac at home there's no answer. When I call his office the phone rings off the hook. "Did you try his private number?" Bobby asks.

"What?"

"His private number that rings directly into his office. Dixie, don't tell me you don't know?"

I stare at Bobby like he's a stranger. But *I* am the stranger.

"Here"—he reaches into his billfold and pulls out a tattered card with a phone number scrawled in ink—"try this." I take the card and look at the number for the longest time as though it's written in a language I can't translate. *Mac has a private number. Who's it for?* "Just call Norma, Dix," Mac always says when I complain that it's impossible to reach him. "She always puts you through, doesn't she?"

"You want me to dial it for you?" Bobby says. He takes the card from my hand and dials. In a minute he hands me the phone. "He's not there, but you can leave him a message."

I listen to Mac's voice. "I'll get back to you," it says. Bobby stands watching me, clearly distressed to have accidentally betrayed Mac this way.

I remember once, more than a year earlier, when Mac and his brothers had been called to Millie's deathbed—a false alarm—Mac had come out of her room as if he were the dying one. On our ride home he was closed tight, nailed shut. "It must be awful to watch your mother dying," I said.

"Everybody has to die sometime."

"I know everybody dies. But it must feel terrible for *you* to watch your mother die."

"She lived a good life."

"I know she lived a good life," I said. "I'm not talking about everybody, or even about Millie. I'm talking about *you*, Mac. Your feelings."

"What about them?" he said.

"I'm asking you how you feel."

He seemed to think about it. "I don't know," he said. "You tell me. You're the one with all the answers."

We didn't speak a word the rest of the way home. He was so dead wrong. I didn't have any answers.

The children and I stay with Thurmond three days after the funeral. He seems lost in his own house. He suffers sudden episodes of weeping on and off throughout the day. He takes long walks around the perimeter of the yard in his bedroom slippers, taking out his pocketknife to cut dead growth off plants trying to flower. Buddy trails behind him silently.

What is Millie thinking about all of this? I find myself wandering around her house talking to her. I'm certain that she hears me—more certain, in fact, than I am that Mac, her living son, hears me when I speak. I tell Millie everything—it just spills out. I imagine her floating just above our heads, wings having burst free from her curved spine, fluttering with excitement, glad to finally be the soul focus of some occasion.

Millie said once, "If I'm sick my boys come to see me at the hospital, and if I have something to say then, they listen."

Will I have to get so sick I almost die before Mac listens to me? Is this the way Millie taught him it works? Rose has never been sick a day in her life. Maybe that's why Daddy thinks her heart is as cold as ice—because he can't break it, the way men are supposed to.

It's late enough that I have my nightgown on. I've only been home from Thurmond's house a week and have seen Mac for no more than a few seconds. When the doorbell rings, I'm afraid to answer it. I tiptoe downstairs and look out the curtains. There stands Ed Lyman, president of HamU, with Sly Martin beside him. Have they come to tell me Mac's been killed by a stray bullet? Have they come to tell me winning's everything?

I invite them inside. They seem embarrassed, as if I'm standing here naked. "Is Mac home?" they say.

"He's still at the office."

"Could you call him, tell him we'd like to talk to him a minute—privately, without stirring up the press."

"Sure," I say. "Have a seat." I nod toward the living room. I go upstairs, dial the private number that Bobby'd given me.

"Gibbs," Mac says into the phone.

"Ed and Sly are sitting in the living room waiting for you," I say. "They look awful."

I offer them drinks, which they accept gratefully. I make them extra strong. Soon, thank God, Mac walks in and shakes their hands. "It's okay, Dixie," Mac says. "You can go on to bed." I turn to go. "Let's talk in the study," Mac says.

Hours later I hear the car doors slam and the engine start. I hear Mac pick up the phone and make call after call. I know he's calling for help. I can't hear what he's saying. I lie in bed as if getting up will throw the world off its axis. It's morning when Mac finally comes upstairs. "Tell me," I say.

"They want me to resign."

"What did you say?"

"I told them it'll be a cold day in hell when I resign."

"I hate you for letting this happen," I say. He stares at me like insanity's the end zone and I've just dodged my way there. "This is my life too, damnit, Mac." I pick up a pillow off the bed and sling it at him hard. It lands on the floor at his feet, an ineffective gesture in every way. "If you can't win, then I *want* you to resign, do you hear me! Just quit!" I'm shouting at him. "This is killing us all, Mac."

He stares at me for a minute like he doesn't know me, like all this time he thought I was the happiest woman in the world. The way he looks silences me.

"*They* want to win. *You* want to win. Okay, then, damnit, we'll win." He looks like you could shoot a bullet at his heart and it would bounce off. "See, the mistake I made, Dixie, was believing this is a game played by a bunch of kids—a *game*. But I see it's just a business. We're not talking win-loss record—we're talking profit line. I've been slow, but I got it figured out now."

Mac looks right through me. "If they'd give me time, I could build a winning team the right way. But if they won't give me time, then I have to build a winning team some other way. And the truth is they don't care how I do it as long as I do it fast—and don't get caught." He picks up his jacket and puts it on.

"Mac, where are you going?"

"To the office," he says. "Where the hell else?"

SARAH

When Jett shows up at the house Mom isn't expecting him. Nobody is. The minute Mom sees him she begins to cry right in front of us. "Mom?" Buddy pats her arm. "Why is she crying, Jett?" Of course, we know. Nobody tells us things, but we know.

"Crying's good for a person," Jett says. "Cleans out your insides. Don't y'all know that?"

Yolanda shows up carrying her briefcase. We're calmed down by then. "Hi, Dixie," she says. "Mac said to meet him here."

"He's in the study," Mom says.

Yolanda gives me the creeps.

Mom makes coffee and I take it to them. Daddy and Yolanda stop talking when I come in. "Thanks, girl," Daddy says. I leave without saying anything. Daddy closes the door behind me.

An hour later Daddy comes out of the study and tells me to find Mom for him. She's trying to work on her column for the *Baptist Bugle*. It's about how we benefit from the hard times in our lives. She read it to Buddy and me. It's all lies. I like the stories she makes up for her writing class at HamU better. She writes some wild stuff. "Daddy wants you," I say. Then I follow her to the study.

"Dix, do me a favor," Daddy says. "Call Columbus. Tell him I need to see him. Now."

I listen to Mom make the call. She sounds like she's inviting him to supper or something the way she says it. "Hey, Columbus. Do you think you could come over?" He's at the door fifteen minutes later. "In there." Mom points to the study.

The next morning we haven't even dressed for school when Jett and Columbus ring the doorbell. Yolanda comes minutes later.

Buddy and I are eating Pop-Tarts when Catfish Bomar gets there. "Hey, darling," he says when Mom opens the door. He kisses her cheek. "Where's my boy?" he says. Mom points down the hall. "Don't look so worried," he says. "This is when the fun starts. This is the best part, honey."

Mom drives us to school in her bathrobe. I hate that.

GIBBS UNDER FIRE, the *Birmingham Post-Herald* says today. COACH PRESSURED TO RESIGN. I find the articles under Mom's bed. She says she's going to make a scrapbook for Daddy—but she's not. Now with Granny dead, I know she never will. She just doesn't want Buddy and me to see them. Like maybe we don't know they're under her bed. She must think we're stupid.

Jett stays and eats supper with us. Afterwards Mom hurries Buddy and me off to bed so she can have Jett to herself. Daddy's gone to his office. They think I'm upstairs, but I'm not. I come down the back way, through the kitchen.

"What's going on?" Mom says to Jett.

"Shouldn't you ask Mac?" he says.

Mom laughs this fake laugh. It's like Mom's giving up when Daddy needs her most. She's so totally selfish it makes me sick.

MARY VIRGINIA

Columbus calls me to say he's gotten Michael's ticket to L.A. "Tell Michael we're set."

The boy's going to Jett Brown's house out there in Hollywood. I told Columbus to get me a ticket too. I'm the boy's mama, aren't I? But Columbus says it'll work against Michael, having his mama trail him around. I don't want nothing going against Michael. He's got the world in front of him.

Michael is the top college prospect in the state of Alabama. College coaches from across the country been calling him and coming to see him. Now, not every coach offers something extra, some coaches just play it straight ahead—you know. But they don't interest me like the ones who see we got needs and try to meet those needs. I don't see why that's so wrong.

I'm poor, but I'm not a fool.

I'll tell you the truth, I been real disappointed in Coach Gibbs over at HamU. I know he wants Michael bad. But as good as he knows us, as much as he knows our situation, our hard times, he has not offered in any way to help us out. I guess he just thinks I'll hand Michael over to him for nothing. I guess he thinks that he don't need to offer us nothing extra since he's been knowing us. But I don't know who told him that.

Mama's scared me and Michael are going to get mixed up in something that'll backfire. You know, like we better not be cutting any deals with these schools. But I look at it different.

I think Columbus, he conveyed to Coach Gibbs just what the situation is, because suddenly Coach Gibbs has taken a real interest in what it is we need.

Tell the truth, I wadn't inclined to let him make up for the way he'd been so cut-and-dry, you know. I didn't ever know Coach Gibbs could be so insensitive, just talking about rules and regulations all the time. I hadn't ever noticed any rules and regulations putting food on the table or buying us some shoes and school clothes. Never mind getting us out this fall-down house. But Coach Gibbs's brother Mr. Bobby Gibbs is coming all the way out here to see me. He's with Jim Walter Homes. Says he just wants to show me what sort of houses they can build. "We're in the business of making dreams come true," Mr. Bobby Gibbs said.

"Well, that's nice," I said, "because I definitely got some dreams."

ROMALEE

When I show Dixie the notes I found she doesn't know what to say. They aren't notes to Walker. They're notes to Cleet that Norma, the secretary, had tacked on his office door. I just happened to see them. So I read them, then I took them down and put them in my pocket. I did this on several occasions when I went to check on Walker. Pretty soon I had a pocketful.

One says, "Cleet, Donna can meet you in New Orleans—Royal Sonesta." Another one says, "Donna needs to talk with you ASAP." Another one says, "Donna called to thank you for the roses."

"Who's Donna?" Dixie asks when she reads the notes.

"I don't know. Walker claims he never heard of her. Norma says she's a guidance counselor. Like that explains anything."

"So you just took the notes off Cleet's door?"

"Yes. I didn't want Frances Delmar to find them. My God, Cleet's mother could find them the way they were displayed for the world to see."

"It's probably nothing," Dixie says.

"I knew you'd say that," I say. "You're the queen of denial, Dixie. You really are."

"So what are you going to do?" Dixie asks. "Tell Frances Delmar? I wouldn't if I were you. It's none of your business really. She might tell you so."

"If Donna was leaving notes for Walker I'd want Frances Delmar to tell me."

"If you want my advice," Dixie says, "don't."

Like this advice should surprise me. Dixie "Don't" Gibbs. But the point is not whether or not this will hurt Frances Delmar's feelings. The point is that we can't let the Donnas of this world get away with this kind of thing. It might be Cleet now, but who will it be next?

DIXIE

Two days after Romalee shows me the notes, Frances Delmar calls. "Dixie," she says, "I want you to do me a favor."

"Oh no," I say.

"Romalee's heart's set on me finding out Cleet's some kind of monster," Frances Delmar says. "I want to prove to her she's wrong. I want to find out for sure."

Frances Delmar comes by to pick me up around seven o'clock. The coaching office is pretty well deserted by then. All the coaches are out of town, recruiting. The secretaries have gone home. Maybe there're a few graduate assistants making clandestine phone calls on the WATS line. Frances Delmar has the key to Cleet's office, so off we go, in search of the truth.

"I feel like a rat," I say. "This is so low, spying on Cleet like this."

"I can't get it off my mind," Frances Delmar says. "I want to stop thinking about it and wondering."

"Why don't you just ask him?"

"Not yet."

We pass the janitor smoking a cigarette in the entryway. "Act natural," Frances Delmar says to me. The football complex is dark so we turn on lights as we make our way toward Cleet's office at the end of a maze of halls. Thank God there's no note from Donna hanging on his door. "See," I say, "nothing."

Frances Delmar unlocks Cleet's office and we go in. I don't know why I'm so nervous. It's a coach's office just like all coaches' offices.

There're pictures of all three kids—two daughters in braces and a son with a cowlick. There's even a picture of Frances Delmar, from when she had her TV show in Mississippi. "I was about fifteen pounds thinner then," she says when she sees me looking at it, "and at least a hundred years younger." There's a plant that needs water and reels of tape and lots of paper in sloppy stacks. There's an ashtray with ashes in it. There're team pictures on the wall. Awards. Plaques. The file cabinet is closed. The drawers are closed. The blinds are closed. "What do you think you're going to find?" I say.

"Nothing. I hope." She pulls out the top drawer of his desk. She picks up a checkbook and looks at it. "What's this?" she says to herself more than to me. "Look."

"It looks like he has a bank account, that's all."

"That's not our bank," Frances Delmar says. "We have a joint account and it's not at this bank."

"So he has an account of his own too," I say. "Lots of people do."

"Do you?" she says.

"No."

"Does Mac?"

"I don't think so."

"Then why does Cleet need one? I'm going to keep this." She puts the checkbook in her coat pocket.

Then she moves a few papers from one side of the desk drawer to the other and there—not even hidden from sight—is a stack of photos. She picks them up. *Let them be shots of the family at Thanksgiving gathered around the turkey with hands folded in prayer,* I think. But I can see I'm wrong. The color drains from Frances Delmar's face. She goes as pale as the backs of the photos with the word *Kodak* printed on them. "What is it?" I say.

"Point Clear. Pictures from the coaches' trip to Point Clear, I guess. Here's Mac."

"Let me see," I say.

She hands me each photo after she studies it herself. Cleet with his arm around a woman wearing a golf shirt and holding a drink in her hand. Cleet and this woman sitting in beach chairs. This woman alone, standing in front of the balcony rail in a hotel room, the beach pounding the shore behind her. Mac and Cleet and Walker in a shot together, probably taken by this woman. This woman and Cleet, looking a little drunk but pretty happy. "She's not a bit pretty," I say, sounding like my daddy.

"I can't believe it," Frances Delmar says. She hands me the last photo and sinks into Cleet's chair.

"Don't jump to conclusions," I say. "They aren't exactly naked and in bed together."

"Yes they are," Frances Delmar says. "I can look at Cleet's face and know that much."

"If this was hard evidence, if Cleet was worried about you finding these, he wouldn't keep them in his top drawer, would he? He'd hide them someplace."

"Nowhere safer than here," she says. "The football office. I never come in here. What, maybe twice a year at most? You know how they make you feel when you come up to the football office, like you're contaminating the place. Like we're back in grade school and they're acting like girls have cooties."

"Frances Delmar, listen to me. You wait and talk to Cleet. Show him these pictures. Ask him to explain. He will."

"What else has he got around here?" She begins to open his desk drawers—all of them—and rummage. "Must be love letters someplace," she says. I stand like a statue and watch her. I don't want to help her ruin her life. "What's this?" She pulls out a pair of men's boxer shorts from the bottom drawer. The words HAPPY BIRTHDAY are printed all over them in red letters. When Frances Delmar stretches the elastic of the waist, a plastic penis shoots out, and she screams. It makes me laugh. I should be crying, but I swear, the look on her face, this huge plastic penis jumping out at her like that. She looks at me with an odd smile on her face. "Can you believe this?" She stretches the waistband and each time the penis pokes out.

"Stop it," I say. "That's ridiculous."

"Cleet always has been a clotheshorse," she says. "Maybe I'll keep these too." She stuffs them into her purse.

"It's a gag gift," I say. "Somebody's idea of a joke."

"Somebody like Donna."

"You don't know that."

"Let's go. If I look any more who knows what I'll find."

I follow her out into the hall and she locks the door to Cleet's office. "Do you want to look in Mac's office," she says, "as long as we're here?"

"No," I say.

"You sure?"

"I'm sure."

"You afraid of what you'll find?"

"Of course not."

"Suit yourself."

We drive home in silence. Frances Delmar is in an odd mood. She isn't screaming and going crazy. She isn't crying.

"What are you thinking?" I say.

"I'm trying to figure out what to do next. I don't want to mess this up."

"Don't do anything drastic," I say. "Promise me. Cleet loves you, Frances Delmar. Whatever else, I know that's a fact."

Frances Delmar looks at me like *I'm* the pitiful one.

MRS. CARPENTER

When Michael signs with Birmingham University, folks go crazy. There're brokenhearted coaches everywhere carrying on like nothing I ain't ever seen. Grown men. If I told you some these coaches was crying and begging, you probably wouldn't believe me. But some these coaches are a desperate bunch.

Coach Gibbs come down to Beasley for the big party. Columbus come right by his side. Mrs. Gibbs come and bring those kids, Sarah and Buddy, too—just for old time sake, I guess. Everybody bunched into this trailer instead of Mary Virginia's house next door, which even though it's been painted blue, still ain't nice as this trailer. Coach Gibbs's brothers, Mr. Bobby and Mr. Terry, they drive down with their wives, Lisa and Janelle. I do know it's the most white people I have ever let into this trailer at one time. I had to tie up the dogs this morning. They been going crazy all day—white people everywhere.

Mary Virginia is dressed to die. She looks like a different girl from who I brought up, like maybe she been born and raised in Atlanta, been living the good life from the start. I didn't raise her to put on airs. She paid more for them shoes than she did that dress and she paid too much for *it*. Went to Montgomery and got her hair straightened too when I know how to straighten her hair. She bought Michael that suit. None my boys ever had a suit that cost that much. Looks like he can't hardly breathe wearing it. But folks keeps on saying, "Y'all look wonderful." Mary Virginia's just eating that up.

"Things are finally going right," Mary Virginia says. "I raised Michael the best I could. It wasn't a bit easy."

"You did a fine job," people say. They don't know I raised that boy as much as she did. I was mama to both of them.

"If his daddy come around now and tried to claim him—well, if he's smart he won't try it," Mary Virginia says. "Of course he's not smart, or he never would have run out on us. But now I bet he's sick knowing what a fool he is. But I been Michael's mama every minute. Not once since he was born have I stopped being his mama. Not once."

After the official signing and the swarm of photographers finish snapping their cameras, and we all done all we know to do, then we drive over to the high school for a party the booster club giving for the five Beasley boys—most especially Michael—who earned themselves football scholarships.

I sit beside Mary Virginia in a folding chair. She's telling Mrs. Gibbs she's getting a new Jim Walter home built on the land where the old house is. "Gonna pull that old thing down," she says. "A crew can take it down in a day. Look." She pulls out a paper with a picture of a house printed on it. "Ain't that a good-looking house?"

"It is," Mrs. Gibbs says. She ain't seen that picture one hundred times like I have. That's all Mary Virginia talks about, Jim Walter. Jim Walter. I stay out of her business.

"Three bedrooms, two bathrooms, a fireplace, a deluxe kitchen— everything," Mary Virginia says. "Of course, some of it has got to be done slow. But it's gon be nice. I'm having Mrs. Ebb—you know her, she's a white woman, down at the dry cleaners—make me up some drapes too. Drapes in every room."

"Mind if I join y'all?" It's Mr. Bobby Gibbs's wife, Lisa, who walks up. "My feet's killing me," she says.

"Sit down," Mrs. Gibbs says. "This is Mary Virginia, Michael's mother."

"We've met." Mary Virginia smiles.

"Yes." Lisa winks at her. "I hope I'm not interrupting."

"Mary Virginia is showing me her house plan." Mrs. Gibbs turns to Mary Virginia. "Lisa's husband, Bobby, is with Jim Walter Homes in Birmingham."

"Sure," she says. "I know."

"Which one did you pick out?" Lisa asks and Mary Virginia shows her the picture.

"Oh, this makes up nice," she says. "I've seen every house finished out, and this one is one of the prettiest ones of all. You know what looks good in here is a sunken bathtub. See, right here, off the bedroom." She points to the plan.

They talk about carpet and kitchen cabinets and wallpaper and I don't know what's wrong with me, but I can't hear it. I can't think about it.

"How you doing, Mrs. Carpenter?" Mrs. Gibbs whispers to me while they still talking. "You doing all right?"

"I'm making out," I tell her.

ROMALEE

COLUMBUS CARPENTER NAMED BLACK BEARS DEFENSIVE COORDINATOR. There's a picture of Columbus smiling in the *Birmingham Post-Herald*. The article says Walker May was promoted to assistant head coach. I read it ten times, then rip it to shreds.

When Dixie calls I'm ready for her.

"I just saw the paper," Dixie says. "Walker's the new assistant head coach, right? Mac didn't tell me he was doing that, but I'm so happy for Walker."

"Don't make me sick, Dixie. It's a subtle demotion and you know it. It's just Mac's way of shuffling him to the side with some figurehead title. It's an insult."

"I don't understand," Dixie says.

"Well, try to understand this, Dixie. Walker quit."

When Dixie pulls up in front of my house there's a crooked FOR SALE sign in my yard. When she knocks on the door I motion for her to come inside. I'm yelling at some fool on the phone. The den is chaos, things torn up, boxes waiting to be packed. I nod for Dixie to sit down. She does.

"Listen, lady," I say. "The paper says Saturday at eight and that's what it means. Yeah, well, the same to you." I slam the phone down. "These bitches. Want to get a jump on my yard sale. No way, I tell them. They pick over all the good stuff, leave the shit nobody wants for the decent customers. Can't sell shit by itself. Got to have the good stuff mixed in with the shit." I light a cigarette. "Judging by the look on your face, am I to believe you didn't know anything about this?"

"Nothing." Dixie looks afraid.

"Mac didn't tell you?"

"You're the one who tells me what's going on," Dixie says. "You're always my only hope of knowing anything."

"If there was ever anybody who didn't qualify to be anybody else's only hope, it's me." I stamp out my cigarette and light another one. I exhale smoke in her direction like it's something to hide behind. Like it can make her disappear.

"Mac took the defense away from Walker with the fancy title assistant head coach," I say. "Walker's crushed, Dixie. I don't know what Mac's thinking—Columbus as defensive coordinator. Give me a break. He's a kid." I suck my cigarette like it's hooked to an oxygen tank and I'm underwater. "Walker's gone to talk to the coach at Pittsburgh and I'm stuck in this damn house to pack up all this crap."

Dixie just sits there staring at me. "Mac thinks the world of Walker," she says.

"That was the old Mac," I say, not looking at Dixie. *What did she come over here for anyway?* I walk into the kitchen and jerk open a cabinet door. It's bare, the contents strewn over the counter. "Do you want a drink?"

"It's eleven-thirty in the morning," Dixie says.

"Can't even find the liquor in this mess." I slam the cabinet door closed, walk into the den, sling papers and sweaters off the sofa, look inside an open packing box, and pull out a half-empty bottle. "Here it is," I say.

"You know I don't drink," Dixie says. "Not this early."

"Well, maybe you should." I get two coffee cups from the kitchen, flop down on the sofa beside her, and pour us each a cup of bourbon. She takes a sip every time I do.

"I could kill Mac," Dixie says.

"Walker's a fifty-two-year-old assistant coach, Dix. He's too old to keep chasing his tail around the country after any scrap of a job he can get. Coaching is a young man's game."

"Mac says that's bullshit. You do what you love."

"Easy for him to say. Mac's a head coach. Who's going to break the news to Walker that he may never be a head coach—me?"

"You can't give up, Romalee."

"Yes, Dixie, *I* can give up. It's Walker who can't give up."

There's a heaviness to my eyes, and the lines of my mouth tug down more than they used to. I've reached that point I've watched older wives reach—which Dixie's going to reach too if she hasn't already—where I'm just tired of it all. So tired. "It wasn't supposed to happen like this," I say.

"It's not going to happen like this," Dixie says. "We won't let it. I'll talk to Mac."

"What good will that do?" I laugh. "No offense, Dixie, but since when does Mac listen to you?"

DIXIE

"Dixie, you've got to talk to Frances Delmar," Cleet says. He sounds like the biggest game of his life's just been rained out. "She says she wants a divorce. I can't talk reason to her."

"And you think I can?"

"The Donna thing was nothing, Dix. I swear. Nothing."

"The Donna thing looked like something," I say. "You had pictures that definitely looked like something."

"I was temporarily insane. That's the truth. I was."

"Somehow I don't think she'll buy that, Cleet."

"I'm not going to let this happen. I'm not going to give her a divorce. I'm moving into the Bear Cave, just temporarily, you know. Just until she cools off."

"I think she's already cooled off, Cleet. I think that's your real problem. The Donna thing just made her know how cooled off she really was, if you know what I mean." I hate to hurt his feelings, but the truth just never seems to register with him.

"Frances Delmar loves me, Dix. I don't care what she says. She'll get over this. Everybody's entitled to a mistake, right? I'm human, right? You don't throw away a seventeen-year marriage just like that. No way." His words are loaded with desperation and every one he speaks sags.

"What do you want me to do, Cleet?"

"Just talk to her for me. Just make sure she knows I love her and

I'm sorry and it'll never happen again. I swear." His voice breaks at the end of his sentence.

"I'll tell her, Cleet. Of course I will. But in the end you're going to have to do your own talking."

Frances Delmar's painting her living room dark red, a color she calls dried blood. She looks like she's been swimming laps in the paint. "Thank God you're here." She holds the roller in her hand. "It gives me an excuse to stop."

"Pretty industrious, aren't you?"

"Why not? I'm getting the sofa reupholstered too. Look at this." She hands me a fabric swatch. "What do you think?"

"I love it," I say. "But does it go with the paint?"

"It doesn't match, if that's what you mean. Matching is so small-minded, Dixie." She leads me to the kitchen, where she opens diet Cokes. "Here," she says. We sit in the half-painted living room on furniture draped in bedsheets.

"I talked to Cleet," I say.

"Really?" She sounds almost disinterested.

"He's upset," I say.

She takes a sip of her Coke and pushes her hair behind her ear. She has a scarf tied around her head but it isn't doing its job. "He's not the only one upset," she says.

"He just wants me to tell you that he's sorry. He loves you. He'll never do it again. That it was nothing. He was insane at the time."

Frances Delmar laughs. "Cleet's priceless."

"So, how are you doing? I mean, *really.*"

Frances Delmar twists a strand of hair around her finger. "I'm okay," she says. "I've cried so much I've gone dry. Look at my eyes. Don't they look awful? But it's been a couple of weeks now, and you know, I'm feeling okay. Actually, I'm getting kind of excited about being on my own, just the kids and me. I have all these ideas about how I want to live. Not just the house, but, you know, my life. A life without football. Right now I think if Donna the guidance counselor walked into this room, I'd shake her hand and say thank you."

"God, Frances Delmar. It'd kill Cleet to hear that."

"I know. But I think I mean it. It feels like I do."

"So you really want a divorce?"

"I called Jerry Chamberlin yesterday."

"Go slow," I say. "Don't hurry this, Frances Delmar."

"If I don't act fast, I might give in."

"Would that be so awful?"

"It's not that I can't forgive Cleet, Dixie. It's more like I don't really want to. I just want this Donna thing to, you know, propel me forward into my own life. Does that make sense?"

It makes sense like a bullet between the eyes. I sit there shamefully sick with envy.

ROMALEE

It doesn't rain. Dixie comes over at six in the morning. Buddy and Sarah come with her. We arrange tables of household odds and ends and football junk—jerseys, programs, cups, socks, pompoms, coaching shirts, anything that says HAM U on it. By seven my yard looks like a souvenir stand at a football game.

Dixie and I wear aprons with pockets so we can collect the money. It's Sarah's job to help people find prices on things. Buddy says he'll patrol for thieves. He puts on some headphones I'm trying to sell and walks around bobbing his head like a rooster. He's a weird kid.

First thing, a heavy man tears open a box and pulls out a football, basketball, two softballs. "Look at this," he shouts to his wife, who's shuffling through old game programs.

Dixie nearly tramples a lady studying a pair of Walker's Sansabelt coaching pants. "Don't touch those balls," she screams. The man drops the balls like they're hot. "Those are her husband's balls," Dixie explains. "They're not for sale."

"They *are* for sale," I say.

"You can't sell those, Romalee."

"I don't see why not."

"It's sacrilegious. Like selling a woman's diary. Or a child's teddy bear."

"If it bothers you so bad, Dix," I say, "just don't watch."

By noon I sit on a kitchen stool beside the ravaged tables, exhausted. It seems like hundreds of people have come and gone. Only a few browsers are left, the tables mostly cleared. I'm on my third or fourth drink, coaxing the stragglers to buy, buy, buy, offering deals of a lifetime. I'm good at this. I swear to God. "Watch this, Dixie," I say. I pick up a Black Bears sweater and put it on, at first to show a man what size it is, but then, instinctively, I grab a retired set of pom-poms and begin a series of cheerleader leaps. Buddy and Dixie laugh like crazy.

"She's drunk," Sarah says to Dixie. The child has no sense of humor. So I cheer myself over to where Sarah stands like a totem pole and put my pom-pom arms around her. "You don't know it yet, Sarah, girl," I say, "but a great spread eagle will come in handy all your life. Look what it's done for me."

Sarah rolls her eyes and pulls away from me.

"Two tits, four tits, six tits, a dollar. All for tits, stand up and holler!" I shout and hop down the driveway like the most earnest cheerleader in the world. Cheering is like riding a bicycle. You never forget how.

"I don't see how you can laugh," Sarah says to Dixie. But Dixie can't stop laughing. We both laugh until the laughter goes sour on us.

DIXIE

The season's over. Recruiting's over. Summer rolls around again at last. We live for summer.

Before the school year ended Sarah had managed to become a force to be reckoned with. The goody-good girls still don't invite her to their parties, but Gabriel has stopped calling her a loser and become her best friend. When I go to Sarah's end-of-school conference her teacher says, "Sarah's a smart girl, but she's a very aggressive child, especially for a little girl."

Thank God, I think.

Buddy hasn't missed a single day of school since after Christmas, mainly because I wouldn't let him. Lilly said, "Sometimes you got to throw a child in the pond if you want him to learn to swim."

Buddy played soccer in the spring. He didn't want to but I signed him up and made him go. He met two boys, Corey and Horton, who like to spend hours at the creek with homemade coat-hanger-and-pillowcase-nets catching minnows, frogs, and even snakes if possible. They're the sort of boys who like science better than sports, but I don't care. Corey's prize possession is a microscope and Horton has a reptile collection in his basement.

"Yes, you can go," I say. "Catch as many snakes as you can. Catch poisonous ones if you want to."

By the time summer's in full swing it's rare that Buddy wets the bed, but he still won't spend the night with Corey or Horton because of his fear of it. He also never invites them to spend the night at our house.

"My mother won't let me spend the night with people," I hear Buddy tell Corey for the hundredth time. "She won't let people spend the night with me either. Not until I'm ten."

"Bummer," Corey says.

"Yeah," Buddy says. "My dad would let me. He's cool. But my mom, she's a real pain."

MARY VIRGINIA

When I take Michael up to the university it like to kills me. It's been him and me for so long. I don't want to cast no shadow on this day by a show of crying and such. I believe if I start to cry, he'll start too. So I'm strong about it.

I get him settled into his room over at the Bear Cave. He got everything he needs—I seen to that. Then I hug his neck and say, "I'm so proud of you I don't hardly know what to do. Don't you do nothing to change my mind about that, you hear."

"Yes, ma'am," he says.

Then I get in the car where Mama's waiting and I cry the whole way home to Beasley. "Lord, you got that boy spoiled," Mama says, "the way you carry on over him."

See, Mama's got ten kids. So she got her feelings all spread out over that many. But I just got one baby—Michael. All my feelings go to him. And they always will.

DIXIE

Smokey's the starting quarterback again this season and it's like he's been waiting all his life to throw the ball to Michael Carpenter. Michael's as elusive as an idea racing across people's closed minds. He can run straight through a wall of opposing tackles like they aren't even there. Afterwards you can't explain how he did it. There's no question he has supernatural powers on the field. He gives people chills. He gives people hope too—makes the fans want to start believing again.

Michael's first season is strange because Frances Delmar and Romalee don't come to the games every week anymore. Once in a while Romalee comes just for something to do, but she makes it clear she doesn't care who wins. It's awkward. I can't watch the game next to someone neutral of heart, especially Romalee.

Even if Romalee doesn't come to the games, she comes to the parties. She's taking better care of herself with Walker gone. "When're you going to Pennsylvania?" people ask her every week.

"Not until I sell the house," she says. Then she just relaxes and enjoys herself and drinks too much.

Cleet brings Donna to the after-game party the third week of the season. I recognize her from the pictures, which Frances Delmar has turned over to Jerry Chamberlin along with the Donna notes Romalee confiscated. In real life, just as in photographs, Donna is remarkable in her ordinariness. This makes her seem interesting. She's likable in a plain sort of way. I have nothing against her, really. It isn't like she's condemned Frances Delmar to a life of agony. All she's done is like Cleet more than she should have. Maybe more than Frances Delmar does. I don't know for sure if that's something to be mad about.

"Why are you bringing that woman *here?*" Romalee asks Cleet in a disapproving tone.

"Donna wants to come," Cleet says. "Frances Delmar doesn't. It's as simple as that."

"*You're* as simple as that, Cleet," Romalee snaps.

Frances Delmar's been hired by Moseley Communications. She does a weekly TV spot called *Healthbeat.* The first one was on menopause. It depressed her, but I don't know why. She's no closer to menopause than Donna is. "At least Cleet didn't take up with a mall-haired teenager like some men do. Donna's every bit his age," I say.

"Well," Frances Delmar says, "let's award Cleet the medal of honor, why don't we?"

Now Donna's sitting next to me at the home games in the seat that used to be Frances Delmar's.

"This is so exciting, isn't it?" Donna smiles. "The thrill of competition and all."

MRS. CARPENTER

After every game me and Mary Virginia wait outside the lockers. The press has learned who we are and likes to ask us for a comment, which Mary Virginia loves to give. "Well," Mary Virginia says, "Michael can't be no one-man team, y'all. Some the rest of these boys has got to do their part too."

After the second game, that close one, them reporters asked me how did I think things was going. So I tell them, "If Coach Gibbs wouldn't try to organize these boys so much I believe we'd have better results out there. I don't know why white people got to overorganize things like they do. These boys got enough talent to be here in the first place, then they ought to just let them play by their instincts and show what they can do."

"So you think the team is being overcoached?" he says.

"I sure do," I say.

They put that in the paper too.

Michael takes after his mother and me when it comes to telling the truth. As stingy as he is with words, the ones he says get right at the point.

"How do you think you'll stand up against Terrell White, that Heisman candidate from Tulane, next week?" they ask Michael with them TV cameras in his face.

"He's fast and he's strong," Michael says. "But I'm faster and I'm stronger."

After we beat Tulane, the fans carry Michael and Smokey off the field up on their shoulders. The press stops Michael outside the lockers. "How do you feel about today's win?" they ask him.

"Fine," Michael says.

"They do anything that surprised you out there?"

"No."

"You played a great game, but so did Terrell White. You still think you're a better athlete than Terrell White?"

"I still think so. Don't you?"

The press, they love this. Michael is never rude or nothing. He speaks soft, but the more he brags, the more they like him. This is because so far he ain't predicted nothing he can't deliver.

Sometimes Coach Gibbs wants to pull out his hair when Michael talks this way. But he can't bring Michael around to his way of thinking—that the less you say, the less the other team got to work with. Michael says precious little, but it still seems like too much.

DIXIE

Inside the dressing room sportswriters mingle and TV cameras scan, but they never seem to catch the essence of it. Not like I see it from my vantage point outside the locker room, the door usually cracked just enough for me to see inside as if by design, year after year after year.

I watch the male celebration ritual that I've witnessed before. Mac talks to the team, pausing occasionally—a signal for them to explode with jubilation. Some players are still in uniform, some in degrees of undress—jockstraps, towels, buck naked. The coaches mingle among them, hugging them, slapping them so hard that some of their backs bear bright red handprints.

I watch men celebrate this way—this one moment when a full range of emotion is allowed them. They scream out nonsensical phrases, then cheer as wildly as teenage girls, jump up and down on locker-room benches, leap onto each other's backs and ride around like cowboys on bucking broncos. They hop into each other's arms and let themselves be carried like screaming babies. Sometimes they jump on each other face-to-face, one wrapping his legs around the other, and shout love phrases to each other.

I think of the slumber parties Frances Delmar and I had growing up, the slumber parties Sarah and Lydia have now, and of how important it is to scream at a slumber party—really scream, until your throat's sore. How important it is to undress in front of each other, exposing breasts as if they were secret confessions, minipads showing through your underpants. There's something powerful in the physical sameness, something even more powerful in the differences this sameness includes. The team does their own version of this, celebrating themselves, their maleness. I watch them.

Why can men love other men so freely, with such abandon and total trust? The way women want to be loved by men—but aren't.

I've witnessed men who seem brain-dead in social settings, whose dullness, whose boringness, is so consuming that they reduce themselves to less than a bump on a log. Nothing to say. No eye contact. No opinions. No presence. But I know you can take some of these same deaf-mute lumps of men and drop them onto a playing field or into a locker room and it'll be like dropping a couple of harmless Alka-Seltzers into a cup of water, the way they bubble up and come to life, so sparkling, so effervescent.

Football is art, body art. I tell myself this. It's like dancing, only the choreography is spontaneous. Maybe the nature of this male dancing is based on trying to escape *really* dancing, the way male talking sometimes seems to me to be based on trying to escape *really* talking. I rarely say so, but to me, football can be almost as beautiful as it is violent. The beauty seems able to survive the violence, to poke its head up above the ruckus and look you in the eye. That kind of beauty. There are elements of flight and fantasy and fear. There is color and contrast. There is crisis and resolution. There is the abstraction of the human spirit made concrete. All of it beyond the necessary. All the nonessential aspects of a football game can seem suddenly essential when they provide the playing field, the backdrop, for the display of what it is to be male. Football is testosterone-driven art. Football makes me rethink beauty. There are times when I think I admire the male body almost as much as I fear it.

Mac has always hated hearing me talk about football this way. "It's just a game," he says. "Don't try to make it more than it is, Dixie." As if I'm the one doing that.

Sometimes I'm startled to think how closely I've observed men, both clothed and naked. I never meant to.

Mac swears men don't look at each other's penises in the locker room. He says, "Dixie, we're naked because we're taking showers. It's purely practical. It's not some sort of beauty pageant." He acts like the very idea that a huge room full of naked men is anything other than a legitimate workplace is really sick thinking on my part. But when I ask him who has the biggest penis, he always knows. I guess somebody must tell him, since clearly he doesn't have the least bit of interest in knowing.

Now I've seen more penises than the law allows. Granted, most of them have been in the resting state, thank God. But I've learned a few things from my years on the outside looking in. For example, I know if that myth about black man's penis is true or not. Some of the wives have discussed this while we wait for coaches and players to get dressed. We've all arrived at the same conclusion.

So I'm not jealous of a penis. I'd just as soon borrow one when I need it as have one of my own. But the truth is I'm jealous of the locker-room high I've witnessed all these years, that explosion into song and tears. I'll admit this: I've wanted to push my emotional self to the limits too, like the half-naked players and coaches do after claiming a victory, large or small. I've wanted to come away with the unbreakable bond that such a team-effort, brotherly-love episode allows. I've wanted to share such a moment with Mac. It seems more desirable than a simultaneous orgasm—to be included, just once, in the most ecstatic and alive moments of his life, when he's stripped down to his essence. But I know I'll never fully experience this. A penis is required for such occasions. I learned long ago that the big *W*, so sought after and revered, does not stand for wife.

The strange thing is, when these same jubilant players and coaches exit the locker room, they do so like somber soldiers, win or lose. It seems they stay in the shower until every ounce of emotion is washed away. They surrender the joy in the locker room and return to the real world as the real men they aim to be—silent, unemotional, shaking their fathers' hands, nodding at friends. People say, "Good game." The players nod in dead seriousness and respond in deep voices, "Thank you."

Mac Gibbs, for one, has never come out of a locker room on any occasion with a smile on his face. He quickly finds me in the crowd, kisses my cheek absentmindedly, and says, "You ready?" as if I hadn't been standing out in the cold or rain or heat of day for a solid two hours, waiting.

One thing never changes though. My heart always leaps a bit when Mac comes out of the locker room looking for me. I love the looks of him. I love that all eyes are on him, trying to read his face, his eyes, trying to hear him say to me, "You ready?" I want to turn to them all, the crowd of players, parents, and fans, and say, "You can guess all you want to, but you will never know what Mac Gibbs is really thinking."

MRS. CARPENTER

Sunday's headlines say MIRACLE CARPENTER WINS IT. Even while I was waiting for him after the game I heard the press pushing their way into the locker room calling, "Hey, Miracle, can we have a couple of minutes, man?" So it's done, Michael's name changed to *Miracle*. Like he's a racehorse or something.

I don't like it.

DIXIE

I'm running late, trying to get packed to leave with Mac for the SMU game. Porter calls to say he's traveling with the team to Dallas. "I'd like to take you out to dinner Friday night," he says. "What do you think?"

Since then I've been excited about the trip. For the first time in a while I think about what I'll wear. All my clothes seem wrong. I settle on basic black. Rose always says, "When in doubt, wear black." I'm in doubt and it's thrilling.

"Porter Warren invited me to dinner tonight," I tell Mac as he unlocks the door to our hotel suite.

"That's good," he says. His mind is already on tomorrow's game, on the steps that'll have to be taken between now and then. Some coaches put on their game faces. Mac puts on his game head. His game heart. His game soul. When you live with a man who never listens to anything you ever say, it becomes really easy to always tell him the truth. "I think I'm going to wear my black dress," I say. "You know, the one you used to like."

"Good," he says.

In the five years since Mac has been head coach I've traveled to every away game with the team. It's not unusual for me to be the only woman on a team bus or a chartered plane or the floor of a hotel. I use the time wisely. I read books. Mac's a silent traveler, although on the way home after a win he might hold my hand. I don't try as hard for conversation as I used to. I know Mac's a man who's pretty much talked out. Maybe women have biological clocks where their ovaries stop producing eggs. But men had language clocks where their mouths stop producing words. We're both right at the edge of our time running out.

HamU takes the other coaches' wives to one away game a year, plus the bowl game at the end of the year. Mac tries to be sure the wives go to the best place—not necessarily to the best game. I nagged him into thinking this way. But the wives appreciate it. The yearly wives' trip is fun because I have good company, people to eat breakfast with, shop with, and sit with at the game. The other away trips I'm left to my own devices. There's CeCe, of course, but she has her own agenda. She acts like a woman running for office. There are dinner invitations from boosters and players' parents, but I've stopped liking to go out with them because too often they have a purpose in inviting me, an angle they want to pursue, a message they want me to deliver to Mac—more playing time for their sons, a switch in position, a move to first string, a second chance, something.

I prefer to stay in our hotel suite, alone, with a good book, and order up room service. Besides, I love hotel rooms. They make me feel sexy even when I'm completely alone. They fool me into thinking I'm a real traveler, a person going somewhere, seeing the world.

Porter knocks on the door to our room at seven o'clock. He looks very clean. We ride the elevator down and walk through the lobby like any two people who have a perfect right to go to dinner together. We take a cab across town to a restaurant where Porter's made reservations. For the first Friday night in ages I forget there's a game tomorrow. "How are you holding up?" he asks me.

"Fine," I say. "How about you?"

"A piece of cake." He smiles.

We eat good food, drink good wine, and talk with high energy and abandon—that's how I get drunk. It isn't the wine. It's the good talk. We do another really amazing thing too. We laugh. God, I love a funny man.

Halfway through dinner my knee bumps against Porter's under the table. "Excuse me," I say. But neither of us moves our knees. They bump together all evening.

We leave the restaurant around eleven-thirty. "So, do you turn into a pumpkin at midnight?" he asks.

"No," I say, "a witch."

He smiles. "I hope you'll cast a spell on me."

"You mean I haven't already?"

When we get back to the hotel we say good-night in the lobby, shake hands like we've just closed a lucrative business deal. "I had fun," I say.

"Ditto."

ROSE

I never loved my husband.

DIXIE

We don't have time to get used to Daddy being sick before we're getting used to his being dead. Once he finds out he has a spot on his liver he just lies down in bed and waits. Daddy doesn't do battle with his disease or death at all. I don't think Rose has forgiven him for that. It's number one on the list of things she hasn't forgiven him for.

In a matter of weeks he surrenders. When Lilly calls Rose to come home and touch him to be sure, he's stone-cold dead.

The last weeks of his life I went to sit with Daddy in the afternoons. He turned off the TV when I arrived and lay with his hands folded over his chest and his eyes closed while I read him the sports pages front and back. If he spoke at all it was to say, "What did *Mac* say about . . ." or "What does *Mac* think of . . ." This had become our pattern long before Daddy's illness. Never had Daddy said to me, *Dixie, what do you think about . . .* But it was especially hard now, during football season, because I saw so little of Mac that I rarely had any fresh quotes to deliver to Daddy. It was like being out of the one tonic that might save him or at least ease his pain. So I just prefaced all my own ideas and opinions with "Mac said" or "Mac thinks." I don't feel bad about lying either. Lies have always soothed Daddy. He made his whole life out of them.

The funeral was at First Baptist Church. It had the looks of a bridge club that had just let out. Women everywhere. There were a few of Daddy's business colleagues, buddies from the golf course, men from the neighborhood, but there was a whole collection of weeping women Rose and I hardly knew, some we'd never laid eyes on before. A few of the women introduced themselves as *a friend of Bennett's* and offered condolences. Others kept a respectful distance.

"Looks like your old man had quite a fan club," Mac says.

Rose looks at the women hovering around Daddy's coffin and doesn't see them. I think they know that and take comfort in it.

It pleases me to think I gave Daddy Mac. Mac was like Daddy's missing son, or his missing self who lived his missing life. When Daddy was sick I'd asked Mac to call him, but he never did. Later he'd say the line was busy. I knew he was lying. But it didn't matter because what Mac did for Daddy was better than a phone call. He evened the score in the family—two women, two men. Daddy had an imagined ally, somebody he believed to be on his side. Mac rescued Daddy from feeling overpowered by Rose and me, the official women in his life. And through Mac I'd siphoned off some of my father's love, a sample, just enough to know what I'd missed. Now he's dead. And I don't feel sad, just tired. Really exhausted.

"Why don't you cry, Mom?" Sarah has cried on and off for two days. "Didn't you love Granddaddy?"

"Of course," I say.

"You have to prove it," she says. "You have to cry."

But I can't.

You never know what shape loss will take in a person. In a matter of weeks Rose signs up for golf lessons at Mountain Brook Country Club. Not group lessons either. She wants private lessons from the pro and she takes Daddy's prize golf clubs with her. His golf bag is so heavy she has to drag it behind her and do battle to lift it into the trunk of the Cadillac Daddy bought himself just a month before the doctors found the spot. It still has that new smell. Now it belongs to Rose.

"What you about to do with them clubs?" Lilly yells as Rose drags the golf bag out of the garage, the strap slung over her shoulder. "You ain't going to pitch them clubs out, are you?" It looks like Rose is heading straight for the trash can.

"Don't be silly," Rose says. "I'm going to learn to play. I always wanted to play."

"What's she talking about?" Lilly says. "Go see what she's talking about, baby. Don't let her throw them clubs away."

I go outside and help Rose get the clubs into the car. It seems to me like a wheelchair we're jamming into the trunk, a symbol of what a hopeless emotional cripple Rose is about to become without Daddy to keep her nailed to her cross.

"There." She slams the trunk closed. She kisses my cheek. "My lesson's at three, honey. Afterwards I might hit a bucket of balls."

Hit a bucket of balls? Who is this woman?

Daddy'd made no secret of the fact that he thought women had no business on the golf course—he didn't care how good looking they were. He acted like women playing golf was some hateful plot they contrived to make men miserable in the one location where men came closest to being happy.

Rose plays golf regularly now. She's not great, but some people say she's pretty decent for a woman, especially one who got such a late start in life.

FRANCES DELMAR

At the end of Michael's first season the Black Bears are 8 and 3, ranked fourteenth in the nation. Even if I don't go to the games anymore, Joe does. He keeps me posted. Now he's begging to go to the Orange Bowl with Cleet. Somehow I've turned into the bad guy here. "Technically, Joe, honey, your dad hasn't invited you, has he?"

"Dad won't care. I can stay in his room with him."

How do you explain to a boy that his daddy's girlfriend is already staying in his room? I'm going to let Cleet be the one to explain that.

Dixie calls me from Miami and says Donna is there with Cleet, like maybe I'll be surprised. "Donna's so happy to be a part of it all that she's really irritating, F. D.," Dixie says. "Every day she dresses herself head to toe in Black Bears paraphernalia. Maybe it's her way of proving her love for Cleet—by dressing like an enthusiastic idiot. She's getting on everybody's nerves with her chronic ecstasy."

I guess this is Dixie's way of making me feel better.

DIXIE

In July my writing professor calls to tell me I've won second place in a short-story contest. I'll get to read the whole story, out loud, to a listening audience.

"Mac, guess what?" I call him out of a staff meeting, so he's expecting me to say one of the children has been run over by a truck. Instead I say, "They invited me to read a short story!"

"That's good," he says.

"You're invited too," I say. "It's on a Thursday night, two weeks from now."

"If it's all the same to you, Dix," Mac says, "I believe I'll just wait until the movie comes out."

I practice reading in front of the mirror every day. Buddy and Sarah let me read to them. "Mom," Sarah says, "that's really good." She looks startled, like I've just done something that she never knew I could do and now she wonders what else I might have up my sleeve. I love her for her suspicions.

The day of the reading I wake up sick with nerves. All day I sip herbal tea and imagine myself in front of an audience. I arrive early and meet my professor in the parking lot. He sees the terror on my face, I guess. "Where's your husband?" he asks.

"Mac couldn't come."

"Too bad," he says.

When I'm finally introduced and I stand to read I'm dizzy enough to faint. The room's spinning. I dive into the story with a shaky voice, glance out at the audience from time to time to be sure they're really there, anchoring me to the moment. My voice gradually calms down. When I finish the last page my hands are trembling, but my voice is strong. At one point my eye was drawn to the side door just in time to see Porter slip in and take a seat in the back. Applause is beautiful music. Better than Percy Sledge singing "When a Man Loves a Woman."

Afterwards my professor says, "Keep writing." It's like saying, *Keep living,* because I know I'll do it or die trying.

"Can't wait for chapter two," Porter says.

"Thanks for coming." I touch the sleeve of his shirt in a sudden surge of gratitude. *Is this the way Mac feels,* I wonder, *when people gather to listen to him?* This is a small, quiet moment compared to Mac's moments before crowds of screaming thousands, but still, I wonder.

Porter walks me out to my car. The summer air is a ripe purple, the night like an eggplant you can make all sorts of delicious things out of. "I don't really feel like going home yet," I say. "Do you?" We get in his truck, go to the nearest 7-Eleven, and buy grape Slurpees in plastic Black Bears cups. We just ride around and listen to oldies but goodies on the radio like a couple of relapsed teenagers. There's just music and wet air and my hair's sort of slapping across my face and Porter's tapping out the beat of each song on the steering wheel and we keep looking at each other and smiling.

I tell him about Daddy's funeral. All the crying women and Rose like a cool statue among them. He tells me about his sister who died when he was young. He remembers hearing his parents crying at night and how he used to get in bed with them because their grief frightened him. He talks about how he waited for his sister to come back, like when his parents told him she had gone to be with Jesus, he didn't know they meant forever.

On our ride back to Birmingham we're mostly quiet. Just good music on the radio. Just two yellow headlights slicing into the darkness.

"How'd it go last night?" Mac asks me the next morning as he is going out the door to work.

"It was wonderful."

"What time did you get home?"

"Late," I say.

I call Mac at the office and make an appointment to meet him for dinner at the Highland Grill. "I have something very important to say to you, Mac."

"I don't suppose you can just say it on the phone?" he says. "I suppose that'd be too easy, right?"

We sit at a table in the back of the restaurant, although Mac doesn't go unrecognized. It isn't until we've had drinks and ordered dinner and buttered our rolls that Mac finally says, "Okay, Dix. Shoot."

"It's about Porter Warren," I say.

"Go on."

"The more you ignore me, the more attention he pays me. And I really like his attention."

"Exactly what kind of attention are you talking about?"

"He came to hear me read, for one thing."

"Extra point for Porter," he says. "What else?"

"He looks at me. He talks to me. He listens to me."

"And I don't?"

"No. Not really."

"So, are you sleeping with him?"

"No," I say. "I'm just spending time with him. I'd see him every day if I could."

"So, what do you want me to say, Dixie?"

"You can say anything you want to."

"Why are you telling me this?"

"Because I want you to know. I wish it were you instead of him, Mac. I really do."

"Look, Dixie. If I'm supposed to be the jealous husband and forbid you to see this guy, Porter, then I hate to disappoint you, but I'm not going to be your guardian. You're a big girl. As long as you aren't sleeping with the guy, as long as all it is, is a lot of talk, then I don't have any problem with it. Look, I know I'm gone a lot. I know when I'm home I'm not the best company in the world. If you've found somebody to talk to, good."

"I was afraid you might be mad."

"As long as you're not sleeping with him," Mac says. "I don't care about the rest."

For dessert we order cheesecake and split it. We haven't shared a dessert in years. It's ridiculously rich and we carve it into tiny bites and eat it slowly in perfect silence.

Sarah and two of her friends are watching *Oprah* in the den. It's about mothers who've stolen their daughters' boyfriends and end up marrying them. It's a sick show, but the girls are thoroughly enjoying it. I can hear them shriek each time the women say something to humiliate themselves.

Buddy's in his room cleaning out his aquarium—it smells terrible.

When Frances Delmar finds me I'm typing away on a short story for my writing class. It's about a woman who picks up a hitchhiker and falls in love with him on the ride to Cheyenne, Wyoming.

"Dixie, you'll never guess who I interviewed on *Healthbeat* today." Frances Delmar takes off her coat, drops it over a chair, and sits down. "Your friend Porter Warren."

I stop what I'm doing.

"We're doing a piece on emergency care, you know. So we interviewed him. He was great." She twists a strand of hair around her finger. "He's sort of sexy or something. Anyway, he said to tell you hello."

I turn the typewriter off to stop its humming.

"I was thinking, you know, since I'm single and all now, I might ask him to lunch sometime. What do you think?"

Celeste Bomar calls Mac from the hospital in the middle of the night. He can barely understand a word she's saying. "What?"

he keeps saying. "What did you say?" He makes her repeat herself so many times she hangs up on him.

I call Rose to come stay with the children, and we drive to the hospital and find Celeste in her nightgown and overcoat in the waiting room. She's making love to a cigarette, her fingers trembling. She hugs Mac like he's her son, come home at last to help look after his impossible father. "Thank God," she says when she sees him.

I take Celeste's keys and go to her house to get her some clothes. When I get back the sun's coming up and Mac's been allowed to see Catfish. "A stroke," he says. "It's bad."

We sit with Celeste all day at the hospital. She's sequestered in a small out-of-the-way room since the hospital is swarming with reporters and newspeople.

I look after Celeste the best I can. She's like a woman cheated. Like a woman who's just had her future snatched away from her. "It's not fair," she says. "We were going to travel together. Now he can't talk. Doesn't even know who I am. It's almost funny, isn't it?"

"I can't believe it either," I say.

"I know he'd rather just die than live on this way."

"Lots of people are praying for him," I say. "The whole state of Alabama and half the country. Everybody."

"I ought to be praying too. But I don't know what to pray." Celeste's hands are frantic, one gripping a cigarette with ashes threatening, the other twisting the button on her sweater until I'm sure it will pop off in her hand. She's chewed the polish off her nails. "Should I pray that he lives or dies?"

"Pray that whatever's best happens," I say.

"I think I need a drink," she says. "Just one drink, that's all. To calm my nerves." Then she makes a noise that sounds like a cat whining to be let out a closed door. It's almost nonhuman, the sound she makes. "I really hate him for this," she whispers.

The rest of the summer Mac makes daily visits to the rehab center. Sometimes I go with him and watch him talk to Catfish—

football talk, the positions, the players, the prospects. It seems to soothe Catfish, but Mac insists, "He doesn't understand a damn word I'm saying." He holds Catfish's hand, squeezing it hard to see if he can get a reaction. He puts socks on his cold feet. He combs his hair for him, making a neat part on the side of his head. He tries to show the nurse how to do it right so that Catfish can at least look like himself, enjoy the familiar comfort of his lifetime part. Mac says repeatedly, "Coach, we got to get you out of here."

Each time I visit Celeste she looks older and smaller. Sometimes I just sit beside her on her bed and we watch soap operas together. Twice I drive her to the beauty parlor to get her hair done. She comes and goes out the back door to avoid being seen. She's started seeing her psychiatrist again, which seems to help. He tells Levinnia to get all the alcohol out of the house and to keep it out. But Celeste is hard to outsmart.

"They've made arrangements to put Coach in a nursing home." Mac sits at the kitchen table gripping the salt and pepper shakers. The children have gone to bed and I'm folding clothes hot from the dryer. "They don't know if he'll ever get any better, Dix. They don't hold out much hope. A damn nursing home." He slings the salt-shaker across the kitchen and it hits an empty glass on the counter. The glass rolls to the floor and shatters.

It's the middle of Miracle's second season. The Black Bears are undefeated. It's like he's kissed a dying corpse and brought it back to life. He hasn't done it single-handedly, of course. Mac is quick to point that out. "Last season we had six seniors," he says. "This season we have thirteen. We also had the best recruiting year I've ever been associated with at HamU. We've got three freshmen starting for us. We're not going to do anything but get better."

I decide to try an experiment. I won't go to the next game. I'll stay home and see what happens. It'll be the first Black Bears game I've ever missed.

Sarah spends Friday night with a friend. She's going to the game Saturday with Gabriel, whom she now thinks of as her boyfriend. Buddy has gone on an overnight camping trip with Corey's family. His parents are academics from up North. Football means nothing to them. So on Saturday morning I wish Mac luck like always when he leaves for the stadium. I rope off the upstairs like usual and stay upstairs in bed in our room. I can hear Butch and his staff rattling around downstairs. I can hear somebody whistling. Maybe they think I've left early for some warm-up festivity or pregame prayer meeting. I doubt it ever crosses their minds that I'm upstairs in my nightgown, listening to the game on the radio. We are leading at the end of the first quarter. I guess that's when I fall asleep.

The word *injury* wakes me up. The way the announcer shouts, *"Oh, no! Oh, no!"* and then takes on a somber tone. "Miracle Carpenter is being carried off the field," he says. "The crowd is giving him a standing ovation. Listen to that." I jerk awake like a jailhouse guard who hears his prisoner escaping. I get up, panicked. I get dressed and dash around getting ready for the party people who'll be arriving soon. *Miracle hurt,* I keep thinking. *No.* Every few minutes I run to the radio to check the score. In the end HamU wins, even without Miracle.

The house is packed with people in no time. The other wives assume I watched the game from the press box with CeCe. Nobody says, "Dixie, where were you?" They say, "Great game, huh? Too bad about Miracle." Nobody has noticed that anything is out of the ordinary. My absence has gone undetected.

The party's upbeat. I feel drugged. Maybe guilt is like a tranquilizer. Maybe it's knowing that I'm totally unnecessary—the fact that people around me knew, but no one told me. Not even Mac. And now I know. I get a glass of wine and sip it. I decide not to stand at the door and welcome people. "Mrs. Gibbs, are you all right?" one of the Beauties asks me.

"I'm fine," I say.

"Dixie, baby," Lilly says, "that Porter Warren is on the phone. Wants to talk to you."

I go upstairs to take the call, close the door to our bedroom. "Hi, Porter," I say.

"I'm at the hospital," Porter says. "Just wanted to let you know about Miracle. He's got a bad back bruise. Maybe a cracked vertebra."

"He'll be all right, won't he?"

"If he takes it easy," Porter says. "He suffered a severe blow to the spine, which is nothing to mess around with. I'll let you get back to your party. Thought you might be concerned."

"Porter?" I pause. "Aren't you coming?"

"Can't," he says. "I'm on duty tonight."

When Mac walks in, Yolanda is the first person to him. She kisses him, leaving a smudge on his face like a pink bruise. "Ten down and one to go," she says. Then he turns—maybe to look for me—but there're hands to shake and hugs to accept. Mac looks happy, has the appropriate expression of a man who is 10 and 0.

When Mac and I cross paths at the party he says, "Miracle is out for the rest of the season. Thank God we play Southwest Louisiana next week. They're two and eight."

"Right," I say.

HAM U WINS CONFERENCE CHAMPIONSHIP. BLACK BEARS GET SUGAR BOWL BID. GIBBS VOTED SEC COACH OF THE YEAR. NATIONAL CHAMPIONSHIP WITHIN GRASP. I tear these headlines out and stuff them in the minicoffins under our bed. *Sports Illustrated* is coming to do a story on Mac. They'll be here Christmas week, then follow the team to New Orleans for the Sugar Bowl.

Not so long ago people wanted to fire Mac. Now he's undefeated and has a chance at the national championship. It's the *Miracle* angle *Sports Illustrated* is after. Mac is the same guy this season that he was last season, isn't he?

Several nights a week Sly comes by with one or two of the somber trustees or Ed Lyman, the university president. Once he brings Senator Billy Harrington with him. They sit in Mac's study and drink and talk about the future of HamU football. This winning season, compliments of Miracle Carpenter and God, has saved Mac's job. Now it's like all the world has fallen in love with him again. All the men in the world, at least. Funny how fast hate can turn into love.

I don't know what's wrong with me. I should be happy.

Word is out that the merchants of New Orleans are disappointed when one of the Alabama universities plays in the Sugar Bowl because instead of flying in and booking all the best hotels and restaurants and cabbing around the city in a shopping frenzy, tipping and eating like maniacs, Alabamians are more likely to drive to New Orleans, book a Motel 6 on the outskirts of town, and bring food from home—or worse, drive their mobile homes, park them near the Superdome, and sit out on the sidewalk in their folding chairs eating Kentucky Fried Chicken or tuna fish sandwiches the wife made.

This is not the reputation Birmingham University wants. After all, we are not a state school like Auburn and University of Alabama. We are private and we need to act like it. So HamU does what it can to counteract the notion that our fans are too thrifty to be taken seriously. Spending money is the way fans thank a city for inviting their team to a bowl game. If you're too cheap it diminishes your chances of being asked back with any enthusiasm. Bowls are partial to inviting one team whose fans have to travel a long way—it's good financial planning—and one team closer to home to increase rivalry and hype.

Sarah and Buddy are proud of their father, so thrilled that during the week in New Orleans they both reach the outermost edges of admiration and come back just as depleted as I am. Sarah trails Mac down Bourbon Street one night to the cheers and crush of fans, seeming to siphon off some of the fans' love for herself, basking in it a little, calling to Mac, "Daddy, wait a minute!" leaving no doubt as to who the slender girl in braces is, struggling to keep up with him and not be left behind.

Buddy rejoices in his own quiet way. Unlike Sarah, he doesn't like people to know who he is. I think he fears their disappointment in him, that it might echo the disappointment he imagines Mac himself feels when he looks at his son, Buddy Gibbs, small for his age, secret reader of books, who studies reptile habits and dreams risky, unsanctioned dreams of making music, jazz maybe, like the music that seeps into the air all around him on the streets of New Orleans.

Aside from official bowl functions I hardly see Mac at all. His week is full of practices, staff meetings, press interviews, talks to this group and that, drinks with this money and that, early-morning devotionals, midnight phone calls. Every night the children and I are dead asleep when Mac finally comes in, never turning on a light, fumbling with his key, sitting on the edge of the bed to slip his shoes off, sleeping in his underwear. Every morning I wake to find that I've wrapped myself around Mac during the night, my legs hooked through his, my arm across his chest, like I'm trying to tie us into a body knot and it's his job to unravel us and set himself free each morning. I know this because when he gets his wake–up call he deftly untangles himself, half waking me, and says, "Go back to sleep." And I do.

One day I wake to find my picture in the *New Orleans Times-Picayune*. I'm greeting Penn State wives, my hand extended, my teeth gleaming. The caption reads: "Dixie Gibbs, wife of Mac Gibbs, welcomes wives from Penn State. A win at this week's Sugar Bowl could earn HamU the national championship."

Another morning, Buddy's picture's in the paper, standing behind Mac, legs apart, arms folded, eyes squinted, headphones on. Buddy is identified in the photograph, whose caption reads, "Like father, like son." Obviously the photographer doesn't know what Buddy's listening to on his headphones, that his mind is a thousand miles away from football. The picture's on the front page of the sports section. Sarah feels slighted and says more than once, "It's not fair." She asks Mac twice if she can be in a picture with him and both times he says, "We'll see."

Two nights before the game the traditional dinner is held to honor members and coaches of both teams. The restaurant's jammed with television crews and camera equipment. Mac stands at the microphone looking out at the crowd. He's done everything expected of him. More. He's done the next to impossible. He's on the brink of winning it all and they love him for this—this winningness. They'll love him even more if he can win this last game, the Sugar Bowl.

"When I was young," Mac says, sipping from his Scotch, "I had a reputation as a passer. Not a very good one." He laughs. The crowd chuckles. "I guess I can thank Jett Brown for that." He pauses. "From time to time people ask me, 'Mac, what's the greatest pass you ever completed? Was it against LSU when Jett made that one-handed catch in the last second to win the conference?'" Mac looks out over the crowd with the expression of an evangelist. "I tell them *no*. I tell them that the greatest pass I ever completed was the one at my wife, Dixie, sitting up here by my side." The crowd bursts into applause.

Mac looks in my direction. "Y'all ever see anything look so good in a black dress in all your life?" The crowd responds with delight—for Mac, for the clever things he can think to say to a woman, about a woman.

"She told me what that dress cost," he says. The crowd roars. They love Mac the husband. "I said, 'Dixie, baby, we could send the kids to college for what that dress cost.'" He smiles. "But I tell you, when she came walking out tonight in that dress looking like a million dollars, I said, 'Shoot, woman, here's my American Express. Go out and get you another one of those damn dresses!'" The women in the audience are beaming—other coaches' wives too. Women who should know better.

Mac ends his remarks by paying tribute to Catfish Bomar. He chokes up asking people to bow their heads in a moment of prayer for the greatest coach who ever lived. Afterwards everyone stands and applauds so long and hard I think for a minute that the building might go up in flames.

Judgment day comes. Actually it's judgment night. Eighty thousand people jam themselves into the Superdome. The excitement is palpable, concrete. If I had a chain saw I could cut it into block-sized chunks, like tearing down a wall. I could get rich selling the hysteria and high hopes. All around me people are doing just that—selling ordinary people dreams of being extraordinary people, *winners*, one and all.

Miracle's back injury will keep him out of the game, but he's on the sideline, in uniform, leaning on a pair of crutches Porter insisted he use. When he takes the field he jogs out, carrying the crutches under his arm like a newspaper. The crowd is on its feet at the sight of him. Their voices sound like a deadly tornado spinning through the dome. The love is deafening.

With six seconds left in the game it's looking like a HamU loss. Already the Penn State fans are celebrating in the stands. I can feel my own blood rise to a near boil. Mac calls his last time-out. I see him talking to Vet, then I see Vet say something to Miracle. The crowd begins to scream. The players on the bench circle Miracle and Vet, bobbing their helmets up and down in the air like corks on the surface of a deep undercurrent.

After a moment of confusion, Miracle jogs onto the field, and the fans erupt like a lid-rattling pot boiling over on its too hot hopes, sizzling itself into blinding steam. *No, Mac,* I think in my prayer voice. *Don't do it. You can't.* I see Porter screaming at Vet, shaking his head, and I see Vet throw his arms up in the air and walk away. *No, Mac,* I pray, *please!* The crowd noise is so great that the referee refuses to let the play begin. Every person is standing and most of them are stomping and screaming too. We have to stand in our seats if we want to see the field. Sarah's praying out loud, *"Please God, please God."* Buddy takes off his headphones to watch. The crowd swallows us with its exhilaration and limitless expectation.

Michael is a beautiful sight on the field. The self-respect of thousands of Black Bears fans rests on his shoulders. The fans subdue themselves long enough for the official to signal play to begin, then the crowd jumps to its feet again, like one giant soul made of a hundred thousand individual souls.

Miracle takes a left lateral toss from Smokey, takes two steps to the left to pull the defense in that direction, then turns and sweeps to the right, dodging through the Nittany Lions like sunlight through a stand of pines. He takes a hit and spins off it, another hit, another spin, the other direction. Just when it looks like he's hit a wall of defensive players, he leaps in the air, climbing on top of and over them, proving once and for all that seeing is *not* believing. *How the hell did he do that?* people gasp. He stumbles across the goal with the ball in one hand and waves it over his head before taking an ambush hit from behind and falling to his knees. A scream is set loose in the blood of thousands of spectators.

The fans push even deeper into their already deeply held conviction that witnessing the winning of a football game is one of the nobler and more satisfying reasons for living a life. And on this night every Black Bears fan in the United States of America has a valid excuse to inhabit the earth. Frenzied fans tear from the stands like they've been set on fire. The officials try to clear the field for the extra point attempt, but it's impossible. Their shrieks more piercing and terrifying than if they were witnessing murder, bystanders swarm the field, tripping each other, sheer joy standing their hair on end. I grab Sarah and Buddy to keep them from being trampled. Fans scream, "Jesus Christ, you see that?" and they run toward Miracle, who lies broken in the end zone before being pulled to his feet and carried off the field on the shoulders of his teammates.

Now Miracle lies on the sideline bench in a fit of pain while Porter works on his legs, so badly twisted that his right foot points north and his left foot south. Hemp and the managers try to hold him down, nail him to the moment, while Porter works on him, shouting orders, his face as red and angry as the flashing siren making its way across the field. I see Vet run toward the ambulance and signal them to hurry. Porter turns his back just long enough for the love-crazed fans to swarm the bench and lift Miracle in exaltation, his feet flopping like two limp fish at the ends of his dangling legs. But the grimace leaves Miracle's face as the crowd lifts him. It's like he feels no pain, like he's being elevated by fifty Kenny Rogers types, all singing "Love Lifted Me," white man's music, and at the moment it's Miracle Carpenter that white men love. They raise Miracle on their shoulders as if it were their job, on this very night, to usher him into the city limits of heaven. He holds on to their pink heads and smiles, even waves, before falling unconscious in their arms.

Then they tear the goalpost down. The police run around the field as useless as gnats on a sore. Eight people have to be taken to the emergency room in ambulances, including Miracle.

PUNT

MARY VIRGINIA

I would of rode with Miracle if I could of stood it, but I tell you the truth, I'm scared of those helicopters, looks like you could fall right out. I made sure they had Miracle tied down good. Then me and Mama drove back to Birmingham to the medical center, praying the whole way. They had Miracle all set up in an intensive care room by the time we got here.

Surgery shows Miracle's got three crushed vertebrae. It's too early to tell if his paralysis come from swelling, which should go away after a while, or from bone damage to the spinal cord, which won't. They assigned one them psychiatrists to his case. The first thing the psychiatrist does is prescribe strong medicine for me. "This should keep you calm," he says to me.

White people kill me. They act like calm's the way to handle near about everything. What's so good about calm? "Don't talk to me about calm," I say to that psychiatrist. "You get my boy up and walking around, then you talk to me about *calm*."

I refuse to leave the hospital for any reason. I don't trust none these people, got needles and bottles, rolling folks from room to room on them carts. It turns my stomach, all of it. I shouldn't never have turned my boy over to football or to this university or to this damn hospital. Now that they got him here, I got to watch everything they say and do. I want them to explain everything that goes on. They owe me that.

I wish I was a Catholic. I like the Catholics because they make a big fuss over Mary the mother. Got her picture everywhere and she's always praying like crazy with that halo over her head. Those Catholics, they respect motherhood. They know a good mother is the hardest thing in the world to be. The Baptists, all they worry about is sin, sin, sin. You ever hear any Catholics worrying about Mary the helpmate? Did Mary submit unto Joseph or not? No sir. They're not worried about how good a wife Mary was to Joseph. Those Catholics don't care about that. It's how good a *mother* Mary was to Jesus that counts. If you ask me that's how it should be.

Today they allowing Coach Gibbs in Miracle's room. He comes up here every day, but can't just anybody go in the intensive care room. You got to be family. But then I said to myself, *Miracle ought to have him a father coming up here to see about him, but he don't.* So I tell those doctors to let Coach Gibbs in, in place of a real father, and they do.

Coach Gibbs sits beside Miracle's bed. "How you doing, son?" he says. I stand in the door and listen to them.

Mama brought Miracle a Bible and told him to keep it in his bed at all times, to sleep with it under his pillow, to read it until he gets tired. Then I read it. We're trying to keep his room filled up with God's word, drown out all that mumbo jumbo the doctors talk in there. "Don't under no circumstances let this Bible out of this bed, boy," Mama said. And Miracle promised. Since then he reads the New Testament until he gets so tired the Bible drops out his hand.

"Let me ask you something, Coach," Miracle says.

"Sure," Coach Gibbs says. "Shoot."

"God got Mary pregnant, right? He never married her or nothing though, right?"

"Well, I guess that's right."

"So Jesus, he was a bastard, right?"

"I hadn't ever thought of it like that."

"But what if God had of married Mary? Then she wouldn't have had to be no virgin, would she? Not if he married her. And say they had Jesus, you know, the regular way, were raising him up and all, then something went wrong, you know, they split. God went his way. The Virgin Mary, she went her way. What then?"

"I'm not sure I'm with you."

"What about Jesus, man? Like what if God and the Virgin, you know, had one of them custody battles. Who would of won?"

"You asking the wrong man," Coach Gibbs says. "I'm a little behind on my Bible reading. What's got this on your mind?"

"I got time to think, Coach. Too much time."

So Coach Gibbs holds Miracle's hand for a minute. "God has not run out on you, son, if that's what you think. I know that."

"How do you know?" Miracle says.

"I just know."

"From where I'm at, Coach, that's not for definite."

MRS. CARPENTER

I can't hardly stand to watch Michael in there in that bed. He don't deserve to suffer. But I say this, don't nobody get what they deserve—and thank God for that mostly. If us sinners got what we deserved, most of us would be struck by lightning the next time it storms. Now and then somebody like Michael got to pay the price for all the blessings the rest of us get that we don't come anywhere close to deserving. You can't watch Michael run and not know the boy has got some angel in him.

So I got to believe God knows what he's doing. I don't agree with God on everything, but I ain't about to go against him over it either. Mary Virginia out there on that cot arguing with God like it's gon do some good. You can't argue with God. She's making people think she's crazy out there talking to herself.

Columbus, he's up at Michael's room every day. He just upsets everybody twice as bad the way he acts. I believe he'd change places with that boy if he could. He'd rip off his good legs, bum knee and all, and give them to Michael. That's why he acts so crazy and moody, getting everybody else upset.

"This ain't right, Mama" is what he says to me every day.

"God got his reasons," I say.

"What kind of reasons God got?" he asks.

DIXIE

Every day I take food to the hospital. Lilly fixes it and packs it in a picnic basket. Mrs. Carpenter's usually in the waiting room watching for me. I set the food on the coffee table, say, "Any news?" and make my silent exit.

It's Porter who keeps me informed about Miracle. Sometimes I call him at the hospital and say, "Tell me," and he does. When I run into Porter on my food deliveries I don't know whether to fall into his arms or stab him with a butter knife. If he was a drug he'd be a painkiller with the potential for addiction, overdose, and certain death. "It's okay, Dixie," he says to me when we collide in the hospital corridor and then back up like a couple of hit-and-run cars pretending there hasn't been a terrible wreck.

"I love Mac," I say to Porter. "Do you believe me?"

"Yes," he says.

"Say it."

"You love Mac."

"Yes," I say. "Thank you."

Recruiting's under way. I watch Mac pack his suitcase—underwear and dark socks, an alarm clock, a carton of Rolaids. Players want to come to HamU now. Number one team in the nation can pick and choose. "Where're you going?" I ask.

"Where do you think?" He doesn't look at me.

"I'll rephrase the question," I say. "Where are *we* going?"

"Straight to hell in a handbasket, I guess." He slings a handful of laundered shirts into his suitcase.

"Mac," I say, "at some point we're going to have to talk."

"Just what do you want to talk about, Dixie?"

"Whether we're still married. Whether we want to be."

"That's up to you."

"Then I want us to see a marriage counselor—together."

He laughs. "Right. That's exactly what I need right now."

"It's not funny," I say.

He looks at me for the first time in longer than I can remember. I feel like I've been stung. He grabs my shoulders and shakes me so hard I know I'll have fingerprint bruises on my arms. "Look. You're the one who's so unhappily married. If you need to see a marriage counselor, fine, go ahead, damnit. I don't need marriage counseling." He turns me loose and goes back to his packing, tosses his shoes into the suitcase so hard they bounce and fly to the floor.

"So you're just going to punish me with silence the rest of my life?" I say. "Is that it?"

"Just who's punishing who around here, Dixie?" He snaps his suitcase closed. "You tell me that."

MARY VIRGINIA

Miracle is so low that he's all of a sudden taken a interest in heaven. He wants to talk about dying and such.

Dixie Gibbs comes in with that lunch she brings and she sits on the foot of my cot. We can see Miracle inside the glass intensive care unit from here. The doctor goes in to jab him with more pins, hoping for pain, you know. I watch this torture every day. I think it will do Dixie good to see it. I want people to know what goes on up here.

The doctor, he's determined. "Here? Here? Here?" It almost makes me scream to watch him do it. He finally leaves with failure all over his face.

Miracle begins to cry. It's just a shaking at first, then he screams out and I go dead inside. Dixie's a mother. I think maybe she knows.

"If you love me you'll bring me a gun," he yells to me. "Do you love me enough, Mama? Do you?"

DIXIE

I'm a real neat sleeper. Ordinarily I sleep like a cold cut between two slices of white bread, sort of waiting for the night to eat me up, but it never does. Lots of times I wake up in exactly the same position as when I lay down. Some people think careful sleeping is unnatural, but I've done it on and off all my life. It's not down like sleep is supposed to be. It's up and floaty, like my bones are gone and I'm a puff of cloud—a dark thundercloud, swollen and cruel. I'm asleep like this when the call comes. That's how I think of it now—the call—like I'm a preacher and it's God claiming my life.

I'm just dreaming, you know, like any other guilty woman, so at first the phone ringing fits right into my dream, but the second ring, the third ring, refuse to submit to the dream, so I slap for the phone in the dark, knocking things over to grab it.

"Dixie? This is Mac."

Before I have time to think how very wrong it is for Mac to be calling me at this hour he says, "I quit."

"You quit what?"

"Football, damnit. Coaching. Every damn thing."

"Mac, where are you? Are you at the hospital?"

"It doesn't matter," he says.

"Mac, you're scaring me. Where are you?"

"I told Sly and Lyman tonight. I said, 'Fuck it, man, I quit.' You know what they said? They said, 'You're doing the right thing, Mac.' They were as happy as hell."

"Mac, you're not making sense. Are you coming home?"

"Hell, no."

"Come home, Mac. Please."

"If I'd thought it would get Miracle up out of that bed I would have quit a hell of a long time ago. People acting like my resignation will have Miracle up and walking around. Okay, so I'll quit. Let's see if that gets him back on his feet."

"Mac, it won't save Miracle. But maybe it'll save you."

Mac laughs into the phone. "Yep, Dix, I knew you'd say something like that. I can always count on you, can't I?"

Then the phone goes dead.

By the time Rose and Lilly get to the house I'm throwing up in the bathroom. I'm down to the bitter yellow bile that means you're empty now, nothing else to get rid of.

"We've got some bad news, baby," Rose says, like something terrible in her life has come loose and fallen into mine.

"Where's Mac?" I ask.

"It's not Mac, honey. It's Coach Bomar. He's dead."

Lilly hands me something from the closet. "Here, you put on something clean. Then get over to see about Mrs. Celeste. I think she's pretty bad."

When I get to Celeste's house Levinnia sends me upstairs. Celeste's as sober as a brown cardboard box. An empty one. "You didn't have to come," she says. She has the TV on but there's just a snowy screen and a buzzing noise. "I'm okay," she says. She looks at me. "You, on the other hand, look awful. What's happened to you?"

"Nothing," I lie.

She pats Catfish's side of the bed. "Take your shoes off," she says, "and lie down right here."

"Do you feel like talking about him?" I ask. "Coach Bomar?"

"No," she says.

The next thing I remember is Celeste waking me up to go home and tell Sarah and Buddy what's happened before they turn on the TV. "Don't let those babies hear the news secondhand," she says.

"They thought the world of Catfish," I mumble.

"Not that news," Celeste says. "The other news." She tries to hand me a newspaper, but I won't take it.

When I leave, Levinnia gives me hot coffee in a paper cup and a banana to eat in the car. I drive across town in the predawn fog and wish I could drive forever with my yellow lights slicing into the fog like two gentle, probing fingers. I pull into my driveway and look at my house.

I get the wet newspaper from the yard, unroll it, and look at the headlines. CATFISH DIES. GIBBS QUITS.

LILLY

The morning of Coach Bomar's funeral I drive over to Mrs. Celeste's house with Rose. They got sports reporters standing all over the yard, TV vans parked on the street. Some the kids in the university band are scattered around, carrying their instruments. One lone boy, he plays his bugle until Levinnia has to send him word to stop it. "It's giving Mrs. Celeste a headache," she tells him. Kids sit on the curb hoping to get autographs. I don't know where their mothers and daddies are.

We see a Boy Scout troop in their uniforms get let out of a station wagon. I watch that den mother park across the street. Them Boy Scouts unroll a paper that says GOD DRAFTED CATFISH IN THE FIRST ROUND! and another one that says FOR GOD SO LOVED THE WORLD THAT HE SENT COACH BOMAR TO BIRMINGHAM U.

"Wonder what badges this earns those boys," Rose says. "Good sportsmanship badges? Death etiquette badges? Sympathy badges?"

"They don't mean no harm," I say. "They got supervision."

A cluster of teenagers stand holding signs that say WELCOME HOME, JETT! Two colored girls are dressed like they think they in Hollywood—got on early-morning sequins and whatnot. I'll tell you, half of what's wrong with this world is mothers have done let loose of their daughters.

It's Jett them girls want to see. Idn't that something? I wouldn't let a daughter of mine act thataway. But I can't wait to lay my eyes on that boy. He calls me up every Sunday, but that's nowhere near enough.

They got policemen—who'd rather be on them motor-cycles leading the team to the stadium with them sirens blaring—standing out in the street directing traffic. Cars circle the Bomars' house like a bunch of snails, knotting the traffic every whichaway, blowing their horns in a grieving sort of way as they go past the house. They acting like it's Christmas and we got this house wrapped in lights, lit up for show.

Levinnia been up most of the night. Butch brought over his crew and set up food service, enough for thousands if you ask me, including a bar with liquor provided by the booster club, which is not right. You not supposed to have no bar at a funeral. Folks is sad enough without liquor setting loose all the rest of the sadness they got bottled up.

Butch got tears in his eyes while he arranges the liquor. He tells me and Levinnia to come out and look what he's got in his truck. Lord God. You ought to see what he's done.

DIXIE

I go upstairs to find Celeste lying in bed fully clothed like a piece of blank paper waiting for death to write its name across her too. Catfish's death envelopes her, like if it's possible to be sealed up in something you can't feel the edges of. My own grief is a dry ocean and I'm drowning in the dryness.

The room's dark. The curtains are drawn. "Celeste," I say, "it's me." I feel for her hand. "Mac'll be here later."

"I can't cry," she says.

"That's okay. You don't have to."

"I've tried," she says.

"Maybe it'll come later," I say, "the crying."

"Did you see all those people outside?" she says. "They act like the goddamn circus is in town."

Levinnia knocks on the door and sticks her head inside the dark bedroom. "Y'all got to come down here and see this," she says. "Butch been working on this thing all night."

"What is it?" Celeste asks.

"Come down here and see," Levinnia orders.

"Shit." Celeste sits up in bed and feels around her nightstand for her sunglasses. She puts them on and stands up and tucks in her blouse. "Okay," she says. "Come on, Dixie. A widow's work is never done."

She looks like a movie star walking through the house in those sunglasses. She's embarrassed for people to see how much she hasn't been crying. The humiliation makes her appear glamorous.

With great ceremony Butch removes the white sheet that veils his masterpiece, placed at the center of the dining room table. It's a larger-than-life ice carving of Catfish.

"Lord!" Lilly says. "If it don't look like his exact head on a plate, only swelled up about the size of God. I ain't never seen nothing like that in my life."

"I had trouble getting his eyes right," Butch says.

I don't know what to think. Everybody will be gathered around the table watching Coach's head melt into a puddle.

"It's nice, Butch," Celeste says. "I'm sure Coach Bomar would have liked it."

"There's nothing in the world I wouldn't do for Coach," Butch says. "I loved the guy."

"Yes," Celeste says. "Everybody did."

The team is bused over by the university and they file into the house in coats and ties wearing their after-losing-a-game expressions, suitable for funerals. I sense they don't believe Coach Bomar's death any more than I do. When they file past his coffin several of them weep openly and have to be led away.

By ten o'clock in the morning the house is bustling with morbid activity. Levinnia has to lock doors to keep people from picking up mementos, combing through Catfish's desk drawers, digging in his trash can, and taking the pictures off the walls. "They is some nosy people in this world," she mumbles.

She goes a step further and ropes off the stairs to keep mourners from wandering into Celeste's bedroom—total strangers sometimes—to offer condolences.

"Don't lock yourself away up here," Rose tells Celeste. "You've got to let people love you through this."

Celeste lets Rose give her assorted death advice and doesn't interrupt or disagree once. Maybe Celeste has heard that Rose is making widowhood into an art form, that she's now an expert on dead husbands. So Celeste is quiet. When Rose finishes she pats Celeste's arm and says, "Sure, you miss them when they're gone, but really you're no lonelier than you were when they were around." Then Rose makes her graceful exit.

"Are you okay?" I ask Celeste.

"No," she says. "Should I be?"

Romalee's wearing black and it's definitely her color. I've never seen her look better. "Dixie," she whispers, "I have to talk to you." She pulls me down the hall to the bathroom, then closes the door and locks it. "Promise you won't get mad," she says.

"What is it?"

"Walker's in town, you know, for the funeral, right? Well, he has an interview with Sly tomorrow morning, you know, for Mac's job."

"Oh," I say.

"You know he's always wanted it, Dixie. You can't blame him. I just wanted you to know."

"Am I supposed to say good luck?"

"Walker has Jackson Smith backing him," Romalee whispers. "He met with him all day yesterday. And wouldn't it be better to have *me* living in your house than some stranger? You could still come over as much as you wanted to—the kids too."

Romalee radiates possibility, the most alluring perfume in the world. "So, just don't be mad, Dixie. Mac had his chance. Now maybe Walker will get a chance. That's fair, isn't it?" Romalee hugs me and leaves a perfect red kiss mark on my cheek. "Come on," she says. "Let's get back out there. I swear this is the saddest thing. I just hate funerals, don't you?"

When Mac arrives he looks like he can't breathe.

I touch Mac's shoulder. "How are you doing?"

"Bad," he says.

Together we watch out the window as Sly and grim-faced CeCe make their way up the walk. Sly's bombarded by the press. "Sly, can you tell us if the search for a new coach is under way?"

Sly pauses for the briefest second and instantly there're fistfuls of microphones aimed at him. "The selection committee met this morning," he says. "We hope to talk to a couple of people in the next few days."

"Can you tell us who the candidates are?"

"It's too early for that," Sly says. "But I will tell you this. Naturally we want a coach who can win, but as always, academics are our first priority at Birmingham University."

I look at Mac. He laughs like a man choking on a dime.

When Danny Boswell arrives the newspeople make a run for him. He's a successful Mississippi coach revered for outwitting the NCAA in three separate investigations. Each time a couple of assistant coaches—and once the athletic director—bit the dust for rule infractions, but Danny managed to come out untouched, like an athletic innocent who never knew, hadn't seen, didn't hear, couldn't remember. He's greatly respected for this. "Any comments, Coach Boswell?" The press clamors around him.

"Ole Catfish was one of the greatest competitors around and he'll be missed," Danny says. Years ago Catfish and Danny had nearly come to blows after Catfish had run up the score on Mississippi and Danny refused to shake his hand after the game. Everybody thought this was very low class. But on this occasion Danny's eloquent. "Today, there is no offense and no defense," he says, "just one big *L* in the column of life." Every hair on Danny's head is in its assigned place as always. He looks so much like Glen Campbell that I half expect him to break into song—a hymn maybe, or "Rhinestone Cowboy."

The house is full of coaches. It's like a who's who of college football—a gawker's paradise. Most Southern coaches don't wear suits. They wear sports jackets and Sansabelt pants, sometimes in bold colors. They wear championship rings on their fingers, gold chains around their necks, and bowl-game watches. They wear polished slip-on shoes. And their hair, if they have any, is nearly always under total control. Show me a Southern coach who can't control his own hair, and I'll show you a coach who's not a true disciplinarian. Their confidence is as unmistakable as their Brut and Old Spice. It's comforting to me to know the house is full of coaches. I know how to be and who to be among them. It's like becoming comfortably invisible—being nobody at all—and today I'm grateful for that.

"How's it going, Mac?" Danny Boswell walks toward us. "It's a shame, man," he says, "your resignation. This is a crazy profession, isn't it? Got to be crazy to do it."

"You sound like my wife," Mac says.

Catfish's body is in the living room in a polished wood casket with HamU spelled out in tiny roses spray-painted gold. Two Black Bear Beauties are assigned to stand on either side of the coffin to smile and welcome people as they file past Catfish's body or pause to say a last good-bye. The Beauties are to make sure no one stays too long, that the line keeps moving, that nobody pulls a souvenir hair from Catfish's head or a button from his shirt. They're also to prevent anyone from depositing a memento in the casket—an old game ticket, a photo, a sealed letter. It's a demanding job. One Beauty weeps steadily through the morning, her nose running so that a handkerchief is no match for it. It's Levinnia who sees this and decides the Beauties should rotate coffin duty in thirty-minute shifts. She sets the timer on the kitchen stove.

I watch Celeste make her way into the dining room, where players are gathered around the table loading their plates with ham slices. They make space for her, the coach's wife, circling her instinctively like she's the quarterback this afternoon and it's their job to see that she doesn't take too many hits.

She signals to me to follow her back upstairs and I do. She locks the door to her bedroom and lies down on the bed in the identical position Catfish is lying in in his casket. It's like she has to assume a death posture every so often, to lie down, close her eyes, and think dead thoughts.

"Are you okay?" I say.

"Don't ever let this happen to you, honey." Celeste folds her hands over her chest and looks me square in the eye.

"Celeste, do you know what I said to Mac? I asked him to go to marriage counseling."

"Darling, football coaches don't go to marriage counseling."

"I know."

"What were you thinking?"

"I was desperate. But I should never have mentioned marriage counseling."

"Believe me, I said many a worse thing than that to Coach Bomar over the years."

"Mac has got enough problems as it is. He doesn't need me to be another one."

"Is that you talking, or him?"

"Him. Me. I don't know."

"Mac's a fool, Dixie. He's a good man, but he's a fool. When it comes to women, most men are."

"Am I a fool too?"

"Probably." Celeste reaches for a cigarette.

"Can I ask you something, Celeste?"

She leans back against the headboard of her bed, which is upholstered in the same fabric as the drapes—a neutral beige pattern, swirly and expensive. Suddenly Celeste looks neutral too, her exhausted, post-swirly blondness blending in so that she seems camouflaged sitting in the bed.

"No, I never had a face-lift." Celeste smiles. "Is that what you want to know? Hand me that ashtray."

"Did you love Coach Bomar?"

She lights her cigarette and sucks on it like it's an old and tired breast and she's an infant desperate for mother's milk. She holds the lighter in her hand, stares at the flame a long time, then snaps it closed. "In the beginning," she says.

"But not at the end?"

"It was hard to tell."

"Do you think I love Mac?"

"I don't know. Do *you* think you love him?"

"I don't know."

"It's a hell of a note," she says, "being a woman. It's like we've got two speeds—love a man too much or not enough. Love is a real killer, honey."

On the drive to First Baptist Church I ride in the limousine with Celeste and Levinnia. Mac rides with the other pallbearers. It feels more like a homecoming parade than a funeral procession. All traffic pulls off the edge of the road and waits for us to pass. Men hold their hats over their hearts. People flash their car lights. The motorcycle police lead the way, sirens sounding, with the same seriousness they use getting team buses through rowdy crowds on game day.

The streets are lined with people dressed in green and gold, waving pom-poms, holding signs that read GOD IS DEAD, COACH BOMAR IS #1, CATFISH WALKED ON WATER. Levinnia's staring out the window like a woman watching a science fiction movie. "White people beat all," she says, then blows her nose.

At the church there's a funeral corsage waiting for Celeste, compliments of a booster who owns a florist shop. It's a white homecoming mum tied with a black ribbon with tiny gold plastic footballs dangling from it. The funeral director pins it lovingly on Celeste's shoulder.

The church is bursting at the seams. The organ music is so loud it has Jesus trembling where he stands in the stained-glass window. The organ music is piped over loudspeakers so people outside, trampling the grass, swooning, can hear too.

• • •

Catfish had brought the football team to First Baptist Church once a year on what's known as Team Day, sort of a homemade Southern religious holiday. And Mac had kept up the tradition. It gives the churchgoers a chance to mingle with the players, pray for them, and quote meaningful Bible verses when they shake their hands after the service. "Praise the Lord!" everybody says. "Bite 'em, Black Bears!"

Pastor Swanson steps up to his podium and clears his throat. Pastor Swanson's known for his Baptist George Jones hair, not unlike coaches' hair—too neatly combed, too perfectly parted, thoroughly sprayed into place. It occurs to me that you can take all the preachers and all the coaches in the South and switch their outfits, and I doubt anybody could tell the difference. I imagine Pastor Swanson in tight polyester shorts, a baseball cap, and a whistle around his neck.

"Charlie Bomar did not just recruit boys for Birmingham University," Pastor Swanson begins emotionally. "Many a boy was drawn out of the darkness and into the limelight at the end of Coach Bomar's recruiting line. Charlie Bomar recruited boys for Jesus Christ, our Lord and Savior!"

"Amen!" someone shouts.

The graveside service is brief. Mac weeps. Celeste pats his hand and whispers, "I know, honey." When it's over Mac helps me into the limousine with Celeste. Before he closes the door Sly Martin approaches and puts his arm around Mac's shoulder. "Glad I caught you two," he says. "This is a bad time, but I know you'll understand. Can't let folks get a jump on us recruiting. Got to get a new coach in here as soon as we can. So do you think you could be out of the coach's house—no hurry—say in two weeks?"

"Dixie and the kids will be out of the house when they're out of the house," Mac says.

"I don't mean anything by it," Sly says. "It's just—"

"We'll get out as soon as we can," I say.

Mac slams the car door so hard I think the window might shatter.

He walks back and gets into a car with Jett. I'm dizzy, like I'm free-falling through a deep hole in the world.

As the line of cars begins to weave its way out of the cemetery I sit beside Celeste, holding her hand, staring straight ahead, reading the bumper stickers on the tails of cars in front of us. An old sticker says AX MAC, a new one says GIBBS IS GOD. But mostly they say, BITE 'EM, BLACK BEARS!

It's nearly midnight. I'm wide awake, sitting up with Celeste, who has at last accepted the loving invitation of prescribed sleeping pills. Downstairs in the den, drinking and telling stories with Jett and Mac, are Catfish's assistant coaches and coaches from rival schools. I sit at the top of the stairs to take what comfort I can in the sounds of their voices.

"Yeah, the Salt and Pepper Shakers." Cleet laughs. "Ole Jett runs out there, a colored boy now, in the middle of fifty thousand rednecks, ole Mac right behind him. Remember that?"

"Still have nightmares about it," Jett says.

"Mac was throwing the ball all over the field, but damn if Jett ain't catching it no matter what sort of missile Mac fires."

"I was scared to miss," Jett laughs.

"Yeah," Cleet says. "Mac always says Jett did as much as Martin Luther King to desegregate the South."

"Mac here always was a real intellectual," Jett says.

"Who needs a drink?" somebody yells.

"Dead. Guys like Catfish don't die." It's Danny Boswell's loud voice. "And Mac, man. Guys like Mac Gibbs don't quit."

"With Mac out of the profession maybe you'll be able to sign somebody, Boswell." Cleet laughs.

"Wait a minute now," Danny Boswell shouts. "I beat Mac on a couple of kids last year. Even beat him on one California kid. Ain't that right, Mac?"

"What were they?" Cleet shouts. "Orphans? You sure as hell never beat Mac on a boy with a mama."

A whooping laugh breaks loose.

"Or a sister!"

"Or a girlfriend!"

"Yeah," somebody yells, "ole Danny's got the best orphans money can buy!"

"So, Mac, old man, what you going to do now?" somebody asks. "I mean football, man, it's your life."

"Guess I better get a new life then," Mac says.

"The way I look at it," Cleet says, "you can sell insurance or you can do TV commentary. What's it going to be, Coach?"

"When I was a kid I used to want to be a dogcatcher," Mac says. "I should have listened to my own advice."

"Shit, man, you'll land on your feet. You always do."

"You'll have a coaching job this time next year," Danny Boswell says. "I have to tell the truth. I'm not going to miss recruiting against you. Do me good for you to take a time-out and play a little golf, man."

"Glad I can do somebody some good," Mac says.

"That kid that's hurt, Miracle Carpenter—you ain't blaming yourself for that, are you, man?" Danny Boswell says. "It happens. Guys get hurt. It's the nature of the game."

"Tell his mama that," Mac says.

It's his shadow I see first, stretching out below me like something lying down. Minutes later I hear footsteps and I see Mac at the foot of the stairs, standing in the middle of his shadow, which is trying to climb the wall. He's rattling a glass of ice in his hands. He looks up to where I'm sitting on the top step. "Celeste okay?" he says.

"She's asleep."

He comes up the steps slowly, dragging his shadow behind him. It's broken into six easy steps. He doesn't look at me. He only looks into his empty drink and watches the ice melt. He sits down beside me, careful not to touch me at all. He's silent.

I wait.

He shakes his empty glass and continues staring into it. I don't feel like a woman sitting beside her husband. I feel like a woman sitting beside the young boy her husband once was. I feel like his mother, whose job it is to understand, but I don't.

He puts the glass to his mouth and sucks out an ice cube, then spits it back into the glass. "Look," he says. "No sense making a federal case out of this, but what I need to know is, what are you planning to do?"

"Do you mean tomorrow? Or the rest of my life?"

"Both, I guess."

"I'm thinking the kids and I might move in with Rose, you know, just for a while. She invited us and she's got plenty of room. Then I don't know. I've been thinking maybe we'll get an apartment close to campus. I might go back to school, finish up my degree maybe."

"Sounds like a plan," he says.

"What about you?"

"Thought I might look for a bridge to jump off of."

"Don't talk like that."

"It's a joke, Dix. A joke. You remember jokes?"

"No, not really."

"Guess I've lost my great sense of humor." He smiles. "I guess you're thinking that's not all I've lost, right, Dix?"

"Suddenly you're a mind reader?" I smile.

"You know what Celeste said to me today?" He holds his glass in his two hands, turning it in circles like it's a small, icy world. "She said she was going to have Coach's headstone carved to say, 'Here lies Coach Bomar. He won lots of games, but he lost everything else.'"

"She can do better than that," I say.

"Like what? 'Here lies a lousy no-good husband who made his wife miserable.' That what you had in mind?"

"I was thinking more, 'Here lies a fucking winner.'"

Mac laughs. "I didn't know you'd learned to cuss, Dix. When did that happen? Is that my fault too?"

"It's my choice. Choice is sort of a new concept to me."

"Seems like you got a lot of new concepts lately. Your man Porter, he's one of your new concepts, isn't he?"

"Maybe," I say.

Mac stands up slowly. "On that note," he says, "I think I'll make my dramatic exit." I watch him walk to the landing, one deliberate step at a time, his shadow like something spilling out of him. His body's always done his best talking for him. His movements are a language I like to believe I can still translate.

I've always loved watching Mac move heavy furniture, lift suitcases, hammer nails into wood, change tires, carry sleepy children to bed. I like the way he walks, the way he smokes a cigarette, the way he enters a room, the way he sits in a car. But most of all, I like watching Mac mow grass. I never loved him more than when he started the mower with one ferocious yank and pushed it steadily across our yard as if he and the mower were merged into one thing, a fine man-machine, bonded inside a deafening noise that keeps the rest of the world from intruding. Afterwards, with sweat pouring off him, Mac would rake the dead grass into little piles and carry it out to the edge of the street by hand. He'd set out the sprinkler, repositioning it again and again until he had it exactly like he wanted it. Then he'd sit on the back steps and drink a cold beer and watch the grass start to grow again. He'd sit a long time, in silence, sometimes with me sitting next to him, barefoot, with one baby on my lap and another one standing on her head in the grass. It was as near to perfect happiness as I could remember.

This had been in the beginning, when our yard was small and simple. Since then our yard's become huge and elaborate. In recent years the university's taken over the landscape, once a week sending over a stranger who cuts the grass slumped unhappily on his riding lawn mower with an industrial-strength leaf catcher trailing him in back.

I hate the telephone. I've never thought of it as a convenience. It's an intrusion. The minute I hear Jay Byrd's voice I feel myself slide underneath the low mood I'm already in. "Mrs. Gibbs, do you have any comment about the lawsuit?" he asks.

"What lawsuit?"

"You haven't heard? I was sure you'd already know."

"Tell me what you're talking about, Jay." My voice is an ice pick.

"Miracle Carpenter and his family have filed suit against HamU and Coach Gibbs for reckless endangerment and breach of promise. They're suing Coach for all he's worth. I've got copies of the suit right here. They claim they've got—"

I hang up the phone. *For all he's worth*—the words are lyrics to a song I used to know all the words to. I turn on the TV, plant myself in Mac's chair, and wait.

Sarah and Buddy bulldoze into the house with Jett right behind them. They'd gone out to get barbecue sandwiches for supper. "Mom?" Sarah's voice cracks. "Did you hear?"

Jett comes in behind her. "They've got tapes," he says. "Miracle and Mary Virginia."

The TV station interviews Miracle from his hospital room. They interview Mary Virginia too, who looks like a case study for the wonders of Valium. She's wearing a church suit. She's had her hair done too. Miracle's sitting in his wheelchair with a blanket Mrs. Carpenter crocheted for him on his lap. I recognize it. He holds up tapes in his hands.

"*Right here,*" he says. "*I got everything on tape.*"

The news plays a small portion of one tape on the air:

> "*There's plenty more where that came from, son. All you got to do is ask.*"
>
> "*Ask who?*"
>
> "*Me. I'll take it from there. Your mama wants a house, right? That can be taken care of, man. You're doing something for us, right? Well, there's folks around HamU who'll do plenty for you too. I mean it.*"
>
> "*What you want me to do, Coach?*"
>
> "*Just keep it down home, son.*"

It's Cleet's voice. It's unmistakable.

The camera zooms in on a photo the newsman is holding.

"Here's my yellow Jim Walter home, the one with the sunken bathtub. They give me the deed to this, Mr. Bobby Gibbs did."

"The coach's brother?"

"Yes, him."

The last thing the newsman says is, "Coach Mac Gibbs could not be reached for comment."

Coach Gibbs could not be reached— I know that hymn too, don't I?

"Did Daddy cheat, Mom?" Sarah asks. "Did he?"

The moving van is scheduled to arrive tomorrow. I love the idea of something large and hollow coming to get us, taking us away from here. I spend the evening wandering through the stripped rooms. It's Jett's job to see that I don't do anything crazy, like set a match to the boxes piled in every room, build a bonfire in the coach's house, which is still university property.

"Here," he says. "Drink this. It's good for you."

"Wine?"

"You can pretend it's rat poison if you want to."

"In that case, thank you."

We sit on the sofa in the den, the one intact item left in the room. "Have you talked to Mac?" I ask.

"Mac can handle this, Dix. Can you?"

I upend my glass and guzzle the wine like it's milk. "How am I doing so far?"

Jett laughs. I love Jett's laugh.

"So Mac helped get Mary Virginia a house? Are we supposed to pretend that's cruel and unusual?" I say.

"It's unusual to have it on tape, girl."

"I'm not naive, Jett. I know Mac's cheated. Let's see—he's seen to it that kids had clothes, and paid for trips home at Christmas, and sent bus tickets so some mamas could see their sons play, and paid for medicine for A. J.'s baby, you know, the one with that heart problem. How's that for despicable? How's that for totally corrupt? Personally, I think they should send him to jail and throw away the key."

"If any of it's on these tapes, they might."

"Bullshit," I say. "Don't forget he won. He won big. Doesn't winning stand for anything anymore?"

"Do I detect bitterness?" Jett smiles.

"Mac's a good man, Jett. Isn't he a good man? Remember when he started out? How much he loved the game? The kids playing the game? He believed all that stuff about good sportsmanship and character building and all that. I know every coach says it, but Mac really *believed* it. I know he did."

Jett stands up, leans over, and kisses the top of my head. He takes the wineglass out of my hand. "Time for a refill."

"You know what, Jett?" I catch his hand as he's leaving. "I begged Mac to win. I threatened to leave him if he didn't."

Jett smiles. "That winning," he says, "it's the whole damn ball game, ain't it, girl?"

"This can't be my life."

"We'll get through this, Dixie."

"So what now?"

"Punt."

ROSE

Dixie and the children have been at my house only a few days when Mac stops by. "Is Dixie here?" he says. I'm half-afraid to let him in. Instead I call Dixie to the door.

Mac's dressed up and smells like Old Spice. "I've called a press conference," he tells her. "I want you and the kids to watch, Dixie. Okay? Five o'clock news. It's important."

"What kind of press conference?" she asks.

"Just watch it, Dix. Please."

We gather around the TV set, all of us, Lilly and Jett too. Dixie sits between Lilly and me on the sofa with Sarah and Buddy at our feet. Jett's in Bennett's La-Z-Boy. On TV Mac stands at the microphone in a crowded room, ready to read a written statement.

"Hold on to your hat," Lilly says.

"I'm here to say a few things I should have said a long time ago," he begins. You can hear a pin drop. *"First of all, Miracle Carpenter is telling the truth, tapes or no tapes. I made him some promises when he signed at HamU. Made some other players some promises too. I did what I could to make their lives a little better, if it meant helping their mamas get into a decent house, or their daddies get a decent job, or getting them a car or paying off some bills. I knew what I was doing was illegal,*

but I looked at it like this. These guys were sure helping me live a better life. The better they played ball, the better I lived, so I tell you what, it only seemed right that I share the wealth a little. I got so single-minded about getting the best players I could get and winning the national championship for HamU that I made the decision to take the risks. Some of our players come from poor homes. I don't have to elaborate on that. Why should they play their hearts out so their coach can live like a king while their own families can't afford the price of tickets to the ball game. The opportunity of an education is a wonderful thing. But the truth is lots of schools are making lots of money off these kids and too many of them come away without their degrees in the end. The last few years HamU's had the highest team graduation rate in the history of the school. That's one thing we've been doing right. So I'm wrong for violating recruiting regulations. But I can't stand here and tell you that I totally regret it. Because the system is wrong too.

"Whatever else I may be guilty of, I'm most certainly guilty of wanting to win. Wanting to win is at the heart of everything I've done in recent years. If Miracle is accusing me of putting winning ahead of good sense, then he's absolutely right. I'm guilty of that. I put winning above my personal integrity, above my family—and for that I apologize to my wife and kids—and above everything that made me love the game all these years. And I'm here to say that I am a living example of failure. One of the surest ways I know to fail is by focusing so hard on winning that you forget what's important, you forget all the things that this great game can teach you, you forget what really matters.

"Looking back, I can't promise I'd do everything different, but I know I'd do one thing different. I would not risk the talent and health of a guy like Miracle Carpenter no matter what. I love Miracle Carpenter. His injury is the greatest regret of my life and I blame myself, no one else. I am guilty of forgetting that he's a human being, of believing he had superhuman powers beyond those of the rest of us. I have no ill feelings toward the Carpenter family for their lawsuit. I would do the same thing in their position. I won't contest it. It seems to me they deserve compensation for all they've lost. I sincerely re-

*gret my part in this tragedy, and once again I apologize for my lapse in judg-
ment and ask their forgiveness.*

"Thank you all for coming and hearing me out."

We switch off the TV set.

"Millie was right after all," I tell Dixie. "Mac did miss his calling.
He *was* meant to be a preacher."

DIXIE

It's after eleven o'clock when Mac calls. I'm in bed. "Look, Dixie, I need to talk to you," he says. "Can I come over?"

I'm waiting on the back steps in my nightgown when he drives up. He seems shy at first and it makes me think for a minute that I'm in love with him again. "I know it's late," he says. "But I had to talk to you. I've been thinking."

"This sounds like trouble." I smile.

He sits beside me on the steps, rests his elbows on his knees, and folds his fingers like he's weaving something together. "I want to talk about us, Dix." Then he goes silent for a long time and I just sit there not making it too easy the way I always used to. Instead I wait. I can outwait him by a mile. If I haven't learned anything else from years of marriage I've learned to wait. "Anyway," he finally says. "I want to talk about us, but damnit, Dix, I'm not sure I know how, so I'm just going to say stuff and hope to God some of it comes out right."

"Okay," I say.

"I don't know how we got to this point. I don't know what all went wrong and when it happened and why. I know most of it's my fault. It must have seemed like I forgot all about you—the kids too—and I guess I did. But one good thing about this mess is that I've had time to think about things. I've thought more the last few weeks than all the rest of my life put together. And I want us to try again, Dixie. I want us to be a family again. I'm getting out of coaching. I'm going to get the kind of job where you come home at five o'clock and eat supper and watch the news, but you're not necessarily *on the news*, you know? I want to move someplace quiet, a small town maybe, and let the kids get some dogs, maybe raise dogs or something. And I'm thinking we could put in a garden. You used to say you'd like that. If I forgot to be married to you, Dix, I'm sorry. I won't forget again. I'll make it up to you if you'll let me."

"I don't know what to say."

Mac's quiet, still weaving his fingers in front of him. "Is it Porter?" he says. "Are you serious about this guy?"

"I like him," I say. "I like who I am when I'm with him."

"But you don't like who you are when you're with me?"

"I'm not anybody when I'm with you."

"We can change that, Dixie. I swear. Give me a chance."

I loop my arm through his and let my hand slide down his arm to see if I can weave my fingers in with his. He squeezes my hand so hard it hurts.

"Maybe," I say.

I begin to imagine a new life with Mac. I imagine him being home to decorate the Christmas tree, watching Buddy's band concert, being there when Sarah gets her braces off. I imagine him laughing about funny things—and being funny again.

It'd thrill Sarah to have Mac home. She spends her life trying to do something he'll notice. She wants him to love her the way she's watched him love his players.

Mac comes by Rose's for a few minutes every day. He brings supper sometimes. He even brought Buddy a couple of tapes once. Country music, but Buddy was grateful anyway. Mac and I take walks and he says Thurmond knows some land for sale in Selma, not a farm exactly, but a nice place in the country. Mac can get a State Farm office there if he wants it. Some guy who's retiring has offered it to him. "How does that sound, Dix?" he says.

"Could you be happy selling insurance, Mac?"

"I can be happy if I have you and the kids."

It's like now that Mac has lost his public life he suddenly wants his private life back. He calls me late one night and whispers into the phone, "Dixie, we could renew our vows. Sort of get married again and start over fresh. I want to do that."

"Me too," I say, surprising myself.

FRANCES DELMAR

HamU hired their new football coach today—Danny Boswell. It's all over the papers. Not Walker, even though he tried to get the job—promised Cleet he'd hire him if he did. Romalee has worn everybody out imagining herself in the coach's house, wanted to turn Buddy's bedroom into an exercise room. Wanted me to help her wallpaper. She told me last night, "I don't know who it is, Frances Delmar, but it's not Walker. He didn't get the job."

"You're not going to shoot yourself over this, are you, Romalee?" I tried to tease her.

"I don't know," she said. "I might."

Walker went back to Pitt today and Romalee's finally ready to go with him. I bet this time next week she'll be in Pennsylvania, house hunting. Look out, Pennsylvania.

Danny Boswell is not keeping Cleet on his staff. I called Dixie and told her as soon as Cleet told me. Fired again. I'm not surprised. Not after Miracle released tapes of Cleet singing, "Keep it down home, son." Cleet wouldn't hurt a fly though—Miracle knows that.

"I'm so sorry," Dixie says. "I'd tell you Mac'll help Cleet get a job, but Mac doesn't have too much clout these days."

"So here we are, Dix," I say.

"Here we are, F. D.," she says.

"Guess what else, Dixie? Cleet's planning to marry Donna. I hope he does too. I've done my time."

ROMALEE

Danny Boswell's salary is more than twice what Mac's was. The only two coaches Danny plans to keep are Columbus and Jasper, who are not on Miracle's tapes. Or if they are, Mary Virginia won't let him release *those* tapes. Like people will believe only the black coaches are honest. Give it up, Mary Virginia. Get a life.

Danny Boswell promises to run a clean program. What a revolutionary concept. "HamU's situation is an example of what can happen when people lose perspective," he says on TV. He promises to recruit players with good grades and character. He promises to put academics first and see that his players graduate—something that slipped his mind entirely at his former school.

Danny Boswell's wife, Kathleen, and their children stand behind him on TV, smiling like they're selling toothpaste. Kathleen's blond too. People say she looks a little like Dixie. Actually, she does too.

At the press conference Danny says all the crap that Mac said when he got the job. The same crap Walker would have said if he'd had the chance.

I can't wait to get out of here.

ROSE

Dixie's upstairs typing when I pound on the door. "Hurry, Dixie," I say. "Mac's on the news, honey."

She comes downstairs behind me. Lilly's already parked in front of the TV. "He's done took a new job," she says.

"What are you talking about?" Dixie says.

"Just what I heard—Mac been named head coach someplace."

"Shhhhhh," I say. "Listen. There he is."

Mac's at the microphone. Behind him is the Spartanburg University emblem. Two years ago they built the biggest stadium in the South. Now they've got to sell enough tickets to fill it up. Bennett used to say they were one of the most underhanded programs in the South.

"I'd like to thank the president, the athletic director, and the people of South Carolina," Mac says, "for this opportunity. As many of you know, I'd pretty much decided to get out of the profession, but Spartanburg University made me an offer I can't refuse." He smiles. "There's a great winning tradition here. I think we can win here again. In fact, I plan to do just that."

Then the press questions come like bullets. Mac looks like himself again—a living target, a happy man.

"I don't believe it," Dixie says.

DIXIE

Mac comes by the house that night, but it's so late I've already put the children to bed. Rose sends him up to my bedroom, where I'm lying in the dark. He taps on the door and comes into the room quietly. "You aren't mad, are you?" he says.

"I'm surprised." I turn to face him in the dark.

"I'm sorry. I should have told you, Dix. I just didn't want anything to spoil this—you know. It's another chance. We can win at Spartanburg. I promise you. It won't be like it was here. God knows the money's good. We'll have more money than you'll know what to do with. We can still buy some land like we were planning, build a house on it. Hell, we can build a castle if you want to." He's pacing back and forth beside my bed.

"I thought you didn't want the football life anymore, Mac."

"Dix, who ever dreamed Spartanburg was going to come along with an offer like this? I thought after all that's happened it'd be a cold day in hell before I'd get another shot like this. I'd be a fool to say no. We got the rest of our lives to take it easy, Dix. Right? We can retire to Selma later on, if that's what we really want. But they believe I can win there. I know I can. I can do it the *right way* this time. This job can make up for the hell we've been through. It's a chance of a lifetime."

"For you."

"Come on, Dix. Don't give me a hard time."

"I'm happy for you, Mac."

"It's going to be great, baby. We'll start all over there. Everything will be better."

"I'm not going, Mac."

"Of course you're going. It'll be a fresh start, Dix."

"No," I say.

"Is it Porter again?"

"No, Mac. It's *you* again."

"Give me a break here, Dix. Be happy for me. For us."

"You need a team, Mac. You don't need me. You don't even need your kids. A coach without a team is like a man without a country or something—a tragic thing. I can forgive your recent insanity. I know you were a man in exile, a man in a state of panic—talking out of your head."

"Dixie, don't."

"Don't what?"

"Hate me." Mac sits on the edge of the bed and takes off his shoes. He loosens his noose of a necktie and lays down beside me in the dark, wraps himself around me the way I used to wrap around him, takes my hand in his, and we automatically lace fingers. We're lying on our sides, facing the wall.

"I don't hate you, Mac," I whisper.

"You won't turn the kids against me, will you, Dix?"

"I won't if you won't," I say.

If beds can float then ours is floating. I can feel our bodies become weightless and the bed lift off the floor, like a raft leaving the dry shore, seduced by the warm licking at its edges, sucked out into the too deep, and left floating there. Seconds pass in which we fall asleep and dream our lives—our pasts—and wake to have them vanish like waves crossing the ocean, swelling as they go, only to break, spill on the shore, and be mercifully taken in again as something other than what they were—our lives, our ordinary lives.

"This is something I've got to do, Dix," Mac whispers, his face in my hair, his words warm on the back of my neck.

"Me too," I say.

"If I was a musician, would you ask me to throw away my guitar? If I was a preacher, would you ask me to step down from the pulpit? Say? I'm a coach, Dix. That's what I am."

"It's okay," I say.

He runs his hand over my face like a man trying to remember. I'm barely breathing, waiting for him to stop. "Mac," I whisper, "I have one request."

"Anything," he says.

"I want you to tell the children yourself."

"We'll tell them together, Dix. Together, okay?"

The bed's spinning now, like one of those mattresses swirling inside the eye of a hurricane, looking like a magic carpet whose riders have been spun off, lost in the spinning. Or maybe like a raft being sucked into a whirlpool, the spinning so fast we can't feel ourselves going down, down. Mac holds me tight, his breathing loud and uneven. "I did, do, and always will love you, Dix," he whispers. "You believe me, don't you?"

"Yes," I say.

And then we sleep.

Mac left for Spartanburg three weeks ago. He gave each of the children five hundred dollars and told them to buy something they wanted. So far neither of them has spent a penny. He also told them to call him anytime they wanted and to come visit whenever they felt like it. He said he'd send them a couple of Spartans sweatshirts as soon as he could. Since then we haven't really heard from him except through the divorce lawyer.

Buddy and Sarah are going to be fine. We're all seeing to that. Sarah says she wants to move away someplace where football is not important. She studies the map of the United States in her spare time searching for a place like that. I got Buddy the snake he's been wanting. It's a boa constrictor. I read that boa constrictors can wrap themselves around you so tight that they can squeeze you to death. "Don't worry, Mom," Buddy explained. "They're just trying to get warm."

I think I can understand that.

Porter comes by now and then and we take long walks or drive someplace in the car. Now and then I spend the weekend at his place. He lives out from town. You have to know where you're going. You have to take dirt roads to get there. It's land mostly, with a pond, an empty barn, and a small farmhouse on it. Some rooms don't have any furniture at all. I could do a lot with his place—I'd start with a little paint. Last weekend we rented a tiller and plowed for a garden.

My first book is being published next fall, *The Gospel According to Gibbs.* It's a collection of my columns about Mac. An Atlanta publisher contacted me and said there's a good market for that now. He says it'll sell like hotcakes in South Carolina. I hope so.

Also recently the editor at Baptist Books contacted me about writing an inspirational book on Mac, *The Mac Gibbs Story: Let Jesus Call the Plays in Your Life,* sort of a biography of a Christian coach. I turned them down, even though I could use the money.

The End

ACKNOWLEDGMENTS

There are people to thank. *Balls* had its inception in George Wolfe's screenwriting class at the University of Alabama. Thanks to George and my classmates for helping convince me that there *might* be a story worth telling.

Over the years, coaches' wives (married, divorced, remarried) shared anecdotes and confessions with me, some of them as unbelievable as they were true, way too far-fetched for the confines of fiction. I'm grateful to them for cheering me on, if not with a collective voice, then at least with a collective whisper. And I'm grateful to coaches' children everywhere, a sensitive, hearty breed, and especially to four that I particularly love, Ali, Leigh, Rich, and Angie, who have small scars maybe but were made strong by growing up in the harsh spotlight of public opinion. They are children who love their fathers, as children will, even when it seems no one else does—maybe especially then.

I'm grateful to Al Kincaid—who laughed in all the right places—for his sense of humor, which never falters, and his gentle spirit, which never fails him, or us.

A special thanks to John Newman—who gave me the pep talk of my life when I needed it most, and who served as my New York translator when I didn't trust my own understanding of the ways and words there—for his encouragement and kindness.

To Tilly Warnock—a wonderful writer who's so smart she scares me, who knows me better than I know myself but is kind enough not to try to explain anything, who loaned me money when debt had me by the throat, and whose advice is always free and good—my thanks.

To Susan Ketchin, whose comments helped to make Dixie stronger and me a little saner. To Lee Smith, the most generous-spirited woman alive, for her constant encouragement and good ear. To Florence Ladd and the Bunting Institute for a magic year, an introduction to a world I never even dreamed of, and the opportunity to work on *Balls* with such wonderful moral support. To Carol Gilligan—who understood what I was trying to do even when I wasn't sure I knew—for her friendship and encouragement.

I'm grateful to my family, who secretly wishes I'd give up fiction and try my hand at something honest—devotionals maybe—for loving me in spite of my profession.

My thanks to Liz Darhansoff—who stood by me through rough times—bless her. And Shannon Ravenel, who, thank God, has season tickets of her own and knows something about balls.

Most heartfelt is my gratitude to Dick Tomey, a brave man, who's teaching me to see the world in new ways. I smile just thinking about him. And last, my gratitude to Southerners everywhere who love their God and their team.

NANCI KINCAID is the author of two previous books of fiction, *Crossing Blood*, a novel, and *Pretending the Bed Is a Raft*, stories. At nineteen, she married a football coach, then raised two daughters, returned to college, received her undergraduate and MFA degrees, and won grants from the National Endowment for the Arts and the Mary Ingraham Bunting Foundation. She is recently remarried—to the head coach of the University of Arizona football team—and lives in Tucson.